R.J. Ellory is the au....................................y
Orion UK, and his ....r–
six languages. He ha............................e,
the Livre De Poche Award, the Strand Magazine Novel
of The Year, the Mystery Booksellers of America Award,
the Inaugural Nouvel Observateur Prize, the Quebec
Laureat, the Prix Du Roman Noir, the Plume d'Or for
Thriller Internationale 2016, the Theakston's Crime Novel
of the Year, both the St. Maur and Villeneuve Readers'
Prizes, the Balai d'Or 2016, and has twice won the Grand
Prix des Lecteurs. He has been shortlisted for two Barrys,
the 813 Trophy, the European Du Point, and two Crime
Writers' Association UK awards.

Among other projects, he is the guitarist and vocalist
of The Whiskey Poets, and has recently completed the
band's third album. His musical compositions have been
featured in films and television programmes in more
than forty countries. He has four television series and
two films in pre-production, and has recently premiered
his first short film, 'The Road to Gehenna'.

Also by R.J. Ellory

Candlemoth
Ghostheart
A Quiet Vendetta
City of Lies
A Quiet Belief in Angels
A Simple Act of Violence
The Anniversary Man
Saints of New York
Bad Signs
A Dark and Broken Heart
The Devil and the River
Carnival of Shadows
Mockingbird Songs
Kings of America
Three Bullets
Proof of Life
The Darkest Season
The Last Highway
The Bell Tower

NOVELLAS
Three Days in Chicagoland:
1. The Sister
2. The Cop
3. The Killer

A DARKER SIDE
OF PARADISE

R.J.ELLORY

ORION

An Orion Paperback
First published in Great Britain in 2025 by Orion Fiction,
an imprint of The Orion Publishing Group Ltd.
Carmelite House, 50 Victoria Embankment
London EC4Y 0DZ

An Hachette UK Company

The authorised representative in the EEA is Hachette Ireland,
8 Castlecourt Centre, Dublin 15, D15 XTP3,
Ireland (email: info@hbgi.ie)

3 5 7 9 10 8 6 4 2

A CIP catalogue record for this book is
available from the British Library.

ISBN (Paperback) 978 1 3987 2402 0

Typeset at The Spartan Press Ltd,
Lymington, Hants

Printed and bound in Great Britain by Clays Ltd,
Elcograf S.p.A.

www.orionbooks.co.uk

'He who fights monsters might take care lest he thereby become a monster...'

Friedrich Nietzsche
Beyond Good and Evil (1886)

I

1975

Morte

I

The rains came, and they did not stop for days.

Ulysses, New York – no more than fifteen miles from the banks of Lake Ontario – caught between the Oswego River wetlands and the tributaries that fed the Finger Lakes – was caught in a crossfire of flooding that gave no respite or sanctuary. When the levees finally broke, the town lost three children within the first twelve hours.

The Oswego, drawing homesteaders towards it with the promise of fertile land for more than two centuries, itself the promise of life and sustenance, was now – once again – a murderer. It was not the first time the river had burst its banks and carried people away to the lakes. Back in 1909, the same thing had happened, but those who were present had long since passed. No one had spoken of it for years. The river had a history of both life and death, the former outweighing the latter in time and memory, and thus the natural human instinct to celebrate that which gave over that which took away prevailed.

On February 15th, 1975, the storm now heading north towards Canada, emergency services, Police, the Sheriff's Department and numerous volunteers from Syracuse and Rochester, began the weeks-long, laborious and heartbreaking process of salvage and recovery.

The body count rose to seven. Beyond that, a further two were missing, presumed drowned, their bodies now lost forever in the depths of the Ontario.

An eighth body was then discovered on Monday 17th – a

twenty-three-year-old schoolteacher called Caroline Lassiter. Caroline did not drown. She was found lying in her own bed, her position one of repose, her hair brushed and laid out across the pillow like some pre-Raphaelite study, clutched in her right hand a carefully-folded piece of paper.

In a precise blocked script were written the words, ABANDON HOPE, ALL YE WHO ENTER HERE.

Present at the Lassiter apartment, charged with maintaining the integrity of the crime scene until the coroner arrived, was a police officer called Rachel Hoffman. Younger than the deceased girl, Rachel was a recent Syracuse Police Academy graduate. On loan to Ulysses from the Patrol Division, her initial posting order had been approved for three months. She had been there for a week shy of six. She had raised this issue with her superiors on two occasions. Each time she'd been told it wouldn't be much longer before she was transferred home.

Caroline Lassiter was the first dead person Rachel had seen up-close and personal. And if her death proved to be a homicide, it would also be the first murder Rachel had attended.

Standing in the neat, very feminine bedroom – as still as a cigar-store Indian – Rachel could not help but feel like an intruder. To her, it seemed that birth and death were somehow sacrosanct, inviolate events that should only be witnessed by those who were bound by blood or friendship to the players in this unfolding drama. Caroline's eyes were open, as dull as old pennies. Had they been closed, she would have appeared to be sleeping, such was her composure. The bedcover was drawn up to her neck, her arms on top of it, her shoulders bare. The stillness of her form was unsettling. Rachel willed the girl to move, to suddenly exhale as if she'd been merely holding her breath for as long as she could. A game, perhaps. A child's game. A prank to scare her siblings.

Rachel stood for close to an hour, and then she heard voices in the hallway from which each room of the small apartment was accessed.

The Tri-County Coroner – early-fifties, bespectacled, his rumpled corduroy suit and woven tie giving him the appearance of a college professor – covered Onondaga, Oswego and Oneida from his office in Syracuse.

He entered the bedroom, looked at the dead girl, then looked at Rachel.

'You've been here alone?' he asked.

'Yes, sir.'

'Sir? We're not on parade here, my dear. What's your name?'

'Hoffman. Rachel Hoffman. Syracuse Patrol Division.'

'Lawrence Hill. I hate it, but everyone calls me Larry.'

Rachel gave a faint smile. 'Then I'll call you Dr. Hill. Or Lawrence.'

'Lawrence is fine,' Hill said. 'And I like you already.'

Hill set down his bag.

'So what do we have here?'

'Caroline Lassiter,' Rachel said. 'Twenty-three. Schoolteacher. That's it. Nothing has been touched aside from the piece of paper that was in her hand. It's over there on the chiffonier.'

Hill laughed. 'Where are we? Nineteenth-century France?'

'Sorry. That's my grandmother.'

Hill crossed the room and looked at the paper. 'So, she wrote this herself?'

'I don't know. As I said, it was in her hand. Apart from removing it and putting it over there, nothing else has been touched.'

'And you did that?'

'No, that was the first responder.'

'Well, we'll know soon enough. There's bound to be examples of her handwriting around the apartment.'

Hill opened his bag and put on latex gloves.

Standing over the body, leaning down until his face was mere inches from the dead girl, he said nothing. The only sound Rachel could hear was that of her own breathing.

It seemed a small forever until Hill stood up once more.

'I need forensics here,' he said. 'I need pictures before I remove the bed cover.'

'As far as I know, they're on the way,' Rachel said. 'Shouldn't be much longer.'

Hill walked to the window and looked out into the street. There was a single police car.

'You're from Ulysses?' Hill asked without turning around.

'Born in Utica,' Rachel replied. 'My folks moved to Syracuse when I was five. And now I've been stationed here for the past six months.'

'And you always wanted to be police?'

'I wanted to be a ballet dancer.'

Hill turned, smiling. 'And why aren't you a ballet dancer?'

'Because it turns out I'm as clumsy as hell. All the grace of a newborn foal.'

Hill laughed. 'Seems to me that a police officer is quite the change of direction.'

Rachel was about to speak when further voices could be heard.

Entering the bedroom, Detective Tom Marcus was accompanied by two forensic technicians and a crime scene photographer.

Rachel had met Marcus before. Laconic, seemingly diffident, she had never warmed to him. During her training, he had given a series of presentations on crime scene protocol, preservation of evidence, fingerprinting, other such things. He wore an expression of perpetual irritation, as if the world provided an inexhaustible supply of things he was obligated to tolerate.

'I know you,' he said to Rachel.

'Hoffman, sir. From the academy.'

'Right. They exiled you to the sticks, then?'

Rachel didn't reply.

'And now you have to deal with a dead schoolteacher and the worst flood in a century at the same time.'

Marcus paused for a second, as if figuring out the best wisecrack.

'Out of your depth?' he asked.

'Funny,' Rachel said. 'You should get a half-hour slot at the Comedy Club. The world shouldn't be deprived of such great material.'

'I need your guys to take pictures before I remove the bedcover,' Hill said, interrupting whatever road Rachel and Marcus were heading down.

Marcus gave instructions. Rachel and Hill stepped out of the room and waited for them to be done.

'Okay, come on back,' Marcus told Hill.

Hill approached the bed once more. He carefully lifted each of Caroline Lassiter's arms in turn, bringing the bedcover down to reveal her breasts, her stomach. He folded it neatly as he went, laying it flat at the foot of the bed. Her naked form was exposed, and – once again – he stepped back to let the photographer take a dozen or more photographs from various points in the room.

'So, whaddya reckon?' Marcus asked. 'Doesn't seem to be any indication of foul play.'

'I'll do my preliminaries here,' Hill said. 'More than likely we won't know until I perform the full autopsy.'

'There's a note, sir,' Rachel said. She nodded towards it.

Using a pen to hold it flat, Marcus read the single sentence.

'What the hell is this?' he asked.

'It was there when I came in.'

'Did you move this, Hoffman?'

'No, sir. The first responder. He said it was in her hand.'

'To see if it was a suicide note,' Marcus said.

'That's what I figured.'

'Well, someone's gonna get a harsh word or two, aren't they?'

Marcus instructed one of the technicians to bag the note and then find a sample of the dead woman's handwriting.

Hill stepped away from the bed. 'I need her on the table,' he said. 'Could be an OD, but I need to do blood tests and all else.'

Marcus turned to Rachel. 'You go on up to Syracuse with the body. I'll clear it with your chief.'

'Yes, sir.'

'You guys all done?' Marcus asked the technicians.

They were. There was nothing to see of any significance. Marcus left with his people.

'Looks like it's just the three of us, then,' Hill said. 'You ever seen an autopsy?'

'No.'

'Brace yourself,' Hill said. 'First few times can be pretty grim.'

2

Grim was an understatement. It was as if Rachel was witnessing the unzipping of a human being. As the scalpel made its way through flesh and muscle – a precise Y from below each shoulder to a point between the breasts, and then down to the navel – Caroline Lassiter's innards were at last being released from twenty-three years of captivity.

'Wait until you get a ripened one,' Hill said. 'A week undiscovered, all swollen up, and it smells like ... well, it doesn't smell like anything, to be honest. That stink stays in your nostrils for days.'

Rachel tried to focus as one organ after another was hefted out of the cadaver and placed on a weighing scale.

'If you need to take a break, do so,' Hill said, recognizing at once that she was struggling.

Standing in a small courtyard behind Syracuse Coroner's Office in a small courtyard, she breathed deeply, quelling the rising wave of nausea that threatened to paint the sidewalk with her lunch.

Rachel was outside for a good fifteen minutes. She didn't vomit, but she retched several times and experienced a wave of dizziness and cold sweats. How someone could get used to such things she didn't know. She had no intention of finding out.

By the time the blood analysis came back, it was past 8.00 in the evening.

'Barbiturates and chloroform,' Hill told Rachel. 'Barbiturates knocked her out so she wouldn't struggle, and the chloroform killed her.'

'I thought chloroform made someone pass out immediately.'

'A very common misconception. Takes a good four or five minutes of uninterrupted inhalation. Someone is going to fight like hell against that. And there are no signs of a struggle, no bruising or lacerations anywhere on the body. And after they're unconscious, it takes a great deal longer for them to ingest enough to bring about death. And the chin needs to be supported from beneath to keep the tongue out of the airway. Hence the barbiturates. At least that's my opinion of what happened here. She was drugged so she didn't resist, and then someone stayed right there and made her inhale enough to kill her.'

'So we have a murder.'

'Undoubtedly.'

'When can we get a report?'

'Tomorrow.'

'And what happens now?' Rachel asked.

'With her? I stitch her up and put her on ice. Your guys inform her family. That's if they haven't already. I'm guessing the charming Detective Marcus or one of the others gets to work on finding your perp.'

Hill paused for a moment, and then he said, 'How do you deal with that? People like Tom Marcus.'

'I deal with it,' Rachel replied.

'Is he threatened by you, or what?'

'I have no idea, and I really have no interest in finding out.'

'Is it this way with all the men you work with?'

'There's always going to be a few, and it would be the same in any line of work. Hell, they even get into head-butting with each other. The amount of time that's wasted by lack of co-operation between different units and departments is incredible. Sometimes it seems that taking the credit is more important than solving the case.'

'Egos, eh? I guess I'm lucky I work with people who can't talk back.' Hill smiled. 'Even when I open them up from gullet to gizzard.'

'This is just a regular day for you, isn't it?'

'I've been doing this a good many years, Rachel. There's not a great deal I haven't seen.'

'And you can just go home, kiss your wife, watch TV, have your dinner and forget about it.'

'All of the above except the wife part.'

'You're not married?'

'No.'

'How come?'

'Just lucky, I guess.'

'You *are* too cynical.'

'Don't get emotional about it. That's the trick. Whoever she was, she's gone. The personality, everything that they were, is not hanging around in cells and bones and blood. The moment the heart stops beating, something goes. Don't ask me what it is, because I sure as hell don't know. The spark goes out, and it's like switching off a light. There's just a hundred and fifty pounds of muscle and bone left behind. It's like a house with no one home.'

'Doesn't change the fact that it's a tragedy. She's pretty much the same age as me.'

'And there we go,' Hill said. 'That train of thought stops right there. You didn't know it was going to happen, and so there was nothing you could've done about it. Now all you have to do is make sure that whoever did this doesn't get to do it again.'

'I'm not a detective. Not yet, anyway.'

'Is that where you're headed?'

'Yes,' Rachel said. 'That's what I want.'

'Well, I guess you better hang out with me a bunch. Get yourself all bullet-proof. You get into Homicide, you're gonna see the very worst that human beings are capable of doing to one another. That's something to look forward to, right?'

Rachel drove back to Ulysses.

Circumventing the roadblocks that were still in place, taking a winding route back towards the center of town, it was past 10.00 by the time she closed her front door behind her.

She took a shower, opened a bottle of wine, and then sat in her kitchen with the lights out.

Trying her best not to think about the events of that evening, her mind was nevertheless assaulted by images of Caroline Lassiter's autopsy. To die so young was a tragedy; to die in such a manner made it so much worse. Perhaps, as Hill had said, you became inured to such things. Not insensitive, not unaffected, but somehow emotionally and psychologically detached. And for any chance of being a detective, detachment and objectivity were key. This was now a homicide investigation, nothing more nor less. She didn't know the victim. They had never crossed paths, never shared a single word. That, in and of itself, did not reduce the urgency or diligence required for the investigation, but that investigation was not her remit. Syracuse PD was running the case, and the best she could hope for was to be somehow kept in the loop regarding its progress. However, if Marcus was primary, then there was very little chance of that. To Marcus, Rachel was little more than a passenger in a squad car, required to merely monitor the radio while the men did the heavy lifting.

Sleep was evasive. Somewhere near 2.00 on Tuesday morning, Rachel drifted off. Her last thought was for the note found in Caroline Lassiter's hands. *Abandon hope, all ye who enter here.*

Whoever had sat so patiently with Caroline as she suffocated had something to say, and if that message was understood then they might be a little closer to understanding who had left it.

3

A week went by.

Tom Marcus was assigned primary on the Lassiter case. As far as Rachel could determine, it had yet to break. Forensics had found nothing indicative of the killer's identity. There were no leads, no further developments, no fragments of information that indicated the motive for Caroline Lassiter's death.

Rachel had accompanied another officer when the woman's parents were informed. She sat and watched; she was required to say nothing, and for this she was grateful. She observed the shock, dismay, disbelief and heartbreak of a mother and father as they tried to absorb the profound weight of the news being delivered. Biased though they might have been, they described their daughter as a gentle soul – caring, considerate, patient and kind. All she'd ever wanted to do was teach. There was no one they could imagine would wish her harm. Of course, they asked why. Why would someone do such a thing? There was no way to answer that question, and thus no answer was given. Until the perpetrator was identified, arrested, interrogated, there would be no explanation, and – even then – the explanation might have no understandable rationale.

Sometimes people were killed for no reason other than that which existed in the mind of the killer. Those reasons could be beyond all reason. Ultimately, it seemed, it was impossible to rationalize irrationality.

The very nature of Caroline Lassiter's death was in defiance of Nature. Parents should not bury their children. That was not the way things were meant to be.

On the morning of Tuesday 25th, Rachel received a call from Lawrence Hill.

'You remember that note in the girl's hand?' he asked. 'Well, it bugged the hell out of me, so I did some digging. I spoke to a few friends, one of whom is an English professor up at the university. He told me it's a line from something called *The Divine Comedy* by Dante Alighieri.'

'Okay, so we need to go talk to this Alighieri guy.'

Hill laughed. 'Unless you have a time machine, that will be something of a challenge. The book was written about six hundred and fifty years ago.'

'Right,' Rachel said. 'In one sentence I have demonstrated how ignorant and uneducated I am.'

'Don't take it personally,' Hill said. 'I'd heard of it, but I had no real clue what it was.'

'And what is it?'

'A poem, essentially. It's about the afterlife, about Purgatory and Hell and whatever. In essence, it's the journey of the soul to Heaven.'

Rachel was quiet for a moment.

'I know what you're thinking,' Hill said. 'You're thinking that maybe we have a crazy out there.'

'Actually, I was thinking that there must have been a reason for whoever killed her to have left that particular line. And that maybe they have more to say.'

'Well, see what you can do with that. Give it to whoever's running the investigation. See whether it sheds any light on anything.'

'I really appreciate the call, Lawrence.'

'You're welcome, Rachel.'

*

Tom Marcus looked at Rachel with such a dismissive expression that she wanted to floor him.

'Why is Hill calling you?' was his first question.

'I guess because I was there for the autopsy.'

'And how does he think this is going to help us any?'

'I don't know, sir. I guess we could check the libraries, see who's withdrawn the book. Seems like it's a pretty unusual title. I sure as hell had never heard of it.'

'You have any idea how many libraries there are in the state?'

'No, sir.'

'And who's to say that whoever did this is from New York?'

Rachel didn't respond. This was going to be a one-sided conversation; she was going to be shot down no matter what she suggested.

'Has there been any further progress on the case, sir?' Rachel asked.

'Nothing that concerns you, Officer Hoffman. Now, don't you have some traffic citations to chase up or something?'

'Yes, sir. Of course, sir.'

Rachel backed up a step, turned and left the office.

At her desk she breathed slowly and purposefully. There was no point getting riled. Men like Marcus would always be men like Marcus. It wasn't even misogyny. It was more basic than that. Such people – inflated with a sense of self-importance that seemingly knew no bounds – treated everyone but their superiors in the same manner. To the captain, Marcus was polite, matter-of-fact, businesslike. He said what was required to curry favor, to protect his reputation, to evade criticism or censure. No doubt Marcus was working whatever angle he could to ascend ever higher in the ranks. His goal was to be in a position where everything could be delegated. From such a vantage point, anything that went well would be something for which he could take credit; everything that didn't would be someone else's fault.

By the end of the first week in March, Rachel knew that Caroline Lassiter's investigation had been abandoned. Marcus was heading up other investigations. That file, along with so many others, would gather dust in a cabinet. The girl would be forgotten, relegated to a statistic, remembered solely by those who knew her and missed her. Why it haunted Rachel, she could not explain. Perhaps their similarity in age, perhaps the mere fact that Caroline had been the first murder case in her police service, perhaps because she believed Caroline's parents when they'd said that there was no imaginable reason for someone to kill her. A truly innocent victim.

There was also the manner of death – meticulous, even surgical. It had not been a crime of passion, nor had it been spontaneous and unintentional as in the case of an interrupted burglary. This has been planned and executed with forethought and preparation. No forced entry, no struggle, no sexual assault, no violence. Caroline Lassiter had been put to sleep. Like an animal. Like a sick, old animal that would merely live to suffer if mercy played no part.

Rachel knew she would have to let it go. If she reacted in such a way to every murder in her career, her mind would be crowded with the dead, each periodically surfacing to the forefront of her thoughts clamoring for an answer. She had no answer, and – it seemed – there might never be one.

Whoever had done this was out there. They walked and talked, they ate dinner, they watched TV, they visited friends and family. They wore a face for the world, and behind that face was another face entirely; perhaps a gallery of different faces, each of them carefully constructed to present a different persona dependent upon the circumstances. They had undertaken research; they had obtained barbiturates and chloroform; they knew that to bring about death the victim's chin had to be raised to prevent the tongue from blocking the airway. Perhaps they had done this before, perhaps not. And, if this was as methodical and conscientious as Rachel believed it to be, then – in all likelihood – there would be another, and yet another. Of this she felt sure, and there sensed a conflict. Motivated by an intense dislike for the attitude of Tom Marcus, she wanted him proven wrong. Against that was the knowledge that in order for that to happen, another human being's life would have to end. If it did, would she carry that on her conscience, as if she had somehow possessed the power to influence an outcome? That was crazy talk. She could not go there.

Perhaps every human being on Earth walked a narrow tightrope strung between birth and death. At some point they would fall, whether through loss of balance, perhaps stepping off voluntarily, sometimes because they were pushed. And maybe that moment was preordained, a destiny that was mapped out before they took their first breath. You live for so many years, in some cases months, other times merely days or hours, and then the lights go out. Darkness descends, and all that remains are the memories of those you left behind.

It was a dangerous thought, as likely to prompt apathy as a hunger for life. We have the time we have. We make the most of it, or we succumb to the whims of fate with no belief in our power to avert them.

4

Raymond Keene was forty-eight years old, and his second marriage had just come to an end.

The first one had begun much the same as most courtships. Each of them had woven a web of lies. He, in truth, had never served in the military; she had never been Homecoming Queen three years in a row. After less than two years, the marriage finally collapsed beneath the weight of falsehoods. One afternoon, facing one another in a roadside diner booth, Raymond and his wife saw one another for who they really were. He said he'd drive her to her folks in Buffalo. She declined, said she'd call her brother to come pick her up. That was the last they ever saw of one another. The divorce had been finalized through phone calls, letters from one lawyer to another. They owned nothing, so there was nothing to divide. There were no children, so custody arrangements never had to be considered.

Four years after the divorce, Raymond met Gayle Willard at an all-you-can-eat buffet in a Chinese restaurant in downtown Rochester. Having unceremoniously failed to make the slightest positive impression at a job interview that same afternoon, he'd decided to book himself into a motel, grab some dinner, and then drink himself into a stupor before heading back to Syracuse the following morning.

As he helped himself to the last four wafer-wrapped king prawns, Gayle – waiting in line behind him – gave an audible sigh of disappointment. Turning to look at her, Raymond apologized and put two back on the hotplate.

'It's okay,' Gayle said. 'You go ahead and eat everything and leave nothing for anyone else.'

And then she touched the sleeve of his jacket. Raymond caught the faintest ghost of her perfume.

'You can apologize with a drink, Mr. Greedy.'

They talked for three hours. They navigated their way through two bottles of wine. Later that night and into the early hours of the morning, they fumbled their way through awkward, drunken sex in Raymond's featureless low-cost motel room.

The following morning, they shared breakfast. She was five years out of a long-term relationship. She wasn't looking for anything serious. This had been fun. She'd like to do it again.

They met weekly for the next six months. By Christmas they were talking about the possibility of getting a place together.

'If we're gonna live together,' Raymond said one Tuesday in January, 'then why don't we…'

'Get married?'

'I mean, I don't want you to feel…'

'If you mean it, ask me properly, Raymond.'

He did. He got down on one knee. He didn't have a ring in his pocket. That could wait. It was the right moment to ask her, and there wasn't going to be a better one.

Gayle said yes.

The wedding was a small affair. They bought a place together in the Syracuse suburbs. Once again, the marriage lasted less than two years.

'The way you look at me, I know you're going to lie before you open your mouth,' she said.

To Raymond, the pitch of her voice gave everything she uttered the ominous sense of an ultimatum. Even when she told him she wanted to make it work, it sounded like a warning.

Raymond understood that when it came to women, he'd spent his entire life trying to figure out the right words without ever realizing that the right words did not exist.

The end of the marriage was like a house fire. A bad one. Kicking through the ash and rubble, there seemed to be nothing worth salvaging.

Their divorce was finalized in April of 1974.

With what little remained of their halved assets, Raymond put down a deposit on a first-floor, one-bedroom apartment in Baldwinsville. He changed jobs, then changed again. Since November 1974, he'd worked in the accounts department of a Home Depot in Rochester. He was responsible for stock control, reorders, returns processing and refund administration. He drank too much. He ate the wrong food. He did not belong to a gym. He drove a crappy car that had too many miles on the clock and rarely started when the temperature dropped. He spent his weekends alone in front of the TV. He'd stopped asking himself when his life would get better.

Returning home on the evening of Wednesday, March 5th, 1975, Raymond took off his jacket, loosened his tie, kicked off his shoes and walked through to the kitchen. He opened the refrigerator and surveyed the contents. Cheese, two eggs, a jar of pasta sauce, an overripe tomato, half a carton of milk. Putting his shoes back on, he figured he'd get a burger and a couple of beers somewhere. He picked up his car keys, paused for a moment, and then put them down again. The way he felt in that moment, two beers would be followed by two or three more, and then he might make everything go away with a couple of shots. He would aim for one of the watering holes within walking distance, preferably a straight line from the apartment so he wouldn't get lost on the way back.

Opening the front door, Raymond turned at the sound of something from the kitchen. He frowned, left the door ajar, and walked back. There was insufficient time for him to consider where the sound might have originated from, but any uncertainty he might have had was resolved when he saw a man standing facing the window ahead of the sink.

'What the hell?' Raymond said. 'Who the fuck are you?'

The man turned. He was a head taller than Raymond. He had on work clothes – jeans and a canvas jacket. His hair was cut short, almost to the scalp.

'Sit down, Raymond,' the man said.

'Who the fuck are you?' Raymond repeated. 'What the hell are you doing in my house?'

From his jacket pocket, the man produced a .38. He pointed it directly at Raymond's head.

'Christ almighty,' Raymond said. 'Okay, okay.'

Raymond took a seat.

'I've got no money,' Raymond said. 'A few bucks, that's all.'

Reaching into his jacket pocket, he took out his wallet. Opening it, he withdrew a half-dozen notes and put them on the table.

'That's all I've got, I swear. I'm not a wealthy guy, mister.'

The man put the .38 back in his pocket. He picked up a bag and set it on the floor by the table. He took a seat facing Raymond. For the longest time he just looked, expressionless but for a faint kind of curiosity in his eyes.

'I don't want your money, Raymond,' the man said.

'Then what do you want? And how do you know my name?' Raymond could feel his heart hammering through his chest.

'For a while, I just want to talk,' the man said.

'Talk? Talk about what?'

The man didn't respond.

'You're not going to hurt me, are you? You're not going to kill me, right?'

Again, the man said nothing.

A profound wave of panic assaulted Raymond. He felt dizzy, nauseous, more afraid than he'd ever been in his life.

'I want to talk about life,' the man said.

Leaning forward, Raymond better saw his face. He was young – perhaps in his mid-thirties – and edging out from his collar was a tattoo, the design of which Raymond could not discern. Everything about the man was quiet. That was the only way Raymond could describe it. When he moved, he moved as if he had all the time in the world. His voice was calm, measured, absent of any identifying accent.

'Life?' Raymond asked.

The man nodded.

'What about it?'

'Its transience. Its fragility. Its lack of meaning.'

Raymond frowned. He shook his head. Was he dreaming? Would he suddenly bolt upright and realize that he'd already been out, already eaten, already drunk far too much, and now he was sitting on the edge of his bed – sick and dehydrated – struggling to slow his heart and dispel the sense of dread that had accompanied a nightmare?

'I don't understand,' Raymond said.

'I know,' the man replied. 'So very few people do.'

They sat in silence – Raymond and the uninvited guest – for a minute.

Wishing to break the deadlock, Raymond said, 'Did we meet somewhere? Do I know you?'

The man shook his head.

'But you know my name?'

'Raymond Keene.'

Raymond hesitated. 'Look, mister. I really don't understand why you're here. You don't want money, but you have a gun—'

The intruder raised his hand. Raymond stopped talking.

'Do you want to be free, Raymond?'

'Free? Free of what?'

'Free *from*, Raymond. It's free *from*.'

'Okay, free from what?'

The intruder raised his hand and indicated the kitchen. 'This. All of this. The ties that bind you to misery and loneliness. The need to do something you hate to support a life that has no meaning or consequence. The empty days, the lonely nights, the sense that you will never feel true joy or peace or worth. Your life is a hollow shell, Raymond. It began and then it will end, and nothing of any true meaning will ever have taken place in the intervening years. I am here to offer you a way out of the trap. I am here to offer you freedom.'

The intruder smiled. He leaned back in the chair – relaxed and utterly self-possessed.

'Is this a gag?' Raymond asked. 'Is this like one of those TV stunt shows? Is there a camera somewhere?' He smiled as he grasped for a fragile thread of explanation.

'Did I win something? Are you going to tell me I've won ten thousand bucks or something?'

'What you have won, Raymond, is priceless.'

Raymond laughed involuntarily. 'Oh man,' he said. 'I knew it! I knew my luck would change one day. Hell, you really had me sweating. You really scared the living hell out of me, buddy! What a stunt, eh? Good job I don't have a weak heart or you might've had a cardiac arrest on the TV, right?'

'Right.'

'So what happens now?' Raymond looked around, expecting any moment to see a cameraman, a pretty girl with a bouquet of balloons, some kind of game show host with a briefcase packed with clean, new fifty-dollar bills.

There was no one. The room and the apartment were silent.

'So, do you want to be free, Raymond?' the intruder asked.

'Well, sure. Who the hell wouldn't want to be free from all this crap? You'd have to be crazy not to want a better fucking deal than this.'

'Because it's been disappointing, hasn't it?'

'I'll say. Disappointing is an understatement.'

'And you have always believed you were meant for better things.'

'Yes. Yes, absolutely.'

'Then we should have a drink together. A drink to celebrate the moment that Raymond Keene secures his freedom.'

'Hell, yeah. I'm always ready for a drink.' Raymond started to get up. 'But I don't have anything here. Maybe we could go to a bar or something.'

'It's okay, Raymond. Sit down.'

Raymond sat.

The intruder reached down and fetched a bottle of bourbon from the bag on the floor. He then produced two glasses. He filled them in turn, sliding one across the table to Raymond.

The man raised his glass. Raymond followed suit.

'Drink,' the man said.

Raymond complied.

The glass was refilled twice, three times, and it was only after the glass was filled for the fourth time that Raymond realized the man had not taken a sip of his own.

'Are you not going to . . .'

Raymond paused. Going to what? The word had escaped him.

'Drink?' he finally said, but the sound left his lips in slow-motion and seemed to hang in the air between them.

The walls moved. That's how it felt. And then the floor beneath his feet seemed a hundred miles below him. An out-of-body experience. He knew about this. He'd watched a documentary one time.

Raymond's eyes were deadweight. He fought to focus, to keep them open. He jolted forward, and the glass of bourbon was swept from the table and clattered against the cupboard door to his left.

'What . . .' he murmured, and then he folded forward, his arms hanging down, the side of his face on the cold Formica table.

As his eyes closed for the last time, he could hear nothing

but the sound of his own breath, the faint murmur of his heart. Throughout his body was a sense of emptiness, as if he was indeed no more substantial than a fairground balloon.

Next came the darkness, and it swallowed him whole.

5

The body of Raymond Keene lay undiscovered for eight days.

Numerous calls were made to his apartment. On two occasions, a Home Depot employee was dispatched to see if he was present. Mail – most of it promotional leaflets and unsolicited junk – accumulated in his mailbox until it started to spill out. It was the mailman who finally called the police.

A squad car arrived in the late afternoon of Thursday, March 13th. The attending officers found the back door open. Entering the premises, they were at once assaulted by the putrescent hydrogen sulfide odor of a decomposing body. They called out for Mr. Keene, knowing all too well that no answer would be forthcoming.

Raymond's corpse was found in the bedroom of his one-level apartment. The cover was pulled up to his neck, his arms over the top of it, his hands across his chest. He was clutching a folded piece of paper.

To all intents and purposes, he appeared to have died in his sleep.

Baldwinsville was Onondaga County, hence Lawrence Hill was summoned from Syracuse. He arrived a little after seven.

Untroubled by the smell, he attended the scene with the two officers. He made a wisecrack about how much sicker they'd feel it if was high summer.

From appearances, Hill guessed Raymond Keene was a bachelor. The mere fact that he'd evidently been dead for a week or more before anyone called it in suggested that he possessed neither a high-powered job nor a vibrant social calendar.

Seeing the note in Raymond's hands, Hill instructed one of the officers to call for a forensics unit. He also told them to find Tom Marcus in Syracuse and get him over there.

Hill waited an hour in the yard behind the apartment. Even he did not need to spend any longer than necessary being assaulted by the vast number of chemicals emitted from the orifices and ruptures of a cadaver in decay.

Marcus could not be located. In his stead, Detective Jim Hibbert arrived with a technician and a crime scene photographer.

Once the preliminaries had been completed, Hill showed Hibbert the note in Raymond's hands.

'We had one of these less than a month ago in Ulysses,' he said. 'If that's what I think it is, then this is now a second murder.'

'And what do you think it is?' Hibbert asked.

'A quote from Dante Alighieri's *The Divine Comedy*.'

'And what the fuck might that be?'

'It's a poem written by an Italian a few hundred years ago.'

Using tweezers, Hibbert removed the note from Raymond's grasp. Sodden with bodily fluids, he tentatively unfolded it on the bed cover. Smudged, though legible, were the words: I DID NOT DIE, AND YET I LOST LIFE'S BREATH.

'Tom Marcus was primary on the last one,' Hill said. 'You should coordinate with him.'

Hibbert gave a wry smile. 'Tom Marcus is right at the very end of a long list of people I don't want to coordinate with.'

'That's as may be, Detective, but it appears you have yourselves a second victim by the same hand in less than a month.'

'Any indication of cause of death?'

'Outward signs, no. Last one was barbiturates and chloroform.

This could very well be the same, but I'll only be able to confirm that upon autopsy.'

'Well, let's get him bagged and in the back of your wagon, then,' Hibbert said. 'Leave it much longer and he'll come away in pieces.'

Bloodwork and analysis gave Hill the answer he didn't want by lunchtime on Friday.

It was same MO. By his reading, the victim was incapacitated with barbiturates and then suffocated with chloroform. He was put to sleep, just as had been the case with the Lassiter girl.

Calling Syracuse PD, he tracked down Marcus.

'Did Jim Hibbert speak to you about the body we found in Palmyra?' Hill asked.

'I only just got in. What's happened?'

'Another chloroform victim with a note.'

'Oh fuck,' Marcus said.

'This was a forty-eight-year-old Home Depot employee by the name of Raymond Keene.'

'So our guy's not just into cute girls, then?'

'Guess not, Detective.'

'I'll come fetch what info you've got and get to work.'

'Seems that'd be the smart move. Family needs to be tracked down. All the usual.'

Marcus hung up without another word.

Syracuse PD authorized a two-man team for 'The Sleeper' as the perp was unofficially named. Marcus was primary, his second a relatively new detective by the name of Michael Ridgway.

Ridgway, keen to make his bones, contacted Hill directly with some pertinent questions.

'Can you tell me the weight of the victim?'

'About one-sixty,' Hill told him.

'So our guy is strong,' Ridgway said. 'Unless something very strange went on, then Keene didn't just lie down on the bed and agree to be chloroformed to death. From what I can see – and this is just hypothesis – there was some kind of exchange that went on in the kitchen. There was a glass on the table, empty, no prints, and then a second one on the floor with Keene's prints on it. I'm going with a loaded drink. Our perp drugs him cold, and then carries him through to the bedroom. Same as with the girl in Ulysses. No struggle, no bruising, no defensive wounds. He lays him out and then he chloroforms him. Does that seem realistic to you, Dr. Hill?'

'Seems as plausible as anything else I could come up with.'

'So something happens that enforces compliance. I'm guessing he's armed,' Ridgway said.

'I'd say so, yes.'

'So we got the method, we have the opportunity, and now we need the motive.'

'Right.'

'And this Italian poetry stuff. You got any insight on that?'

'I have a friend up at the university,' Hill said. 'He was the one who identified the line from the first killing. It comes from a book about the journey the human spirit makes after death. You know, through Hell, Purgatory and then to Heaven.'

'Like a religious thing, right?'

'I haven't read it, but I would assume so.'

'You think your friend would be willing to talk to us?'

Hill smiled. 'There's two things you need to know about university professors, Detective Ridgway. One, they love the sound of their own voices. Two, they never pass up an opportunity to show off about how much they know.'

Hill gave Ridgway a name and number.

'I appreciate your time, Dr. Hill.'

'You're welcome, Detective Ridgway, and I wish you the best of luck.'

The call ended, Hill dialled the police department in Ulysses. He asked for Rachel Hoffman.

'Rachel, this is Lawrence Hill.'

'Hey, how are you?'

'I'm good. Look, the reason I'm calling is to let you know that there was another murder – same MO as the Lassiter girl. This time in Palmyra. A man in his late forties. Your buddy Tom Marcus is on it, but there's another detective called Michael Ridgway. I just got off the phone with him. He seems very motivated.'

There was silence at the other end of the line.

'Rachel?'

'Yes, yes I'm here.'

'I just thought you might want to know.'

'Yes. And thank you. I don't know that I'll be able to do anything about it. I'm still out here in Ulysses. And no one's given me a Detective Shield since we last spoke.'

'I have no doubt that'll come in time. I guess I just wanted to let you know in case you were still stuck in the *Is there anything I could have done?* mindset. Whoever's doing this is intent on doing it. He's crossed counties. Who's to say he won't go out-of-state for the next one?'

'If he does, it'll be federal.'

'Well, let's hope Marcus and Ridgway get something substantive, eh?'

'Sure thing.'

Hill was set to end the call.

'Oh, Dr. Hill?'

'Yes.'

'There was a note, right?'

'There was, yes.'

'What did it say?'

30

'I'm assuming it was another line from the same book. It said "I did not die, and yet I lost life's breath."'

'I'm thinking someone needs to read that book.'

'Well, if you want to wade through several hundred pages of medieval Italian verse, then knock yourself out. I gave Detective Ridgway the name and number of a friend at the university. He'll be able to shed some light on it.'

'I hope they make some progress.'

'And even though it's always a pleasure to speak to you, I hope I don't need to call you again.'

'You take care, Dr. Hill.'

'You too, Rachel.'

Rachel called Syracuse. She asked for Ridgway.

'This is Detective Ridgway.'

'Hi. My name's Rachel Hoffman. I'm Syracuse but on loan to Ulysses. I was on crime scene at the Lassiter girl's place.'

'Okay. What can I do for you?'

'I just spoke to the coroner. He told me there was a second murder, same MO, and the perp left a note just as he did here in Ulysses.'

'And if that's true, why would the coroner tell you this, Officer Hoffman?'

'I was there. I went up to Syracuse with the body.'

'And…?'

'I'm interested, Detective Ridgway. That's all there is to it. I'm not chasing a shield or whatever. I just spent a good few hours with a girl that should be teaching kids in school right now, but she's dead.'

'And you want me to keep you posted?'

'I'd just be interested to know if you make any progress on this.'

'Give me your number.'

Rachel did so.

'I'll call you,' Ridgway said. 'When that will be, your guess is as good as mine. But if there's news, I'll let you know.'

'Appreciated, Detective.'

The line went dead.

6

It was Tuesday the 18th before Professor Allan Cambridge, Head of Syracuse English and Literature Department, could make time to see Detective Michael Ridgway.

Cambridge was apologetic as he showed Ridgway into his office. The walls, lined floor-to-ceiling with books, the desk laden with piles of papers, the floor a maze of further texts, volumes and pamphlets, was exactly as Ridgway had imagined a university professor's office would be.

Once seated, Ridgway explained who he was, why he was there, that Lawrence Hill had directed him to Cambridge for some information.

'As I understand it, you have a well-read killer on your hands,' Cambridge said.

'I have someone who kills people and leaves notes at the murder scene. Those notes are lines from a book—'

'But not just any book, Detective Ridgway. Do you know anything of this text at all, or its author perhaps?'

'I don't, sir.'

'The book is called *The Divine Comedy*. The author was an Italian poet, writer and philosopher by the name of Dante di Alighierodegli Alighieri. He's now simply referred to as Dante. He was born in Florence in the middle of the thirteenth century. He wrote a great many things, but *The Divine Comedy* is considered not only his finest work, but also one of the greatest works in European literary history.'

'And it's a religious text?'

'Religious, philosophical, imaginary, prophetic, mythical, realist, surrealist. It encompasses so many ideas and themes that it's impossible to classify it as any particular genre.'

'So, for an uneducated cop...?'

Cambridge sat back. He seemed genuinely pleased to be given the opportunity to explain something. His manner was neither condescending nor superior.

'Very simply, there's a pilgrim called Dante. In that sense, the author is speaking of himself. Dante has to make a journey to Heaven. He must pass through Hell and Purgatory to get there. He has a guide called Virgil. Virgil represents human reason. Once he reaches Heaven, Dante's guide is Beatrice. She represents divine revelation, grace, faith and other such things. In the last part of his journey into *Paradiso*, he's accompanied by Saint Bernard of Clairvaux. Bernard was an twelfth-century mystic, an abbot, and a founding member of something called the Knights Templar. That's a different subject entirely and not necessarily relevant here. Anyway, back to the point. Dante begins his journey in a dark wood. The wood is widely considered to represent sin. He cannot find his way. He is lost. He is rescued by Virgil, and they start off towards Hell. In Hell, the punishment for each sin is what's known as a *contrapasso*, a sort of poetic justice if you like. Whatever sins have been committed in life, the punishment is the reverse. For example, a gambler spends every tormented hour losing money. A promiscuous person is forever denied release from their sexual urges. That kind of thing. Anyway, Virgil guides Dante and they find their way out of Hell to Purgatory. Purgatory is symbolized by a mountain on an island. There are seven terraces on the mountain, each corresponding to the seven deadly sins.'

Cambridge looked at Ridgway. 'You've heard of those, right?'

'Yes, of course. I don't know that I could name them, but I have heard of them.'

'Wrath, envy, pride, gluttony, greed, sloth and lust. All of these correspond to the way in which love can be tainted and debased by humanity. Maliciously, love becomes wrath and envy. Love that is too strong becomes greed and lust. You get the idea.'

'Yes, of course.'

'And then finally we have Heaven, or *Paradiso* as it's known in the text. Here are celestial spheres that symbolize prudence, fortitude, justice, temperance, faith, hope and love. That's a simple version of things because there's also spheres that relate to Medieval astronomy and the true essence of God.'

'Okay, so ...'

'So how does this text relate to a motive for someone killing another human being?'

Cambridge smiled. 'I have not the faintest idea, Detective Ridgway. I am an English teacher, not a criminal psychologist. All I can say is that people have been using religious texts as a justification for murder, for war, for genocide for thousands of years. "My God is better than your God" and all that.'

'Is the book rare?'

'No, not at all. I would imagine it could be found in pretty much every library in the world. Most bookstores would carry it, too. Like I said, it's considered one of the most important works in European literature, and – depending on your viewpoint – one of the most important in the history of the written word.'

'Which doesn't help me.'

'No, I can see that, Detective Ridgway.'

'I would ask you to keep all of this to yourself, Professor Cambridge. The presence of a written note, the connection to this book. That's not something that has been made public.'

'Oh absolutely. Not a word shall pass my lips.'

Ridgway got up.

'Thank you for your time.'

Cambridge showed him to the door and they shook hands.

'Let me know if there's anything else you think I might be

35

able to help with. Tragic though it is, I have to say it's injected a little excitement into what is a very quiet, academic existence.'

'Of course, sir, and thank you again for seeing me.'

Cambridge smiled. 'Let's hope you can find your own Virgil to guide you out of Hell.'

7

Upstate New York was home to the Adirondack Mountains. Part of the New York Forest Preserve, the range possessed over two hundred thousand acres of old-growth forests, within it endless tracts of fallen trees, as if giants departing had discarded their broken furniture. Close to ten million tourists – hunting, fishing, canoeing, trekking, climbing, those who sought merely space and air and nature – visited each year.

At the northernmost point of Lake Ontario, up through Mexico Bay towards Watertown, the Black River began its southerly journey to Lyons Falls. On its route, and just below Fort Drum, was Carthage – a *blink and you miss it* village on the edge of Wilna, Jefferson County.

Arriving in the late afternoon of Friday, April 18th, accompanying a group of retirees who planned a week of walking and sightseeing in the mountains, was Maria Fischer. Maria was a registered nurse employed under seasonal contract by a Syracuse-based outfit called Wilderness Wonders. Offering 'unparalleled adventures for the young at heart', Wilderness had established itself as a respected and thriving vacation management company for those seniors who gravitated towards the outdoors. Trips to Niagara Falls, the Great Lakes and the Adirondacks were their specialty, and they prided themselves on value for money, attention to detail and their flawless customer service. With each party, a nurse was assigned. So as not to spook the clientele, the nurse was called a 'Wilderness Care Manager'. Prior to final booking confirmation, prospective vacationers were obligated to inform the Care Manager of ongoing treatments, medication schedules, adverse conditions such as high blood pressure, respiratory issues, any recent illnesses, and any long-term health contraindications. Throughout the April mountain week, Maria would be on hand to deal with any and all medical requirements or emergencies, fully qualified to administer first aid, also to provide information to attending medical personnel in the event of a serious illness or life-threatening condition.

In the third week of April, Maria's party was comprised of twelve guests – four couples, three single women, one single man. The youngest was sixty-one, the eldest seventy-seven. They were booked in at the Lakeland Retreat, a substantial hotel and cabin complex that sat between Carthage and the banks of the Black River. Lakeland was a preferred facility for Wilderness. Guests could stay in the hotel itself, or choose a self-contained cabin. The setting was picturesque, the accommodation more than comfortable, and the mark-up that Wilderness added for themselves was generous.

The first meal, as was tradition, was held in the hotel restaurant. This was an opportunity for Maria to introduce herself properly, to tell the guests that she was there for anything they might require, and also for those assembled to get to know a little of one another. As was so often the case, the exuberance and enthusiasm of the gathering was contagious. Wine flowed, stories unfolded, and it was well past midnight by the time the ensemble began to disperse, some of them to their respective hotel rooms, others chaperoned by a member of the hotel staff to their cabins.

John 'Frenchie' Wilson and his wife, Vivian, were one of the couples who'd selected a cabin. His nickname – even used by his wife – was the only name by which he was known. No one called him John. No one called him Mr. Wilson. He was just Frenchie, plain and simple. He used the name with pride, and he had no reservations when it came to telling people exactly how he'd earned it.

On June 6th, 1944, by then a corporal in the 82nd Airborne Division, Wilson – one among the dozens dropped by twelve planes – parachuted into the marshes south of Carentan and entered a German-occupied town called Grainges. The battle that ensued was bloody and brutal. Finally the Americans were overrun. The Germans killed over forty civilians and a number of US soldiers. Despite their surrender, the battalion surgeon, two medics and fourteen paratroopers were divided into two groups. Five were marched at gunpoint to a nearby pond, bayoneted and thrown into the water. The remainder were marched over three miles to a field near Le Mesnil-Angot. Here they were forced to dig a pit, to kneel ahead of it, and then they were shot in the back of the head.

The SS that remained in Grainges looted it for valuables, killed civilians, and then torched it.

Wilson had evaded capture and survived. Having manned a mortar position for fourteen hours straight, he then headed south and joined another infantry company moving east.

Following the end of the war, Wilson remained in France until 1948. He learned the language, acted as an interpreter for French Jews who'd survived the Holocaust, and when he returned to New York just before Christmas of that year, he brought one of those survivors with him. Marrying her, they settled in Albany. They raised four children, the youngest – Benjamin – now a thoracic surgeon at Hartford Hospital in Connecticut.

Both Frenchie and Vivian were in good shape for their age. Though Vivian suffered a little with rheumatism, she was never one to complain. Periodically, Frenchie drank a little too much, and that welcome dinner at Lakeland was one of those occasions.

By the time the lights went off in their cabin a little after one in the morning, Frenchie was out-for-the-count. Inured through close to three decades of experience, Vivian was not troubled by her husband's sometimes thunderous snoring, and the day had been long and tiring. Her breathing slowed gradually, her body welcoming the warmth beneath the generous covers, and she drifted into a sleep from which she would never awaken.

The absence of Frenchie and Vivian Wilson was noted by Maria Fischer on the morning of Saturday the 19th of April.

The first of the group's daily trips into the Adirondacks was scheduled to depart by bus into the foothills a mile or two west of Fort Drum at 10.30. The remainder of the guests – a little worse-for-wear, certainly a great deal less vociferous and rowdy than they'd been the night before – had all shown by 9.00. Breakfast, as had been the case with the previous evening's dinner, was a buffet in the hotel restaurant.

At 10.00, leaving the remainder of her charges to their own devices, Maria went to the hotel reception desk and asked to see a plan of the resort. Identifying which cabin housed the Wilsons, she headed over there alone. Knocking repeatedly on the locked front door and getting no response, she walked around the cabin. Every window was closed and curtained.

Back at the hotel, Maria requested assistance from security. Hearing this, the duty manager came out of his office.

'I'm Carl,' he said. 'I'm the early shift manager.' He asked her what was happening.

'I have a couple,' Maria explained. 'Mr. and Mrs. Wilson. They're in one of the cabins. They're supposed to have joined us for breakfast.' She glanced at her watch. 'The trip we're scheduled to take today is due to leave in ten minutes.'

'And you've been out to the cabin?' the manager asked.

'I have, yes. Nothing. Not a sound.'

Unable to disguise his concern, the manager said he would accompany her.

Fearing the worst, Maria was overcome by a sense of foreboding. Her mind, needing to find some rationale for what was happening, refused to give up on an explanation. She was not unused to death. She was a nurse, after all, and had specialized in the care of the elderly for much of her career. People died. That was just the way things were, and there was nothing that could be done to prevent the inevitable. If one of the Wilsons had died, then the other would have wasted no time in alerting someone. However, in that moment, she vaguely recalled reading of a case some years before. A wife had died in her sleep. The husband, distraught, lost, confused, had stayed with her for two days until he'd finally gathered sufficient will to make it out of the bedroom to call someone. Was that what had happened here? Would they enter the room and find a heartbroken and utterly devastated husband or wife holding the hand of their loved one?

The door opened into semi-darkness, and Carl stepped back to let her inside.

'Mr. Wilson? Mrs. Wilson?' Maria called out. 'It's Maria. Are you alright?'

Silence greeted her.

Carl then called out for them. Again, no response.

'That's the bedroom,' he said, indicating the door to the right.

Everything slowed down. The world beyond the walls disappeared. Her heart raced. There was moisture on her palms, so much so that as she tried to open the door the handle just slipped between her fingers.

'Let me,' Carl said, and Maria stepped aside.

Inside the bedroom, it was even darker. Nothing moved. The silence was almost physical in its intensity. And the smell – that of disinfectant, but somehow sweeter, more cloying – filled her nostrils.

Ether, she thought. *I can smell ether.*

Carl walked to the window and drew the curtains.

The recumbent forms of Frenchie and Vivian Wilson, their eyes closed, the cover drawn up, lay beside one another with their arms down by their sides. The fingers of the hands that were closest were entwined, as if – in their last moment – they'd each held onto the person that meant more to them than anyone else in the world.

They had survived war and death and indescribable horror together. They had made their way out of Hell – hand-in-hand, side by side – and then, as they'd taken their final breaths, they had departed life with a gesture that symbolized their resolute unity.

'Are they dead?' Carl asked.

'Yes,' Maria said.

'Are you sure?'

'I'm sure.'

'Oh my God,' Carl said quietly. He backed out of the room and left Maria alone with the Wilsons, her heart in her throat, her eyes filled with tears.

8

The Cause of Death report was submitted to Carthage PD by the Tri-County coroner. John and Vivian Wilson had died of chloroform poisoning. The small slip of paper that had been discovered at the crime scene – on it the words, O HUMAN RACE, BORN TO FLY UPWARD, WHEREFORE AT A LITTLE WIND DOST THOU FALL? – was filed as evidence and catalogued in lock-up. Perhaps it would have remained there indefinitely, never once coming to the attention of either Tom Marcus or Michael Ridgway had it not been for the insistence of the youngest of the Wilsons. Dr. Benjamin Wilson, he of Hartford Hospital, took it upon himself to call Carthage PD repeatedly until he threatened to go to the press if someone in a position of authority didn't take his call. Carthage – ill-equipped to deal with a double homicide – called in assistance from Major Crimes Unit, Homicide Division. A week later, Benjamin Wilson arrived at the office of Lieutenant Ross McCarthy in Syracuse.

McCarthy listened to Wilson. He expressed his commiserations for the loss of his parents, and assured him that everything that could be done was already being done to bring the perpetrator of this terrible crime to justice.

Wilson was used to dealing with officials of all sorts – from over-eager hospital accounts managers all the way up to the Head of Surgery and the Hospital Administrator. He knew when he was being sold a bill of goods and he wasn't buying.

'Who's running the case?' Wilson asked.

'Ultimately, I am,' McCarthy replied. 'We're responsible for pretty much every homicide investigation in most of the counties between Rochester and Albany. We cover the north as well, and that's why Jefferson County falls under our jurisdiction.'

'So if Jefferson County is under your jurisdiction, why did I have to phone Carthage a hundred times to get anyone to do anything?'

'All I can do is apologize, Dr. Wilson.'

'But you have a team of detectives, right?'

'We do, sir, yes.'

'So which detective is heading up this specific investigation into the murder of my parents?'

'I don't have that information to hand at this very moment, sir.'

'Then I'll sit here until you find out.'

'Sir, if you could—'

'Just nothing, Lieutenant. My parents were killed. They were supposed to be on vacation. Someone broke into their cabin and killed them. My father was a decorated World War Two veteran. My mother was a Holocaust survivor. They were hard-working, tax-paying, contributing members of society. They raised four children, all of them career professionals. My sister happens to be an attorney. I have no doubt that police negligence and ineptitude would be manna for the *Journal* or the *Tribune*—'

'I fully appreciate how you must be feeling right now, but—'

'Oh fuck off, Lieutenant. You have absolutely no fucking idea how I feel. My parents are dead. From what I understand, they were killed with chloroform. Do you have even the faintest idea how hard that is? I am a surgeon. I know medicine, seemingly a great deal better than you know police work. Such a thing would take preparation, time, care, precision. This wasn't some crime of fury. This wasn't some random drive-by shooting. This was calculating, premeditated, and very, very intentional. Now, are we going to sit here and bullshit one another for the rest of the afternoon, or are you going to tell me what the living fuck is going on?'

Thirty minutes later, Benjamin Wilson was in an interview room with Michael Ridgway. As yet, the case had not yet crossed his desk. Perhaps, had Wilson not shown up, it might never have done. Ridgway listened, took notes, asked questions, and gave Wilson the very definite impression that he knew what he was doing. Though the interview gave Wilson no further information about what had happened to his parents, and – more importantly – nothing regarding the identity or motive of the perpetrator, it did reassure him that someone in Syracuse PD gave a damn.

An hour later, Ridgway located the note that had been left in the cabin. He arranged to have it faxed from Carthage. As soon as it arrived, he was in McCarthy's office.

'We now have four, sir. The first in Ulysses, a schoolteacher called Caroline Lassiter. The second was in Baldwinsville, a guy called Raymond Keene. And now we have the Wilsons. That's four with the same MO, and at each scene the perp left a handwritten note. I have all three notes, sir, and the writing is the same. I've done some legwork on this already, and I want to go primary.'

'You were running the first two?'

'No, sir. Detective Marcus was primary. Let Marcus run with the cases he already has. Give me this one, and give me an officer to handle the admin and cover the phones.'

'And where the hell am I supposed to magic you up an assistant from, eh?'

'There must be someone who can be transferred, even if it's for a short while, just until I get this thing off the ground.'

'Let me take a look.'

'There was an officer out in Ulysses. She was stationed at the first crime scene. She's on loan from here.'

'Her name?'

'I have it written down, sir.'

'Get it for me. I'll check it out.'

9

Rachel Hoffman stood inside the doorway of Michael Ridgway's Syracuse PD office. It was Wednesday, May 7th. The call had come in for her to transfer back from Ulysses the previous afternoon.

On a board to her right were pinned pictures of the four chloroform victims – Caroline Lassiter, Raymond Keene, Frenchie and Vivian Wilson. Beneath them were copies of the three notes that had been left behind at the crime scenes.

'You asked for me, didn't you?' Rachel asked.

'I did.'

'You said you'd keep me posted.'

'I did say that, yes. I forgot. My mind was elsewhere.'

Rachel turned and looked at the board.

She indicated the Wilsons.

'Elderly couple,' Ridgway said. 'Found dead in a vacation cabin outside of Carthage. Side by side in bed.'

'What is that, Jefferson County?'

'Yes.'

'You have the coroner's tox report?'

'I do.'

'Barbiturates and chloroform?'

'Yes.'

'That's four dead in two months.'

'That we know of,' Ridgway said.

'And you know about this book, right? Where the quotes come from.'

'A basic idea, yes. I went over to the university and spoke to a professor there. The coroner on the first two introduced us.'

Rachel looked at the faces. A young schoolteacher in her early twenties, a Home Depot employee in his late forties, a retired couple.

'For someone who is so prepared and methodical, it seems to me that there must be some sort of link between these people,' Rachel said. 'Surely, this can't be a case of random selection.'

'That's what we're here to find out.'

Rachel turned and looked at Ridgway. 'And I'm not just here to make coffee and photocopies, right?'

'You're here to help with every aspect of this investigation, Officer Hoffman.'

'And what about Tom Marcus?'

'What about him?'

'I'm assuming that you've now been assigned primary on this. Marcus was primary on Caroline Lassiter. Is he not going to be pissed that you've taken over?'

'Tom Marcus has more than enough work to be getting on with. Don't concern yourself with what he might or might not think.'

Rachel nodded. 'I'll do my best.'

'So, we're gonna need everything. Caroline Lassiter's parents, siblings, work colleagues, friends. Same for Keene. People at the Home Depot where he worked. Ex-wives, girlfriends, neighbors. As for the Wilsons, I met their youngest son. He's a surgeon over in Connecticut. He's threatened to go to the press if we don't get moving on this. The father was a World War Two veteran, the mother a Holocaust survivor. Public relations-wise, we need to keep a lid on that. That's precisely the kind of story that the *Tribune* would headline. Police incompetence an' all that. You know the deal.'

'And the notes are something only the attending officers and the respective coroners know about.'

'Yes. You, me, Detective Marcus, my Lieutenant, crime scene photographers, Forensics and Coroner's office staff.'

'We have means and method, but no clue as to motive.'

'Right.'

Rachel stepped back from the board and sat facing Ridgway. 'Criminal psychologist?' she asked.

'We can look at that, yes, but first we need to get as much information about all of these people as we can. We put a picture together of their lives, professional and personal. We see if we can't find any connection between them. If there is, then we're some way towards identifying the reason for their selection. If not, then we look at other angles.'

'You ever been primary on a homicide before?' Rachel asked.

'Once, yes. It was closed within a week.'

'So we're both green as grass on this kind of thing.'

'We are, but the basics are the basics. Information is everything. The more we get, the better. Then it's a matter of prioritizing. Eliminate the irrelevant, hold onto whatever remains. The trick is to know what's important and what's not.'

'Is that a quote from detective class?'

'Yes, absolutely. And once we'd learned it verbatim, we got to do coloring and jigsaws.'

Rachel looked towards the window. 'Can I ask you a personal question?'

'Sure.'

'Are you single?'

Ridgway smiled and frowned simultaneously. 'What?'

'You don't understand the question?'

'Sure I do. I'm just surprised to be asked. And yes, I'm single.'

'Okay.'

'Why did you ask me that?'

'I guess it doesn't make a great deal of difference. Married guys can be worse sometimes.'

'What? You think I'm gonna hit on you?'

48

'Fifty-fifty.'

'I have absolutely no intention of this being anything other than a professional, working relationship.'

'That's what you say now, Detective Ridgway. And after we've spent countless hours together, after we've stayed up nights, eaten crappy take-out food, after we've sat here poring over statements and testimonials until we can no longer keep our eyes open, things can get awkward.'

'Is this something you've experienced?'

'I'm sure you can guess what it's like to be me in a work environment like this.'

'Whatever guys you're talking about, I'm not one of them.'

'I'll take your word for it.'

'So, are we gonna discuss sexual harassment in the Syracuse PD, or are we gonna get to work, Officer Hoffman?'

'In here, you can call me Rachel. And yes, we're gonna get to work.'

IO

The investigation unfolded exactly as Rachel had predicted.

Throughout the following six weeks, herself and Ridgway interviewed everyone they thought might give some indication of the direction they could take: Home Depot cashiers and delivery drivers, employees at the Lakeland Retreat, the staff of both Wilderness Wonders and Caroline Lassiter's school, relatives of each of the victims, their numerous friends, work colleagues, previous employers and ex-partners. They went back through every aspect of the four autopsies. They listed medical centers, schools, veterinarian clinics, chemical companies and pharmaceutical suppliers who stocked chloroform. They approached every university medical department in the state, made enquiries about drop-outs, failed graduates, anyone who'd left any kind of lasting impression on the relevant professors. They looked for earlier instances of barbiturates or chloroform being employed in any crime, no matter what it was.

Rachel also bought a copy of *The Divine Comedy*. She lost count of the nights she fell asleep with the book on her face.

There were late nights and early mornings; there was endless driving, bad food, too much coffee, too little sleep. The edges wore thin. There were days when Rachel Hoffman and Michael Ridgway struggled to remain cooperative and amicable.

Finally, as they started into the third week of June, they came to the bitter and blunt conclusion that they really were no farther forward then they'd been at the outset of May.

The office that had now become their second home was

crowded with files, photographs and an endless stack of note-books. The frustration was palpable. Ridgway's lieutenant was making noises about transferring Rachel back to routine duties. Yes, she could stay in Syracuse, but he needed her out in a squad car, not locked up in an office poring over reams of paperwork. Despite the endless hours invested, they had yet to progress the investigation at all.

The identity and motive of 'The Sleeper' was as much an enigma as they'd been when Rachel first stood in Caroline Lassiter's bedroom back in February.

'We need something else,' Ridgway said. 'Some other angle, some other approach.'

'You want to get a psychologist in on this?'

Ridgway shrugged. 'And what would that do? Give us a hypothesis, sure. At best, a bunch of possibilities about the type of person that might do this kind of thing?'

'So what do we know? I mean, really, what do we actually know? Physically able, sufficiently strong to carry a man from his kitchen to his bedroom, familiarity with medical procedure, certainly as far as the use of barbiturates and chloroform are concerned. We don't know his age, race or height. We are assuming that he wrote the notes. If we're going to get a psychologist involved, then we should also get a graphologist to analyze the handwriting.'

'I asked about that.'

'And?'

'It was met with the expected degree of cynicism. The general consensus seems to be that handwriting analysis is even less reliable than a lie detector.'

Rachel leaned back in the chair and closed her eyes. She was exhausted – psychologically and physically. She needed a haircut, a week of good food and adequate rest. In truth, she needed a vacation.

'How long do you think we have before we get shut down?' she asked without opening her eyes.

'Honestly, I guess a week. Two at most.'

'So we need another victim.'

'What?'

Rachel sat up. 'We need another one, Mike. Face facts. The only way we keep this thing on the tracks is if there's something that warrants the continuation of the investigation. We need another body, and we need him to make a mistake.'

'If you place any credence in the power of thought, then you have just sentenced someone to death.'

Rachel took a calendar from the desk. 'Okay,' she said, counting out the days. 'From Lassiter to Keene, we have twenty-four days. From Keene to the Wilsons, it's thirty-seven. It's now been fifty-eight days since those bodies were discovered.'

'And there's always the possibility that there are more victims that haven't been found. Or maybe they've been found, but in entirely different states.'

'And we've sent out memos, followed them up, watched the newspapers, done everything we can aside from go to the press with this.'

Ridgway was quiet for a moment.

'What are you thinking, Michael?'

'I am thinking that maybe someone else could go to the press.'

'Are you serious?'

'The Wilson guy. The surgeon. He threatened it. If he'd done it we'd have heard about it. Maybe he needs some encouragement.'

'No,' Rachel said emphatically. 'You can't do that, Michael. You have any idea the kind of shitstorm that would blow up if you got found out? We've somehow managed to keep this whole thing under wraps. Every single person we've spoken to, we've impressed upon them the necessity to say nothing to anyone. And now we're going to break the cardinal rule ourselves?'

Ridgway didn't reply.

'Michael. Tell me you're not going to do this.'

'Okay, okay, for Christ's sake.'

Ridgway got up. He walked to the window. He buried his hands in his pockets.

'So where from now?' he asked, almost to himself.

Rachel had no answer, and so she said nothing.

Ridgway turned back. 'Like you said, he needs to make a mistake. He needs to give us something, any fucking thing. It doesn't matter what it is, there just needs to be something, some new element, a thread we haven't seen before—'

The phone rang.

Rachel stood up. Ridgway took a step forward.

It kept on ringing and neither of them moved.

'If this is—' Ridgway started.

Rachel snatched the phone from the cradle.

'Syracuse Homicide. Officer Hoffman speaking.'

Even as she listened, the color drained from her face.

II

Once more, standing silent and emotionally subdued in the presence of yet another terminated life, Rachel Hoffman could not conceive of anything as absolute as death.

Here was the end of things. Whatever story had been told through the chapters of this life had come to a close. There had been minutes, hours, days and months, all of them crowded up against one another, and now there would be no more happiness or heartbreak, love or loss, moments of dark self-inspection against those times when everything had seemed so very bold and bright and beautiful. The rare occasions when the world did not seem so cruel and unforgiving were few and far between, and perhaps the most difficult to remember.

'You okay?' Ridgway asked. 'You need to go outside for a while?'

Rachel shook her head.

'Dr. Hill's on the way. Forensics and the photographer, too. I'll go out front and wait for them.'

'Okay,' Rachel said. She crossed the room and looked out of the window. The stillness was palpable, as if time itself had stopped.

They were in Van Buren, a town just ten miles north-west of downtown Syracuse. It was a neat, well-maintained house in a quiet street. The owner and occupant was a fifty-one-year-old seamstress called Brenda Forsyth. The call had been made by Kyle Webster, twenty years old, who lived with his folks just three doors down. Kyle worked in construction. He was Brenda's go-to-guy for odd jobs and home maintenance. She'd arranged for him to come over on Saturday, just two days earlier. He'd knocked, received no answer. He'd tried again on Sunday. Again, no answer.

By the time it got to Monday morning, still not a sound from within the house, Webster took it upon himself to enter the property. He had keys, had been in before when work was required in Brenda's absence.

'Did you find that unusual? Her asking you to come over and then not being here?' Ridgway had asked him.

'For Brenda? No, not particularly. She was always forgetting things. And she has a sister with kids. She often goes over there at a moment's notice to look after them or just hang out.'

'Does she have children of her own?'

'No.'

'Husband, ex-husband, boyfriend?'

'She's never been married,' Webster said. 'And if she had a boyfriend, I didn't know about it.'

'So she lived here alone?'

'Yes.'

'Do you know if her parents are still alive?'

'They're not, no. They died a good while back. Mother first. Cancer, I think. Her dad was killed in a work accident. That's what she told me. She didn't give me any details, and I didn't ask.'

'Were you close?'

Webster shrugged. 'She was a nice lady. I didn't see her so often. I really only came round when she needed somethin' fixed or whatever. I'd see her in the street, sure, but we didn't socialize.'

'Was she friends with your parents?'

'No. She was quiet, you know? Kept herself to herself. Lonely, I guess, but maybe that's the way she wanted it.'

Ridgway left Webster in the care of the first uniform that showed up. Webster would give his statement, but Ridgway doubted there was anything he could tell them that would help.

Once that was complete, Webster would be driven to Syracuse so his prints could be taken for the purpose of eliminating him from the crime scene. Ridgway and Rachel would canvass the neighbors, locate both family members and those in whatever social circle Brenda had maintained, just as had been done with Caroline Lassiter, Raymond Keene and the Wilsons.

Though Ridgway's experience was limited, he knew enough to understand that the vast majority of murders were committed by those who were known to their victims. People killed their parents, their husbands and wives, even their children. It was always the first line of inquiry. The most challenging of all were the random or premeditated killing of strangers. Ridgway was certain, as certain as it was possible to be, that the individual who had racked up five murders over the past four months was as much as stranger to the victims as he was to those now working to identify him.

Sitting there alone in Brenda Forsyth's living room, Ridgway could hear Kyle Webster once again detailing precisely what he'd seen when he entered the house. Perhaps, in that moment, he questioned – if only briefly – the wisdom of having insisted that he assume primary on this. He was no stranger to self-doubt. He had not been a bold and confident child, and that lack of self-assurance had continued into his teenage years. Joining the police had not only been a career choice, but also a means by which he'd believed he could overcome some of his own lack of confidence. In the main, it had worked. He had adopted an attitude that facing whatever was in front of him was the only way to overcome his anxiety about that something. Better to try and fail than never to try. But this? This was in a different league altogether. This was, undeniably, a matter of life and death, perhaps even for himself and Hoffman. The perpetrator was utterly unknown to them. They had no leads, no tangible physical clues, not even the most fragile element of circumstantial evidence to narrow the limitless possibilities ahead of them. Everything about the killer remained a mystery. He and Hoffman had worked – diligently and conscientiously, devoting hundreds of hours to this investigation – and what they had to show for it was another dead woman.

Ridgway's exhaustion was not merely physical, it was mental and psychological, a deep-seated fatigue that consumed his energy to think. He did not want to be sidelined. He did not want the case taken from him by those more experienced and authoritative. He wanted to see it through; he *needed* to see it through. If he didn't, he would carry the unforgiving burden of that failure indefinitely.

Rachel heard Hill's voice from the front hallway. He entered the room and smiled.

'Rachel.'

'Lawrence.'

'How've you been?'

Rachel shrugged.

'I know your guy out there,' Hill said. 'Detective Ridgway. He called me about the Lassiter girl. I sent him over to a friend of mine at the university.'

'Right.'

'I heard there was another couple. Old folks out in Carthage. Is that right?'

'It is, yes. This is number five.'

'Let's step out for a while,' Hill said. 'Let the snapper and the science nerds do their thing, eh?'

As the crime scene protocol was executed, Hill, Ridgway and Rachel waited in the kitchen. Surrounding them were the everyday things of an everyday life. Plates stood in a rack on the drainer. A kettle sat on the stove. A floral hand towel hung from a hook beside the sink. A box of English Breakfast tea was on the counter.

'I didn't see a note,' Hill said. 'Was there one?'

'There's an envelope,' Rachel said.

'Where?'

'It's under her pillow. You can see the end of it sticking out.'

'Okay, so right now we're assuming that this is number five. This could be something else entirely. This could be a suicide.'

'It could,' Rachel said, 'but I think it's number five.'

'Based on what?' Hill asked. 'Intuition?'

Rachel looked up at him. 'Because I want it to be.'

Hill frowned.

'Michael and I have been doing nothing but this for the last six weeks. We've spoken to everyone, looked at everything, gone back through every single document, every statement, every photograph, every shred of evidence. I've even read half of that book he's quoting from. We have absolutely nothing, Lawrence.'

'And you're hoping that this is another one, that he's slipped up, given you a lead, right?'

'Right.'

Hill looked at Ridgway. 'And you?'

'What Rachel said. We've covered every inch of this thing and wound up nowhere. If we don't get something they'll shut us down and it'll all have been for nothing.'

'Morally dubious, but I guess it's not a great deal different from disease research. Trial and error, right? Kill a half dozen in the process, but find a cure that saves countless other lives.'

'I'm dead-tired, Lawrence,' Rachel said. 'I want it to end. I *need* it to end.'

'And if it doesn't, what then? Say you do get shut down and sent back to the sticks. And say your guy moves on, winds up in a different state and starts all over again.'

Rachel said nothing.

'This is the life, Rachel. You chose to do this. You're not obligated.'

'I chose to do it, yes, and because I chose to do it I am obligated.'

'So stop feeling sorry for yourself.'

Rachel looked up, her expression angry, hurt even.

'The world is crowded with people aspiring to things they will never achieve. They lie to themselves, they lie to everyone else. You're doing something valuable here, something that only a very few people could do. You do your level best. That's what you do. That's all we can ever ask of ourselves. If it feels like a duty, then yes, you've got no choice. Only you will ever know if you gave it everything. There's no applause for this. There's no great reward at the end. You solve this and they won't name a street in your honor or throw you a party.'

Hill leaned forward. He looked Rachel dead in the eye.

'But you'll sleep at night, and there will be a great many more who'll be sleeping easier because you stopped this nightmare.'

'I know,' Rachel said. 'I know.'

'So far, your track record for making it through the bad days is a 100%. There'll be more bad days. A great many more, I have no doubt. You'll make it through those, too. And in the meantime, you do what needs to be done, keep yourself focused, stay diligent and conscientious and professional. That's what we all need you to do, because there's no one else out here who's got the guts to take this on.'

Rachel smiled. 'You my life coach now?'

'If that's what you need, sure, but I don't think you need one.'

Hill turned to the door.

'We're done in the bedroom,' the photographer said. 'There's a letter. It was in an envelope under the pillow. Forensics said you might want to see it before they took it for prints and saliva.'

Hill got up, Rachel too. Ridgway followed them back to the bedroom.

Laid out flat, already in a polythene evidence bag was the letter, carefully printed by the same hand.

The three of them stood in silence and read it.

DEAR FRIENDS,
JUST LIKE PROMISES, HEARTS WERE MADE TO BE BROKEN.
  I AM NOT WITHOUT SENSITIVITY AND COMPASSION. I
UNDERSTAND THAT THERE WILL BE THOSE WHO WILL NEVER GRASP
THE REASONING AND RATIONALE THAT LIES BEHIND MY ACTIONS.
  AS HAS BEEN SAID BEFORE, IRRATIONALITY CAN NEVER BE
RATIONALIZED. BUT WHO MAKES SUCH A JUDGMENT? WHERE IS
IT WRITTEN THAT WE CANNOT EACH HAVE OUR OWN PERCEPTION
OF WHAT IS RIGHT AND WRONG? ARE WE NOT ALL GUILTY OF
CRIMES OF THOUGHT, OF MOTIVE, OF INTENTION, OF HURTING
ANOTHER OUT OF GREED, JEALOUSY OR MEAN-SPIRITED
REVENGE? HUMAN BEINGS WILL FOREVER BE INCLINED TOWARDS
THAT WHICH SERVES THEMSELVES, AND THOUGH THERE ARE
THOSE WHO PROFESS TO LEAD LIVES OF SELFLESS DEDICATION
TO THE WELFARE OF ALL, THEY ARE LIARS. EVEN THE PIOUS SEEK
PERSONAL REDEMPTION AND ETERNAL SALVATION.
  INEVITABLY, THERE ARE TIMES WHEN THE DARKEST ASPECTS
OF HUMANITY EXPLODE ONTO THE WORLD, PAINTING THE
LANDSCAPE OF OUR LIVES IN COLORS BOLD AND BRUTAL. THIS IS
NOW ONE OF THOSE TIMES.
  I EXTEND AN INVITATION TO ACCOMPANY ME ON THIS JOURNEY.
THERE IS A DESTINATION. WHAT THAT MIGHT BE, YOU WON'T
KNOW UNTIL YOU ARRIVE. AND THEN – PERHAPS – YOU MIGHT
COMPREHEND THE MEANING AND SIGNIFICANCE OF WHAT HAS
BEEN DONE.
  DO NOT LET THE BLIND GIVE YOU DIRECTIONS.
  INSTINCT IS EVERYTHING.
  WHEN YOU TRUST YOURSELF AS MUCH AS YOU TRUST ME,
THEN EVERYTHING WILL BECOME CLEAR.
  ADIEU.

  DANTE.

60

12

Dr. Philip Conrad, resident psychologist at St. Francis University Hospital, had, for a considerable number of years, also served as a consultant psychologist to Attica Correctional Facility, a maximum-security facility in the town of the same name.

Among those for whom Conrad had submitted psychological reports for various trials, sentence hearings and parole applications were the Black Panther Party leader, H. Rap Brown, the New York Westies hitman, Edward Cummiskey, and Vincent 'Jimmy' Caci, the New York mobster who – after being released from Attica – then moved to LA to become a Southern California *caporegime*.

Conrad, now in his early sixties, was – by his own admission – no expert in criminal psychology. Nevertheless, he was the one who most readily agreed to meet with Detective Ridgway and Officer Hoffman.

In the days between the autopsy of Brenda Forsyth – an autopsy that confirmed she had been drugged with barbiturates and then chloroformed to death – Rachel had completed a thorough and comprehensive summary of all she and Ridgway considered relevant in their investigation. Included were copies of the three notes and the letter from Dante. The handwriting on the letter was identical to the notes, and thus there seemed no doubt that Dante had written them. Forensic analysis reports had come back from the Forsyth crime scene. There was no saliva on the envelope, and thus blood-type and serology tests had not been undertaken. There were no identifiable fingerprints, no skin cells beneath Brenda's fingernails, nothing in her hair, nor any bodily orifice that indicated the presence of another person. In essence, the crime scene was clean, just as had been the case with the previous three.

It was early afternoon on Wednesday, June 25th, when Conrad ushered Michael Ridgway and Rachel Hoffman into his office. It had been a long drive, and much of it had been in silence. The report they had compiled had been with him since the previous morning, delivered by police courier.

Sitting across from Conrad at a wide desk, on it an odd collection of objects – a snowglobe, a small wooden skull, a tray of assorted pens and pencils, a copy of *The Muses are Heard* by Truman Capote – Rachel felt as if she'd been sent to the principal's office. Conrad's manner was somewhat formal, not at all relaxed it seemed, but then he smiled, and there was such genuine warmth in that smile that she realized he was perhaps not the person she'd expected him to be.

'I read your report,' Conrad said. 'It was rather like a good mystery yarn, but with no denouement, obviously. Or should I say no denouement as yet. Seems to me that your "Sleeper" seems intent on depriving you of sleep.'

Rachel looked at Ridgway. Ridgway managed a half-hearted smile.

'So what can you tell us, Dr. Conrad?'

'Where to begin?' Conrad asked. 'Psychology is *psyche-ology*. The study of the psyche. It means breath, life, spirit. It is a study of the animating force of a human being. But, if you're venturing into the field of the human soul, then you are also walking around the edges of religion, faith, belief in a God, a Creator, a Divine author. That division between what is mind and what is soul has been challenging us for as long as we've existed. And then you have the physiological aspects of the human state. What is governed by brain? Where are memories stored? What governs personality? How can you have two seemingly identical twins – same parents, same upbringing, same education, same diet – and yet they are entirely different personalities? One of them is a space research scientist, the other is a vagrant.'

Conrad leaned back, his elbows on the arms of his chair. He pressed his palms together and then steepled his fingers.

'In the letter, your Sleeper raises a question. Who judges what is reason and what is not? What is right and what is wrong? Killing a man is wrong, except when it comes to war. It's also wrong, punishable by death, even now, unless you are killing someone who has killed others. In truth, all I can give is my opinion. Someone else, perhaps with greater experience, greater intellect, might give you a different analysis of what this could mean.'

'Anything you can tell us can only help,' Rachel said.

'Unless it points you in the wrong direction,' Conrad replied.

'As it stands right now, we don't have any direction at all,' Ridgway added.

'And thus you have an open mind. Sometimes that's better than making an incorrect assumption and pursuing it.'

'We just need you to tell us what you think,' Rachel said.

'Okay, just as long as you don't take what I'm saying as gospel.'

Conrad picked up his copy of the sleeper letter. Rachel could see that he'd made numerous notes in the margins.

'*Dear friends,*' Conrad said. 'That could be directed to you, or it could merely be predicated on the fact that more than one person would be attending the scene. However, the fact that he uses any introduction at all, and especially the word *friends*, suggests the desire to establish a rapport. He wants to include you. He wants to make you feel part of this.'

'Part of this?' Ridgway asked.

'Whatever he's doing is a performance, Detective. What's theater without an audience?'

'And then he says, "*I am not without sensitivity and compassion*".

Well, by his actions, he is completely devoid of sensitivity and compassion, at least by our standards. This leads us to the next line, where he says that there will be those who will never grasp the reasoning and rationale behind what he does. This is narcissism in its purest form. Your Sleeper is certain of his own superiority.'

Conrad put the letter on the table. He took a pen and underlined a section.

'*Are we not all guilty of crimes of thought, of motive, of intention...*' et cetera. And then we have '*Even the pious seek personal redemption and eternal salvation*'. Here he is minimizing what he's doing. Here he's telling us that he's no worse than anyone else. It's justification, of course. It's an effort to not only make himself right for what he does, but also, in a sense, blameless. Such a personality cannot bear criticism. What's there to criticize? He's done nothing wrong. What he's doing is so very often considered for the greater good. Take Hitler, for example. His successes were his. His failures were the fault of those around him, and then – finally – the German people themselves.'

'So he's right, no matter what?' Rachel asked.

'Not only right, Officer Hoffman, but more right than anyone else. Those who can't see that, well, that's down to their lack of intellect and vision.'

'And what about the killing itself?' Ridgway asked. 'What possible motive could he have?'

'There's two factors to look at here,' Conrad replied. 'First and foremost, we have the matter of taking a human life. There's a huge difference between what is happening here and what we could term a comprehensible motive. The husband who kills his unfaithful wife. The man or woman who kills another in the execution of a crime. The fugitive who kills a police officer to evade capture. They're still murders, of course, but they have a reason that we can understand. Multiple homicide is a different thing altogether. And even more so in this case because there appears to be no appreciable similarity between the victims. He's not killing only blonde teenagers or bank managers or men that weigh more than three hundred pounds. He's killing because he wants to kill, sure, but he's killing for a reason that only he understands. As he says, he's inviting you to accompany him on a journey. He's going somewhere. There's a destination. You won't understand it until you get there because ... well, because you aren't as smart as he is. He's telling you not to trust anyone but him. Don't let the blind give you directions. Who are the blind? Everyone is blind, as far as he's concerned. He is going to open your eyes. He will be your guide, your teacher, and thus he will bring you to enlightenment.'

Conrad once again leaned back.

'I would say he's self-educated. I would say he's of above average intelligence. I would say he's somewhere between twenty-five and forty years of age. I would hypothesize that he doesn't have a career per se, but rather a vocation.'

'A vocation?' Rachel asked.

'A calling. Something he feels he has to do, rather than something that promises wealth, position, social stature et cetera. Whether he has a criminal record, I couldn't tell you. There's nothing to indicate that one way or the other.'

'Okay,' Rachel said. 'Is there anything else you can tell us?'

'One final thought,' Conrad said. 'At the end he uses the word *Adieu*. That's unusual. Why that word? To me, it suggests an intent to continue the correspondence. It's not as final as a "Goodbye". But there's another possibility, again nothing more than a hypothesis. "Adieu" comes from the Latin, "ad Deum". It means, literally, "I commend you to God", but "commend" in the sense of "entrust". Like, "Into thy hands I commend my spirit". Is that what he believes he's doing with the victims? Commending their souls into the hands of God? The fact that he calls himself Dante tells me that he believes he's on some sort of divine mission. The book itself is a journey through Hell, Purgatory and onwards to Heaven. Is that where he believes he's going? And, if so, what is the "Heaven" he's taking himself and us to? Again, we go back to this notion of a higher purpose, something that us mere mortals cannot comprehend.'

As he returned the report, Conrad said, 'I really don't know that anything I've said has been useful, or whether or not it will help focus your investigation. You may already know this, but there's a very interesting project now ongoing with the FBI. A couple of years ago they established something called the Behavioral Science Unit. As far as I understand, they're conducting extensive interviews with multiple murderers and the like, all with a view to establishing some sort of criminal profiling index. I don't know all the details and I don't know who's running it, but that might be an avenue worth exploring.'

Ridgway got up. Rachel followed suit.

Conrad was thanked for his time and contribution. He told the detectives to come back to him if there was anything else he could do to assist.

'So?' Ridgway asked once they were back at the car.

'Interesting, sure, but I don't know that any of that helps us.'

'Maybe we should talk to the Feds.'

'Or maybe it's time to go to the press. Officially. A public statement.'

Rachel didn't respond.

Ridgway started the car. As they made their way back to Syracuse PD, she looked from the window. Passers-by, other drivers, people waiting at stop signs, people leaving stores, people going on about their lives, all of them utterly oblivious as to what was happening in their midst.

Aside from one, of course. Someone out there knew precisely what was happening, and until he'd reached whatever destination he was heading for, he was going to keep on doing it.

Rachel knew that more people were going to die. In that moment, she was overwhelmed by the feeling that there was nothing she could do to stop it.

Though there had been squibs in both the *Journal* and the *Tribune* regarding Caroline Lassiter and the Wilsons, no connection had been made between the five murders that had taken place in Syracuse and the surrounding area. The deaths of Raymond Keene and Brenda Forsyth had not been reported at all.

At first, Lieutenant Max Kolymsky was reticent. Kolymsky had headed up Syracuse PD Homicide for eight years. He did not trust the press, and he wanted to do everything possible to avoid the inevitable, sensationalist feeding frenzy that would ensue if the world was alerted to the fact that they had a multiple murderer in their midst.

It was Rachel who managed to convince him otherwise, arguing that they had to get the public on board, that all earlier lines of inquiry and investigation had come to nothing. As far as she was concerned, this wouldn't stop until they approached it from a different angle altogether.

'And what about this Fed thing that the psychologist told you about?' Kolymsky asked.

'We can ask,' Ridgway said. 'But what will that give us? I'm guessing nothing more than the same sort of guesswork that we got from Conrad.'

'I don't know,' Kolymsky said. 'Experience has taught me that journalists are motivated solely by the need to exaggerate the facts and manufacture as much fear and drama as possible. They're there to alarm people, not allay their fears. They want red banner headlines. They want to shock people.'

'What if we work with one journalist?' Rachel asked. 'What if we have someone as an exclusive point-of-contact?'

Kolymsky laughed dismissively. 'Yeah, for an hour. Once this gets out, this place will be besieged. When did one newspaper ever let another newspaper run with a story and not jump all over it themselves?'

Rachel glanced at Ridgway. *Back me up here, for Christ's sake,* her expression said.

'I think Hoffman is right, sir,' Ridgway said. 'We have to go wider on this. We've got an office full of paperwork and we're no closer to anything substantive. The public are often the last line of approach on these things, and yet they're very often the ones that give us the leads we need.'

'And you know this from how many successful homicide investigations, Detective Ridgway?'

'What would you do in our position, sir?' Rachel asked.

'What would I do? I'd go back through everything with a fine-toothed comb—'

'We've done that, sir. Twice.'

Kolymsky looked at Ridgway. 'She always this combative?'

'Yes, sir. Much more so, usually.'

'Okay, look, I get it,' Kolymsky said. 'It's frustrating, but good solid policing is the only thing that works. You have five murders. I don't believe that there's not a single shred of evidence in one of those locations, nothing from Forensics, nothing from the coroner's office that doesn't give you some avenue to pursue on this thing.'

'If there is, we're not seeing it,' Rachel said. 'And if you feel so certain that that's the case, come spend a day with us in the office. We'll go through everything together, page by page, photograph by photograph, and you can show us what we're not seeing.'

Kolymsky looked at Rachel implacably.

Ridgway didn't know whether he was going to shout at her or send her back to patrol. Rachel didn't move a muscle, holding Kolymsky's gaze until he finally nodded his head.

'The *Tribune*,' Kolymsky said. 'Not the *Journal*. Find out who's

on the crime desk and bring them in. I want to see them personally. You can be here, but I'm going to be doing the briefing and
answering the questions.'

'Thank you, sir,' Rachel said.

She got up, Ridgway too, and they headed for the door.

'Are you after a shield, Hoffman?' Kolymsky asked. 'Is that
what this is really about?'

'No, sir. What it's really about is defending and protecting
the public.'

13

Carl Sheehan was a novelist. This was what he told people. Though he was – as yet – unpublished, it didn't change the fact that he was a novelist. That he was still working on a long-incomplete first book – a coming-of-age road trip set in the Deep South in the 1950s – also didn't prompt him to modify his stated occupation. When asked, as he always was, 'Can I perhaps read something you've written?', he would respond with, 'Soon. You'll be able to read something soon.'

In his own estimation, having worked for the *Syracuse Tribune* for four years, having accumulated a hundred or more bylines, counted for nothing. He'd talked his way into the job with little more than a handful of community college credits to his name, and after a year of covering charity bake sales, civil ordinance meetings and the openings of new car dealerships, he'd been transferred to the city desk. Following the unexpected departure of another journalist, Sheehan had persuaded the editor-in-chief to give him a shot at crime. For six months he'd struggled, forever late in the game, and it seemed he was destined to return to the banality of community journalism.

In March of 1972, as the nationals covered Nixon's diplomatic mission to China, Sheehan caught a break. At the time he'd been dating a triage nurse from Syracuse General. She'd made a comment about conflicting paperwork. Sheehan asked her what she meant.

'What we're treating them for and how they're being billed.

Sometimes it just doesn't make sense, you know? I can understand a handful of errors, but not as many as we're getting.'

Sheehan went on to expose a three-year-long medical insurance scam that involved two senior consultants, a surgeon, an accountant, an administrative clerk and the hospital administrator. Jobs were lost, criminal and civil charges were filed, and Carl Sheehan was awarded Investigative Journalist of the Year by the Syracuse Press Association.

He was no Woodward or Bernstein, but he had secured his position at the *Tribune*. Now, at twenty-six, he was heading up the Crime Desk. He was methodical, hard-working, committed to honest reporting, and he did – every once in a while – feel that he was doing something of worth. Despite this, Sheehan had no burning aspiration to be headhunted by the *New York Times* or the *Washington Post*. Journalism was his job; it paid the bills; it gave him a reason to get up in the morning. He was, after all, a novelist, and once he'd completed his book and published it to wide acclaim, he would leave the *Tribune* and everything it represented without a second thought.

Just after 10.00 on the morning of Monday 30th, he received a call from Officer Rachel Hoffman of the Syracuse PD Homicide Division. She asked if she and Detective Ridgway could meet with him. They didn't want to meet at their respective offices. Would he be willing to meet them at a diner?

Intrigued, Sheehan agreed. He arrived at the specified rendezvous less than an hour later. He found Hoffman and Ridgway waiting for him.

After ordering coffee, Sheehan sat and listened to what they had to say.

'And so what would be required of me?' he asked.

'To report on the story,' Rachel said. 'To do it in a measured and matter-of-fact way. To sensationalize it as little as possible, but not to minimize the seriousness of what we're dealing with here. You'll have access to information, of course, but there will be certain things that we'll ask you to keep out of your articles. Things that we want to hold onto so we can use them to confirm or eliminate suspects, verify eyewitness accounts, the usual, you know?'

'Yes, of course.'

'Do you have any questions?' Ridgway asked.

'Am I the only journalist you've approached?'

'So far, yes.'

'Why me?'

'Because you head up the Crime Desk at the *Tribune*. Because we'd prefer to run this with your paper rather than any other. Because you have a track record of solid investigative work.'

'But the primary purpose of this is to encourage anyone who might know something to come forward, right?'

'Right.'

'Is there a reward for information?' Sheehan asked.

'Not at this time,' Rachel replied, 'but if this generates the sort of public outcry that I think it might, then there's always that possibility.'

'And I would have it as an exclusive.'

'Yes. Of course, as soon as it gets out, the *Journal* and every other paper will want to run with it, but you would be the only direct contact for us.'

'Where do I sign?'

'You'll need to meet our Lieutenant,' Ridgway said. 'He has to give final approval. If you're available, we could do that now.'

Sheehan reached for his jacket. 'Let's go, then.'

Kolymsky, despite reservations about Sheehan's age and experience, approved a first discussion with Hoffman and Ridgway. He would need to see the piece that Sheehan prepared. He would have final approval. Sheehan would also be required to sign a confidentiality declaration.

For the remainder of that afternoon and into the early evening,

Sheehan read the witness statements and crime scene reports. He asked questions, looked at photographs, clarified points that he failed to grasp. Finally, the three of them sat in Ridgway's office to discuss how best to approach an article.

'It needs to be along the lines of "Police seek assistance",' Ridgway said.

'Covering the fact that it's a similar MO, that written communications left at the scene leave no doubt that it's the same perpetrator, but without giving any specifics regarding what those communications are,' Sheehan said.

'Exactly,' Rachel said.

'And who will we be directing callers to?'

'This office,' Ridgway said.

'Are we giving out your names?' Sheehan asked. 'Taking into consideration the fact that you have a complete psycho on your hands, do you want him to know who's looking for him?'

'Yes,' Rachel said.

'You're sure about that?'

'What if he calls? What if he gets off on the idea of taunting us?' She looked at Ridgway. 'I don't know about you, but I don't want to miss any opportunity we might get to have a direct exchange with him.'

'I agree,' Ridgway said. 'We'll handle it so everything that comes through the switchboard is sent here. There's gonna be occasions when neither one of us is available, sure, but I want to manage this as closely as possible. We can't afford to have messages and information winding up on half a dozen different desks.'

'You've got to make the same decision too, you know?' Rachel said.

'I'm well aware of that,' Sheehan replied.

'You're not obligated. You can just byline it to the Crime Desk.'

'If you're willing to be named, then so am I.'

'Okay,' Ridgway said. 'When can you have a draft for us?'

'Before lunchtime tomorrow,' Sheehan said. 'I need to brief my editor. I'll tell him only what he needs to know. I'll run a hard copy and bring it over. Kolymsky can check it, and if we're good then I can get it in Wednesday's first edition.'

'Good,' Ridgway said. 'So, we're out of here, unless you've got any more questions.'

'Have either of you read this book?'

'I'm reading it now.' Rachel said.

Ridgway shook his head. 'Nor me.'

'I have,' Sheehan said. 'A good deal of it, anyway. Back at college. It's hard work. Profound stuff. Makes me wonder if what we're dealing with is a far grander plan than just killing some people.'

'Meaning?' Rachel asked.

'Maybe this is a precursor to something. I mean, I don't know. I'm just spit-balling here, but what if we're dealing with a really committed off-the-wall crazy who hears God talking to him through the water pipes or whatever?'

'So this is Hell?' Ridgway asked. 'Is that what you're saying?'

'Not Hell, no,' Sheehan replied. 'You've got to die before you get to Hell. He's not chopping people up or decapitating them or whatever. He's putting them to sleep. In a way, he's killing people in the most humane way, like euthanizing a sick animal. Maybe he's sending people to Hell. That's where they begin their journey, right?'

There was silence in the room.

Rachel looked at Ridgway, and then they both looked at Sheehan.

'I mean, I'm just saying,' Sheehan said. 'What if this is only the beginning?'

14

SYRACUSE TRIBUNE

WEDNESDAY, JULY 2, 1975

Carl Sheehan – Crime Desk

HOMICIDE DIVISION SEEKS INFORMATION IN HUNT FOR KILLER

Detective Michael Ridgway and Officer Rachel Hoffman of the Syracuse PD Homicide Division are seeking assistance from the public following a spate of murders in Upstate New York over the past four months. The body of schoolteacher, Caroline Lassiter (23), was discovered in her apartment in Ulysses, Oswego County, on Monday, February 17th. Subsequently, a further four victims of the same killer have been identified as Raymond Keene (48), a Home Depot employee from Baldwinsville, John and Vivian Wilson (65 and 64 respectively), Syracuse residents holidaying at the Lakeland retreat in Jefferson County, and Brenda Forsyth (51), her body found by a Van Buren neighbor on Monday, June 16.

Syracuse PD Homicide Division has established a telephone hotline to which calls can be made in confidence. Those with information pertinent to the individuals named above, or anyone who believes they may be able to assist the police in their enquiries, are urged to make contact at the earliest opportunity. All calls will be treated with the strictest confidentiality.

When asked for comment, Lieutenant Max Kolymsky, heading up the Homicide Division, said: 'There is no doubt that we are investigating a highly dangerous individual. However, I urge the public to remain calm. I have assigned a team of dedicated and highly-experienced officers to this case, and I have no doubt that this individual will be swiftly apprehended. In the meantime, I can assure all Syracuse residents that our task in ensuring their safety and well-being is, above and beyond all else, our foremost priority. And to the individual responsible for perpetrating these heinous crimes, I would urge them to surrender themselves to the police immediately. I give my personal guarantee that they will be afforded their full rights to counsel and due process of law will be adhered to unequivocally. If they do not surrender, then my officers will take whatever measures are required to eliminate this threat and bring an end to this campaign of unjustified and seemingly motiveless killing.'

15

The telephones didn't stop ringing for a week.

Michael Ridgway and Rachel Hoffman barely left the office. The number of calls reduced significantly in the evening, and thus they spent the latter hours of the day sifting through one message after another. They snatched a few hours' sleep here and there on alternating shifts. Most of the information could be readily ignored. A woman was convinced her husband was the killer. A clairvoyant had received a vision that the killer – even at that moment – was breaking into a home in Chicago. Yet another stated categorically that the perpetrator was a serving officer in the Syracuse PD.

The *Journal* picked up the story, as did regionals in many of the surrounding counties. By the end of the week, banner headlines were proclaiming *UNSOLVED DEATH RAMPAGE TERRIFIES CITY* and *POLICE DEPARTMENT FLOUNDERS AS KILLER STALKS STREETS*.

Inevitably, the manner of killing was identified. Such a thing would not have been difficult. The names of the victims had been published. All it would have taken was a few calls to known relatives or friends, perhaps even the nurse who'd been accompanying the vacationers at Lakeland, and the killer's MO was in the public domain. The first article – headlined *CHLOROFORM KILLER CLAIMS FIVE* – ran in the *Courier*. Within twenty-four hours the stories referred to the perpetrator as 'The Surgeon', 'The Sleeping-Beauty Killer', 'The Syracuse Sleeper' and 'Doctor Death'.

There was no mention in any article about the letter, the notes, or the book from which they'd come. There was also no mention of Dante.

On Thursday, July 10th, Kolymsky met with Hoffman and Ridgway in his office. He let them speak in turn, each of them detailing leads that had come in, the work that had been done to follow them up, the considerable effort that had been made to identify from where the drugs used in the murders had originated. After they were done, Kolymsky sat for a good thirty seconds in silence.

At last, he said, 'So, in essence, we still have nothing.'

'Nothing substantial, sir,' Ridgway said.

'Don't sugar-coat it, Detective. You have no leads. Nothing. Zero. That's the blunt truth, isn't it?'

'Yes, sir.'

'So, do you have any theories? Anything at all that would even suggest a connection between these victims?'

'Aside from the fact that they have no real dependents, no,' Rachel said. 'Three people without partners or children, and an elderly couple whose children have long since grown up and moved away.'

'So, what you're telling me is that our guy has a heart.'

Neither Rachel nor Ridgway responded.

'I would ordinarily pass this over to my crackteam of hard-nosed detectives, but it seems that you are it. You are what I've got. There isn't anyone else. I can't ignore the work you've done, and I certainly can't ignore the commitment and man-hours you've dedicated to this. However, I also can't ignore the pressure from the media, the public, the captain, the Mayor's Office and whoever else considers they have a say in this matter. So tell me, what are you going to do now?'

'We want to talk to the FBI,' Ridgway said.

'The FBI? What the hell has this got to do with the FBI?

Unless there's been a murder out-of-state that you're not telling me about.'

'They have a Behavioral Science Unit,' Rachel said. 'They are establishing a criminal profiling index.'

'What, like an address book? A telephone directory for all the psychos in the country?'

'No, sir. But with what we have, we believe they might be able to help us narrow down the age, race, likely occupation, educational background, perhaps even physical characteristics of our guy.'

'And this would mean a few days vacation for you pair in Virginia?'

'We'd need to go there,' Ridgway said. 'They're not going to send anyone here to help us.'

'Have you asked?'

'No, sir.'

'Well, why don't you start by calling them up and seeing if there's anything they could do? Seems to me that might be a good idea before I even look at approving a budget. With the additional administrative staff we've taken on to field these calls, and with both of you out of the running for any other investigation that's ongoing, you are already costing me more than any other single operation in my tenure in Homicide.'

'I'll call them,' Ridgway said.

'You go do that, Detective—'

Kolymsky stopped mid-sentence as a dispatcher knocked on the door and then came through without invitation.

'Sorry, Lieutenant, but there's a call for—'

'Who is it?'

'He just said that it was time to speak in person. That it was the right time on the journey.'

16

'This is Detective Michael Ridgway—'

'Get me Rachel.'

Ridgway hesitated. People scrambled across the office to get onto the call. Kolymsky indicated that if recording hadn't already begun, it needed to begin right that second.

'Can I ask your name?' Ridgway asked.

'You know who this is. Get me Rachel, Detective Ridgway. Ten seconds, Rachel is on the line, or I'm hanging up.'

Ridgway looked across at the adjacent desk. Rachel stood there with a receiver to her ear.

'This is Rachel Hoffman,' she said.

'Hello, Rachel.'

'Who am I talking to?'

'You know exactly who I am, Rachel.'

Rachel stepped back and sat down. She could feel her heart in her chest. She could feel her pulse in her temples.

'Can you tell me something to—'

'Barbiturates. Chloroform. Abandon hope, all ye who enter here.'

'Okay.'

'So, how are you?'

'How am I?'

'Yes, Rachel. How are you?'

'I'm tired. That's how I am.'

'I'm sorry to hear that. I guess it's been a rough few weeks for you and your people.'

'Everyone here is tired. We want this to end.'

'And it will.'

'When? How?'

'Soon, Rachel. Soon.'

'Don't you think you've made your point already?'

'Made my point? And what point do you think I'm trying to make?'

'That you're in control? That you can kill anyone you wish to kill? I don't know. I imagine that there must be some reason for this.'

'Which you are struggling to comprehend.'

'Yes.'

The caller remained silent for a few moments. Rachel could hear his breathing. It matched her own exactly.

'From where I'm standing right now I can see the corner of Trent and Machin. There's an old woman crossing the street. From the way she's moving it seems that everything hurts. Every bone, every muscle, every nerve.'

Kolymsky pointed at Marcus. He gesticulated towards the door. Marcus and his partner started running.

'You just told me where you are,' Rachel said.

'I told me what I can see. And if you think for a second that the people that are now being sent to find me are going to get here in time, then they're very much mistaken.' He paused. 'Anyway, as I was saying. The old woman. The woman who wishes for death with every fragile breath in her body. I feel for her. She wants to rest. She wants to lay down and close her eyes and never open them again. She wants to find peace.'

'Is that what you're giving these people? Peace?'

'In a way, yes. Perhaps.'

'Because you think that's what they want?'

'People don't know what they want, Rachel. They have no idea. None at all. Even you have no idea what you really want.'

'I want to stop you.'

'You don't need to.'

'Because you're going to stop yourself?'

'Because there's one last thing I need to do, and then I'll be ready.'

'Ready for what?'

'The answer to the eternal question. The question that no one has ever been able to answer.'

'And what's that?'

'What happens afterwards?'

'Afterwards? After what?'

The caller didn't respond.

'After we die,' Rachel said.

'After we die, Rachel.'

'Is that the destination you spoke about in your letter?'

'Oh no, not at all. That is something else entirely.'

Out of the corner of her eye, Rachel could see that Kolymsky was sending out more people. They were moving swiftly and quietly across the office.

She wondered how many phone booths had a line-of-sight to Machin and Trent. Two, maybe three.

'I'm going to go now, Rachel. It's been good to share this time with you. There's every possibility you and I won't speak again. Not if things go as intended.'

'Wait—' she said.

The line went dead.

Rachel sat there for a good ten seconds, the receiver in her hand.

Ridgway called her name.

Rachel looked up at him, her eyes wide. She just stared at him without blinking.

There was the indescribable feeling of something crawling beneath her skin. Her forehead was varnished with sweat, her mouth dry, and across the back of her neck was the sensation of a thousand insects.

She felt invaded. That was the only word that came to mind. The voice, the calm directness with which he spoke, the self-assurance with which he uttered every word and answered every question.

'Rachel!' Ridgway repeated.

She snapped to, stood up, for a moment light-headed.

'For Christ's sake, let's go!'

17

It was rapidly established that there were only two phone booths from which the junction in question could be seen.

Both were cordoned off within minutes of squad cars arriving. Forensics teams were dispatched to each.

Standing on Machin as people watched and wondered what was going on, Rachel considered the possibility that the call might have been made from a residence. It was unlikely. Even with the very basic technology they possessed to trace calls, they would be able to determine through which of two or three exchanges the call might have been transferred. That would narrow down the search area to less than half a dozen suburban districts. That would not be in keeping with all other aspects of the MO. The complete absence of any physical evidence at each of the four crime scenes indicated a man who prepared everything meticulously, someone who paid attention to detail, someone who intended to give up only that information he intended to share. And he had now shared something important. He'd told her that they were not going to stop him. He had one more thing to do, and then he was going to stop himself.

That final act, as far as Rachel was concerned, had to be another killing. And then what would he do? Turn himself in? Kill himself? The latter seemed most probable. After all, hadn't he said that he'd then be ready for the answer to the eternal question?

The disquiet she felt was unlike any emotion she'd ever experienced. She was disconnected, somehow distant, as if three or four feet behind herself. She watched herself move, she heard words coming from her own lips, but the thoughts that prompted her movements and responses were somehow separate in time and space.

She managed to focus her attention as Ridgway explained that they had a number of clear prints from each of the phones, even a full palm print from the interior Perspex of one of the booth hoods.

Ridgway drove them to the lab, and he and Rachel waited there in the corridor while the technicians isolated and hard-copied each impression they'd found.

It was late in the evening by the time they were done. They had eighteen distinct and identifiable prints. Whether or not their perp was among them, they didn't know. They would have no idea until as many people as possible could be requisitioned to go through fingerprint records. And then there was always the possibility that Dante had no arrest record, had never been processed through the system. But what else could they do? This was a lead they had to pursue, and they had to pursue it with as much dedication and manpower as could be mustered.

They would begin with Syracuse itself, and then widen their search through every surrounding county. If needed, they would call for assistance from Buffalo, Rochester, Utica and Albany. If Dante had left a print, and if that print was on record, they would find him.

Leaving the lab a little before 10.00, Ridgway said he would drive Rachel home.

'We should get started—'

'Get some rest,' he told her. 'We have a huge amount of work ahead of us. We need to be sharp. Right now, as tired as we are, it could mean the difference between seeing something and missing it. And we can't miss.'

Rachel was more than willing to have the decision taken out of her hands.

'I'll call Kolymsky,' Ridgway said. 'I'll get as many people as I can for first thing in the morning.'

'Okay,' Rachel said.

Ridgway drove. Rachel closed her eyes and tried not to think.

Rachel stood in the dark and silence of her kitchen.

As Ridgway turned the corner in the street below, the head-lights of his car threw shadows of the window blinds across the ceiling. The sound of the engine faded into the distance.

She closed her eyes and breathed.

An image of her mother, her father, the last time she'd seen them. Was that January, February? Christmas had been and gone; that much she knew. They'd been in Philadelphia, her mother predictably three sheets to the wind, her father talking like he had only so much time to use every last word in the dictionary.

It was the same madness, the madness she'd known throughout her childhood, her teenage years, all the way to that final decision to leave the circus of their lives and find her own way.

How many times had they moved in those first fifteen years – ten, twelve? – and always driven by her father's insistence that the *next big thing*, the *incredible opportunity*, the *This is it now, this is the one!* was just one step away. Like the last time, and the time before that.

As a child, it had been strangely exciting – new schools, new friends, new neighbors. She'd been swept along on the wave of her father's enthusiastic self-belief, her mother's indefatigable trust in him. Later, wiser, realizing that what he said and what he did were so very rarely the same thing, Rachel had seen the cracks in the façade. In truth, her mother had never believed in him at all. She'd humored him, and in so doing had consigned herself to a life of unpaid bills, skipping creditors, sudden depart-ures from motels and rental homes in the middle of the night.

'Are you ready for an adventure, sweetheart?' her father would excitedly whisper as he woke Rachel in the cool half-light before dawn. 'Get your things, just as much as you can carry. No, you don't need that. We'll get you a new one when we get there.'

'Where are we going, Daddy?'

'You'll see when we get there. Come on, hurry, hurry.'

They would drive for hours, the irreducible minimum of their life's possessions crammed into a car with outstanding payments. Rachel remembered one time her father asking her if she had any money for gas. Anything at all. She'd been twelve.

Her mother hadn't started drinking until Rachel was sixteen.

The first time she saw her mother drunk, Rachel thought she was ill. Awkward movements, as if her planned physiology had been left incomplete, she held onto the edge of the sink and looked at Rachel with a thin smile, a smile that had been corrupted by a lifetime of disappointments.

Her eyes were empty, vacant.

'Are you okay, Mom?'

'You know what my father used to say to me, Rachel? He used to say, "Give everyone a second chance, never a third." I've lost count of the number of chances I've given your father. That man is going to die with his pockets full of IOUs and his heart swollen with disappointment.'

'Are you sick?'

'Sick? No, sweetheart, I'm not sick. But then again, maybe I am. Sick with worry, sick with anxiety, sick with trying to change someone who doesn't want to change. In fact, someone who doesn't even see that there's a need to change.'

'Can I do something to help?'

'The only person you can help is yourself. And the only way to do that is to get away from us as soon as you can.'

Rachel had often asked herself if her career had been nothing more than a means by which she could establish a routine. She didn't even need to choose her clothes in the morning. They were the same clothes every day. She had no boyfriend, no pets, not even a houseplant. If needed, she too could pack her whole life into a car and move. Maybe she didn't want people and possessions because she never wanted to leave them behind. She never wanted to lose anyone or anything again.

She possessed sufficient self-awareness to appreciate that her career was a remedy for the way she'd lived before. Now she had certainty, now she had predictability; now she had a place to go and a reason to go there.

These past months had been trying in every way. When she'd said she was tired, she'd meant it. But this was no fatigue that would be remedied by a few good nights' sleep. This was not the sort of exhaustion one shrugged off little by little with each day of a vacation. This was something deeper, something altogether more profound.

This man – this killer, this sociopath, this nightmare – had drained the very essence of her being. He'd managed to inveigle his way into her psyche and draw out of her everything she possessed. It had become a relationship – the most toxic kind of all – but it was not something from which she could walk away. This was truly dangerous, for not only had it been enforced against her will, it was also a direct and immediate threat to life itself.

It was in that precise moment that Rachel experienced a sudden rush of terror. There was one more thing he had to do. That's what he'd said. One more thing and then he would be ready.

Was she the one thing? He'd asked for her by name. He'd wanted to speak to her and no one else. He knew who she was, and there was no doubt in her mind that he knew where she lived.

Slowly, attentive to every sound she was making, Rachel took off her shoes. Drawing her gun, she made her way from the kitchen to the living room, easing the door open just enough to see along the edge of the frame. Her eyes had grown accustomed to the dark, but she was not only looking for what she could see in the faintly-lit spaces between shadows, she was also listening for the slightest sound.

Her nostrils cleared like ammonia. The hairs on the back of her neck prickled. There was a tension all over her scalp that increased as each minute passed.

From the living room to the bathroom, and then to the bedroom, her eye on the tall wardrobe that stood at the foot of her bed.

Edging ever closer, moving sideways so as to present as narrow a target as possible, she felt her grip tighten on the gun. Her heart did not race. It slowed. Her breathing was shallow. She could feel the nap of the rug beneath her feet.

Stepping to the right of the wardrobe, she crouched. She paused for a moment, her ear just an inch from the side. She held her breath. She listened. She waited.

With her left hand, she reached towards the handle. She would snatch it, pull the door open suddenly, roll down and ahead of it, her gun raised.

She counted to three. She moved. Her shoulder met the edge of the mattress, and she fell awkwardly.

The door swung slowly open.

She was on her back, her head up, her gun aimed unerringly at a long overcoat and an old robe she kept meaning to throw out.

Silence. Everything was still.

Rachel released the hammer of her gun and put it on the bed. She lowered her head to the rug. She closed her eyes and breathed deeply. She stayed right where she was until the turmoil of nerves in her stomach had eased.

Not my time, she thought. *Tonight is not my time to die.*

18

Of the eighteen individual prints that had been lifted from the two phone booths, only three of them existed within the Syracuse PD system.

Late on Monday, after exhaustive work by more than twelve officers and four administrative staff, the names were actioned as priority for location and questioning.

Though the second name, that of a sixty-one-year-old auto shop owner who'd been arrested for selling stolen tires back in 1969, was discounted as being a likely suspect, Kolymsky still sent people out there. The others – Marvin Lewis O'Dowd and Robert Leonard Marshall Jnr. – were both of considerably more interest.

O'Dowd was a career criminal. Fifty years of age, he'd spent a good third of his life in juvie or jail. His last term – four and a half years in Attica – had seen him released just seven months earlier. O'Dowd was a thief, plain and simple. Didn't seem to matter what it was, O'Dowd would take it. Jewelry, clothing, artwork, cars, trucks full of furniture and white goods; if it could be sold on then it was fair game.

Rachel, seeing Kolymsky dispatch Tom Marcus and his partner to find O'Dowd, believed it would be a waste of time. There was nothing on O'Dowd's record to indicate any violent or homicidal intent. O'Dowd had never been arrested for assault, and the robberies he'd been convicted for were not armed.

Marshall was born in Albany, his father a military-contracted budget administrator, and thus the family had moved from one six-to-twelve-month posting to another at numerous bases across the US. With a first criminal caution at just nine years of age, Marshall had racked up a lengthy yellow sheet. Much of it was juvenile, and thus the three strikes policy had yet to come into force. Only two charges of any gravity were on his adult record, that of breaking and entering and public indecency. Marshall was twenty-eight at the time, his father on contract to Fort Irwin, the family in rental accommodation in Barstow, California.

On the night of Saturday, September 20th, 1969, Marshall had gained unlawful access to a residence housing female community college students. One of the students, Catherine Levitt, had woken to find a naked Robert Marshall standing over her bed. It was only later that she discovered that Marshall had masturbated while she slept and ejaculated into her hair.

Considering the nature of the crime and his previous juvenile record, Marshall was jailed for three years. Additionally, a recommendation was made by the court that Marshall undergo a psychiatric evaluation. There was nothing in his record that indicated whether or not that evaluation had been carried out.

Rachel assumed that Robert Marshall had been registered as a sex offender, but there was no confirmation of this in his file. He'd served thirty-one months, and all she had was the address he'd given back in August of 1972 when he was released – Vails Gate, Orange County, just ten or fifteen miles north of West Point on Route 32. The address was that of his parents, the father then employed on the financial program attendant to West Point's intended inclusion of female cadets.

Looking over the file with Ridgway, they concurred that Marshall Snr. and his wife would more than likely have transferred away from West Point to some other base. Whether or not their son had moved with them was unknown. They relayed their findings to Kolymsky.

'Hoffman, you call West Point,' he said. 'Find out where the

91

father went. Ridgway, get hold of New York Probation Services and see if there was any other address for him.'

Ridgway came back with nothing. Rachel had better luck. West Point gave her a contact name and number for the U.S. Army Budget Department in DC. It took some persistence, but she finally tracked down someone who had access to the necessary data. Marshall Snr. was now on contract to Fort Campbell in Kentucky.

It was early evening before Rachel reached him.

'I ain't seen him nor heard from him since we left New York,' Marshall said. 'He in trouble again?'

'There's no warrant out for him, sir,' Rachel said. 'We just need to find him. We're working on a case up here in Syracuse and we need to eliminate him from our enquiries.'

'All I can tell you, Officer Hoffman, is that if there's some trouble then it wouldn't surprise me a damn if my boy was up to his neck in it. That's one disturbed young man, let me tell you.'

'Why d'you say that, Mr. Marshall?'

'That shit that happened in Barstow. You know about that, right?'

'Yes, sir, we do.'

'Damn pervert stuff. Makes me sick to think of it. He was raised right. How the hell he wound up all crazy had nothing to do with us.'

'In what way crazy?'

'In and out of psychiatric treatment, on pills for this, that and the other. Sayin' shit that didn't make no sense at all. Got into some weird religious ideas for a while. Just a mess.'

'And you have no idea where he went after your contract finished at West Point?'

'Not a damned clue.'

'Do you know if he might have come here to Syracuse?'

'I'm sorry,' Marshall said. 'I can't help you. Boy always had his own mind, did his own thing. He could be anywhere.'

'Once we find him, I'll be sure to let you know.'

'You needn't do that. We're just fine not havin' to worry about what the hell he's up to.'

'Thank you for your time, Mr. Marshall.'

Marshall hung up.

Rachel briefed Ridgway and Kolymsky on the call.

'Get onto the DMV first thing tomorrow,' Kolymsky said. 'Find out if he has a driver's license and where it's registered to. If that goes nowhere, start calling psychiatric clinics and hospitals with a psychiatric department. If that's a dead-end, I want an APB and I want that journalist back in here so we can run a picture in the *Tribune*. I want this guy found, and I want him found yesterday.'

19

They did not find Robert Leonard Marshall Jnr.

DMV had no record of him. As far as they could see, he'd never possessed a driver's license.

Three days of calls to psychiatric clinics and hospitals, and they came up empty-handed.

On Friday the 18th, Carl Sheehan was back in Kolymsky's office. Kolymsky wanted a front-page piece with Marshall's police mugshot.

'This is 1969,' Sheehan said, looking at the image he'd been handed. 'You don't have anything more recent?'

'We have what we have, Mr. Sheehan. People don't change that much in six years.'

'But he's not officially a suspect, right?'

'Not officially, no, but he used that phone booth, and that's where our caller contacted us from.'

'That you know of. As far as I understand, there were two booths that the call could have originated from. And who's to say he didn't use the phone for something entirely unrelated?'

'For Christ's sake,' Kolymsky snapped. 'Are you a fucking journalist or his defense lawyer? We gave you this, and you owe us. You put that out, and as and when we get him, you get the story. That was the deal.'

'There's a fine line here, Lieutenant. What if this man has absolutely nothing to do with this?'

'Then you can write a goddamned article about police fucking harassment for all I care. I am at my wit's end with this. We need to find this man, if only to eliminate him from the investigation. Now, are you gonna do this, or should I call someone at the *Journal*? I am quite sure that they wouldn't get into a debate about journalistic ethics with me.'

'I'll do it,' Sheehan said. 'But I'm not going to say he's a suspect. I'm gonna say that you want to talk to him because you believe he might have information that could assist with the inquiry.'

'You can say he's the second coming of Christ if you want. I need his picture on the front page of your paper, and that's all there is to it.'

Leaving Kolymsky's office, Sheehan saw Rachel at her desk.

She was on a call, and he waited until she'd hung up.

'Mr. Sheehan.'

'You know what I'm being asked to do, right?' Sheehan asked.

'I do.'

'And?'

'And what?'

'And what if this is not your guy?'

'Then we'll know to stop looking for him,' Rachel replied matter-of-factly.

'I don't mean that. I mean, what about the effect it will have on him? People get it into their heads that this is your perp and all it'll take is another crazy to see him and you'll have a shitstorm on your hands.'

Rachel sat back and looked at Sheehan.

'It won't be the first time something like that has happened, Officer Hoffman.'

'And what if he is the guy?' she asked.

'Then I have no doubt that all of you will get citations and commendations from the Chief of Police and you'll have fast-tracked your way to detective.'

'I can't make out whether you're the exception that proves

the rule about journalists, or you're concerned about the effect it might have on your career.'

'Believe me, I don't give a fuck about my career,' Sheehan said.

'You're not angling for a Pulitzer?'

'Pulitzer was an asshole. Ironic that the prize for the best journalist was created by a man who created the yellow-sheet tabloid press. Hearst gets all the blame, but Pulitzer was just as bad.'

'Look, all I can tell you is that we have a profound interest in tracking this guy down. He may be our killer, he may not. But, until we find him, we have no way of knowing. We have exhausted pretty much every route we can. Now it's down to an APB and the public, and that's where you come in.'

'Do you have anything on him aside from the print in the phone booth?'

'We have sufficient information to suggest that he may not be the most upstanding and law-abiding citizen.'

'Which means he has a record,' Sheehan said.

Rachel said nothing.

'Your silence speaks volumes.'

'What did Lieutenant Kolymsky say?'

'He said that I can either run this, or he'll call the *Journal*,' Sheehan replied.

'Well, based on my experience, he's a man who does what he says he's going to do.'

'I'll do it,' Sheehan said. 'And I sure as hell hope we're right.'

'If we are, we'll have saved some lives. If we're not, then we'll jump off that bridge when we get there.'

Sheehan's piece ran in the morning edition on Saturday the 19th. It was brief, matter-of-fact. It did not state that Marshall was a suspect, merely that he may have information that could assist in the investigation.

That afternoon the phones started up again. There were people who said they'd seen Marshall, others who said they knew the man but his name wasn't Marshall. Even Wilson, the surgeon from Hartford, called to ask if this was the man who had killed his parents.

Expecting a similar response to the first of Sheehan's articles, Kolymsky brought in a half dozen additional officers to man the phones.

By eight on Saturday evening, the office was once again silent. The APB had gone out statewide. As yet, there had been no sightings, not even suspected sightings.

At 9.00, Rachel Hoffman and Michael Ridgway called it quits. Frustrated, frayed at the edges, dismayed that the hundreds of hours they'd devoted to this had – in truth – come to nothing, they left the office and went to a nearby Chinese restaurant.

Neither one ate a great deal. They spoke even less. Ridgway dropped Rachel at home, said he'd see her in the morning.

'What's your gut on this?' Rachel asked him through the open window of the car.

'Regret from inaction is the worst kind of regret,' he said without looking at her. 'No one can say that we haven't given it everything. Maybe it will be as he said. Maybe he'll do whatever he's planning to do, and then he will kill himself, or he'll do suicide by cop. Or maybe he'll turn himself in so he can be a celebrity for a few days.' Ridgway looked up at her. 'I don't fucking know, Rachel. I really don't fucking know.'

Ridgway put the car in gear and headed off.

Rachel watched him go. She didn't think about Marshall being in her apartment. She didn't think about what was going to happen tomorrow. She thought about what else she could have said to Ridgway. The man was battered – mentally and physically – but he'd worked as hard as anyone could have asked of him. She had done the same, but there was something about his manner that told her he was taking it personally. He was primary. The burden was on him. He had asked for the case, and he'd been given it. It was not a matter of ego or pride. He was not that kind of person. It was a matter of duty, of professional responsibility. More than anything, it was that he cared. His motivation was genuine and sincere. She knew almost nothing of his personal life, but she sensed that it was as insignificant as her own. There was no one waiting for him at home; no one to ask him about his day, to express a few encouraging words, to distract him – even for an hour or two – from the pressure he was feeling.

With that thought, Rachel regretted staying silent.

20

Michael Ridgway was not a man who needed to be acknowledged. For as long as he could remember, he'd known he had to do something of importance with his life. His father – a difficult, angry man who'd become only more difficult and more angry as he'd gotten older – was burdened by the knowledge that he'd always taken the path of least resistance. Perhaps wishing that his son would not follow in his footsteps, he'd challenged him ceaselessly to do better. That those challenges felt like an endless barrage of criticism resulted in a quiet and resentful teenager. An only child, Michael sought refuge in his mother's encouragement. When Michael left for college, she quit the marriage.

'You're on your own,' she said. 'I wish it didn't have to be this way, but it does. I can't take it anymore. The idea of staying with your father for the rest of my life hurts me more than the idea of leaving you. I know you won't understand that, at least not now, but if I stay then I will just disappear into nothing.'

Three years later – having only seen her a half dozen times – she died. The doctors said *natural causes*. What could have been more natural than guilt and a broken heart?

After graduating, Michael moved away. It was not that he held his father responsible for what had happened, but he knew that if he remained, his father's bitterness and cynicism would poison him against the future.

It took a long time to find his self-belief. It was subdued and fragile, but it responded to the presence of other people, one girl especially who encouraged him to study, to persevere, to make friends, to connect with life. That their relationship only lasted two years didn't make it any less important. She had her own demons, and she carried them purposefully. Finally, her grades insufficient to enable her to pursue her own aspirations, she gave up and went back to Seattle. It seemed that her ability to encourage others did not work on herself.

Michael had never considered the police as a vocation. In truth, he'd never possessed a clear idea of what he was going to do with his life. Law enforcement happened by accident – a brief conversation with a stranger, a story of a murder that had happened in their apartment block, and the seed was planted. It seemed that further threads were destined to pull him in that direction, none of them individually significant, but – working together – they became a rope by which he was bound.

Michael didn't tell his father what he was doing. His father would want no part of it. They hadn't spoken in years. The last time had been a brief telephone call one Christmas. His father had been drunk, had rambled about how Michael's mother had betrayed him, how she had let them both down. And then he talked about himself as a father, how he was sorry if Michael had misconstrued his intentions.

'I tried my best,' he said, 'but maybe some of us are just not cut out for that. I know I failed you, and I hope you don't hold it against me. I can't go backwards and fix it. Whatever shit you're dealin' with as a result, you're gonna have to fix it yourself.'

Michael Ridgway graduated with honors from the Police Academy. Within seven years he was a detective. Having spent much of his time in the shadow of people like Tom Marcus – veterans, embittered and disillusioned by an endless catalog of frustrated prosecutions and allegations of coerced confessions – Ridgway had also become cynical. He recognized it in himself, and worked to undo the psychological fatigue that it occasioned.

Partnering with Rachel Hoffman had been different. Sure, the investigation was more frustrating and challenging than anything he'd yet experienced, but he was a firm believer in dogged perseverance. If he could bring this to an end – secure an arrest, a successful prosecution – then he knew he stood a chance of no longer playing second fiddle. He would seek primary assignments whenever he could. He would get his gold shield. He would make a difference.

Once inside his own sparsely-furnished apartment, he shrugged off his coat, removed his tie, and went to the refrigerator.

Opening a can of beer, he sat at the kitchen table for a while. He wasn't yet ready for sleep. Sleep would come, perhaps restless, unsettled, but it would nevertheless be a brief hiatus between one day and the next. Tomorrow, even though it was Sunday, and despite the fact that was not officially on the duty roster, he would be back in the office. Hoffman would be there too, and they would push on this thing until it broke. It had to break. It was a fundamental law. The more pressure they applied, the more likely they were to find the fault line. Criminals of this nature were egocentric narcissists. Caught between their desire to evade capture and an inherent need to be recognized for their self-styled genius, they made mistakes. Ultimately, no one wanted to be invisible. And this guy, with his barbiturates and his chloroform, his letters and his phone call, seemed to be a man with a perverse compulsion to be infamous. This was a performance, a series of set pieces, each of them seemingly unrelated, and yet there had to be a thread that tied them all together.

A schoolteacher, a blue-collar worker, a retired couple, a woman living alone who seemed to have never done anything to impress herself upon the world. They had been put to sleep. That was the only way to describe it. Painless, more than likely unaware of what was happening to them, they just drifted away and never returned. If anything, it was strangely merciful.

As for motive, it was something known only to the perpetrator himself. Psychotic, sociopathic, whatever term you employed, it all meant the same thing. Some deep-seated and profound reality existed in the mind of such a person, a reality that was theirs and theirs alone. It burdened them with an intensity that could not be alleviated by any other means. They were solving something, and though that something did not actually exist in any universe but their own, it required a very particular solution. The solution was as deranged as the problem itself, and until they found the person they would never come close to an understanding. Even then, they might never comprehend it. The perpetrator could very well go to trial with no coherent explanation for their actions. They could very well be judged unfit to stand, and thus spend the rest of their lives in some high-security facility, forever being probed and provoked by doctors and psychiatrists, all of whom would come to their own independent conclusions about what could drive a man to commit such acts.

In essence, understanding was not Michael's job. His mission was to identify, locate and prevent such a person from continuing along this road of horror and destruction. Five people had died, and he could not bear the thought of any further loss of life through his own lack of diligence and conscientiousness.

A little after 1.00 on the morning of Sunday, July 20th, Michael lay down and closed his eyes.

Sleep came quickly, and it was welcome. Such was his depth of exhaustion that he did not hear someone entering his apartment, nor did he stir when that someone came through the bedroom door and stood over him.

The thing that woke him was a sudden sensation of pain in the side of his neck – an insect bite, a pinprick – and he opened his eyes.

The next thing he felt was the pressure on his forehead. Cold, hard, right above the bridge of his nose. He sensed the presence of someone before he saw them, his eyes becoming accustomed to the darkness, the vague silhouette of the figure standing over him becoming clearer and more defined.

'Don't speak,' the intruder said. 'There is nothing you need to say.'

Michael started to move. It was instinctive, immediately defensive.

'Stop,' the intruder said. 'This is a .38. It will punch a hole right through you.'

Michael lay still. His breathing shallow, his heart barely discernible in his chest, he knew what was happening. More importantly, he knew what was going to happen next.

'Who are you?' Michael asked, even though he knew the answer. His voice sounded like someone else's, or – more accurately – as if it was his own voice coming from some other place, a different room, perhaps from the street outside his window.

'I am Robert Marshall. The one you're looking for.'

'What do you want?'

'What do I want?' Marshall echoed.

Michael felt his vision begin to blur. He struggled to focus, to maintain as much self-awareness as he could. He was fighting against an incoming tide. It was darkness and depth and silence and nothingness. He was slipping into a tunnel, and the walls of the tunnel were closing against him as he went. He tried to move his fingers, but they did not respond.

'I want redemption,' Marshall said. 'The same as everyone.'

There was a sense of being swallowed, consumed, absorbed into something featureless and unforgiving. Wherever he was going, Michael knew he wouldn't be coming back.

Trying to form words, trying to translate those thoughts into words, his face unresponsive, his whole body like a mass of unyielding solidity, his every sense blunted, inhibited, becoming slowly redundant, Michael tried to fight it but it was futile.

'You'll sleep soon,' Marshall said. 'Just accept it. Acceptance is best, you know? Sometimes things happen and there's nothing we can do about them. Resisting is just a waste of energy and attention. What is happening can't be undone. Everything is inevitable.'

There was a feeling then that he was unravelling – snapshots of his life, his present, even those things he'd imagined for his future – all woven together like a patchwork quilt that was coming apart at the seams. He was not afraid. He did not have the presence of mind to feel afraid. He felt almost nothing, and then he felt nothing at all.

After Michael Ridgway was dead, after the hypodermic needle, the chloroform, the mask he himself had worn so as not to be affected were set aside, Marshall pulled the covers up to Michael's neck. Leaving Michael's arms exposed, he then brought them up so as to cross at the wrists over his chest. From his coat pocket he took a small slip of neatly-folded paper. Placing it between Michael's hands, he then stood back and closed his eyes. He remained motionless for a minute or more – breathing slowly, his heart-rate accelerated only a little – and then he opened his eyes and smiled.

Undressing, neatly leaving his clothes over the back of a chair, he then took the revolver and walked around to the other side of the bed.

Removing the pillow, Marshall then lay down beside Michael.

Closing his eyes once more, he placed the muzzle of the gun beneath his chin.

'Into thy hands I commend my spirit,' Marshall whispered, and then he pulled the trigger.

21

SYRACUSE TRIBUNE

TUESDAY, JULY 22 1975

HUNT FOR KILLER ENDS IN TRAGEDY

By Carl Sheehan

An exhaustive investigation undertaken by the Syracuse PD Homicide Division into a series of recent killings ended in tragedy in the early hours of Sunday morning with the death of Detective Michael Ridgway. Ridgway, a dedicated and highly-regarded officer, was found murdered in his apartment, thus becoming the sixth victim of Robert Leonard Marshall Jr. (34). Born in Albany, New York, Marshall spent much of his early life moving from state to state with his father, a contractor for the US military. Though he possessed a criminal record, Robert Marshall had never previously been arrested or charged for any violent crime. The motivation for his killing of Caroline Lassiter, Raymond Keene, John and Vivian Wilson and Brenda Forsyth, the deaths of whom have previously been reported in the *Tribune*, remains unknown.

When asked for comment, Lieutenant Max Kolymsky, heading up the Homicide Division, said, 'The loss of such an exemplary officer in the line of duty is a deeply-felt tragedy that has profoundly affected not only my Division, but the entire Police Department of this city. Detective Ridgway was both a role model for those who worked with him, and the community as a whole. His dedicated efforts to bring this individual to justice were the epitome of what it means to defend and protect. The fact that he gave his life in the pursuit of this commitment tells us all we need to know about the man he was. My sympathies are with his family and those who knew him.'

According to the official police statement, Marshall entered Ridgway's apartment unlawfully and administered barbiturates with a hypodermic needle. Ridgway was then suffocated with chloroform in the same manner as the previous five victims. After having murdered Ridgway, Marshall then took his own life with a handgun. Their bodies were discovered by Ridgway's investigative partner, Officer Rachel Hoffman, in the latter part of Sunday morning. Hoffman was unavailable for comment.

Though no explanation for Marshall's actions has been forthcoming, resident psychiatrist at St. Francis University Hospital, Dr. Philip Conrad, had earlier been consulted during the investigation. Conrad was reticent to make any official statement, making it clear that he had no prior knowledge of Marshall and had not viewed any records relating to his personal history or psychological profile. When asked for an opinion, Conrad said, 'It is not within our remit to hypothesize, and it would be unfair to do so. The motivations for such acts of heinous cruelty and the wanton destruction of human life are often unfathomable, even to those who are trained in the field of the mind and human motivations. Though the tragic death of Detective Ridgway has cast a profound shadow over this investigation, it is now concluded and the residents of Syracuse and the surrounding areas can be assured that the reign of terror enacted by Robert Marshall has come to an end.'

Posthumously commended by the Syracuse Police Department, Detective Ridgway's funeral service will be held at a private chapel, the mourners expected to include members of his family, colleagues and civil dignitaries only.

22

The image of Michael Ridgway's body beside that of Robert Marshall, the contents of the man's head having left a wide arc across the wall, was something that Rachel believed she would never forget. An abyss of shock and horror had given way to a numb, matter-of-fact pursuance of routine.

She'd told the officer accompanying her to call it in. Within fifteen minutes another squad car was at the scene. Within another thirty the forensics team and Lawrence Hill had arrived. Hill tried to speak to Rachel, but Rachel was incapable of responding. Hill had her taken from the room. She'd kept trying to go back, but they hadn't let her.

It had been more than an hour before they were done, and then Ridgway's covered body had been carried out of the apartment and put on a gurney. From the kitchen window, Rachel had watched them manoeuver him into the back of the coroner's wagon. Hill had stood beside her in silence.

'There was a note,' Rachel had finally said.

'Yes, there was.'

'What did it say?'

'Eternal, and eternal I shall endure.'

'Jesus,' she'd said, more an exhalation than a word.

'It's over,' Hill had replied.

Rachel had looked up at him, her eyes wide, her face absent of color.

'You need to go,' Hill had said. 'Go back to the office, do what you need to do, and then take some time out.'

'I don't want to be alone.'

'Then don't be alone, Rachel, but you can't stay here. He's gone, and there's nothing you can do about it.'

Lowering her head, Rachel's eyes were filled with tears.

'Look after him, Lawrence,' she'd said, and then she'd turned and left the kitchen.

Michael Ridgway's funeral was held at St. Jude's Evangelical Church on Wednesday, August 6th, at 2.00.

Carl Sheehan was there, and – just as he'd said in the article – those in attendance included colleagues and dignitaries. On the family side were just a handful of people. One of them bore a striking resemblance to Ridgway, and it was he who later approached Rachel. He introduced himself as Michael's father, and then he asked if she had known his son.

'We worked together, Mr. Ridgway,' she said. 'Just for a few months, but it was daily. I got to know him. He was a good detective. A good man.'

'A good man,' Ridgway Snr. replied. 'I doubt he'd have said the same about me.'

In his expression was a sense of self-pity, as if he needed forgiveness for his failure as a father.

'His mother died a long time ago. We were separated before that. We weren't a close family. Hard to say, but it's the truth. I wasn't even there when he graduated the academy. I was wrapped up in other things, out of state, you know? I could've been there, but I wasn't, just like pretty much the rest of his life.'

Rachel wanted to get away. She glanced to her left. Sheehan caught her eye. He got the message.

Sheehan walked towards them.

'I'm really sorry, sir,' Sheehan said, taking Ridgway's hand. 'Your son was a credit to the Police Department, and I know that he will be sorely missed.'

'Thank you,' Ridgway replied.

'Unfortunately, I have to take Officer Hoffman away. There's some things we need to attend to. Official things.'

Ridgway nodded. 'I understand.'

Sheehan started walking. Rachel reached out and touched Ridgway's arm.

'I'm so sorry,' she said, and then she followed Sheehan to the exit of the church.

Outside, Sheehan was waiting for her.

'Thank you for that,' Rachel said. 'I know I should have stayed and talked to him, but—'

'You don't need to say anything,' Sheehan replied. 'I get it, completely.'

'No siblings. No girlfriend. Estranged from his father. It seems his only friends were people from the department.'

Sheehan didn't reply. He looked out towards the parking lot as the line of squad cars started towards the cemetery.

'Are you coming?' Rachel asked.

'No,' he said. 'This is a police thing.'

'Come,' she said. 'You knew him. And you can extricate me from any more conversations I don't want to have.'

'I don't think your people would want a journalist there.'

Rachel smiled briefly. 'My people are human beings, too.'

'Do you want me to come?' Sheehan asked.

'Yes,' Rachel replied. 'And then maybe we could go get a cup of coffee or something. Unless you've got somewhere else you need to be.'

'No, I don't have anywhere else to be, Officer Hoffman.'

'Call me Rachel.'

'Carl,' Sheehan replied.

Traveling in Sheehan's car, following on behind the motorcade, they didn't share a word. Sheehan didn't question why she didn't wish to travel with her colleagues. Perhaps solely because she knew Sheehan would say nothing and that was what she needed.

Rachel also stood beside him at the rear of the ranks of uniforms as the committal service was performed. He sensed her unease as the gun salute was performed, and once the coffin had been lowered into the ground he did as she asked and took her back to his car.

'There'll be a thing,' she explained. 'Some bar somewhere. They'll get really drunk. I can't deal with that right now.'

'Where can I take you?' Sheehan asked.

'Home so I can change, and then maybe some diner, some coffee shop. Anywhere aside from the places I know.'

'Are you hungry?'

'I don't know, Carl. I don't know what I am right now.'

'It's okay,' he said. 'You can let me make the decisions.'

Rachel Hoffman took a week's leave. Until she returned to work on Thursday, August 14th, the only person she spoke to was Carl Sheehan. He offered no opinions; he didn't try to make her feel better; he shared no meaningless platitudes about 'Moving on with her life' or 'Being strong for everyone else'. He listened, and he never seemed to become impatient. True to his word, he expected no decisions of her. He brought food, he took her outside and they simply walked until they'd walked enough. Sometimes she cried. He let her cry. Sometimes she sat silent at the other end of the telephone and he never said a word. The grief was a deep well, but he knew that little by little she would see footholds and places where she could gain some purchase to bring herself out. She would surface when she was ready, and not before. Recovery from such shock and grief could not be forced or hurried. It was a process, and it would take its own time.

Though they spoke of the case, neither one of them could offer up any plausible or rational explanation of what had happened. Marshall's motivation for what he'd done had died with him.

Rachel thought about that last note that Marshall had left —*Eternal, and eternal I shall endure.*

Perhaps, in some strange way, it was fitting. Long after Robert Leonard Marshall had vanished from her mind, the memory of Michael Ridgway – not as he was in death, but as he was in life – would still be present.

It was her duty to remember him, and remember him she would.

II

1980

Inferno

23

The world was a darker place. Of this, Detective Rachel Hoffman had no doubt.

Since her promotion and transfer to Syracuse Criminal Investigation Division a year and a half earlier, her world had been populated by a cast of broken and brutal characters. Long days, short nights and irregular meals were the norm. Shouldering not only the weight of primary assignment to numerous cases, she was also aware that being a woman in such a male-dominated environment continued to lend its own particular burden. Running a case with a male second had a tension all its own. Officially, she was the superior. In reality, she had to walk on eggshells so as not to dent pride or aggravate ego.

Struggling to comprehend the once-familiar city, Rachel was aware of schisms and rifts – social, racial, political – that worsened with each passing year. Every headline and TV news report had something to alarm and terrify the population.

New York was ravaged by crime; people were ghettoized and disconnected. Drugs were prevalent, as were the crimes attendant to addiction – robbery, assault, gang conflicts and territorial warfare. The New York Mafia – having declined in the 70s – was as strong as it had ever been. And then there were the killings. Not the murders of passion or greed or organized crime, for they were at least understandable. The individual campaigns of multiple killings were becoming more frequent.

Out in Menard Correctional Facility, Illinois, was a man called John Wayne Gacy, the 'Clown Killer'. Charged with the brutal drugging, rape and murder of more than thirty young men, his trial had started in February.

Ted Bundy had been sentenced to death for the third time in Florida. Again, more than thirty victims – co-eds and teenage girls, their innocence and dignity destroyed before their too-short lives were violently ended. Echoing her own thoughts, Bundy had said, '*How could anyone live in a society where people they liked, loved, lived with, worked with and admired, could the next day turn out to be the most demonic people imaginable?*'

It was a question she'd asked herself, still doubtful she'd ever find an answer.

The one case that had obsessed her more than any other had been that of David Berkowitz. Just four or five hours' drive from her home, the self-styled 'Son of Sam' had killed six and wounded seven. What had drawn Rachel to the case were Berkowitz's letters – first to the *Daily News* in May of '77, then the *New York Post* in September of the same year. That first letter – on the back of which he'd written *Blood and Family – Darkness and Death – Absolute Depravity – .44* – had begun with, '*Hello from the gutters of NYC, which are filled with dog manure, vomit, stale wine, urine and blood.*' In the *Post* letter, Berkowitz had alluded to demonic possession and declared, '*There are other Sons out there, God help the world.*'

Berkowitz was in segregation in Attica. Rachel had considered going down there. She wanted to know why he'd felt the need to write to anyone. She knew it wouldn't help her understand what Robert Marshall had done, but the need to comprehend such motivations and actions was sufficient to override her reasoning.

And then there was Zodiac, yet another homicidal sociopath who felt the need to write letters, to communicate in symbols and codes that only he could fully comprehend.

In all such investigations there were hypotheses and theories, all of them open to interpretation, none of them bearing the stamp of irrefutable fact. Every case was unique, and even the work of the FBI's Behavioral Science Unit – though significantly farther forward than it had been five years earlier – was up against the fundamental challenge of understanding the human mind. Perhaps that was the one great mystery that would never be solved by Man, because Man could not view himself objectively. Each explanation was biased by the perceptions and preconceptions of the observer. Simplistically, Tom Marcus's often-expressed viewpoint – *Opinions are like assholes; everyone has one, and they're usually full of shit* – was perhaps the closest he would ever come to the truth.

Rachel would never forget Michael Ridgway. She'd heard it said by so many of her peers and colleagues: *There will be a case that you'll never solve. Your career will end before you find a resolution, and it will haunt you until the day you die.* The prospect of never knowing the truth troubled her. Truth was addictive, perhaps the most powerful drug of all, and she was hooked. But, then again, perhaps the addiction felt by killers was even more compelling – the need to find an ever-greater rush of adrenalin that came with the terror they inflicted. There was the need to elaborate, to add drama and substance, all in the hope that they would once again find that first high. Maybe that was the reason that some wrote letters, that others left cryptic clues. Perhaps the need to prove their superior intellect became part of the theater. *I am here, but you will never find me.* Narcissism and ego knew no limits, and then – in a final act of defiance, if only to prove that they could not be judged – they took their own lives. Just like Robert Marshall. It was a world of gray shades and indefinite lines, a world where the worst of humanity took every possible opportunity to paint the world with nightmares.

On the morning of Thursday, March 13th, Rachel arrived early at the office. Lieutenant Kolymsky, now a handful of years from retirement, looking increasingly browbeaten and frustrated, called her into his office.

'You're going to Virginia,' he said with no preamble.

'Virginia? Why?'

'Because the Feds are doing some seminar or something. It's three days. You leave on Sunday.'

'A seminar about what?'

'On fucking origami, Rachel. What the hell do you think?'

Rachel sat down. 'You know, sometimes you are just a bear with a sore head. What the hell is wrong with you?'

'Wrong with me? There's nothing wrong with me. Oh, aside from funding cuts, endless bullshit paperwork, people off sick, people not pulling their freight, people looking busy when they're doing absolutely fucking nothing of any value. And that's just today.'

'And if I don't want to go to Virginia?' Rachel asked, knowing full well she would go but in a mood to goad Kolymsky.

'Then I'll second you to Tom Marcus. You can spend a month being told to fetch coffee and wear shorter skirts. How's that for a start?'

'I'll go,' Rachel said. 'Three days of Virginia springtime sounds wonderful.'

'You're not going to look at the fucking countryside. You're going to go find out what this criminal profiling crap is all about.'

'I'm guessing you don't put a great deal of stock in it.'

'Get the hell out of here. Go do some work. Jesus Christ, you people.'

Rachel leaned forward and placed her hand gently on Kolymsky's.

'You know, Max, I've always thought of you like a father. Your warmth, your sensitivity, your compassion has always been an inspiration to me.'

Kolymsky pulled his hand away.

'Rachel ... right about now would be a good time to fuck off.'

24

Arriving at Washington National Airport on Sunday evening, Rachel was greeted by Joseph McCullin. No more than thirty, McCullin had that scrubbed and pressed look of so many young Federal guys.

'I'll be driving you and some of the others to Quantico,' he said. 'We've got you in a nearby hotel. It's nothing fancy, but you'll only be sleeping there.'

'How many are attending?' Rachel asked.

'I guess about a hundred and fifty.'

'All PD?'

'No. There's some NCIS people, some from Army CID. Mostly Police, but it's a mix. New York, Pennsylvania, Maine, Vermont, Virginia of course, and then a few from further afield.'

'And it's all for Behavioral Science?'

McCullin smiled. 'Everything will be explained tomorrow, Detective Hoffman.'

Three more detectives showed up while they were waiting – two out of New York, one from Philadelphia. One of the New Yorkers, Ray Ward, offered to carry her overnight bag. Rachel thanked him, but carried it herself.

As they reached the car, Ward said, 'Don't mean anything by it, but aren't you a little too young and a little too pretty for this line of work?'

Rachel smiled. 'You know, that's pretty ironic, 'cause I was just thinking that you were maybe a little too old and a little too ugly.'

'Busted,' Ward said. 'I didn't mean any offence.'

'None taken,' Rachel said, taking his case and hefting it into the trunk of the car. 'Wouldn't want you straining those ancient bones, right?'

'I think you an' I are gonna get along just fine,' Ward said.

'Let's not find out, shall we?'

The hotel was just as McCullin had said – clean, functional, absent of any decor. He said he'd be there to pick them up at 8.00 in the morning.

'You don't need to bring anything with you,' he added. 'Everything you need will be provided.'

The others headed off to a nearby restaurant. Rachel wasn't hungry. More to the point, she didn't much care for an evening of cop banter and bullshit.

Rachel slept soundly. She rose early, showered, took coffee and eggs in the hotel restaurant, and was outside in the parking lot before 8.00. The other three detectives showed up shortly after. Ward, in particular, looked a little worse for wear.

'Rough night?' Rachel asked.

'I don't sleep so well in strange places,' he said.

'And you old folks have to keep getting up for the bathroom, right?'

'Sure we do.' Ward didn't crack a smile. 'And I guess they're gonna have picture books and coloring stuff for you today, right?'

'I fucking hope so,' Rachel said. 'And there better be glitter and glue or I'm gonna hold my breath until I die.'

They laughed; the awkward tension from the previous day was dispelled.

'Where you from?' Ward asked.

'Syracuse.'

'You?'

'Twenty-plus years in New York Homicide. The belly of the beast.'

'Things seem to be getting worse out there.'

'Place is coming apart at the seams. That old-school Mafia thing about not selling drugs doesn't seem to apply to the new guys. Epidemic fucking situation, and all the shit that goes with it. But I stay out of that. Homicide is more than enough for me.'

'And I guess we're here to find out how to do our jobs better.'

'You do know you have to be selected for this gig, right?' Ward said. 'Your Lieutenant will have put you forward. Anyone else from your squad here?'

'Just me.'

'Then you're the one they wanted. I guess they think you've got potential.'

'Or they're being careful. Must have a token girl along for the ride, right? Don't want the Feminist Movement all up in arms about discrimination, do we?'

'Cynical,' Ward said.

'Honest,' Rachel replied.

After registration in the administration center, they were directed into an auditorium. Multiple hushed conversations created a low rumble of sound like haulers on the freeway. Up ahead of them was a podium, behind it a large projector screen. The assembly waited patiently until an agent came up the steps at the front of the dais and took his place.

'Welcome,' he said. 'My name is Scott O'Brien. I am a Senior Special Agent assigned to the Behavioral Science Unit. I've been in this unit for the past three years alongside Agents Ressler and Douglas. We've been working tirelessly to establish not only a centralized database, but also a profiling system that's designed to assist law enforcement with multiple-homicide investigations. Some of you may have had some experience in this area, but our hope is that the next three days' work will help your approach become more systematic, method-based and effective. We're going to start with basics, and then, as we prioritize in certain areas, we're going to put you into different groups and we'll be able to deal with more specialized questions.'

O'Brien paused to ensure his preamble had landed.

'So, to begin, we're going to look at criminal investigative analysis. This is a process of reviewing criminal acts from both a behavioral and investigatory perspective. We look at what was done, when it was done, how it was done, and then the environment of the act, the physical and circumstantial evidence, all other facets of the perpetrator's modus operandi. This will include observations of first responders, on-scene detectives, photographers and forensic teams, autopsy results, coroners' reports, everything that contributes to building a comprehensive picture of the offender. What is now beginning to emerge from our numerous and thorough interviews of incarcerated perpetrators is that there is always a specific and individual rationale.'

He gave a wry smile.

'Yes, we will touch on criminal psychology, but there is an inherent flaw in our subject material. We're interviewing and analyzing the means and methods of individuals who have been arrested, tried, convicted and imprisoned. Some of those individuals are serving lengthy prison terms, often life without parole, others are on death row. Ego enters the fray. They resent us. They challenge us. There can be a conscious effort to muddy the waters and confuse us as much as possible. By their very nature they are liars, many of them intent on demonstrating their intellectual superiority over those that curtailed their campaigns of murder and mayhem. And so, when it comes to understanding the mind of such a person, we are the very first to admit that we don't know everything. In fact, we know very little at all. What we do know is that there are patterns. There are repeated routines and rituals. There are things that they feel they have to do – whether it's taking a token from the victim, an item of clothing, some hair or jewelry – or leaving something behind to tell us that they've been there, that they have again outwitted us.'

Rachel, making notes, looked up. She thought of Marshall and the quotes from *The Divine Comedy*.

'In summary, criminal profiling is a method of suspect identification based on what we can glean from a crime scene about the suspect's physical and psychological states. It can be things as simple as height, weight, physical strength, whether or not the perpetrator leaves a body at the scene or moves it to another location. However, it can include less immediately obvious things. The perpetrator kills in a manner that suggests some understanding of human anatomy. The perpetrator tortures a victim before killing them. Our subject positions the victim in a specific way, or removes a body part such as an eye or an ear. The variations are limitless, and though we'll perhaps never reach a point where what we interpret from a scene will take us directly to an arrest, we are also optimistic that what we're doing here may shorten investigation time or guarantee a greater conviction rate.'

O'Brien looked around the room to ensure that he hadn't lost the attention of his audience, and then he said, 'So, let's begin with the case of David Berkowitz, the so-called 'Son of Sam'.

The lights went down. On the screen ahead of them, a larger-than-life image of Berkowitz appeared. Smiling bemusedly, almost as if surprised that anyone would be interested in who he was, the killer of six looked out over the assembly.

'Hello from the gutters of NYC,' O'Brien said. 'My name is David Berkowitz, and I am possessed by demons.'

25

That second night at Quantico, now restless and troubled, Rachel asked herself if this was a road she wished to travel.

The things she'd seen and heard that day were beyond all human reasoning. The torture, the infliction of pain, the desire one human being possessed to subject another to terror and agonizing death. The rapes, the mutilations, the decapitations, the methods employed to dispose of bodies – burning, dismemberment, burial, dissolution in acid and lime, and all of it motivated by an incomprehensible dictate more powerful than the threat of arrest, imprisonment, even execution.

As a child, she'd been told her concentration was poor. In time, she'd understood that this was a superficial explanation. When she was interested, her focus was intense, almost obsessive. Her first impulse had been to better understand what had happened in the case of Robert Marshall, but now it went beyond that. She was drawn to the Bundys, Gacys and Berkowitzes of the world. Such individuals were not only particular to her line of work, but an inherent part of the society within which she lived. People killed in self-defense, to protect families and possessions, to defend territory, to repel aggressors. And then there were those who killed in rage, out of jealousy, hate, even passion. Here she was confronting the darkest aspect of the psychological spectrum: those who killed for the simple pleasure of killing; those who relished the emanation of distress and terror when pain was inflicted. Here were the sadists, the sociopaths, those without moral compass, those without any vestige of humanity.

Taking this road would mean such people would become her mental and emotional bedfellows, her neighbors, her vocation.

O'Brien had quoted Nietzsche at one point: *He who fights monsters might take care lest he thereby become a monster.*

Was this the inevitable destiny of people who spent their lives tracking the most evil of human beings? Was their deranged psychology like a virus, insidiously infecting everything that came within its field of influence? And, if so, who would she become?

Rachel knew she was a moth to a flame. She sought the truth, but the truth was so often fierce and brutal. As with the moth, that final moment of brilliant exposure resulted in the extinguishing of life.

During one break, Rachel spoke to Ward. He proved himself nowhere near as cynical and embittered as she'd expected.

'Keeping your shit together is a matter of imposed and enforced self-discipline,' he told her. 'I have a wife, three kids and a house in the suburbs. Sure, there are long days, and sometimes I'm on a case for months at a time, but when I get home I've left all that behind. I don't talk about it with my wife. I don't discuss this stuff with my buddies.'

'And you can just let it go,' Rachel asked.

'It's not always easy. Sometimes my wife tells me to go take a drive for an hour, look at the sunset, come back when I'm ready to behave myself. But she doesn't judge and she doesn't complain.'

'But she married into it.'

'She married a rookie beat cop. Now I wear a suit and tie and I go poking around dead people for days on end. It's a different thing altogether.'

'I can do this,' Rachel said. 'I'm just not sure that I want to do it.'

'Well, only you can figure that out. Evidently, whoever signed you up for this jamboree has the notion that you'd be good at it. And if you don't do it then someone else is gonna have to, because – believe me – there's a never-ending supply of fucking whackjobs out there.'

'Thanks for talking to me,' Rachel said. 'I figured you for an asshole, but you're actually a good guy.'

Ward laughed. 'Hey, you better keep that to yourself, sweet-heart. I got a reputation to maintain here.'

O'Brien was a little late on Tuesday morning. He apologized, said he'd been arranging some practical exercises for them. He then commented on the fact that the number of attendees had dwindled by a good twenty-five percent.

'Not everyone can do this,' he said. 'This is a psychological assault course. This will test your nerves and your stomachs. We're going to drop you in at the deep end. If you feel like you're drowning, just say so and we'll pull you out.'

There were murmurs from the gathering, but that was all.

'Today, we're getting into physical crime scene analysis,' O'Brien went on. 'The bodies are real. These are people who requested that their cadavers be used for this purpose to fur-ther scientific research. We're going to look at stab wounds, exsanguinations, the effect of bullets at long and short range, blood spatter, and everything else that can exist around a murder victim that you'll need to record. If you get sick, go be sick. For some of you, it will be the first time. There are others among you who've seen this kind of thing many times. Either which way, this is absolutely necessary in our line of work.'

With that, O'Brien walked off the stage and towards the door. Other agents appeared and started to hand out protective coveralls, face masks and gloves.

'So let's go do the fun part,' Ward said. 'Like the Ted Bundy Theme Park.'

*

The next morning, standing ahead of the bathroom mirror, Rachel ran her hand across the steamed glass and looked at herself. She believed she wouldn't recognize herself in the street. Something had changed. Some deep shift had occurred in her psyche. She'd voluntarily walked through the gates of Hell and come out the other side – intact, yes, but the pieces of herself had been reconstructed in a different way. She was hardening to this; she was becoming inured to death, her emotional responses blunt and matter-of-fact. People died. Sometimes they died in truly awful ways. This was the nature of things. It had been happening since the first human being had hefted a rock or fashioned a club to take another's life.

That night she would head back to Syracuse. With her she would take a certificate stating that she had completed a National Center for the Analysis of Violent Crime Training Program. She would be called upon to act as Police Department Liaison in the event of a Federal investigation in her jurisdiction. More importantly, she would be first on deck if there was a multiple murder case on her home turf.

Rachel had made her decision, though there was still a degree of self-doubt attendant to it. Only with time and trial would she know whether she was capable of fulfilling everything that would be asked of her. People would depend upon her – not only her superiors, her colleagues, the Police Department itself, but the families and loved ones of those whose lives were taken. She was twenty-seven years old. Her childhood and teenage friends were unknown to her now, but she imagined that they would be leading regular lives – working sociable hours, pursuing careers, getting married, raising families. These events played no part in her life. The events she would celebrate would be arrests, convictions and prison sentences.

If that was the way her life was going to count for something, then so be it.

*

That final afternoon, they were divided into groups of ten or twelve. An agent was assigned to each to take questions. O'Brien himself was chairing Rachel's group, and she took the opportunity to broach the Robert Marshall case.

'Based on what we've covered here,' O'Brien asked, 'is there anything you'd do differently?'

'I would have impressed upon everyone involved that they needed to proceed with greater caution,' she said. 'My understanding now is that such people want attention. The reason will be different in every case, of course. These people don't wake up one morning and decide they're going to kill. This is an impulse that's been present for perhaps their entire lives. That sequence – the harming of animals, random acts of cruelty, arson, all the things that lead up to the urge to take a life. That's something that's part of their make-up. And how better to get attention than to demonstrate superiority of intelligence over the people that are working to prevent you from fulfilling your *raison d'être*? That's what I see now. That we have to be aware of the possibility that we might become targets.'

O'Brien listened without comment, and then he said, 'I'm not going to disagree with you, Detective Hoffman. All I'm going to say is that in the vast majority of investigations there is very little purpose in looking at what might have been done better. To be honest, you can drive yourself crazy going down that road.'

'I get that, but we can learn from our mistakes.'

'Sure, but the next case won't bear any similarity to the last one or the one before that. Every case and every perpetrator is unique. Every psychology profile is unlike any other. You can gain experience, you can caution your colleagues to be mindful for their own safety, but can you really know how a sociopath will respond to the progress of an investigation? I don't think you can.'

'So in every case we are flying blind?'

O'Brien leaned back in his chair. 'We've spent thousands of

man hours interviewing people, creating hypothetical scenarios, identifying commonalities, trying to isolate patterns in how these things play out. If they exist, we haven't yet found them. We'll keep on working, and the more cases we address, the better our understanding will be. But do I believe that one day we'll crack some code that enables us to identify a perp after the first murder, the second perhaps? No, I don't. I don't think that's even possible.'

'Then why are we doing this?'

'Familiarity. So we can distance ourselves from the emotion of the thing. So we see things objectively, unclouded by panic and disgust. To look past the dead body in front of us and see the things that others can't see.'

'And feel nothing.'

'Nothing but the need to find the truth.'

Later, as Rachel was signing out and preparing to leave, O'Brien appeared in the reception area.

'How are you feeling?' he asked.

'Are we getting in touch with our feelings now, Agent O'Brien?'

'I guess that was a bit too Haight-Ashbury.'

'I'm fine,' Rachel said. 'I guess I need time to integrate every-thing into my old way of thinking.'

'Or just abandon your old way of thinking altogether.'

'Perhaps, yes.'

O'Brien's expression changed. It was fleeting, but there was a moment when Rachel believed she saw the man behind the badge.

'This may seem out of left field,' he said, 'but have you ever considered working for the Bureau?'

'Me, a Fed? You're not serious.'

'I'm not here on some sort of recruitment drive, but you're

very bright and very able, and you seem to have taken to this very easily.'

'Not so easily, believe me. I'm questioning whether this is even something I can do as a detective.'

'Oh, I don't doubt you'll do just fine,' O'Brien said. 'But we need people dedicated to this line of work. I genuinely believe that you could become an expert in this field.'

'And what does it do to you?' she asked. 'I mean, how do you function in an ordinary world with ordinary people when you're living with this kind of thing on a day-to-day basis?'

'You very quickly come to the realization that there is no ordinary world and there are no ordinary people. There are just people, and some of them are crazy.'

'Some of them belong in Hell,' Rachel said.

'Well, maybe that's where they came from, and it's down to people like us to send them back.'

'Let me get back to work,' Rachel said. 'Give me some time to think it over.'

'You take all the time you need, Detective. The crazies keep getting crazier, and they don't look like they're about to stop anytime soon.'

26

The very last thing Rachel had expected when she arrived in the office on Friday was a message from Carl Sheehan. Seated at her desk, she stared at the slip of paper in her hand.

Call me, it said. Urgent.

Beneath it was a phone number.

That day, after Michael Ridgway's funeral, August 6, 1975, she and Carl had gone to dinner together. The following day they'd spoken on the phone. A week later, it was a movie and take-out at her place. The assumption, initially, had been that they were merely desirous of company, someone to talk to who understood what had happened. The prospect of a relationship had never entered her mind, and yet that was exactly what had occurred.

Rachel could remember the precise moment it had happened, even though it was the better part of five years ago.

Carl had known, just as she had, that such a thing was not a good idea. Born out of loneliness, a sense of isolation, the simple human need to feel that someone was there for them, they had buried their reservations. They'd entered into some kind of tacit, unspoken agreement that they weren't really a couple, that they were merely collaborating in some sort of mutually-beneficial arrangement that would serve to minimize their alone-ness.

By Christmas of 1975, they were talking about living together. It would be more practical, less costly, and even though Carl was then considering a move to one of the papers in New York, such a prospect was not yet on the horizon.

They never did move in together, and though the relationship lasted for another eighteen months, finally coming to an end in June of '77, Rachel knew that the possibility of commitment had somehow been the very thing that had tilted things on its axis. They'd talked about something, and then neither one of them had done anything practical to realize it. She'd waited for Carl to make the first move; he had done the same. Each had wanted the other to be the initiate, and each had failed.

Carl was complex. He carried a deep sense of personal insecurity. Not about his work; when it came to his career he possessed an indomitable sense of self-assurance and professionalism. But behind that persona was a troubled man. His father had died when he was just twelve. It tore a gaping wound through his world, and that wound had yet to heal. Left reeling, barely able to reconcile himself to the new reality he faced, his mother had been there for him as best she could. Together, they navigated their way through the deep, emotional currents that assaulted them.

Three years after his father's death, his mother had remarried. Carl had believed it was a mistake, and he'd held onto that belief. From their first introduction, the man had considered it his prerogative to tell Carl how he should behave, how he should dress, which friends he considered acceptable and which he did not. Already a rebellious teenager, Carl felt a deep resentment towards him. Time had not alleviated the depth of that resentment. And it wasn't only the negativity directed towards Carl, it was the fact that his mother had become less and less herself as the years elapsed. Carl knew that she'd been drowning, just as he had, and that she'd clambered aboard the first life raft that reached her. That the boat was riddled with holes, endlessly taking on more water than could be bailed, was something she couldn't admit.

That Carl saw his mother so infrequently concerned him. He knew he should be less troubled by his stepfather's slights and derogatory innuendos, but he'd long since reconciled himself to the fact that his mother's life was hers to live as she chose. Nothing he could say or do would ever bring her to an understanding of how she'd been worn down into submission and reconciliation, forever seeking to placate, appease, to maintain the status quo instead of standing her ground. Carl loved his mother, respected her, admired her. She had supported him in every decision, listened when he needed to be heard, been an anchor in every emotional storm he'd endured. But she'd made a choice, and that choice had been carved in stone. She'd sided with her husband in order to keep the peace, and thus her son had thereafter been relegated to a secondary position.

As was the case in so many toxic relationships, the prospect of loneliness was greater than the present threat. There was pride too, for to admit that her judgment had been ill-advised was to admit being wrong. No one wanted to be wrong; they kept on suffering, all the while telling themselves they were right.

Rachel had met Carl's mother and stepfather. She sat quietly in the man's shadow, seeming forever to be cautious of saying the wrong thing. The man had built an invisible wall between mother and son, and there seemed to be nothing Carl could do to reach the woman he'd once known.

His solution was to distance himself from it, but that resulted in a sense of guilt that he'd abandoned her.

The simple truth was that both Rachel and Carl had arrived out of dysfunctional families. Their respective concepts of how relationships worked had been skewed by their own childhood experiences. It was not an excuse or a justification for failing to maintain what they had, but it was a factor in its collapse. There were things about themselves and about one another that they seemed incapable of reconciling, and thus the end was inevitable.

The catalyst for the break-up had been Carl's career. An opening had become available at the *New York Courier* crime desk. It was not the *Wall Street Journal* or the *Times*, but it was a step up from the *Syracuse Tribune*. Carl knew he needed to go, and

Rachel had not disputed that. He'd asked her to go with him. Such a thing was not only unlikely, it was also unrealistic. The PD didn't just move people randomly from one jurisdiction to another. They could maintain the relationship, see each other at weekends, perhaps. In reality, they had been unable to maintain it when they'd lived within walking distance of one another. They were bound together by a thread of insufficient substance to keep them from falling in opposite directions.

The relationship had come to some sort of natural conclusion. Carl's departure for New York was the excuse they both needed so each could remain blameless.

They had spoken only once since their awkward goodbye nearly three years before. Carl had called her in the fall of 1978 to tell her that his mother had died. He said he didn't know why he was calling her, didn't know why he felt she should know, but there it was: she was dead.

'I'm so sorry,' Rachel had said. 'Are you okay?'

There had been silence at the end of the line for a small eternity.

'I still think about you,' he'd finally said. 'I miss you.'

'Carl—'

'I'm sorry, Rachel. I know I shouldn't say it, but...' He didn't finish what he was going to say.

'You take care,' Rachel said. 'It's going to be okay. I know it must be tough, but you're going to be okay.'

Again, there was an uncomfortable silence, and then Carl had hung up the phone.

Perhaps any regular person would have called him back, or at least felt some obligation to do so. Rachel felt nothing. Carl was no longer part of her life, and she had no wish to be dragged back into his.

If the reason for now reestablishing contact was a personal matter, then surely he would have called her as he did before. He was in New York, presumably still at the *Courier*, and thus she couldn't dismiss the possibility that his request had something to do with a feature he was working on. Perhaps it was something to do with Marshall, and to ignore it would have been disrespectful to the memory of Michael Ridgway.

Rachel procrastinated for an hour, knowing full well that she would call the number and find out what was going on. She busied herself with paperwork, made some coffee, a twisted knot of tension growing ever tighter in the base of her stomach.

What was she afraid of? How many worst-case scenarios could she invent between deciding to call and then making the call? An unlimited number, it seemed, and finally, just so she would no longer remain in mystery, she picked up the phone.

It was perhaps no more than thirty seconds before Rachel heard Carl's voice at the other end of the line, but during that brief interlude she saw their entire history unfold in her mind. In amidst the times they'd been utterly incapable of communicating, there had been moments of true affection and mutual respect. Had she loved him? Did she know what love was? Did anyone truly know? Had she felt loved? That was a question with no clear answer, as there was very little with which she could make a comparison. Broken, awkward people doing their best to be something else.

'Rachel?'

'Carl.'

'Thanks for calling me back.'

'Are you okay?'

'Yes,' Carl replied, 'and no.'

The knot of tension in Rachel's gut dissolved into a feeling of anxious anticipation.

'There's been a murder,' he said. 'A bad one.'

'Okay.'

'It looks like a copycat.'

'Of what?' Rachel asked, knowing what he was going to say before he said it.

'They left a note. Like the others. The same book.'

Rachel had no words. She wanted to hang up. She didn't want details. She didn't want anything to do with this.

'Rachel? Are you still there?'

'I'm here, Carl.'

'So, like I said, there was a note. It was a quote from the Dante book.'

'No, I got that. I just don't know why you're calling me about it. Surely the PD in whatever precinct is dealing with it?'

'They are, Rachel, but there's something you need to know.'

Rachel didn't speak.

'Rachel?'

'What, Carl? What do I need to know?'

'The note was addressed to you.'

27

New York was a blunt assault to the senses.

Rachel hadn't been for several years, and what she saw from the cab as she drove through Queens to Astoria Boulevard was a city that bore no resemblance to the American Dream. Here seemed to be the birthplace of a nightmare. Boarded stores, garbage crowding the sidewalks and gutters, the incessant noise of music from cheap speakers, huddles of disheveled people around streetlights and in doorways, the pimps and hookers, the dealers and junkies, all of it coalescing into a subliminal discordant grind of disillusioned humanity.

Defining how she felt was impossible. Everything was awkward, everything was uncomfortable. Too many thoughts. Too many questions. Too much emotion simmering beneath the surface.

Directed upstairs and through to the 114th Homicide Suite, the door was opened before she knocked.

'Detective Hoffman?'

'Yes.'

'Thank you for coming down so quickly. I'm Maurice Quinn. I'm primary on this mess.'

Quinn extended his hand, and they shook.

'Can I get you anything? Some coffee, some water?'

'I'm good, thanks.'

Quinn was in his late-forties, heavy-set, his hair thinning on top. He wore a good-quality suit that had seen better days. He seemed agitated. Even his manner of breathing seemed anxious, as if concerned that the air in the room was in limited supply.

Quinn sat down at his desk and looked at Rachel. She guessed he wanted her to say something, but she waited for him to speak first.

'You know a journalist called Carl Sheehan?'

'I do, yes.'

'How do you know him?'

'Professionally and personally,' Rachel replied. 'He covered an investigation I did back in '75. Then we had a relationship for about eighteen months. That ended in the middle of '77.'

'And you've maintained communication with him since?'

'No.'

Quinn reached for a file on his desk.

'What does this have to do with your case?' Rachel asked.

'Mr. Sheehan is on the crime desk at the *Courier*, as you know,' Quinn explained. 'We had a homicide the other night. Obviously, word got back to Mr. Sheehan and he showed up here looking for a story. How he got the information we still don't know. We can only assume that someone leaked it to him, and we're looking into that. Nevertheless, it was Sheehan that came to see me as the assigned detective, and that's the reason you're here.'

'There was a letter. That's what Carl told me. Can I see it?'

Quinn withdrew a page from the file on his desk and passed it to Rachel. Evidenced by the minor variations in spacing and character height, the letter had been typed on a manual typewriter.

Dear Friends,

So, here we are again. It has been a while, hasn't it?

I want to take this opportunity to welcome you on this next stage of our journey together. I trust that the bureaucratic formalities of the New York Police Department will not be so thoughtless as to exclude Detective Hoffman from the proceedings. And if you are reading this, Rachel, let me join those who must have already congratulated you on your promotion. I have been following your work as and when I can, and I know that you are a conscientious and diligent officer.

Pleasantries aside, we have work to do, and here you will find my first offering.

I trust you will appreciate my contrapasso. Even if I say so myself, it possesses a certain elegance and wit.

I sincerely hope that one day we will have an opportunity to speak in person.

Until then, lest untoward events transpire, I wish you adieu.

Dante.

Rachel read the letter twice, unease invading her body like a virus. The hairs rose on the nape of her neck. Across her scalp, a thin film of cold sweat broke out.

'You see why we asked for you,' Quinn said.

'This is a copycat,' Rachel replied. 'The perp back in '75 is dead. He shot himself after killing my partner. Whoever wrote this must have accessed information that was never released to the press.'

'Maybe Sheehan was careless with his notes, or someone broke into his place and found them. He says not. There's also the possibility that it came from someone at Syracuse PD.

However it happened, it doesn't change the fact that whoever sent this has a personal interest in your involvement.'

'And what can you tell me about it?'

'That it's one of the most disturbing things I have ever witnessed,' Quinn replied. He reached for another file on his desk, opened it, and selected a number of photographs.

At first, Rachel struggled to understand what she was seeing.

Suspended from a hook in the ceiling of a darkened room, a naked figure was bound with red straps of some description that hung to the ground. Upside-down, the wrists and ankles had been roped in such a way as to bend the body in half. The fingers of each hand had been removed. The head was tilted back, and where eyes should have looked back at her there was nothing but empty, black sockets.

Quinn passed her another print. It was a close-up of the face. A third was a section of the strapping, blood red in color. They were ribbons, a good three or four inches wide.

'You've ID'd the victim?' Rachel asked.

'Christopher Wake. We had him on record here. Sexual molestation, attempted rape. He did eight years in Attica. Released about a year ago.'

'His job?'

'Well, he was an optometrist. Had a practice here in Queens before he was busted.'

'The *contrapasso*.'

'I looked that up,' Quinn said. 'Some religious thing, right?'

'It means "suffer the opposite". It comes from a book called *The Divine Comedy*. It means that people in Hell will suffer in a way that's a kind of karma for their sins on Earth. Hence the hands and eyes.'

'He looked and touched what he shouldn't have.'

'Seems so,' Rachel replied.

'And "Dante" was the sign-off in the letters in your case up in Syracuse?'

'Yes.'

'And the ribbons?'

Rachel shook her head. 'Not a clue. They'll be there for a reason. You'll need to get some kind of expert to figure that one out.'

'An expert in what? Bondage?'

'My guess would be an image from a religious text. Some representation of Hell, maybe? That's what I'm getting with the *contrapasso*.'

'I'll make some calls,' Quinn said.

Rachel looked at the photographs once more, and then she put them back on the desk.

'And this place?' she asked.

'A disused lock-up. The owner died some years ago with no estate benefactor. There's six of them in a row. Technically, they now belong to the city. They've been slated for demolition, but no one ever got 'round to it.'

'And nothing in the other lock-ups?'

'Junk, garbage. People have slept rough in them. We didn't find anything of any relevance.'

'And Wake's place?'

'Also Queens. We went through it thoroughly. Nothing.'

'So what do you want from me?' she asked.

'I want you to speak to Sheehan.'

'Why?'

'See if you can figure out how our perp might have accessed the police reports on your Syracuse gig. Or maybe that Sheehan told someone about it.'

'You can't have one of your own people do it?'

'I could, sure, but he'll be more relaxed with you. Like I said, he's not a suspect. We're not interrogating him. According to the coroner, Wake was hanging there for twenty-four hours at most. He was still alive after his fingers were cut off and his eyes were removed. Cause of death was asphyxiation due to the constriction of his chest in that position.'

'And say we figure out what happened, or say we don't, what then?'

'Your name's in that letter, Detective Hoffman,' Quinn said. 'Whoever this sick fuck is, he wants you on board. I'm guessing you'd really rather not be involved, but we're past that point. I know your Lieutenant will want you back as soon as possible, but you've got history on this kind of shit. We could use your input.'

'Are you asking me or telling me?'

Quinn smiled. 'I guess I'm asking in a telling kind of way.'

'And you want me to speak to Carl Sheehan today?'

'I can have him brought over now.'

'Not here,' Rachel said. 'You want to make this unofficial, then let's have it be unofficial. I'll meet him in a diner or something.'

'As you wish.'

'Just so you know, I've never discussed the Syracuse case with anyone outside law enforcement. I went over it with some Behavioral Science people at Quantico, but I didn't get into the finer details. If Carl really has no idea how this information got out, then I think this meeting isn't gonna give you anything new.'

'I'm not holding out for some revelation here, Detective Hoffman, I just gotta work every angle possible. You know the beat, right?'

'I do, yes. I'll talk to him. You got somewhere close we could meet?'

'Turn right out of the building, couple of blocks down there's a place on the corner. It has booths in the back where you'll get a bit of privacy. It's called The Java House.'

Rachel glanced at her watch. 'Call him. Tell him to meet me there as soon as he can.'

'Will do,' Quinn replied, and reached for the phone.

28

Rachel stood up when Carl came through the door of the coffee house.

He saw her and smiled. He'd grown a beard, and his hair was longer. It suited him. As he walked towards her he seemed more assured than she remembered.

'Rachel,' he said as he took a seat across from her in the booth.

'Carl.'

'You look well.'

'I look like I need a haircut.'

'How are you doing?'

Carl glanced round for a waitress, caught her eye. He ordered coffee, strong and black.

'Smart enough to get into trouble,' he said. 'Not quite smart enough to get out of it. The usual.'

'I can't believe it's been nearly three years.'

'Same,' he said. 'And a lot has happened.' He paused, looked away for a moment. 'I'm going to be a father.'

'Seriously?'

'As serious as it gets,' he said. 'My girlfriend, she's an ICU nurse at General. Two months pregnant.'

'Congratulations,' Rachel said. It was the right word, but the wrong emotion accompanied it. She didn't know what she was feeling – jealousy, a sense of loss. Carl had always said that he had no wish to start a family. She had concurred. They both had careers to consider. But here he was, a parent-to-be. He had wanted a family; he just hadn't wanted a family with her.

'Completely unplanned,' Carl said, as if reading her mind. 'Totally unexpected. But now it's happening, we have to deal with it.'

'And your girlfriend—'

'Suzanne,' Carl interjected. 'She's as surprised and ill-prepared as me. We talked about it. A lot. We decided that we couldn't consider not having it.'

'That's not what I was asking.'

'But I was,' Carl said.

'I'm sure you'll make a great father.'

He gave a wry smile. 'Let's hope so, eh?'

The coffee arrived. They sat in silence for a few moments.

'How things ended—' Rachel started.

'Were how they ended. Let's not do that. There's no point. And that's not why we're here, right?'

'No, it's not. All I want to say is that I missed you a great deal more than I thought I would.'

'Same for me,' Carl replied. 'But we've moved on. You have someone?'

Rachel shook her head.

'There's been no one for three years?'

She laughed. 'I'm not a nun, Carl. But no, nothing serious, nothing that's lasted.'

'And now you're a detective.'

'I am, and so I need to ask you some detective-type questions.'

'You want to know how I found out about the letter.'

'Detective Quinn wants to know.'

'Someone told me,' Carl replied.

'From the 114th?'

Carl didn't reply. He picked up his coffee cup.

'I get the protection of source stuff, Carl. I just need to know for myself.'

'So you can rule me out as a suspect?'

'Sure, yes. That's the reason why. Don't be a dick about this.'

'Someone in the 114th, yes,' Carl said. 'But that's between you and me.'

'You don't tell me their name, I can't tell Quinn.'

'And so it doesn't matter. I just got word about the letter. That was it. I haven't seen it. I just know that it had your name in it and it was signed "Dante".'

'It was the same kind of thing as before. It even began "Dear Friends".'

'So this guy was killed by someone who knows as much about the Marshall case as we do.'

'That's what it looks like, yes. I know I didn't discuss it with anyone. Did you?'

'Not a word.'

'Then Syracuse has a far more significant issue with confidential information than the 114th.'

'So it would seem,' Carl said. 'And what's your take on it?'

'I don't have a take. It's a copycat. That much is clear. Not the MO, but *The Divine Comedy* connection. Beyond that, there's one dead guy – that we know of – and they want me here because I'm now involved.'

'Because you were invited by whoever did this.'

'And that someone knows I am now a detective. They congratulated me.'

'Congratulated you?'

'Even told me they'd been following my career. They said I was conscientious and diligent.'

'And what can you tell me about the victim?' Carl asked.

'I can't tell you anything.'

Carl frowned. 'Oh come on. There has to be some give-and-take here, Rachel.'

'I can tell you it was a male. I can tell you there was some theater involved.'

'Theater?'

'It was dramatic. Not like Syracuse. Someone didn't only get put to sleep.'

'Bad?'

'Very.'

'And they have anything?'

Rachel shook her head. 'As yet, no. There's some indication that the crime scene was staged, maybe made to look like something. What, we don't know, but we'll be getting in touch with people who might point us in the right direction.'

'So you're here for the duration?'

Rachel shrugged. 'I don't know, Carl. I don't want to be here, but I don't think I'm gonna have a great deal of say in the matter.'

'Well, if you need something in the press, you know who to ask, right?'

'Sure.'

'So, is that it? Are we done here?'

'For now, yes.'

Carl finished his coffee and got up.

'If you end up staying here a while, you should come over and meet Suzanne.'

Rachel looked up at him. 'And why would I want to do that?'

'Because … Christ, I don't know, Rachel, I guess I'm just being polite.'

'You don't need to be polite with me, Carl. You've got your own life. Aside from this, I'm not any part of it. I think it's best we keep it that way.'

Carl stood silently for a moment. Rachel guessed she'd made him feel awkward.

'You're right,' he said.

'It was good seeing you.'

'You too. Let me know if there's anything you need, okay?'

'I will.'

Carl smiled. He turned and walked away. Rachel watched

him go. He didn't look back. There was a good possibility that she wouldn't see him again, at least in anything other than a professional setting. How she felt about that, she didn't know. She didn't want to think about it. He was going to be a father. He had moved on, definitively so. Maybe she hadn't, at least not completely, and now there was no way to recover what had been lost.

Rachel ordered a BLT to go.

29

Detectives Maurice Quinn and Rachel Hoffman spent the next three days canvassing Christopher Wake's family, friends, neighbors, even those with whom he'd spent time in Attica. They tracked his last-known movements on the day he was murdered. They trawled through his yellow sheet to see if anything might flag up a lead. There was nothing.

Following Wake's release back in April of the previous year, he'd attended sex offender counseling as part of his probationary conditions. His probation officer, a hard-headed pragmatist whose manner was as tough as his job, told Rachel that there was no indication of Wake having returned to his previous behavior pattern. As far as the PO was concerned, Wake's stint in prison had been enough for him to get the message.

Unable to resume his practice as an optometrist, Wake had worked for a construction company out near Elmhurst. His foreman had had no issue with him. He was a hard worker, punctual, didn't cause any problems, willing to take any overtime that was available. He didn't socialize with the other workers, but that was not unusual for those on probation. Such people tended to keep themselves to themselves. The company had hired guys right out of prison many times before. The boss, according to the foreman, had had his own troubles in the past and believed that everyone deserved a second chance.

The *Courier* ran a piece about the murder. It was short and to-the-point. It did not go into detail about the way in which the body was brutalized. There was no byline, so Rachel didn't know if Carl Sheehan had authored it. Neither the *Times* nor any other paper picked it up. Wake was just another homicide in the homicide capital of the world.

Quinn had been good to his word as far as reaching out to anyone who might have some understanding of the crime scene. He'd sent out a brief description of the body position and the red ribbons that had been tied around it to Cornell, Fordham and others. On Tuesday 25th, a call came in to the Homicide Suite from a department head at NYU's Institute of Fine Arts. Professor Richard Boyer said he might very well have something that could be relevant.

Quinn drove. Boyer met them, seemed all too eager to help. Once in his office, he produced a series of prints.

'These are from a book called the *Hortus deliciarum*,' he explained. 'It means "Garden of Delights", and it was an illumin- ated encyclopedia produced nearly a thousand years ago by a nun called Herrad of Landsberg.'

Boyer selected one print. 'It depicts some scenes of Hell, and this is what I thought of when I saw the reference to the body's positioning.'

Both detectives stood and looked at the image. Against a background of flames were what appeared to be a series of four levels. Along each level were figures enduring grotesque forms of torture. There were cauldrons of people over fires, and around the margins on each side were countless burning bodies. Up in the right-hand corner, suspended upside-down in the exact manner as Christopher Wake, was a figure surrounded by red flames.

'In the description I received, there was mention of red bind- ings or ribbons,' Boyer said, 'but perhaps they were employed to symbolize the flames of Hell.'

There was no doubt about it. The similarity between the photographs Rachel had seen from the crime scene and the image before her was undeniable.

'And this book,' Quinn said, 'you have a copy here?'

'Oh no,' Boyer said. 'It was housed in a place called Temple Neuf in Strasbourg. It was bombed during a siege in the late 1800s and the original was destroyed. However, parts of the volume had earlier been copied and so we have at least some pages of it.'

'So how would someone know about this?' Rachel asked.

Boyer shrugged. 'Anyone with a significant interest in medieval manuscripts, early religious artworks, illuminated texts and the like would have come across it. It's a well-documented volume.'

'Can you make a copy of this picture for us?' Quinn asked.

'I made these for you already,' Boyer said. 'You're welcome to take them with you.'

Rachel thanked Boyer for his help and they left.

On the way back, Quinn asked her about the Dante book.

'It's an allegorical journey,' she said. 'A man called Dante is taken through Hell, Purgatory and on to Heaven.'

'I get that, but if this homicide was intended to symbolize Hell, then what the fuck was going on in Syracuse?'

'Death,' Rachel said matter-of-factly. 'That's the conclusion we came to at the time. Someone has to die before they begin the journey. Those people were euthanized. That's the only way to describe it. They were drugged and then put to sleep, like you would with a sick animal.'

'And there's no doubt, I mean no doubt whatsoever, that this guy Marshall was the perp?'

'None,' Rachel said. 'He committed suicide with the final murder.'

'Your partner, Ridgway.'

'Right. And there was no physical evidence of anyone else present. All the things he used were there. Only his prints on them.'

'But someone else could have been there, right? That's all I'm saying. And that someone is now here.'

It wasn't a possibility that Rachel had realistically considered, but it couldn't be dismissed altogether. Leaving nothing at a crime scene was simple enough. Gloves, shoe covers, even full protective gear as was used by Forensics, a thorough walk-through after the fact to ensure that nothing incriminating had been left behind.

'I mean, it's something we have to consider,' Quinn said. 'That there were two people in Syracuse. One of them's dead, and the other one shows up here five years later. It would sure as fuck explain why they know everything about Syracuse. This *Comedy* book, the letter, that you were on the original investigation. Whoever it is asked for you by using the name 'Dante'. That's only gonna come from inside Syracuse PD Homicide itself, or from a direct involvement in the original murders.'

'I want to believe it's a leak,' Rachel said. 'I want to believe it's a copycat.'

'I understand,' Quinn said, 'and if it was me I'd want to believe that as well. But we can't fall into the trap of assuming something and then trying to interpret everything to fit that premise. We need to remain open-minded, and so we have to take this into account.'

'And why wait five years?'

'Christ, how the fuck would I know? Why even do this kind of shit in the first place? Because some people are just fucking crazy. Isn't that explanation enough?'

'Okay, so we take it into consideration,' Rachel said. 'I'll get everything sent down from Syracuse. We'll go through it together and see if there's anything to substantiate what you're saying.'

'If nothing else, we rule it out, right?'

'Right.'

Rachel closed her eyes. As clear as day, she saw the dead body of Michael Ridgway, beside him the blood-spattered form of Robert Marshall. She pictured Caroline Lassiter, Raymond Keene, the Wilsons and Brenda Forsyth. She remembered how much time it had taken to let it all go, to blanche her mind of those memories. And now they were all coming back. So much time had elapsed, and yet it now seemed like yesterday.

Neither she nor Quinn spoke again until they reached the 114th. They headed on up to the Homicide Suite and Rachel put a call in to Syracuse. The records she needed would be sent down the following day.

Rachel then busied herself with preparing a case board. She pinned up a copy of the Dante letter, the crime scene photos of Christopher Wake, beside them the photocopy that Boyer had given them from the *Hortus deliciarum*.

Looking at them now – side by side – there was no mistaking it. A man had suffered his *contrapasso* – a piece of grotesque theater – and she'd been personally invited to this performance by the author himself.

30

Waking in a strange bed in a cheap hotel room in Astoria, Rachel was lost. It took a handful of moments to get her bearings, to remember where she was and why she was there. Cognizance arrived as an unrelenting pressure – emotionally, psychologically – and she lay motionless for a good ten minutes, staring at the beige, grubby ceiling, forcing herself to remain optimistic, to find a belief that the end of this would come swiftly and with finality. Try as she might, she was not optimistic, and she did not believe.

She thought of Carl Sheehan, his soon-to-be fatherhood, of a nurse in the ICU at General who'd been able to hold him down long enough to establish some roots. Rachel knew she'd not been able to do that. She'd been unable to create any real foundations at all. Her apartment was featureless, devoid of photos or plants or paintings. There were no cushions, no throws, no childhood keepsakes on mantles or shelves. Her life was a vacuum into which only the darkest human endeavors gained access. And she allowed them in, welcomed them perhaps, for in this way she could convince herself that her life had meaning and purpose.

Assaulted by a sudden and intense wave of nausea, she rushed to the bathroom and retched dryly into the sink. Her throat and chest burned. She ran the faucet, scooping up handfuls of cold water and dousing her face. Simultaneously she felt both young and naïve, old and weary. She wanted to talk to someone about what was happening. There was no one she could think of but

Carl, but he would be the last person to whom she'd reach out. Whatever they'd had was gone, and there was nothing she could do to recover it.

NYPD 114th had loaned her a car. She drove over there, arrived around 8.30.

Quinn was already in the office.

'Did you sleep?' he asked.

'Enough, yes.'

'I didn't. Not really. I kept waking up thinking about what our vic must have gone through. Coroner said that suffocation like that wouldn't be quick. Imagine hanging there, knowing that you're going to die. There's nothing you can do. It's all over. And the pain he must've felt.' Quinn shook his head. 'It defies imagination.'

Rachel sat down. 'We have to have a game plan.' she said, 'We've got no eyewitnesses, no one among Wake's contacts that have given us anything, no physical evidence at the scene that points us in any particular direction. In truth, we have nothing. So what do we do when we have nothing?'

'We do something,' Quinn said. 'We provoke a reaction.'

'Whoever did this will do it again. I don't doubt that for a second. There were five killings in Syracuse. If this is a copycat, then he's going to do as many, if not more.'

'You don't know that,' Quinn said.

'I don't know anything, and neither do you. So we consider all possibilities. It's either a copycat or it's not. If it's not, then we're looking at a second person who was there in Syracuse. Then we have to ask ourselves why wait five years? Then we need to look at how these victims were selected, or if it was completely random.'

'Not in the case of Wake,' Quinn said. 'He was a sexual predator. He was killed in this manner because of what he'd done.'

'So let's look at his victims.'

'His victims were young women.'

'Sure, I get that. But what about a father, a brother, a husband? Wake did eight years, but maybe someone held onto their hate until he got out. Maybe someone didn't feel that eight years was sufficient punishment.'

'We can look,' Quinn said, 'but I'm not buying it. If someone killed Wake out of revenge, then why not just kill him? Why go through all this drama? This took some planning and preparation. And there's too much coincidence there. Wake abuses some girl, and a relative not only decides to wait until he's released from prison, but also gains access to information about the Syracuse case that could only have come from the PD itself. And if you were going to kill someone in a manner that would then be attributed to someone else, you would choose an ongoing case, not an MO that came from a perp who's dead.'

'I'm pitching anything I can think of, Maurice,' Rachel said.

'I understand that, and it needs to be done, but I think that line's going nowhere.'

Rachel got up. She walked to the case board and looked at the images of Christopher Wake. She looked at the letter.

'His first offering,' Rachel said. 'That's what he writes. This is his first offering. That tells us as clear as day that he intends to give us at least a second. *Lest untoward events transpire.* What would be an untoward event? I guess it means that if we catch him. That would be untoward, right?'

'For him, yes. Not for us.'

Rachel breathed deeply. She tried to focus.

'So, as far as physical evidence is concerned,' she said, 'we have the body, the rope, the ceiling hook, the ribbons, the letter and then the lock-up space itself. We also have the fact that the eyes and fingers were removed from the scene. We have Wake's criminal record. We have a reference to Dante and this medieval bookplate that we got from Boyer. So what don't we have?'

'Every-fucking-thing else,' Quinn replied. 'Motive, opportunity, prints, eyewitnesses, you name it.'

'And of those things, what could we potentially get that would help us the most?'

'Well, we know we don't have prints or witnesses, so that leaves motive and opportunity.'

'The motive is the motive,' Rachel said. 'We can only guess at that. That leaves us with opportunity. Wake was taken or he went there voluntarily. If he was taken, then he had to have been taken against his will. That means he was drugged, bound, transported.'

'No drugs according to the tox report.'

'So let's assume that he went there voluntarily. Why would he go? To meet someone, perhaps. Who would he want to meet? What could have been sufficiently enticing for him to turn up at a block of disused lock-ups?'

'Sex? Drugs? What would a lowlife like Christopher Wake want?'

'You say these things were slated for demolition. He was in construction. Maybe someone offered him a job on the side, cash, no questions asked?'

'Sure, but that could've been a conversation in a bar. That could've happened anywhere.'

'But whoever approached him knew who he was, that he was a sexual predator. And if they met him somewhere, even an apparently casual meeting, then they had to have known something of his routine.'

'So we canvass bars?'

'*A* bar, more than likely,' Rachel said. 'He was unmarried, no girlfriend, no siblings, no living parent. The people who'd know something about his life outside work would be the people he worked with, his PO, and those who attended these counseling groups with him.'

'Long shot,' Quinn said.

'You got a shorter one?'

'Nope.'

'So let's go back and speak to them. What else are we going to do right now? The Syracuse files won't be here until later.'

Rachel waited for a response.

'For Christ's sake, Maurice, you can sit there as long as you like waiting for the cavalry. They ain't coming.'

Quinn opened his mouth to say something.

'I don't want to hear it. Just get your fucking coat already.'

31

As far as Anthony Yates was concerned, everything that had happened throughout his life was someone else's fault. Everything bad, at least.

The world owed him, and it owed him plenty. He was still waiting for his dues, and he would wait as long as it took. He would get what he deserved, and then everyone who had wronged him, everyone who'd hurt him or shamed him or ridiculed him would feel something of what he'd suffered. And he had suffered. There was no doubt about that. He'd been abused by foster parents, bullies at school, kids in juvie; he'd been hurt so many times that he expected nothing but more hurt. He didn't want it, he didn't wish for it, but it happened. And it kept on happening until he learned to hurt back. That, it seemed, was the only thing that eased his mind.

When he was fifteen he killed a dog. It was a ratty, dirty fucked-up creature, a whining stray who hung around in the street where he lived. The dog died slowly. It bled out from a puncture wound in the gut. It looked at him like he could do something to stop it. Maybe he could have, but he didn't. He crouched near it, stroked its head, talked to it, told it that what was happening was inevitable, and the dog looked at him with these big watery eyes and its breathing started to falter and then it went still and its eyes just stared at something Anthony couldn't see.

The people he'd lived with back then were equally dirty and fucked-up, but in a very different way. The man was strong and he held Anthony down and he punished him for things Anthony didn't understand. That dumb fuck was dead now, but Anthony could still see his face, still feel the sting of tears in his eyes as he was made to stand against the wall, legs apart, knees bent, forehead to the wall, until every muscle in his frail, malnourished body screamed for respite. And the woman – drunk, ugly bitch – just laughed and mocked him, told him he was a weak boy, a pathetic boy, a boy who'd never grow to be a real man. Where she was now, Anthony didn't know, but he hoped she was dying of cancer or something. He prayed that she was being eaten alive by some terrible wasting disease for which there was no cure, no drug to ease the pain, laid up on a filthy mattress, writhing and crying and screaming and praying for it to end.

And they were not the only ones. There were others. Even the ones who tried to be kind and patient and understanding, even those who professed to empathize with what he'd experienced in his miserable, shitty life, were hypocrites and liars and only in it for the money. He knew that, because as soon as the money stopped, they would kick him back to Child Services and let him be someone else's problem.

A year later, some other house, some other family, he'd killed their cat. He hit it with a hammer. It died instantly. There was no reason for killing the cat. He'd just wanted to, and so he did.

That's when he went to juvie. He was there for six months. He thought a lot about the dog and the cat and how it had made him feel. Powerful. That was how he'd felt. Like there was something he could control, something he could dictate, something he could make happen that no one else could stop.

When he was nineteen he set a car on fire. He smashed the window and poured gas inside and then he stepped back and flicked a lighted match through the hole in the glass. The sound was extraordinary – *Whoomph!* – and the flames ate up the car and the smoke funneled up into the sky and it was black and orange and the other windows just cracked and imploded and the smell was like nothing he'd ever smelled before. He watched the paint bubble and peel. It was red, but it browned and blackened and then flaked away and floated upwards, still glowing, incandescent, and it was like his own personal firework show.

There was no one inside. It was just an empty car, but it made him think about how he would have felt had there been someone inside. That notion aroused him but he suppressed it, held it deep down inside. He didn't want to kill anyone. Not really. That kind of thing got you in serious trouble, and he'd already had enough trouble to last a lifetime.

No one ever found out who burned the car. Maybe no one cared. For sure, whoever owned it got insurance money and bought a new car and life went on like it had never happened. That was the way of things. Shit happened, but the world didn't top.

There had been other cars, one time an empty house, and he'd stood down the street and watched as the fire engines came and the hoses were unrolled, and then other people came out on the street in their pajamas and robes and watched it collapse to its foundations and in the morning there was nothing left but wet, blackened remnants of someone's home. It was a skeleton, all broken-up and filthy, and here and there were odd fragments of a life – a picture frame, a melted vase, a single scorched shoe.

Nothing lasted forever. Everything had to die.

In August of 1968, Anthony had been arrested on suspicion of arson. He said nothing, just like his lawyer told him, and the detective who questioned him went round and round in circles trying to catch him out. The detective got angry and frustrated and Anthony thought, *Fuck you, you pigfucker*, and he kept on saying nothing until they had to let him go for lack of evidence. They told him he'd been cautioned. The told him they knew it was him who'd burned down the carpet store. They told him they were going to keep an eye on him, that they would get him one day.

That was out in Red Bank, New Jersey.

Anthony didn't care for people keeping an eye on him or trying to get him one day, so he upped sticks and moved to New York. He never saw or heard from those pigfuckers again.

On July 4th, 1972, Anthony had his own Independence Day celebration. It was just a small store. It was owned by Chinese-looking people. Three days earlier, he'd gone in there asking for change for a dollar so he could use the phone. They pretended they didn't understand him. He heard them laughing after he'd left.

On the night of the 4th, he went back close to midnight and broke a window. He poured almost a gallon of gas into the building and then walked backwards to make a trail along the ground.

The rush he felt as the flame moved ever-so-slowly to the wall was nothing short of life-affirming. When it went up, it went up fast. The fire was a living, breathing monster. It was so hungry. It swallowed and swallowed, and the more it swallowed, the bigger and greedier it became.

Someone saw him. Anthony ran, but he didn't run fast enough. There were crowds in the streets and they got in his way and he slipped and fell. There was gas on his clothes and on his shoes, and the person who saw him picked him out of a line-up and he was arrested and charged. He didn't know their name. Later he found out it was an off-duty pigfucker cop and that's why everyone believed what he said. Anthony knew that cops were some of the worst liars in the world, but that didn't seem to matter.

The Public Defender was a blonde woman. She told Anthony to say nothing at the trial, but Anthony couldn't help himself. He told them all to go fuck themselves in the ass and die.

They sent him to Attica. He was twenty-three years old. It was October 17th, 1972, a Tuesday, and outside it was raining. They said he was going away for eight years, but he was only there for six years, four months and a handful of days. When he came out it was a Tuesday and it was raining. That was the way of things. Shit still happened, and the world didn't change.

Attica had been bad. Worse than any foster home, worse than juvie. Worse than the nightmares he'd had after standing for hours with his knees bent, his forehead against the wall, every muscle and nerve on fire, praying and praying and praying that he didn't piss himself. Attica had been worse than all of them together.

He'd been out close on a year. He had a room in a house in Astoria. He worked the graveyard shift at a white goods warehouse. He didn't like the foreman. He was Polish and fat and an asshole and a pigfucker, even though he wasn't a cop. He figured one day he'd torch the place with the guy inside and see how it felt.

But not today. Today was going to be different because things were looking up. Anthony had been offered a job. Out-of-the-blue, a driver had started a conversation with him. He said his name was Melvin and he was from Philly. It was just small talk while the crew unloaded the shipment. He was a funny guy, but he also said that the world was fucked and most people were dumb as shit, and then he told Anthony that he could get him a position as a driver. The pay was better than some shit-stinking warehouse job and he could work at night or during the day or any hours he liked. He could be his own boss. Fuck all of these people telling him when to piss and when to eat and when he could go to the bathroom. Fuck them all.

Melvin gave Anthony the name of a bar up on 3rd Avenue, made him swear he'd show up.

Anthony swore and they shook hands and Melvin drove away.

32

A little after seven on the evening of Friday the 28th, a call came into Quinn's office. A body had been found in a wrecking yard. Quinn asked for the call to be transferred to another detective. He and Rachel had spent two days questioning and re-questioning every contact of Christopher Wake they could find. The only thing that had come of it was that Wake, at his last PO meeting, had said that he'd been offered another job. What that job was, where the offer had come from, he hadn't said, and the PO hadn't asked.

Quinn was tired; he wanted to go home; he wanted a beer and a baseball game. The last thing he needed was another homicide.

The Desk Sergeant explained to Quinn that he'd been instructed to put the call through to him specifically.

'Something about red ribbons,' the Sergeant said.

Quinn took down the address. He and Rachel left immediately.

Forensics were on-site already, and the unit chief explained that though it appeared that the body had been burned in the car, the car itself had burned out a good while before.

'So someone transported an incinerated corpse and left it inside this vehicle. That's what you're telling me?' Rachel asked.

'That's what I'm telling you.'

'What else you got?'

'As yet, nothing. We need to finish up and then the coroner can take him.'

'You know it's a man.'

'Height, build, bone structure. It's definitely a man.'

'Is the coroner here?' Rachel asked.

'En route. We need another half hour or so, and then he's all yours.'

Rachel stood back behind the crime scene tapes with Quinn.

'Your second offering,' Quinn said. 'A burnt one.'

'Not funny,' Rachel said.

'Just trying to lighten the mood.'

'Lighten the mood on your own time, Maurice.'

The Coroner showed up a half hour later. Her name was Marion Adams. She looked like she'd come from a dinner engagement.

'I don't usually wear cashmere to crime scenes, she said as she suited up. 'It's my wedding anniversary.'

'I'm sorry,' Rachel replied.

'That I'm married, or that my dinner was cut short?'

'I guess that depends on your husband.'

'Oh, he's a good one. He's used to this. He'll head home and watch some sleep-inducing sports documentary.'

Quinn joined them.

'Who's primary?' Adams asked.

Quinn looked at Rachel.

'This is Detective Quinn,' Rachel said.

'There's no primary,' Quinn said. 'Detective Hoffman is down here from Syracuse to assist on this.'

'What, you're some kind of hot-shot psycho hunter?'

'That'd be me,' Rachel said.

'So what we got?'

'Forensics Chief says the body was burned elsewhere. This is a secondary site.'

Adams zipped up her protectives and ducked beneath the tape.

With a torch, she surveyed the interior of the car.

Looking back at the detectives, she said, 'What's the deal with the ribbons?'

'Calling card,' Rachel explained.

'So you've had another one?'

'We have,' Quinn said. 'Not burned. Last one was hung upside-down without his fingers and eyes.'

'Creative,' Adams said. She went back to looking over the body, a Dictaphone in her hand.

Five minutes elapsed. Adams recorded her observations in detail.

Returning, she asked for assistance in getting the body out of the car and onto a gurney. Flesh and bone had fused. Whatever clothes the vic had worn were charred to fragments. Pieces of fabric came away like dried leaves. Forensics collected and bagged them.

The body, laid on its side, fixed now in a seated position, wouldn't go in a bag. Adams covered it with a black polythene sheet and taped the sheet to the gurney.

The Forensics Chief assisted her in getting the gurney into the wagon.

'You'll want me working weekends, right?' Adams asked.

Rachel didn't reply. Her expression gave the answer.

'I'll be in at 8.00 in the morning. Give me a couple of hours and then come over,' Adams said. 'You're not gonna get prints. I can get you height, weight, blood type, tox, dentals, identify the accelerant, approximate time of death. That's as good as it's gonna get.'

Quinn and Rachel thanked the coroner. They watched in silence as she drove away.

'You want a beer?' Quinn asked.

'Two,' Rachel replied. 'At least.'

On Saturday morning, Rachel met Maurice Quinn at the coroner's office. It was a little after 10.00. Rachel had skipped breakfast. Quinn evidently hadn't. There was a streak of egg yolk on his tie. Rachel waited for him outside the restroom while he sponged it off.

Entering the theater, Rachel was assaulted by the smell. It was unmistakable, unlike anything else. That raw rotten funk invaded the nostrils, permeated the pores of the skin. Approaching the table where the vic's body was mid-autopsy, Adams saw her wince. Handing her a small plastic tub, she said, 'Menthol. Put some on your upper lip. It doesn't handle it, but it helps.'

'You get used to it?' Rachel asked.

'Hell, no. I've been doing this for years and it still bothers me.'

Standing six feet or so from the cadaver, Quinn asked what she'd found.

'Male. Late twenties, early thirties. Five-nine. Give or take – a hundred and fifty pounds. Accelerant was acetone. Nasty stuff. Smoke in his lungs says he was burned alive.' Adams nodded towards another stainless steel table against the wall. 'Your ribbons are over there. I kept them as intact as I could. They were tied around him after the fact, obviously. I'll get those over to Forensics to see if they can find anything.'

Reaching to her left, Adams produced a steel kidney dish.

'This, however, was the most interesting thing.'

Rachel took latex gloves from her jacket pocket and snapped them on. She took the dish from Adams.

At first look, it appeared to be a length of black rubber, perhaps two inches, a half-inch in diameter.

'That's a steel tube,' Adams said. 'On the outside is your vic's burned flesh. You'll completely incinerate a body at about 750 Celsius. Steel is double that. Whoever put it there wanted it found. Inside the tube was a message.'

Adams produced an evidence bag. Within it was a slip of paper.

Rachel knew what it was before Adams handed it over.

It was the same typed font as the letter found at the Wake crime scene.

> I have come to lead you to the other shore;
> into eternal darkness; into fire and into ice.

'That means something to you?' Adams asked.

'It does, yes,' Rachel replied. 'It's going to be a quote from Dante's *The Divine Comedy*.'

'So there's a backstory to this.'

'This is the second that we know of, and it's connected to the case I worked on in Syracuse five years ago.'

'Well, if I find anything else I'll let you know, but you'll want an ID on this guy as a first step. I've got the forensic odontologist coming over. We'll get X-rays and a summary over to you later today. You're out of the 114th, right?'

'Yes,' Quinn said. 'If whoever couriers it can bring it directly to the Homicide Suite, that'd be appreciated.'

'Consider it done,' Adams said.

'Can we take this?' Rachel asked, holding up the evidence bag.

'I need to get it photographed and logged,' Adams said. 'I'll send it over with my autopsy report and the X-rays.'

33

'Attica,' Rachel said. 'That's where we check first.'

It was early afternoon. On the desk was Adams' couriered package.

'Wake did eight years. Maybe this guy was there too.'

'As good a place to start as any,' Quinn said. 'I'll call them.'

Rachel had pinned up the photographs of the second victim along with a photocopy of the note. The original and the steel tube in which it had been found had already been secured in the 114th Evidence Lock-up. While Quinn went through channels at Attica to get the help they needed, Rachel went down to the Precinct Commissary and got coffee for them both. On her way back, she remembered the *contrapasso*.

'Arson,' she said as she came through the door. 'People in Attica for arson.'

'Attica don't have their own in-house dentist,' Quinn said. 'They sub-contract to a state-registered facility in Binghampton.'

'How far?'

'Three, three and a half hours drive,' Quinn said.

'Call Attica back. Ask them to give us a list of everyone released in the last five years who did time for arson. Give me the name of the place in Binghampton and I'll tell them we're coming.'

'It's Saturday,' Quinn said. 'They're dentists. They'll be on the fucking golf course.'

'Then we're gonna spoil their game, aren't we? Just like we spoiled the coroner's anniversary dinner.'

The fax signal started up. The list had come back from Attica. 'Seventeen names,' Quinn said.

A recorded message at the dental facility gave Rachel an emergency number. She called it, got a switchboard, found the name of the senior dental practitioner. Despite the fact that she identified herself as a detective from the 114th, the switchboard operator held her ground. She was not authorized to release personal telephone numbers. Rachel didn't get into a fight with her. Instead she called Binghampton PD, tracked down a home address from a three-month-old parking violation. She got the telephone number from Information. She called the number, got no answer. She said they should drive up there and appear on the guy's doorstep.

'If he's not there, that's six hours in the car for nothing,' Quinn said.

'What, and you don't like my company?'

Quinn shook his head resignedly and fetched his jacket from the back of the chair.

Dr. Thomas Delaney lived in an elegant mock Georgian house in the suburbs of Binghampton. A middle-aged Hispanic woman opened the door. The detectives were asked to wait in the foyer.

Delaney came down a curved stairwell in tennis whites.

'Detectives,' he said.

'Hoffman,' Rachel said. 'And this is Detective Quinn. Apologies for the intrusion, but we've come to ask for your help.'

'My help?'

Rachel explained the situation. She showed Delaney the list from Attica and the X-rays from the odontologist.

Delaney indicated a mark on one of the images. 'This is a root canal,' he said. 'But not one of mine. And this here's a wisdom that should probably have come out a good while ago. This man didn't take very good care of his teeth.'

'Can you help us?' Quinn asked.

'Sure I can, but the records are at my practice.'

No more than twenty minutes away, Delaney's surgery was an impressive facility with rigorous security provisions.

'We take care of the folks from Attica off regular hours,' Delaney explained. 'They come down here with escorts, obviously, but we're state-registered, and that means we have to have a designated section. No windows, double doors, the works.'

Delaney walked them through to the rear of the building. Along a short corridor, they came out into an annex that was altogether more functional. Whereas there had been leather furniture, coffee tables and wall art in the front of the facility, here there was nothing.

Through a door accessed by both key and electronic combination pad, they found a small office, the walls of which were lined with filing cabinets.

'Patient records going back fifteen years,' Delaney said. 'The teeth of everyone in Attica, correctional staff included.'

Delaney went through one file after another, removing X-rays from each and sliding them into retainers on an illuminated screen on the wall. Half an hour. That's all it took.

Delaney turned from the screen, a file in his hand.

'This is your man,' he said. 'Anthony Yates. Date of birth, January 7, 1949. That'd make him – what? – thirty-one years old. Here's the impacted wisdom, and here's the root canal. That, detectives, is quite as unique as a fingerprint. It's marked for transfer. That means he must have been released. If his file is still here, then we've not received notification of where he's now registered. However, looking at the general state of his teeth, I don't think dental care has ever been foremost in his mind.'

Rachel couldn't thank Delaney enough. He seemed genuinely pleased to have been of assistance. He drove them to his home and they headed back to New York.

An hour into the journey, Quinn said they should look into the Attica connection.

'I'm thinking that maybe it's someone who was inside with them.'

'First thing is to find out who he was, what he did.'

'Which only we can do,' Quinn replied. 'Not even release dates are made available.'

'So we're looking at police, correctional staff, probation, courts, lawyers, Social Services, sex-offender register administration, inmates, and then outside the system you've got friends, family, employers, work colleagues—'

'I get it, I get it,' Quinn said. 'But we have to agree on how we approach this.'

'We need help,' Rachel said.

'Sure we do. I'll speak to my Lieutenant. But, knowing the workload, the best we're gonna get is maybe a couple of uniforms.'

'I don't mean that kind of help,' Rachel said. 'We need to go public.'

'Seriously? At this stage, I really don't think it's a good idea to get journalists involved.'

'Just one journalist,' Rachel said. 'Carl Sheehan.'

34

Margaret 'Maggie' Silva was a realist.

No matter who they were, no matter their history, everyone was out for themselves. Call it whatever you wanted – selfish, mean, inconsiderate – it was all the same thing. The dumb ones didn't see it. The smart ones called it something else.

There was greed in peoples' eyes and in their words. Whatever you had, they wanted more. And even when you were left with insufficient for yourself, they wanted that too.

Since childhood, Maggie had known these things, and the older she got, the more she knew they were true. In fact, the only thing that had happened was that people had gotten worse.

Her own parents were all up in the Jesus thing. Church on Sundays, church at Easter, Christmas, Thanksgiving, and any time anything happened they would get down on their knees – in the kitchen, out in the yard – and they would pray. If things were good, they prayed their thanks. If things were bad – which they mostly were – they would pray for the strength to keep on going.

'These trials are sent to test us,' her father would say with that mealy-mouthed, weak-willed smile. 'You must trust in the Lord's plan.' And then he would hold her hand and pull her down to her knees, and start reciting some meaningless crap from the Bible.

Maggie hated it. She hated them. She hated church and school and public holidays and people who said 'Have a nice day'. She hated the whole fucked-up world.

When she was thirteen she jerked off the school janitor in a bathroom stall. He gave her ten bucks. She told him if he didn't give her ten more she'd tell a teacher that he'd molested her. He gave her the ten bucks and made her promise to never say a word. She didn't. She jerked him off a few more times, and each time he made sounds like he was going to die and then he gave her a twenty. One time he told her to put his thing in her mouth. She told him to fuck off.

In February of 1956, just fifteen, she was expelled from school for stabbing a girl with a pencil. She didn't stab her hard. The pencil only went into her leg about half an inch. The principal told her father that he should send her to reform school, that Maggie was very, very lucky that the other girl's parents were not going to press criminal charges, that if Maggie didn't change her ways then she could only look forward to a life of escalating trouble. Her father said he would deal with it.

Dealing with it meant daily prayers and more church and endless chores around the house. It meant being schooled by her mother. It meant being grounded for weeks on end. Just a couple of weeks shy of her sixteenth birthday in December of the same year, Maggie took off with three hundred and eight dollars from her church Christmas charity drive. She hitched her way across New Jersey from Somerville to Trenton, and took a motel room. She paid in cash and they didn't ask questions. She turned tricks most nights, sold weed, some pills, even helped the motel manager with a couple of scams.

By the time she was twenty, Maggie had her own apartment in downtown Trenton. It wasn't a palace, but it was better than a motel room. She'd fucked more than enough strangers, and she was focusing on coke and pills. The mark-up was way better than weed. And then she made a mistake. She agreed to meet a new supplier in a bar. He'd been referred to her by a regular. The guy in the bar seemed legit. He said the right things and he acted the right way, and the price that he gave her for coke was a good ten percent less than what she was paying. She bought ten grams.

Three days later, the cops raided her apartment. The whole thing had been a set-up. They had her regular on some other beef; the guy in the bar was a narc. Sure it was a set-up, but what the hell was going to happen?

In June of '61 she was sentenced to twelve years in Clinton Correctional. Her Public Defender was a waste of skin and oxygen. He didn't even file an appeal. New Jersey was all hot on dealers, and Maggie caught the sharp end of the stick. With good behavior, she could've been out in seven, but people fucked with her so she fucked with them back. She even did six months in solitary after choking her cellmate unconscious.

Released in May of 1973, Maggie was thirty-two years old, had no education, no money, no home. She hadn't heard from her folks since she'd left Somerville. She guessed they were nothing but pleased about that.

Leaving Trenton, planning never to return, Maggie moved to New York. The Big Apple was crowded with lowlifes – gangsters, dealers, junkies, pimps, whores – and it wasn't long before she gained a foothold. This time she was smart. She kept everything on the down-low. She dealt only in coke, and she dealt to uptown types, people with no shortage of money, people who had something to lose. She got a supplier she trusted. She never discussed her business, and she never agreed to meet anyone who offered a better price or a better grade of powder. She made a lot of money. Stupid money. By the time she was thirty-five she was the owner of a hair salon, a car wash, and a comfortable, spacious apartment in Greenwich Village. Sure, her legitimate ventures didn't make as much money as the coke, but they were above board. She even paid taxes. The last thing she needed was the US Treasury on her ass. Maybe they could get Capone that way, but not Maggie Silva.

*

When Maggie arrived home on the night of Sunday, March 30th, 1980, she showered, put on her robe and poured herself a glass of wine. She switched on the TV to dispel the silence in her apartment. She sat near the window of her living room, the lights of New York out ahead of her, and she closed her eyes. Most times she thought about little else but money, about when she would have enough to just disappear quietly into obscurity. She knew she'd never have a family of her own. It was something she'd never yearned for, but the notion of finding some place away from the noise of the city appealed to her.

She was tired. It had been a long day. She would finish her wine and go to bed.

Leaning forward to set her glass on the coffee table ahead of her, she started to get up. It was then that she sensed something. What it was, she didn't know. It was a feeling, a perception. She turned. Whatever it was – whoever it was – was quick. She barely had time to register the shape, and then the blow against the side of her head arrived with such force that she just folded to the floor.

Slurring into consciousness, Maggie was on her back. She was naked, her hands and feet tied to each corner of the bed. The room was dark, but she knew someone was there.

She opened her mouth, but the figure stepped forward suddenly and placed a gloved hand over her mouth.

Maggie pulled against the ties. She tugged and kicked and wrestled with as much energy as she could muster, but she was held fast. A sick, numb terror overwhelmed everything. The hand over her mouth relaxed.

'Please... please...'

'Sssshhh now, Maggie,' a voice said. 'Not another word or I will have to hurt you.'

Eyes wide, breathing fast and shallow, a cold sweat over her entire body, she knew she was going to die. She was going to be raped and butchered. Or worse. And she was sorry then, perhaps for the very first time in her life she was truly sorry for all the things she'd done and the people she'd hurt and abandoned and lied to and cheated.

The man sat down on the edge of the bed and she saw the outline of his face. In the darkness, she couldn't see clearly. If he stayed right where he was and didn't put the light on, then there was no way she would ever be able to identify him. She would tell him that. She would tell him to do whatever he was going to do and she would never breathe a word to anyone. On her life, she would never breathe a word.

With his hand still over her mouth, the man leaned over and switched on the bedside lamp.

Maggie closed her eyes. She would lie right where she was and keep her eyes closed and he could do his worst and then leave and that would be the end of it.

'Look at me,' the man said.

Maggie turned her head away.

She felt the vice-like grip of his hand beneath her jaw. He turned her head towards him.

'Look at me, Maggie.'

Everything loosened inside her. Every muscle, every sinew, every nerve. She was made of nothing but air. She was a shadow, an empty shell, a vacuum.

She opened her eyes. He let go.

From somewhere inside his coat, the man produced a bag. He opened it and set it on the table beside the bed. He had a spoon in his hand. A small one, silver, reflecting the light from the lamp. It was one of hers. He'd taken it from the kitchen.

Dipping the spoon in the bag, he once again closed his hand beneath her jaw.

'Open wide,' he said.

Maggie wrestled against his grip, kept her lips tightly closed.

'Open wide, Maggie, or I'll cut a hole in your face.'

Maggie opened her mouth.

She knew what it was. Coke. He was feeding her coke. Feeding her coke by the spoonful. Her mouth was dry and she started to cough.

'Swallow,' the man said, 'or we're going to be here all night.'

A second spoonful. A third. She felt the rush then, and she knew this was no baby laxative, talcum powder cut-down shit. It was strong, and it flooded her body with a fierce wave of adrenalin.

And he kept on going, one spoon after another, and he was careful not to spill it, careful to ensure that she was swallowing everything he gave her, and while he did so he talked to her in a low, almost soothing voice.

'Midway upon the journey of our life, I found myself within a forest dark, for the straightforward path had been lost. Ah me! How hard a thing it is to say, what was this forest savage, rough and stern, which in the very thought renews the fear.'

Muscles tensing, her body seizing violently, her chest filled with fire, and then Maggie started to retch. Vomit filled her throat and mouth, and then spilled through her nose and down her cheeks.

And still he kept on feeding her – one spoonful, yet another, and his voice became a whisper as he leaned closer towards her.

'So bitter is it, death is a little more...'

Lurching upwards, her heart seemed to burst in her chest. Everything went black, and for just the briefest moment there was a sense that she was looking down at herself.

And then there was nothing.

35

It took until late on Sunday evening for Rachel to track down Carl Sheehan.

He'd been away for the weekend, he explained, visiting with Suzanne's parents.

'We need to talk to you,' Rachel said. 'Can you come over to the 114th in the morning?'

'Tomorrow's gonna be difficult,' Carl said. 'Tuesday would be better.'

'It needs to be now, as soon as possible.'

'What's happening?'

'I'm not going to get into it over the phone,' Rachel said. 'I just need you to be here.'

'So, if I'm going to cancel everything that I've got going on, I need a little more than that.'

'What you need is to trust me,' Rachel said. 'I'll be there by 8.00 latest. Don't let me down.'

'I'll make some calls.'

'Carl—'

'Jesus Christ, Rachel, okay. I got it. I'll be there.'

Rachel was at work before 7.00. She seemed to be running on little else but caffeine and adrenalin. Once again, she'd fallen asleep reading the *The Divine Comedy*. She was nearing the end, and had still to find anything in it that helped focus her thoughts or indicate a motive.

Quinn arrived a half-hour later with a case file and she went to his office. He looked as rough as Rachel felt.

'You know, Maurice, I don't even know if you have a family.'

'I have a family, yes.'

'How do they deal with this shit?'

'Let's just say that my wife has reconciled herself to the fact that this is the way it has to be for now. I guess at some point she might run out of patience, but I guess I'll deal with that when we get there.'

'I don't see how I could reconcile the two.'

'Have you ever tried?'

Rachel didn't reply.

'You do realize that after this—' He looked over towards the case board. 'After whatever the hell this has finished, there'll be another one and then another one, and if my brief experience with you is anything to go by, then you'll be just as fixated on that one as you are on this.'

'You think I'm fixated?'

Maurice gave a wry smile. 'You're a little intense.'

'You don't think this warrants being intense?'

'I think it warrants being professional, conscientious, methodical, realistic. I think it warrants your undivided attention when you're here. Outside of here, I think there's other things that should engage your energies. If you don't learn to separate the different parts of your life, then this becomes your life.'

'You're getting a bit philosophical, Maurice.'

'You're smart, Rachel. Whip-smart. You're really focused and driven. I respect that. You've come down here from Syracuse and thrown yourself into this with as much as anyone could ask of you. But if you keep on running in fifth gear, then you're gonna start shaking things loose. You can only do as much as you can. You have to ease up every once in a while, step back from this, you know? You've been here ten days. Have you even been out to dinner? Did you go see a movie? Have you even talked to any of your friends on the phone?'

'I don't have friends. I mean yes, I have friends I guess, but they're people I work with.'

Maurice frowned. 'You're telling me that you don't know anyone socially outside the department?'

'I talk to my neighbor sometimes.'

'And what about your folks?'

Rachel shrugged. 'We're not close. I saw them last Christmas, briefly.'

'You have no brothers or sisters?'

'No.'

'Okay, well I'm definitely no fount of wisdom on the subject, but I've been doing this for more than twenty years. You need to get some other things going on in your life. You can't just do this and nothing else. You won't stay the course. You'll wind up with a nervous breakdown. I've seen it happen, and it happens to the ones who seem to be the brightest and the best.'

'So I need to go bowling or take up knitting or I'll go crazy, right?'

'Joke all you want, Rachel. I'm just telling you what I've seen. You spend all your time dealing with this kind of shit, you start to believe that the whole world is this way. It's not. This is the dregs. The kind of people who do this are in a tiny, tiny minority. The vast majority of people are good and decent and hard-working. Trust me, there's a great deal more light than there is darkness.'

'I'll take your word for it.'

'Getting back on track, this is Anthony Yates. Arson. Did six years plus in Attica. Released a month after Wake, so I'm thinking that we might take a trip out—'

Quinn stopped mid-sentence. Carl Sheehan was in the doorway.

'I'm sorry,' Sheehan said. 'If I'm interrupting something I can come back.'

'No,' Rachel said. 'Come in. We were just talking. Nothing important.'

Sheehan walked into the room. He saw the case board.

'You have another,' he said. He looked at the photographs, at the photocopies of the letter and the note from the Yates crime scene.

'What the fuck is this?' he asked, almost to himself.

'Take a seat, Mr. Sheehan,' Quinn said.

Sheehan did as he was asked.

Quinn leaned back in his chair.

'Detective Hoffman tells me you're a good guy,' Quinn said. 'I have to be honest, I have learned to trust journalists about as much as I trust lawyers. However, I do trust Detective Hoffman and if she says that you can help us, then I'm gonna run with it.'

'Trust me to do what?' Sheehan asked.

'From what we can see, we have a copycat. I know that you were asked about the letter. You haven't told us how you came by it. I could make an issue of that, but I'm not going to. I appreciate that there is – let's say – a kind of give-and-take between the press and the police department, and I also appreciate that confidential sources need to remain confidential for a reason.'

'All I can tell you—'

'Let me finish, Mr. Sheehan. What I was going to say was that whoever your source is, and whatever you had to do to get the information you got, well that's between you and them. If, however, we later find out that your source was in any way involved in these crimes, like they also passed information on to the perpetrator, then you're gonna find yourself pulled into the same hurricane of shit as them. Do you understand what I'm saying?'

'I get it,' Sheehan replied.

'So, seeing as we understand one another, is there anything you want to tell us?'

'The person who told me about the letter was not PD. Not directly.'

'And do you have any reason to believe that this person might have—'

'If you're asking whether or not I think this person is giving this information to someone else, then no, I don't.' Sheehan replied.

'And what makes you so sure?'

'Because I know them. I know what kind of person they are.'

'And this person that you know so well, are they connected to this investigation in an official capacity?'

'They are, yes.'

'And are they being paid to give you information?' Quinn asked.

'No, they're not.'

'So they're just leaking confidential data about ongoing investigations out of the goodness of their heart?'

'They owed me. They got into some difficulty and I helped them out.'

Quinn was silent for a moment. He looked at Rachel. Rachel said nothing.

'Are you going to tell me why I'm here?' Sheehan asked. 'Is this what this is about? You're just trying to find out how I knew about the letter?'

'No, Mr. Sheehan, it's not why you're here. I just need to be certain that you and whoever you're talking to has no direct connection to this, that you're not compromised.'

'The person was there, okay? At the crime scene.'

'So we're talking Forensics, Coroner's Office, crime scene photographer, right?'

Sheehan didn't reply.

Quinn leaned forward. He looked directly at Sheehan. 'Detective Hoffman believes that we need to enlist some public assistance with this case. I'm reticent, but I'm also conscious of the fact that we have two deaths, no substantive clues, no firm leads, nothing circumstantial that's pointing us in any particular direction. She also told me that you worked with her back in Syracuse, that you did what she wanted, that you didn't take advantage of the situation.'

'Rachel and I had an understanding,' Sheehan said.

'And if we asked for your assistance again?'

'Well, you'd get it. Tell me what you want. You want something in the paper, I can put something in the paper. You want me to look into something unofficially, I can do that too.'

Sheehan looked at Rachel as if for support.

'Look,' he said, 'I'm not some sensationalist hack, Detective Quinn. I'm a journalist, sure, but not every journalist is a muck-raking, two-faced, lying sack of shit that would sell their own kids for a byline. I know what happened in Syracuse, and I know how much Rachel was affected, not only by what Marshall did, but also the fact that she lost her partner. And just like you didn't become a cop so you could play the big man and get kickbacks and bribes and whatever the fuck, I didn't become a journalist to invent bullshit news stories for my own gratification. If you want my help, then ask for it. If you don't, then I'll fuck off and do something else.'

'Okay,' Quinn said. 'We're going to have to trust one another, all three of us, and see if we can't get something out there that will help us find this guy.'

'Well, alright,' Sheehan said. 'So tell me what you know. No notes, no recording, just tell me what's been happening and we'll go from there.'

'How long you got?' Quinn asked.

Sheehan shrugged. 'Rachel told me to clear my desk and show up. I cleared my desk. I showed up.'

'Good enough,' Quinn said. 'Rachel can tell you everything. I'm going to get coffee.'

36

NEW YORK COURIER

WEDNESDAY, APRIL 2, 1980

Carl Sheehan – Crime Desk

RED RIBBON SIGNATURE IN
DOUBLE HOMICIDE

New York Police Department 114th Precinct Homicide Division have issued an appeal to the public for information regarding two recent murders.

Following the unexplained deaths of Christopher Wake (35), a construction worker from Queens on 19 March, and Anthony Yates (31), a warehouseman from Astoria on 28 March, anyone with information regarding the whereabouts and activities of the aforementioned individuals in the days leading up their deaths should contact Detective Maurice Quinn on the toll-free number given at the end of this article. Any information will be treated in the utmost confidence.

Though circumstances differ, the murders have been attributed to the same perpetrator. The body of Christopher Wake was found in a disused lock-up in Queens. Cause of death was given as suffocation by the Coroner's Office, but Wake had suffered a number of violent injuries prior to his death. Anthony Yates' burned body was found in an abandoned car in a wrecking yard, also within the jurisdiction of the 114th. Both men had prior criminal records and had served custodial sentences in Attica Correctional Facility. Wake and Yates were released within a month of one other in early 1979.

Present at each scene, thus indicating a connection in the seemingly unrelated homicides, were numerous red ribbons. Police are working on the basis that the perpetrator had some personal connection to each of the victims, and that the signature bears some – as yet unknown – relationship to the motive. Their respective manners of death also bore a similarity to the crimes for which each of them were convicted and incarcerated.

Leading the investigation, Detective Quinn issued a statement urging anyone who might have knowledge of either victim to come forward. 'Sometimes it's the smallest, seemingly insignificant details that prove to be the most helpful, and thus I encourage anyone who knows anything to make contact as quickly as possible,' he said. 'I can assure the public that we are dealing with this investigation as a priority, and that every available resource is being applied to ensure that the individual responsible for these horrific crimes is identified and brought to justice as rapidly as possible.'

37

The decision not to run the article on April 1st had been Sheehan's. He understood the urgency, but he'd discussed it with his editor and the editor had agreed. They concurred it would be inappropriate, that – alongside all the customary spoof pieces – it would lose its impact.

The decision to keep Rachel's name out of the piece had been Quinn's. If the killer believed that Rachel was no longer involved, he might send another communication to insist that she be reassigned. Any communication they received could only give them more with which to work. As for omitting any reference to the Syracuse homicides, Rachel believed it would only add fuel to the fire. She knew the article would get attention, that encouraging speculations about copycat killings would be counterproductive. She also had no wish to see her own history dragged through the press. More than that she had no wish to see a regurgitation of all the sordid details about Robert Marshall and the murder of Michael Ridgway.

The article did get attention, but not in the way they'd hoped. The *Courier* ran its piece in the morning edition. That evening, the *Times* issued a sober variation, but the smaller regional papers had a field day *–RED RIBBON KILLER, BRUTAL DOUBLE HOMICIDE BAFFLES COPS, EX-CONS ON HIT LIST FOR SAVAGE KILLER, RED RIBBON JUSTICE FOR SEX ASSAULT DENTIST*, each article somehow managing to outdo the next in terms of shock-effect and intent to alarm the public. They had no new information to offer, of course, but they'd somehow managed to exaggerate Sheehan's article into something as lurid and sensational as possible.

What those articles did do, however, was prompt a call from Detective Wayne Trent from the 6th Precinct.

'We have something that might interest you,' Trent told Rachel. 'Dealer. Forced overdose. Found her Monday night in her apartment.'

'And why do you—'

'This shit with the red ribbons, Detective Hoffman. Red ribbons draped over the bed where we found her.'

Emerging from the Queens-Midtown Tunnel beneath the East River and heading into Manhattan, the Empire State up and to her right, Rachel realized that she'd barely seen the sky since she'd arrived in New York. Her days had been spent in the office, her nights in a featureless motel room.

Heading past the Flatiron and turning left on 18th, she wondered if the case – now crossing two jurisdictions – would be taken from her. Maybe the respective captains of each precinct would conclude that this was now a New York matter, that some unknown quantity from Syracuse was the last thing they needed. If such a thing happened, how would she feel – resentful or relieved? Would it fuel an already-incipient self-doubt about her own ability? She wanted to stay in New York. She wanted to see this thing through to the end. And, no matter which way she looked at it, and despite the fact that he was tied into a long-term relationship with a child on the way, she wanted to see Carl Sheehan again. Theirs had been the longest relationship of her life. It had meant something – what, she wasn't sure – but she was tied to something and it kept pulling at her. If she could go back now, would she work at it, would she make different decisions, would she have come with him to

New York? She didn't know – could never know – the answers to those questions. All she knew was that something within her had been fearful of making such a commitment.

Trent was waiting for them. Expecting some kind of territorial resentment, she was surprised by the man's reception. He was young, perhaps in his early thirties, and had yet to carry that shadow of frustration and disillusionment that so many detectives seemed to possess.

Ushering them into his office, he thanked them for coming over.

On his desk was the case file – the crime scene photographs, the coroner's report, the initial summary of his findings when attending the first call.

'Margaret Silva,' Trent said when all three of them were seated. 'Thirty-nine years old. Originally from New Jersey. In and out of trouble as a teenager. Did twelve years in Clinton Correctional on a narcotics charge. Released May of '73. She came here, set up shop. Coke mostly, bits and pieces of other stuff too. Her apartment's in the Village. She owned a hair salon and a car wash, both legit.'

'When was she found?' Rachel asked.

'Monday evening. The door of her apartment was left open, evidently on purpose. Coroner says she died within the previous twenty-four hours. Had upwards of eight grams of coke in her system. Tied to a bed, as you can see, and force-fed. Pretty fucking horrific way to go.'

'And did you get anything from the scene?' Quinn asked.

'Clean as clean can be,' Trent replied. 'I mean, we're still processing some stuff, but as it stands there was nothing that gives us a direction to go in. It was clinical. That's the only way to describe it.'

'Neighbors?' Rachel asked.

'Heard and saw nothing, or if they did, they're not talking.

There's a couple of other interesting characters in that building and they make it their business to cooperate with us as little as possible.'

Rachel picked up the photographs. Once she'd looked at each, she passed them to Quinn.

'It's the ribbons, right?' Trent asked. 'That's what connects these things.'

'That, and the manner of death,' Rachel said. 'Our first guy was a sex offender. Did eight years in Attica. Had his eyes removed and his fingers cut off. Second one was an arsonist. He was burned alive.'

'What, so this is some kind of whacko vigilante shit?'

'It's a little more complicated than that,' Quinn said. 'This is connected to a case that Detective Hoffman ran back in 1975 in Syracuse. Five murders, all of them killed with chloroform. The perp offed himself so there's no explanation of why he did what he did. Our guy here is a copycat. He knows a good deal about Syracuse, even used the name 'Dante' in a letter at the first crime scene. That tells us that he's got access to police files, court files, who knows. Anyway, the first guy leaves notes behind—'

'We got a note,' Trent interjected. He opened the file, withdrew a photocopy and handed it over.

AND HAS A NATURE SO MALIGN AND RUTHLESS, THAT
NEVER DOTH SHE GLUT HER GREEDY WILL, AND
AFTER FOOD IS HUNGRIER THAN BEFORE.

'You know what that means?' Trent asked.

'It's a quote from a book,' Rachel said. 'Same notes both in Syracuse and now here.'

'Surely this was in the papers back then,' Trent said.

'It wasn't, no,' Rachel replied. 'We had a few pieces on it, but none of them gave the full story. The only way to have these details is from official records.'

'So it could be a cop? Someone out to clean up cases that didn't convict?'

'Sure, it could be,' Quinn said. 'Right now we're blind. We've got all the files from Syracuse, but we just haven't had the time to trawl through all of it yet.'

'Right, right,' Trent said. He leaned back, looked at each of them in turn. 'So, how do you wanna play this?'

'Play it?' Rachel asked.

'This is your case, active and ongoing. Okay, so the Silva woman's in our jurisdiction, but I can clear it that you have authority. Believe me, that's not going to be an issue. We have more than enough on our plates as it is.'

'Who do you need to speak to?' Quinn asked.

'I already did. Told my lieutenant. He said he didn't have a problem with you guys taking over on this one.'

'I was kinda hoping you might have someone who could work on it with us,' Rachel said. 'There's just the two of us, and we've got a double homicide already.'

'Sure, I can ask. I'm just being realistic when I say it's unlikely.'

'Ask,' Quinn said. 'We could do with a fresh perspective on this.'

Trent got up and left the room.

'It fucks our Attica theory,' Quinn said.

'But she's still an ex-con,' Rachel said. 'Which tells us that our guy has access to records.'

'You think Trent's right? You think it could be a cop?'

'Only as much as it could be a PO or someone in the court system.'

'So let's go there. Let's go through the arrest records, probation files, see if there were correctional officers who served at both Attica and Clinton—'

Trent came back into the office. From his expression, Rachel knew the answer to his request.

'I'm sorry,' Trent said. 'You're either gonna have to take the case as it is or leave it with us. An inter-precinct collaboration isn't gonna fly.'

'Because?' Quinn asked.

'Politics, overtime, budget, existing workload, all the things we don't want to think about. I did my best, but it was a no.'

'Can you get all of this logged out to us? Physical evidence, everything.'

'Sure I can.'

Picking up the case file, Rachel said, 'But I want to take this now, okay?'

'Sure, but you'll need to come down and sign for it.'

'And send everything over to the 114th as soon as you can.'

'Hopefully within twenty-four hours,' Trent said. 'If there are any problems, I'll let you know.'

Rachel got up. 'If there are any problems, we're coming back to get it.'

38

Rachel and Maurice Quinn went back over every piece of paper-work they had to hand. They listed first responders, arresting officers, detectives, forensics crew, crime scene photographers, court officials, lawyers, judges, probation officers, even staff who'd worked at the juvie where Yates had been incarcerated. They hadn't even started on the correctional officers in Attica and Clinton. The 6th Precinct files on Margaret Silva had yet to arrive. Already, they had in excess of three hundred names.

'This is impossible,' Quinn said. 'We just don't have the resources to find these people, let alone question them. We could spend hundreds of hours on this and come back with absolutely nothing.'

Rachel was tired. Everything was frayed. Whatever seams were still holding her together were being tested to breaking point.

Getting up from the desk, she walked to the case board. She looked at the pictures again – Wake, Yates, now Silva. The ribbons. Red ribbons. Across the three crime scenes it was yards of the stuff, and – aside from the notes – it was the only piece of physical evidence that linked the murders.

'This ribbon is the same at each scene,' she said without look-ing back at Quinn. 'It's going to be a particular color, a particular composition, and there are going to be only so many places where you can buy it.'

'Garment District?' Quinn suggested.

'Where's that?'

'Back where we were. Manhattan. Whole area around Penn Station, sort of between Fifth and Ninth.'

Rachel turned around. 'And they have fabric suppliers.'

'Sure they do. Suppliers, designers, manufacturing, fashion houses, stores everything. But—'

'I know what you're going to say, Maurice. And no, I don't for a second believe that we're going to walk into some place that sells fucking ribbons and they're going to give us a name and address. However, I would like to know if there's anything particular about it. I would like to know what it's made of, where you can buy it, how much it costs. Let's get a sample from lock-up and go ask some people. I just need to get as many details as possible clear in my mind, okay?'

'Sure, sure,' Quinn said. 'We can take a drive over there.'

'So let's do that, even if it's only because it'll make me feel like I'm trying.'

'Trying?' Maurice smiled. 'Detective Hoffman, you are the most trying person I've ever met.'

Within an hour of their arrival, they knew the ribbon was silk, that it was alizarin crimson, and that there were only a handful of manufacturers in the city where it could be obtained as a bulk order. The reassuring fact was that the manufacturers were trade only. You couldn't just walk into the place and order dozens of yards of it.

The information came from a dressmaker off West 38th called Alice Woloch. She was no more than five two or three, had to be seventy years old, and wore a carnival of outsized costume jewelry.

'It's not cheap, but then quality never had been cheap, has it?' she told Rachel. 'Everything's going synthetic these days. You want silk, it's going to cost you.'

'I'm not concerned about the price,' Rachel said. 'I just want to know where you can get it.'

'Garment Directory,' Alice said. 'They have everything in there.'

'And where can I get one of those?'

Turning to a shelving unit behind the reception desk, Alice produced a heavy volume. It landed with a thump on the counter.

'Right here is where.'

'And the ribbon places are listed in here. How do I find them?'

Alice smiled. 'You look under *R*, sweetie. And then you go down and you find *RI*, then *RIB*. You get the idea, right?'

Rachel glanced back at Quinn.

'Detective stuff,' he said.

Rachel noted the name and address of every ribbon manufacturer in the book. There were seven in total, all of them within a radius of a dozen or so blocks.

'Is this for some kind of Police Department party or something?' Alice asked before they left.

'Something like that,' Rachel replied.

Alice raised her eyebrows. 'Now I know why there's never enough money to fix the damned roads.'

They started walking. Quinn knew the area, so he led the way.

'If we find something,' he said, 'then this is gonna be the flimsiest of leads that ever solved a case.'

'You were the one who asked the public to come back with anything. If I remember correctly, you said the smallest details sometimes proved to be the most helpful. Those were your words, right?'

'Not my words. Departmental Press Office words.'

'Nevertheless.'

'You do understand that a manufacturer like this is going to be sending stuff all over, don't you? Not just the US, but the world.'

'Maurice, if you want to go back to the office and start calling probation officers and court stenographers, you go ahead. I'm doing this with or without you.'

'I wouldn't feel good about letting you walk the streets of New York alone, Rachel. Small-town girl like you.'

'I have a gun.'

'Even more reason you shouldn't be unaccompanied.'

Two hours in, the working day approaching its end, Rachel felt she was chasing a ghost. In the main, the difficulty was incomplete and disorganized records. The places they visited were hives of activity, dozens of workers at endless rows of machines, the din overwhelming. Locating specific individuals who could answer their questions was the primary challenge. People had left for the day, were on vacation, were off at some other site out of the city.

Ready to quit and return the next day, Quinn agreed to visit one more factory. It was the fifth they'd tried.

First Class Fabrics was a good half a dozen blocks from where they'd parked. It was housed in a five-story building, the two lower floors of which were occupied by a bridal gown outlet and a design studio.

The owner, a middle-aged Korean, was immediately on-edge. Rachel guessed he had unregistered workers, cash-in-hand labor, more than likely a catalog of fire and safety regulation violations.

'We're just interested in orders placed, Mr. Hyun,' Rachel assured him. 'Nothing else.'

Hyun showed them through to a tiny office at the far end of the floor. No one looked up from their work. Heads down, the noise close to deafening, Rachel could barely imagine what it would be like to spend day after day in such a place.

Once inside the office, Rachel showed Hyun the ribbon.

'Yes,' he said. 'You want more?'

'This is yours?' Quinn asked.

'Silk,' Hyun said. 'We have very good silk here.'

'Was this made here?' Rachel asked.

'We can make this here, yes.'

Rachel glanced at Quinn.

'Mr. Hyun,' Quinn said. 'We're asking whether or not this particular ribbon was made right here. You understand?'

'I don't know,' Hyun replied. 'Maybe here, maybe somewhere else. But we make red ribbon. Any color you want.'

'Do you keep your order forms?' Rachel asked.

'Order forms. We have them, yes.'

'Can we see order forms for ribbon for the past year? Is that possible?'

'It's possible, yes. Why do you want order forms? You don't want more ribbon?'

'For now, we just need to see the order forms, Mr. Hyun. If you can get them for us, that would be really appreciated.'

'I don't want no police trouble,' Hyun said.

Quinn smiled. 'You're not in any trouble, Mr. Hyun. That's not why we're here. We just need your help. We need to find out if you processed an order for red silk ribbon.'

Hyun hesitated. He looked at each of the detectives in turn, as if gauging their intent.

'This is a good business,' Hyun said. 'Jobs for many people.'

'I promise you,' Rachel said. 'We just need to see the order forms and then we'll leave.'

'No police trouble.'

'No police trouble,' Quinn said.

'Okay, come.'

Hyun eased past them and left the office. They followed him to the very end of the floor and into a narrow corridor. To the right was another office.

Opening it, Hyun showed them where the records were kept. Boxes, dozens of them, lined the walls. They were stacked ceiling high in some places. The boxes on the floor had been crushed.

'Orders,' Hyun said.

'Christ,' Quinn said under his breath.

Rachel stepped inside. The boxes weren't dated, nor was there any indication of order type.

Hyun pointed towards the lower boxes. 'Old ones,' he said. He indicated the upper boxes. 'New ones.'

'We need to look,' Rachel said. 'Is that okay?'

Hyun nodded. 'Look, but don't take, okay?'

'Thank you,' Rachel said.

Hyun glanced at his watch. 'I leave in one hour. My brother will come for night workers. I'll tell him you here.'

'You're open all night?' Quinn asked.

'All night,' Hyun said. 'Good business. Lots of work. Make money for many families.'

Rachel thanked Hyun again. Hyun left them standing speechless inside the mountain of paperwork.

A little before 4.00, on the morning of Friday, April 4th, Maurice Quinn – exhausted, starving, at the very limit of his patience – stopped dead with a piece of paper in his hand. He read it, read it again, and then he said, 'Here.'

'You have something?' Rachel asked.

Quinn didn't reply. He just handed her the order form with an expression of disbelief on his face.

Rachel frowned, took it from him. 'What is it?'

Quinn just nodded at the paper.

It was there, right there in her hand, but she almost didn't want to look.

Twenty yards of Alizarin Crimson silk ribbon. The order had been placed on Tuesday, January 15th, 1980. The address given was on Steinway Street, Astoria. It was not the fact that they'd found an order for the ribbon, nor that the address was just four blocks from the 114th Precinct, but that the name on the order was Michael Ridgway.

'Rachel,' Quinn said. 'I know you must—'

'Don't say anything, Maurice,' she replied. 'Please just don't say anything right now.'

39

Less than two hours later, New York coming to life around them, Rachel and Maurice Quinn stood on the sidewalk looking at an empty storefront on Steinway Street. It had once been a bakery called *Perfect Pastries*, but looked to have closed down some considerable time ago.

Whatever hell their Ribbon Killer was trying to create, it had now become very personal indeed. Rachel knew she couldn't process what she was thinking and feeling, and so she didn't try. They'd been up all night, they'd eaten barely a thing, and she knew the only way she could continue was if she shut down everything except the protocol of the investigation itself. She had a job to do. That was all she had to do. The explanations – the whys and hows, the rationale behind what was being done to her – would all come later. It was intentional; it was purposeful; this has been premeditated and planned to terrorize her, to shake the foundations of everything she was. And it had worked. She felt invaded, every aspect of her life for the past five years laid bare for all the world to see. It was as if someone out there knew more about her than she knew of herself.

And here she was. She'd pulled the finest of threads, and everything had begun to unravel. This was what he wanted. This was a trail of breadcrumbs that she'd been meant to follow, and follow it she had. Dante had called her conscientious and diligent. He knew she'd get there, that she'd latch onto something that connected the crime scenes and trace it back. He'd chosen silk, he'd chosen the color, he'd made a theater of everything to lead her in the right direction.

'We need to find out which driver delivered the order,' Quinn said.

'Did you get the name of the delivery company from Hyun's brother?'

'Express Transit,' Quinn said. 'They have a depot near LaGuardia.'

'So let's go.'

'You need to rest, Rachel, seriously.'

Rachel turned and looked at Quinn. 'Like I'm going to lie down and go to sleep right now, Maurice.'

'We'll go there, okay?' Quinn said. 'But let's at least get some coffee and something to eat first.'

'Fine,' Rachel said. 'But we go right after and we find this driver today.'

Express Transit was a sizeable company that covered commercial deliveries across the entire New York metropolitan area. The LaGuardia depot was one of six out of which they ran deliveries, but it did cover east Elmhurst, Jackson Heights and everything west up to the East River, including Astoria.

The duty manager, Ralph Nevitts, had also run the night shift. He was due to leave at 9.00. It was Friday, and he was overwhelmed with time-sensitive deliveries that needed to be out before the weekend. He directed the detectives to a processing administrator called Marcia Lomax.

'It's an order that came out of a company in the Garment District called First Class Fabrics,' Rachel explained. 'The order was placed on January 15th this year, but we don't know when it was shipped. We do know the address it went to, but it's an unoccupied storefront in Astoria.'

Marcia looked at Rachel with a defeated expression.

'So,' she said, 'you want me to find a single order to an address that doesn't really exist that could have been delivered by any one of a hundred or more drivers sometime during the last however many weeks.'

'That's what we need,' Rachel said.

'You have any idea the number of orders we deliver each day?' Marcia asked. 'Thousands. Literally thousands.'

'They're not computerized?' Quinn asked.

'Don't talk to me about computers, detective,' Marcia said. 'Seems to me a computer is only as good as the information you put in it, and if you don't have the time or the people to enter that information, then they're little more than furniture.'

'So, your delivery orders are—'

'Taken over the phone, written by hand, put into a schedule. The deliveries get signed off by the driver, and he comes back here with all the dockets. They're filed by date and zipcode... they're supposed to be filed by date and zip code, and then we put them in storage.'

'Here?' Rachel asked.

Marcia glanced back over her shoulder. 'We have a warehouse full of them.'

'Do you separate them by company?' Quinn asked.

'That would mean a file for each client, and we have an endless number of one-offs. That would just be impractical. Sure, some of the bigger clients that have been using us for years have their own area in the warehouse, but most of them are too small to bother.'

'Do you know if First Class Fabrics is a regular customer?'

'Not a clue,' Marcia said. 'If they're in the Garment District, they could be one of dozens of small outlets that use us from time to time. I'm afraid that if you want to find a specific delivery note then you're gonna have to wade in there and look.'

Marcia showed them the way. It was a reprise of the night they'd just spent – a mountain of paperwork, but this time stacked on a vast acreage of shelving units.

'Over there to the right is this year,' Marcia explained. 'It's meant to be separated by month, but it isn't.'

'Thank you,' Rachel said.

Marcia made to leave, and then she paused. 'Can I ask why you're after this in particular?'

'It's a homicide case,' Quinn said. 'It's just a lead we're following. It might come to nothing, but we have to look.'

'Right,' Marcia said. 'So the sooner you find it, the better.'

'Absolutely.'

'I've got a couple of drivers downstairs. They're not going on runs until 11.00. You want me to send them up to give you a hand?'

'That'd be really appreciated,' Quinn said.

Once again, it was an unenviable task. Express dealt with everything from single item, confidential deliveries between legal companies and official city authorities to trucks filled with wallpaper, furniture and white goods. Much to Rachel's dismay, the original order forms and delivery notes were all bundled together. The entire thing was random.

The drivers – Lucas and Ron, both in their early thirties, both of them having worked for Express for more than a decade – explained that a failed delivery always came back to the depot.

'If there's no one there to sign,' Ron said, 'then it comes back on the same vehicle. We try again the next day. If that's a fail, then we notify the sender. They get twenty-four hours to sort it out, and if we don't receive instruction to deliver again, sometimes to a different address, then it goes back to where it was picked up.'

'But there has to be someone there with ID who can sign for receipt,' Rachel said.

'If it's a company, then we don't need ID. Same goes for a private residence.'

'And a storefront?' Quinn asked.

'Same as a company. If it's a legitimate business, then we just deliver to the address and that's that.'

'We can only hope that there's a name,' Rachel said. 'Either the addressee, or that whoever signed for it has a legible signature.'

The four of them went through page after page. Eleven o'clock came, and the drivers had to leave. Rachel and Quinn kept on going.

Just before noon, Marcia appeared.

'Nothing yet?' she asked.

'Not yet, no,' Rachel said, 'but we're through a good deal of this.'

'And if you don't find it?'

'Then we're going to need to speak to the drivers who cover Astoria, see if they remember.'

'Seriously?'

'It matters that much,' Rachel said.

'And I thought being a detective was all about eating donuts and chasing bad guys with guns.'

'Donuts are just for beat cops,' Quinn said. 'Once you make detective you can't have more than one a week or you'll not be able to chase anyone.'

Marcia smiled. 'I'll leave you to it, then. If you find what you're looking for, maybe the Police Chief'll let you have a donut as a reward.'

'One can only hope, Marcia. One can only hope.'

By the time Rachel found the delivery note her head was aching and she was finding it hard to focus. They'd been at it close to four hours. She sat back on her haunches, the pale blue slip of paper in her hand, and she said, 'Maurice, I got it.'

Passing it to him, he read it aloud. 'First Class Fabrics to Perfect Pastries, Steinway Street. One consignment. Fabrics. Delivered Thursday, February 7.'

'There's a name, Maurice. At the top.'

'John Fletcher.'

'We have a name, Maurice. We have a fucking name.'

'You don't actually believe that this guy would've been dumb enough to use his real name, do you?'

'Right now, I'm ready to believe anything. Give me that much, will you? It's something. It's more than we had yesterday. Yesterday we had three dead people and a bunch of ribbons. Now we have an empty storefront and someone who signed for a delivery. That means whoever it was must have been inside that building. So that's where we go look.'

'We'll need a warrant.'

'So, let's get a fucking warrant, Maurice.'

Quinn got up. He held out his hand and helped Rachel to her feet.

'I'm taking you home,' he said. 'I'll request the warrant. Even being optimistic, it's gonna take a while to go through channels. I'll need to put something together to give it some weight.'

'I'll come with you.'

'Let me do it,' Quinn said. 'And as soon as it's done, I'm gonna go home and get my head down for a few hours. I need some sleep, Rachel, and so do you.'

'Tell whoever to call us as soon as it's signed off. I want inside that place as soon as possible.'

40

Rachel had as good as collapsed. She'd intended to shower, to wash her hair, to take a little time to unwind, but instead she'd kicked off her shoes and lain down on the bed. *Just for a moment* she'd told herself. *Just let me close my eyes for a moment.*

She slept right through until daylight woke her on Saturday morning.

Before she showered and changed, she called the 114th. Quinn had not arrived. She asked for his home number. No one answered.

Unsettled, she got ready and drove to the office. Her thoughts were dominated by the death of Michael Ridgway. She'd lost a partner, a friend, and she had no intention of losing another. Of course, she knew it was irrational, but that didn't limit what she was feeling.

Quinn was there when she reached the Homicide Suite.

'Nothing on the warrant yet,' he said. 'Had there been I would've called you.'

'Did you get some sleep?'

'Out for the count,' Quinn said. 'And you look a great deal better.'

'You looked up Fletcher?'

'That's what I'm doing. So far I have ninety-six in New York state alone.'

'Ninety-six?'

'So far. There's gonna be more.'

'And then we narrow it down to the ones with records. We check those out first.'

Quinn looked at Rachel.

'You know what you're doing,' Rachel said. 'I'm sorry.'

'I gotta tell you, it's a hell of a thing we did yesterday,' Quinn said. 'I ran the warrant request through my Lieutenant. He said if you want a job here, you've got it.'

'You can tell him that's very kind of him, but I want to get this guy and then go home.'

'I wasn't sure what to make of you when you arrived, but you're a hard worker.'

'Isn't this what we're paid for?'

Quinn smiled. 'Oh, believe me, there's a whole bunch of guys here who just clock in and clock out. Irreducible minimum, know what I mean?'

'Well, I believe that you either do something or you don't do it, and if you do it, then you do it to the best of your ability.'

'And that's why you'll wind up with a gold shield, and then you'll get a Division, and then you'll be Chief of Police by the time you're forty.'

'Not a prayer,' Rachel said. 'The last couple of days I've handled enough paperwork to last me a lifetime.'

The phone rang on Quinn's desk.

'Okay,' he said. 'On the way down.'

He hung up, reached for his jacket.

'Warrant's ready,' he said. 'They're giving us a couple of uniforms, too.'

Rachel had no doubt that the building would be empty, but she was reassured by the presence of two patrol officers. She and Quinn were advised to stay back on the sidewalk while they did a full external reconnaissance. The officers returned within minutes. Access was possible through a broken door at the rear.

They hadn't yet been inside, but – from every indication – it appeared that the property was vacant.

Regardless, all four of them went in guns drawn. The man they were looking for, whatever his name was, had killed three people.

The interior was shadowed and dirty. Dust was thick on the work surfaces and ovens. Bags of flour, now rotten, lay on the floor. The smell was cloying, damp and musty. Through the rear kitchen Rachel could see into the store itself. The light from the street was sufficient to pick out the shelving and glass-fronted display units. There was ample sign of recent foot traffic, but it was scattered, smudged, and she didn't see a single clear footprint.

Quinn followed her into the front room. 'We need to get all this glass printed,' he said. He asked one of the patrol officers to call in a forensics team.

While the call was patched through, Quinn followed the second officer up the stairs to a small landing. There were three doors. Opening one, it revealed a room devoid of furniture. Empty boxes were strewn about, a filthy blanket, some old magazines and newspapers. The second gave into a larger room, still no more than ten by twelve, but on the floor was a bedroll, a towel, a couple of empty wine bottles and a pair of shoes. The third room was a toilet with a washbasin. Everywhere was a film of greasy dust, save around the faucets and the bowl of the sink itself.

Quinn went back to the top of the stairs.

'Rachel!' he called out. 'Come check this out.'

Standing beside Quinn in the room where someone had evidently slept, Rachel felt something was wrong. Had she been asked to define it, she wouldn't have been able to do so. It was a sense, a perception perhaps, but it told her that this was too easy, too simple. She put on gloves, carefully lifted one of the wine bottles by putting a pen into the neck. She rotated it slowly, looking carefully.

'Prints,' she said.

'Of our guy, or some homeless guy who lucked out.'

'I guess we'll find out soon enough.'

'If it is our guy, then he's been really fucking careless.'

'That's what bothers me,' Rachel said, 'but we're jumping to conclusions. We need all of this photographed, everything printed. We need the full works.'

One of the patrol officers came through to find them.

'There's something you should see,' he said.

Rachel followed him to the small bathroom, Quinn right behind her.

The officer indicated a small, mirrored cabinet above the sink.

'I put on gloves,' the officer said, and stepped aside.

Rachel looked into the cabinet. There on the shelf, as if left for her and her alone, was a newspaper clipping. It was Sheehan's *Tribune* piece from July of '75. Five years old, yellowed at the edges, it had been kept for this moment. Lifting it out carefully, she showed it to Quinn.

'Hunt for Killer Ends in Tragedy,' Quinn said. 'Is that what I think it is?'

'It's the piece Carl Sheehan wrote after Michael Ridgway was killed.'

'So our guy was here,' Quinn said. 'He slept in there, washed in here. He was right here.'

'Maybe,' Rachel said.

'What do you mean, maybe?'

'It's too much,' she said. 'Too neat, too clean. We identify the ribbon, we find the place it came from, we find where it was delivered, and now this? You can't seriously believe that someone so organized, so methodical, would make a mistake like this. We were meant to come, meant to find this—'

'It's called police work, Rachel. That's what it is. Can't you take some credit for your efforts?'

'It feels wrong, Maurice. It feels so very wrong, but I don't know why.'

'Put that back,' he said. 'Let's get Forensics here. Let's get all the evidence we can, see if we can't nail the prints. If those prints come back John Fletcher, then what else is there to say?'

'I don't know,' Rachel replied. 'But this was here for me, wasn't it? I mean, how else can you see it? This newspaper article was left here for me.'

'So, the guy wanted to taunt you. He figured himself smarter than you, but he wasn't, was he? You tracked him down, you found out where he was staying, didn't you? People like this are crazy, and crazy people make mistakes. Can't you accept that you did a remarkable job and—'

'There's something else going on, Maurice,' Rachel said.

Quinn looked at her. There was a certainty and a determination in her expression that exceeded anything he'd seen before.

'This is about me. This is about Michael Ridgway. This is about what happened back in Syracuse.'

'I know it is, Rachel. It's some whacko copycat—'

'No,' she said. 'There's more to it than that.'

'Okay,' Quinn said. 'You said already that we were jumping to conclusions. We need to stick with the evidence, alright? Just the evidence, and nothing else.'

Rachel returned the newspaper clipping to the cabinet.

'I need to get outside,' she said. 'I need some fucking air.'

41

Forensics didn't come back to Rachel until late on Sunday the 6th.

The prints on the wine bottle matched those on the medicine cabinet, the rim of the sink and half a dozen other places in the empty store. Quinn ran them against every John Fletcher with a criminal record in New York and came back empty-handed. He then requested that the prints be checked against every Attica inmate for the last decade. Again, there was nothing. Quinn not only widened the remit, but located the earlier tenants of the Steinway Street property so he could eliminate their prints. It was going to take days perhaps, and there was nothing they could do but wait.

By the end of Tuesday, Rachel was questioning everything. That same nagging sense of doubt about such a thin thread of evidence leading them to the perpetrator wouldn't let her be. It was the same as Syracuse – the prints on the phone booth. Sure, people made mistakes, even those who believed they had taken all precautions, but she couldn't get past the idea that she was being played.

While Quinn oversaw the ID of the prints, Rachel went back through every case file from 1975. She re-read the initial crime scene and coroner's reports, reviewed the photos, went over Robert Marshall's yellow sheet. Then she started work on background for each of the victims. There appeared to be absolutely no connection between any of them and no connection between them and Marshall. She was looking for something unknown, something that no one had previously seen, and yet with no clear idea of what that could be. She checked previous addresses, current and previous occupations, doctors, dentists, hospital visits, even birth dates and star signs. Whichever way she looked at it, Rachel came back to the conclusion that Marshall's victims had been selected at random, or based on some pattern or connection that was known only to himself.

The New York victims – Christopher Wake, Anthony Yates and Margaret Silva – were different. They were all convicted criminals, and each had died in a manner that was connected to their criminal history. There was a rationale behind what had been done to them. Why they had been selected was unknown; perhaps some earlier relationship to their killer, though – again – perhaps they had also been selected randomly. There was certainly no shortage of sex offenders, arsonists and drug dealers in New York from which to choose.

Prevalent in Rachel's thoughts was the urgency with which they had to act. Syracuse had seen five victims. In New York they already had three, and notwithstanding the possibility that there were more undiscovered, she didn't want to find herself called out to another murder scene. She was exhausted, but it went far beyond the physical. This was a slow-motion hell through which she was being been dragged by someone who was still out there, perhaps even in that moment perpetrating yet another hideous act of brutality against an unsuspecting human being. Moral judgment aside, no one deserved to die in such pain and terror.

It was a little after 10.00 that night. Rachel was alone in the office. Her head hurt, her body ached; she'd barely eaten a thing all day. She'd concluded that there really was nothing further to be accomplished that night. She would go back to the hotel, sleep as much as she could, come back to it tomorrow.

Getting up from her desk, she reached for her coat.

Quinn came in through the door, behind him a patrol officer.

'We got him,' Quinn said.

Rachel didn't speak. She looked at him, her expression somewhere between disbelief and confusion.

'The prints,' Quinn said. 'Charles Gregory Wagner. He had a yellow sheet, did five years on Rikers for stabbing someone in a bar fight.'

Still, Rachel had no words.

'We've got an address, Rachel,' Quinn said. 'Down by the river. We've got a SWAT team heading out. We're going now.'

'Are we sure of this?'

'What d'you mean, are we sure of it? We've got a positive ID on the prints. We've got a felon with a history of violence—'

'I know, I know. It's just that—'

'Just nothing, Rachel. We are going there right the fuck now and you're either coming or not.'

Rachel put on her coat. 'Go,' she said. 'I'm right behind you.'

Four cars and a SWAT vehicle carrying a ten-man team made its way from beneath the precinct and out onto Astoria Boulevard. They went without lights and sirens.

Rachel and Maurice Quinn were in the lead vehicle. Behind them was a patrol car with two officers, then came the truck, following on behind a second patrol car with a further two-man team. The patrol officers would cordon the street at both ends, then station themselves with a line-of-sight to the rear of the property.

'As far as we can see, the property to the right is empty, the one to the left a good fifty yards clear,' Quinn told Rachel.

'But no confirmation that this Wagner guy is there.'

'That's what we're going to find out.'

Rachel knew that Quinn believed they were reaching the end of the investigation. Quinn believed that the man they were looking for was nothing but some psycho copycat killer, that his arrest or death would bring all of this to a satisfactory conclusion. Rachel felt very differently, but did not voice it. She'd believed that whatever had taken place in Syracuse was the end. It hadn't been. She felt certain that it had only been the beginning – of what, she didn't know – but it was a feeling that she could not relinquish. There was some other more significant drama unfolding, and this was merely the second act. Had she been asked to explain her rationale, she would have struggled to phrase it in terms that could be understood by anyone but herself. Perhaps Carl would get it, but he would be the only one. This was not a matter of probative or circumstantial evidence, but rather a matter of trusting her own intuition. It went beyond a hunch. This was something deeper, more profound. There was a sense of being one of the *dramatis personae* in a piece of theater. She was acting a part. There was a set, a director, other actors around her. There was a script, but those on stage hadn't seen it, and thus didn't know their lines. Regardless, the acts were unfolding one by one, and she – along with everyone else – was having to improvise.

That feeling – that her cues were coming from off-stage, that someone in the shadows was prompting all of this – was beyond a feeling. It was close to certainty. She was being led along a road, destination unknown, and what was happening now was simply part of a greater story.

A little before 11.30, the SWAT team leader, Sergeant Dean Kluge, coordinated final clearance. Cordons had been established, snipers had been positioned, and between the SWAT and patrol officers they had every exit route covered.

Kluge came back to the car where Rachel and Quinn were waiting.

'No sign of anyone in the building,' he said. 'There's lights on in the back, but that doesn't mean your guy's inside. Two floors, a basement, front door, rear door. Windows on the left of the building that give onto an alleyway. We're ready to go.'

'Then go, Sergeant,' Rachel said.

Kluge radioed his men. Sixty seconds, front and rear access simultaneously.

'Alive,' Rachel said. 'That's what I want. If he's in there, I want him out alive.'

'We'll do our best, detective, but if he's armed and initiates fire—'

'I know,' Rachel replied.

At 11.41, Kluge gave the order to breach the building.

From the street, Rachel watched as men seemed to enter from all sides. Flashlights bounced back and forth within, their beams visible through windows.

The thing that struck Rachel more than anything was the silence. The street was dead. Nothing moved but the officers on scene. There was no shouting, no gunfire, no sirens. That, more than anything else, seemed to be the most disturbing aspect of the entire scenario.

Five minutes elapsed, perhaps less, and Kluge exited through the front door and walked across the street.

From his expression, Rachel knew. She heard his words before he even said them. She looked sideways at Quinn, and – to her – it appeared that Quinn also knew.

'Fuck,' he said under his breath.

'He's in there,' Kluge said. 'In the basement. You coming in, or you gonna wait for Forensics?'

'I'll call Forensics,' Quinn said.

Rachel looked at Kluge. 'Lead the way, Sergeant.'

It was Wagner.

Despite the distorted features, the swollen tongue, the discoloration of the skin, there was no doubt. Hanging from a rafter in the basement of the property, he'd been dead a good twenty-four hours. On the floor was a bedroll, much the same as the one found in the Steinway Street bakery. There were discarded food tins, bottles of water, and over against the wall a large cardboard package, through the open top of which Rachel could see the ribbon that had been ordered from First Class Fabrics.

In that moment, it seemed like the last pieces of a jigsaw had come together, but the image now represented was not what she'd imagined it would be.

She was overcomplicating things. That's what she told herself. A felon with a history of violence had somehow gained access to police or court records. He'd taken it upon himself to copycat elements from a five-year-old case. This kind of thing had happened before. She had no doubt it would happen again. In a month all of this would be forgotten. There would be some other insanity dominating the headlines. If everyone else could let it go, then so should she.

Quinn came down the basement stairs. He looked at the body, then at Rachel.

'Forensics are on the way,' he said. 'We need to get out of here, let them do their thing.'

'Yes,' Rachel said. She turned and looked at Quinn. 'I want to go home, Maurice. Patrol can stay here. I don't even want to think about an incident report until tomorrow.'

42

On Thursday, April 17th, the investigation into the Charles Wagner triple homicide was officially closed. Wagner's death was ruled a suicide.

Through the previous eight days, from the first notification of Wagner's death to the statement made by the 114th's press office, Carl Sheehan had run the story in the *Courier*. Other papers had picked up on it, but Sheehan's were the only pieces that gave a comprehensive picture of all that had happened.

For no reason other than confirmation of information, Sheehan and Rachel had spoken three times. On the third occasion, Monday the 14th, Rachel told him that she would soon be going back to Syracuse.

'You want to meet up?' he'd asked. 'Just have a drink or something, you know?'

'No, Carl. I don't think it's a good idea.'

'I'm not looking for any inside info,' he said. 'I'm done with the Wagner story. This would just be a social thing. To say goodbye before you leave.'

'Carl—'

'Okay, okay, I get it. Well, I guess that's it then. You take care, and well done, okay? I'm sure plenty of people have congratulated you, but it was a great piece of police work.'

'You take care too, Carl,' Rachel said, 'and I wish you all the best with the baby.'

*

Later that Thursday afternoon, Quinn came to see her.

'Lieutenant tells me you should be out of here tomorrow,' he said, 'but you have to get cleared by the department shrink.'

'What?'

'It's routine, Rachel. We all have to go visit her after a case like this. Homicide, kidnapping, even suicides. It's protocol.'

'Not in Syracuse.'

Quinn smiled. 'Well, we ain't in Syracuse, are we?'

'And what the hell is it supposed to accomplish?'

'Christ, I don't know. Make sure you aren't all traumatized and weirded-out, I guess. Make sure you're emotionally stable, that you don't need some leave or whatever. Just go talk to the woman. She's harmless enough. It'll be an hour, tops.'

'And if I don't want to?'

'Then you'll never leave New York. You'll be forever consigned to spending your days with lowlifes, scumbags, junkies and thieves, and that's just the guys in this precinct.'

'This is bullshit. You know that? I'm fine. I just want to go home.'

Quinn raised his hands. 'Not my request, Rachel. Take it up with the Lieutenant. Good luck with that. Seems to me it'd be a great deal easier to just go answer a couple of questions and be done with it.'

'What? I just show up and knock on the door?'

'I don't know if she's available right this second, but I can check.'

'So check,' Rachel said. 'If I've got no choice, then the sooner we get it over with, the better.'

'You want an explanation,' Dr. Claire Brandon said. 'And very often you'll never get one.'

Rachel had been put at ease by the woman. She had even begun by apologizing for taking up Rachel's time, and that she had no reason to be concerned about Rachel's welfare.

'It's what we do,' she explained. 'There are instances, especially with less experienced officers, where the aftermath of murders can have a profoundly disturbing effect. And then with the veterans, we find that a long history of seeing this kind of thing has made them inured to it. They lose empathy. They find it increasingly difficult to relate to people in their familial and personal environments.'

Rachel was asked to give an account of everything that had happened with the Wagner investigation – right from Friday, March 21st, and her arrival at the 114th to the moment she'd seen Wagner's body in the basement.

Rachel skimmed over it. Her account was as succinct as she could make it.

Dr. Brandon had listened attentively, and then told her that she'd read the investigation report already.

'So why ask me to tell you?'

'To see if there was anything else you would mention. Memory is fluid. Some things only occur to you days or weeks later.'

'I don't have anything else to tell you,' Rachel said. 'The only thing I have is questions.'

'For me?' Brandon asked.

'No, for Wagner.'

'About why he did what he did?'

'Doesn't everyone want to know?'

Brandon smiled. 'No, Detective Hoffman, not everyone does.'

'So people just let go of all of that, just move on, never give it a second thought?'

'A few, sure. Others figure out something that explains the behavior of such people to their own satisfaction. And then there are those that worry at it relentlessly.'

'And I'm one of those?'

'I don't know. I guess we'll have to wait a few months and see if it still bothers you.'

Rachel leaned back in the chair. 'Okay,' she said, 'so you tell me why people do this kind of crazy shit.'

'My opinion?'

'Sure. You're a psychologist, right? You have all the answers about motive and impulses and people who are schizophrenic and whatever.'

'I have some answers,' Brandon said, 'but I still have as many questions as you. Maybe more, to be honest.'

'So tell me some of the things you know. Maybe it'll help me figure out how to let go of this.'

'Do you feel you need to let go of it? Is it troubling you on a personal level?'

'No, not on a personal level,' Rachel said. 'It's not like that.' She paused. 'Okay, so I handled a case back in Syracuse five years ago—'

'Robert Marshall.'

'You know about that?'

'I read the newspaper reports, I asked some questions. I also spoke to Detective Quinn. He gave me the backstory on that.'

'So you know that we were treating this as a copycat.'

'Yes, I do.'

'So, here's the deal. We don't know how Wagner got hold of the information on the people he killed. He had to have known something about their individual criminal histories to have killed them in the way he did. That wasn't coincidence. That was as specific and individual as possible. And I don't know why we aren't chasing that. To me, that seems like an important thread to follow.'

'Because Wagner is dead,' Brandon said. 'With his death, the case is closed. It's as simple as that.'

'Except it's not, is it?' Rachel said.

'If the PD had the manpower, the resources, the time—'

'I'm not questioning that.'

'So what are you questioning, Detective?'

'I want to know why. I want to understand what was going on in that man's mind. I want to know why he focused on the Syracuse case, why he felt the need to copy it, to leave the same kinds of messages from the same book.'

'Then maybe you should have become a psychologist.'

'But you said yourself that you don't know. If you don't know, then who does?'

'I'm not a criminal psychologist, and I'm certainly not a pro-filer. I guess for that, you'd have to speak to Behavioral Science at Quantico.'

'So give me your educated opinion, the one that comes with the degree and the Master's and the letters after your name.'

'But then we wouldn't be talking about you.'

'Well, if we're interested in my psychological well-being, then the only way to feel better about this is to have some insight into what I was dealing with.'

'People process experiences differently,' Brandon said. 'You can have two children, brothers, even twins, raised in the same family. Let's say there's an abusive father. Each child gets treated the same. The father is violent, the mother is also abused and is therefore unable to mitigate the suffering of her children. All of them are impotent in the face of this rage and fury. You could hypothesize that each of us has a fundamental drive to survive, and in this scenario the father is perceived to be the one who is surviving best, if only from the viewpoint that he's the only one not being tormented and bullied. So, we have one child who starts to identify with the father figure. He exorcizes his pain and trauma by tormenting others. Maybe he kicks the family dog, maybe he hurts defenseless animals, maybe he bullies smaller kids at school. He's adopted the persona and behavior of the father because he sees that's how you can not only release the negative emotion, but also because he has this twisted interpretation of what being in control of your own life actually means. That make sense?'

'Yes,' Rachel said.

'And then we have the other child. Maybe he's emotionally stronger. Maybe he has more of his own innate will to survive. Maybe he's not as impressionable as his sibling. He suffers the same abuse, but he somehow manages to retain his own identity. He clearly identifies his father as a domineering, anti-social character, and he refuses to behave in the same way. He manages, somehow, to finally escape the environment. Maybe the abuse is stopped by some outside agency. Maybe the father dies. Something happens that brings about their separation. Now we have two brothers, one cast in the mold of the father, the other dedicating his life to assisting abused children.'

'Okay, so we deal with things differently. What doesn't make sense is why someone like Charles Wagner or Robert Marshall would feel the need, because it is a need, to torture and kill people, to put them to sleep with fucking chloroform of all things, and how that relates to ... to what? A solution to a problem? An imaginary problem?'

'That's the dividing line right there,' Brandon said. 'That's the marker between sanity and insanity. I know you have the legal definition. The ability to differentiate between right and wrong. But whose right? Whose wrong? Mine? Yours? Some judge in some court case decades ago who had to determine whether or not someone could be held legally responsible for their actions?'

'So, it really is that simple? Or that complex, depending on which way you look at it?'

'Sometimes it's simple, other times complex, Detective Hoffman. Seems to me that the only time the police are ever truly interested in the motive for someone's actions is when it will contribute to the identification of a perpetrator. Motive, method, opportunity, right? Those are the questions you ask at the outset of a case.'

'There's no manual for this, is there? There's no "Psychos Handbook" I can read that will make any of this more comprehensible.'

'You need to accept the fact that a small minority of people are truly sociopathic. They don't think the same way as us. They certainly don't process emotions as we do. They lack empathy. They lie without compunction. They think nothing of hurting and harming others to serve some unknown end. They can be seemingly ordinary individuals. They can be smart or stupid. They can do menial jobs. They can be utterly inconspicuous. Other times, they rise to positions of great power and destroy societies and nations. History is littered with them. Are we really any closer to a useful understanding of the causes of such behavior? Probably not, no. We see the consequences, sure, and then we try and figure out why.'

Rachel had no more questions. In essence, she'd been told the same thing back in Syracuse by Conrad, the resident psychologist at St. Francis University Hospital.

'So, I'm good,' Rachel said. 'I'm ready to get back to work.'

'There's nothing else you want to talk about?'

She shook her head.

'Well, if you run into difficulty, make sure you tell someone. In an ideal world, you'll get better and better at separating out your personal and work lives.'

Rachel smiled.

'What?'

'The personal life,' Rachel said. 'That's something I need to figure out at some point.'

'I know what happened on this investigation, Detective Hoffman. I can see how single-minded and hard-working you were. You are a credit to the Department. I can only imagine how many more people might have died if you hadn't conducted this inquiry so effectively. Maybe the sense of accomplishment that comes with that knowledge will have to be enough for you.'

'I guess we'll see, eh?'

'I guess we will.'

43

Rachel flew into Syracuse on Saturday morning.

Prior to leaving, she'd gone out to dinner with Maurice Quinn. They didn't talk about the case, they just had dinner. When they parted company, he told her that it had been a pleasure to work with her. She expressed the same sentiment. He told her to stay in touch, and that if she ever found herself back in New York, she should give him a call. As the cab pulled away, she'd glanced back and raised her hand in farewell. The possibility that she would again experience the loss of a partner had occurred to her several times during the Wagner case. She believed that such an outcome would have been too much for her to bear. She also knew that the likelihood of herself and Quinn ever crossing paths again was nigh impossible. Why, she didn't know, but she believed she'd neither see him nor hear from him ever again.

On Monday morning, Max Kolymsky told her she'd been cited for a commendation. He also told her that if she wanted to take some leave – a few days away, get out of the city, maybe spend some time with her family – then she should do that.

Rachel told him she was fine, that she was keen to get back to work.

In one of his rare and compassionate moments he told her not to neglect herself, that she was a valued member of the team, that everyone needed a breather from the madness.

'I appreciate your concern, but it's okay. I'm good, Lieutenant, really.'

It took less than a month for Rachel to realize that she wasn't good. Not at all. She was haunted. That was the only word she could find to describe how she felt.

She wanted answers, and answers of a great deal more substance and weight than those she possessed.

She thought about asking for a transfer, perhaps somewhere quiet like Ulysses. She considered a request to stay out of homicide investigations. She thought of many things, but none of them were right.

It took a little longer – a couple of weeks, perhaps three – but she finally realized what she'd been trying to avoid. The way out of this was neither avoidance nor escape. There was no avoidance, and there would be no escape until she had answers for every question that remained. She knew then that there was perhaps only one place in the world she would have a hope of finding those answers.

In the first week of June, seated at her desk, she lifted the phone and asked for an external line.

Reaching the Federal Law Enforcement Training and Research Center in Quantico, she asked for Senior Special Agent, Scott O'Brien.

She waited patiently, watching her fellow detectives at their desks, wanting to ensure that her conversation was not overheard.

'Agent O'Brien speaking.'

'Agent O'Brien. This is Detective Rachel Hoffman. I don't know if you remember me—'

'Yes of course, Detective Hoffman. What can I do for you?'

'Back in March, just before I left Quantico, you asked me a question.'

'I did, yes.'

Rachel was silent for a moment.

'You have been thinking about it, haven't you?' O'Brien asked.

'I have, yes,' Rachel replied. 'And I wanted to see if we could meet.'

III

1985

Purgatorio

44

Thunderous heartbeat. Blood hammered through her veins and temples; breath came fast and shallow; a deep well of fear erupted from the base of her gut like something feral and hungry. Crouching then, down on her haunches, her back against the wall, her gun raised, the constricting weight of the bulletproof jacket an encumbrance. *If he comes out now*, she thought, *there's no way I'm going to get out of the line of fire.*

Rachel glanced back towards the top of the stairs. Ben Landis motioned for her to get to the other side of the door.

She shook her head. She indicated that she would cover him as he moved along the corridor. Landis nodded in agreement. He hunkered low, almost on his belly, and he moved along the dirty linoleum floor towards her. As he passed, he glanced up at her. They had the same look in their eyes – heightened senses, tension, fear, everything that accompanied a moment like this.

From inside the apartment, there was nothing. Not a sound. Maybe the woman was already dead. Maybe he'd choked her or broken her neck or cut her throat. Maybe he'd dragged her to the window and thrown her to the sidewalk below.

They needed more people; they needed back-up, a tactical team, a breach unit, a cordon at each end of the street. But they didn't have them, at least not yet. The call for reinforcements had gone out only minutes before. They'd be on their way, but how long that would take she didn't know. Five minutes? Ten, twenty? They didn't have that much time. They had to get into the apartment and get the woman out before she was killed.

Then again, maybe he had no intention of killing her. Maybe in whatever disjointed alternate reality he lived in, she was his ticket out. He couldn't possibly believe that, but then he'd taken her from the bank, dragging her kicking and screaming out of the front door, money spilling from the bag he carried, the gun in his hand, passers-by fleeing amidst screams and shouts of panic. And how much had he taken before the alarm went off, before the cops were dispatched to the scene? Ten thousand, twenty, fifty? However much it was, it wasn't worth a life.

Rachel and Ben Landis were now on either side of the door.

The pressure was palpable, claustrophobic, more than she could ever have imagined. In the past four years, after all the training, mock scenarios, tactical exercises and range practice, there was nothing – absolutely nothing – that could have prepared her for the psychological tension that a real-life situation occasioned.

'FBI!' Landis shouted. 'Back up away from the door. Lower your gun!'

Silence. Deafening silence.

Rachel reached to her right, and with the side of her clenched fist she hammered against the door.

'FBI!' she shouted.

There was a moment's hesitation, and then 'Fuck you!'

'Lower your gun!' Rachel said. 'Back away from the door! Get on the ground, face-down!'

'You go fuck yourselves!'

'You have ten seconds!'

'You come through that door, she's fucking dead! You hear me? She's fucking dead, okay?'

The woman screamed. It was sudden, piercing, a desperate cry for help. There was a thud. The woman screamed again.

Rachel motioned to her left. One of them needed to get outside, to coordinate back-up. This was now a hostage situation, and there was no way they were going to handle it alone. The risk was far too great.

Landis started back along the hallway, past her, down to the top of the stairs, and then he descended slowly, silently. Reaching the bend in the well, he glanced back at her.

'Go!' she mouthed, and urged him away.

Landis disappeared out of sight.

Rachel closed her eyes and breathed as best she could. She tried to quell her heart, her pulse, the feeling that everything inside her was unravelling faster than she could hold it together.

This was new. This was different. This was something she had never before experienced.

Somewhere in the distance she heard sirens. Back-up. Thank fucking Christ.

Easing down against the wall, Rachel lowered her gun a fraction. She realized her hand was covered in sweat. She wiped it dry on the leg of her pants. Gripping it once again, she shifted her weight from one leg to the other. Her calf was cramping fiercely. The feeling in the base of her stomach was as if everything was twisted together. A Gordian knot of nerves and sinews.

The sirens crescendoed. Within minutes the street would be cleared, snipers would be on rooftops and looking out of windows in the facing block, a cordon would go up, and a tactical unit would come up to relieve her. Before she knew it, she'd be back down in the street with Landis and all of this would be behind her. Then the adrenalin rush would stop, the feeling that she was on a knife-edge where the slightest wrong move could wind up in a homicide, or – worst-case scenario – her own death, would be replaced with a sense of disconnected professionalism, albeit forced, and she would perhaps be able to review what had happened with a detached eye.

She had been here before, but never alone. There had been raids, breaches, arrests, even times when she'd levelled her gun at a man and brought them to surrender, but this was the closest she had ever been to an actual one-on-one confrontation with an armed assailant. She needed the woman out of there, the perp in cuffs, and she needed to breathe.

There were voices now, filtering through from the street. They were faint, but they carried the urgency of official action.

There was movement to her left. She looked back, her gun aimed unerringly at the top of the stairwell. Landis's hand appeared over the top riser. Rachel exhaled. She hadn't been aware that she'd been holding her breath.

Landis emerged slowly. He gave her a thumbs-up. He motioned for her to come back towards him, that others would now take control of the hallway outside the apartment.

Rachel started to move, and that's when she heard it. It was instinctive, a sense rather than a clearly audible sound. There was movement inside the apartment. She raised her hand. Landis stopped. The silence was breathless.

Another sound, clearer, much closer to the door. Tension ramped up. Her nerves were taut. Her heart started hammering in her chest once more, loud enough to fill her ears with the pressure.

Surely not. There was no way this guy was going to try and get out into the hallway. He couldn't be that dumb, or could he?

Rachel slid back a foot or two. She went down on one knee and raised her gun.

The weight of the weapon seemed greater than ever before. Deadweight. Her index finger flat against the breech, her eyes wide, holding her breath once more.

Another sound, a whimper, a cry, the sound of someone gasping for air.

Was she hearing it, or was it imagination?

Another movement caught her eye. A shadow at the foot of the door. It was there, and then it was gone.

Rachel looked back at Landis.

Inside, she motioned. *Movement behind the door.*

Landis nodded. He crawled forward and crouched at the end

of the hall, gun raised, immobile, his eyes fixed unerringly on the doorway.

Sounds again, more of them, and then the unmistakable *click* of the latch being freed from the striker plate. The handle was turning. Someone was coming out. Someone was definitely coming out of the door.

Rachel steadied herself. She did not doubt for a second that the hostage would emerge first. If she was in such a scenario, that's what she would do. She had to put herself right into the middle of this situation and ask herself how she would think. There was no other way. Put the hostage in the line of fire, use them as a shield, a means by which uncertainty could be introduced. Cause a moment's doubt, a moment's hesitation, and the perp would have time to fire first. But would he resort to killing law enforcement in order to escape? Couldn't he understand that there was no way in the world he would ever get out of that building? But in such a moment actions were not driven by reason, but by desperation. Evasion and escape, by any means, would be at the forefront of his mind. He needed to get out. That would be the only thing he would be thinking. Holed up in an apartment on the fifth floor of a building that was surrounded on every side, he was a rat in a trap. There was no option but to run.

The light at the base of the door increased fractionally. It was being opened, no question now, and Rachel had no way of knowing if he would come out slowly, inching forward, the woman ahead of him, or if he would push her into the hallway and then rush them. She had to be prepared for either, but how could anyone ever be prepared for such a thing? You learned to drive, but when it came to a highway pile-up everything you knew about controlling a vehicle was as good as useless.

Rachel prayed then. To whom, to what, she didn't know. Didn't even try to understand what she was experiencing. She would have a second, less than a second, and she would have to act. If she got it wrong then the hostage, Landis, and herself would be wounded or dead. If it was the hostage, then all hell would break loose. Maybe her career would be over. Maybe she would be sidelined into a nowhere office to keep her head down and shuffle papers. Maybe she would be wounded, invalided from the Bureau, unable to pursue any kind of career in law enforcement.

All these things occurred to her in less time than it took for the door to open. And it did open – slowly, silently – and then she saw a foot, a woman's shoe, and she knew that right behind her was an armed and potentially dangerous individual who would stop at nothing to make his escape.

The speed with which Rachel moved was reflexive, without consideration, instinctive. Rolling forwards and sideways simultaneously, she reached out and grabbed the woman's leg, pulling her down with every ounce of strength she possessed. The woman screamed, caught by surprise, and before she had time to react in defense, she was on the floor. Rachel was in the doorway, down on her knees, the gun ahead of her, and for a split-second she saw nothing.

A sound from another room.

Landis was behind her then, pulling the woman back along the hallway to safety, telling her to lay flat, to stay absolutely still. Landis followed Rachel into the apartment.

Rachel was ahead of him. She indicated to the left and through a doorway.

Landis nodded.

The sound of a window opening. The perp was aiming to get out and onto the fire escape.

Rachel rushed the door, came through it at speed, caught sight of the perp – one foot on the kitchen counter, another, out through the window, his left hand holding the lower frame, in his right hand a gun.

He looked back at her.

'FBI!' she hollered. 'Stay right where you are! Lower the gun! Lower the fucking gun right now!'

She saw fear, doubt, a split second of uncertainty.

He did not lower the gun.

'Now!' Rachel screamed.

The gun moved, and it moved the wrong way.

Rachel dropped to her knees and turned sideways just as she'd been trained. Reduce yourself. Limit the size of the target.

She saw it then – in his eyes, his body language, a sort of faint darkness that seemed to pass over his features, like the shadow of a cloud across a field – and then he raised the weapon.

Within the confines of the room, the sound of gunfire was extraordinary. There was nothing but the sound. It was like some vast hammer against an anvil, a roar, a thunderous barrage of force and noise, and when she pulled the trigger the second time the recoil was sufficient to snap the gun upward and send shockwaves through her forearm, her elbow, right into her shoulder.

The first bullet hit the perp in the right side of the torso, the second in the gut. He didn't make a sound. He dropped like a stone. He landed awkwardly, his one foot still up against the counter, his left arm twisted beneath him. The impact of his head against the floor knocked him out cold. He still held the gun. Held it like a lifeline.

Rachel kicked the gun away and knelt to find a pulse. There was one, but weak.

She looked back at Landis.

'Get the woman out,' she said, 'and get the medics up here.'

Landis went. She heard him running out of the apartment, the words he spoke to the distraught woman in the hallway, the sound of her voice, the sobbing, and then feet on the stairs. It seemed like the whole world was coming to find her, and she heard all of it like faint echoes of reality beneath the incessant ringing in her ears.

Her hand still on the man's neck, she felt the pulse stutter and weaken.

'No,' she whispered. 'No.'

Even as the medical crew came into the apartment behind her, she felt it go.

Withdrawing her hand, she sat back on her heels. She holstered her gun.

'I think he's—' she started to say, but then someone was helping her to her feet. She was escorted out of the room and into the hallway.

From within the apartment, she could hear the futile efforts that were being made to revive the gunman. She heard the labored breathing of someone doing CPR; the hum of a defibrillator, the command to *Clear!*, and the thump of charge as it rushed through the body. Again a second time, a third. And then someone said, 'Call it,' and Rachel knew.

She looked up. Landis stood ahead of her.

'Let's get you out of here,' he said.

Rachel was unable to move.

Landis put his hand around her shoulder. He guided her back along the hallway and down the stairs. At the head of the well she looked back, made an attempt to return to the apartment.

'It's done,' Landis said.

Rachel looked back at him. Her expression was as empty as her mind.

'The woman's okay,' Landis said. 'She's outside and she's being taken care of.'

'I killed him,' Rachel said.

'Better that than him killing you. Or killing an innocent woman.'

'Yes,' she muttered. 'Yes, of course.'

'We're leaving now,' Landis said. 'There's nothing left to do here.'

Rachel let Landis escort her down the stairs and out into the street. There were people everywhere. It seemed the entire street was nothing but uniforms and official vehicles. There were lights, barriers, tapes, police units, others from the Bureau office, and it all blurred together into a vague kaleidoscope of colors and noise.

Still the ringing in her ears was the only clearly definable sound.

She wondered if she would hear it for the rest of her life.

45

'When did you graduate?'

'June of '81,' Rachel said. She leaned back in the chair. It was the morning of Monday, August 19, and she'd had the first halfway sufficient night's sleep since the shooting. Now she was having to go through it with the Bureau psychologist – a stern-looking woman called Frances Burroughs. Rachel had been told it was standard protocol after every agent-involved shooting, even if the shooting had not been fatal.

'And before that you were in the police department in Syracuse?'

'I was, yes.'

'For how long?'

'Doesn't it say in my file?'

Dr. Burroughs smiled. It was the first time she'd given any indication of a genuine human emotion.

'It is, Rachel, but we need to talk and I always feel it's better to get to know a little more about you in your own words.'

'I joined the PD when I was twenty-one. I was there for a little over six years.'

'All of that time in Syracuse?'

'Yes. I mean, I was assigned to different counties, but I was always Syracuse PD.'

'And did you always want to be in law enforcement?'

Rachel smiled. 'I wanted to be a ballet dancer.'

Burroughs' expression communicated that she didn't know whether Rachel was joking or not.

'And why did you leave the police?'

'To do more,' Rachel replied. 'To understand more.'

'About what?'

'Why people did the things they did. What drives a person to kill. Where that kind of motivation comes from.'

'And you thought you would find the answers here?'

'Behavioral Science appealed to me. However, I have a way to go before I get there. There's some things I missed in school that need to be fixed.'

'And what about your family?'

Rachel frowned. 'What about my family?'

'What do they think of your vocation?'

'I don't think they have any opinion at all,' Rachel replied. 'I don't really have anything to do with them. My father's ... well, let's just say he doesn't really think about the world in the same way as most people.'

'Meaning?'

'He's running from something. What, I don't know. There's always something better on the horizon. He's irresponsible, unreliable, doesn't pay his bills, doesn't keep his promises, but if you confront him with those things he looks at you like you're crazy. I gave up trying to understand his rationale a long time ago.'

'And your mother?'

'She accepts him, tolerates him, suffers him. She drinks.'

'When did you last see them?'

Rachel paused. She had to think. 'A year? Maybe longer. I can't really remember.'

'And you have siblings?'

'No.'

'They didn't want any more children, or they couldn't have more?'

'I don't think they wanted me.'

Burroughs moved in her chair. She leaned back and looked at Rachel for a few seconds.

'What makes you think that?'

Rachel turned towards the window. She could see a clear, cloudless sky. She tried to focus. It was difficult. She kept going back to that moment in the kitchen, the certainty she'd possessed that the man in front of her was not going to do what she asked. She'd known she would have to shoot him. What she hadn't known was whether he was going to shoot her first. It unhinged things. It frightened her more in hindsight than it had in the moment. Then, there had been no time to think. After the fact, there was little else she could consider. Her own death. Her own mortality. The end of everything.

'I don't know,' Rachel said. 'Maybe because I felt like a piece of luggage that had to be dragged along in whatever new adventure my father had planned. I say "planned", but I don't think he ever really planned anything in his life.'

'Were you happy to come to Pennsylvania? To leave New York?'

'I didn't have a choice,' Rachel said. 'It's protocol that we're assigned to a different part of the country from where we enrolled.'

'Okay, but that doesn't answer the question, Rachel.'

'Was I happy to leave New York? I guess so. I lost a partner. I didn't really have a social life. A relationship ended. There were a number of things that made me feel like it was a good idea to go somewhere else and make a fresh start.'

'And do you have those things now? A social life? A relationship?'

'I have a relationship,' Rachel said. 'Though how much longer it's going to last, I don't know.'

'What's his name?'

'His name is Alex.'

'And how long have you been in a relationship?'

'A year and a half.'

'What does he do?'

'He works for the city. He's a civil engineer.'

'Do you live together?'

'No, we don't.'

'Why not?'

Rachel was irritated. She was uncomfortable. She wanted to get out of the office, out of this pointless conversation.

'You want to leave?' Burroughs asked.

'I just don't really see the point of asking me about my personal life. I'm sorry, but what has this got to do with anything? I shot a man. I killed him. It happens. It comes with the job. Whether or not I live with my boyfriend is—'

'Why do you think that your relationship with Alex won't last?' Burroughs interjected.

'Because he wants to get serious. He wants to settle down. He wants us to live together, start a family. All the stuff that normal people want.'

'And you don't want those things?'

Rachel shook her head. 'No, I don't. Does that make me abnormal?'

'Do you think it makes you abnormal?'

Rachel laughed reflexively. 'I have a pet hate,' she said.

'What's that?'

'People who answer questions with a question.'

'I'm sorry,' Burroughs said. 'It comes with the job.'

'I don't think there's such a thing as "normal",' Rachel said. 'I think all of us are crazy in our own particular ways. I don't believe that anyone really understands the human mind or motivation or why people do the things they do. I think a lot of psychology is based on personal opinions, and those opinions can't help but be influenced by the person's own irrationalities. Freud was nuts, right? Goethe, Kant, the lot of them. All a

241

special type of crazy. If there really was a scientific structure and methodology to an understanding of the human condition, then they would agree with one another. But they don't. That tells me that a huge amount of it is not only opinions, but opinions that can then be interpreted a million different ways by a million different people.'

'I can't argue with that,' Burroughs said.

'Then what are we doing here? Filling out forms? Ticking boxes? Going through the motions?'

'How do you feel about having ended someone's life, Rachel?'

'How do I feel about it? I don't know that I really feel anything. The individual I killed was armed, attempting to flee the scene of a kidnapping, had already robbed a bank, and was planning on shooting his way out of a police and federal cordon.'

'And so it was necessary.'

'Inevitable.'

'Except if you had wounded him.'

'I fired in self-defense, Dr. Burroughs. The first hit, in my split-second judgment, did not sufficiently incapacitate him to ensure he would not shoot back, or that he wouldn't continue to try and make his escape.'

'Do you wish that he hadn't died?'

'What would be the point of thinking that?'

'I am just trying to ascertain whether there's some residual of guilt attached to the shooting of this man.'

'No, I don't feel guilty. I can see that it might have been better if he'd given himself up, but he didn't, did he?'

'So, in your estimation, you did the very best job you could do in what must have been an extraordinarily difficult and stressful situation.'

'Yes.'

'Good,' Burroughs said.

'Is that it?'

'Unless there's anything else you want to discuss.'

'No.'

Burroughs smiled. 'That was a little too quick.'

'Meaning?'

'Just take a moment, Rachel. Think about your personal life, your career, your service here, the loss of your partner back in Syracuse, your family situation. Just step back and look at everything as objectively as you can and ask yourself if there's anything else you'd like to talk about, any advice you could use, anything at all that feels like a burden, mental, emotional or psychological. You've been here four years and you and I are meeting for the first time.'

'It's the first time I've killed someone.'

'You don't have to kill someone to come and talk to me, you know?'

Just to placate Burroughs, Rachel was silent for a time. What she actually thought about was the last conversation she'd had with Alex. They had both skirted around the edges of an ultimatum. It was never stated, but it was there. There was no denying it. He wanted what he wanted, and Rachel would never be able to give it to him. It wasn't complicated, and she really didn't need to discuss it with someone else. Rachel and Alex each had their own minds, their own purposes, directions, hopes for the future. If they were incompatible, so be it. Things started; they ended, too. That was just life.

'I'm good,' Rachel said.

'Okay, then,' Burroughs replied. 'I'm signing you off.'

Rachel got up and walked to the door. Pausing for a moment, she turned back.

'Don't think that I don't appreciate your time, Dr. Burroughs,' she said, 'but I'm not fragile. I've seen more than enough craziness to last me a lifetime, and I still get out of bed and come to work. This is what I do. I think it's what I'll always do. I think it matters. If I didn't, I'd do something else.'

'I know you would, Rachel,' Burroughs said. 'You need me, you know where I am.'

Rachel left the office, closing the door quietly behind her.

46

Back at her desk in the Allentown FBI Office on Wednesday morning, Rachel completed the reports on the shooting.

The perp – Damien Hunter – had been under surveillance as part of the office's action against organized crime within the city. Believed to be part of a much wider conspiracy, a number of armed robberies had taken place in the previous six months, the proceeds of which were more than likely intended to fund a greater enterprise. What that was – drugs, real estate, construction, arms – was unknown, but the players in this particular theater were all known to the Bureau.

Though the PD was aware of the surveillance program, they had not been directly involved. The fact that Rachel and Ben Landis had been monitoring Hunter's whereabouts and activities at the time of the robbery was the sole reason for their pursuit. Had they not been, it would have been a police matter, but they'd seen what was unfolding before the bank's alarm was even activated. Had Hunter not taken a hostage, things might have been different. Perhaps they would have let the PD deal with it as per protocol, but in the moment – an innocent woman's life endangered, a potential escalation of shooting and public mayhem – there was no doubt in Rachel's mind that she'd done the right thing.

Her supervisor – Senior Special Agent Joy Willis – had said as much.

'Do the report,' Willis told her. 'I've got your back.'

*

Since meeting with Burroughs, Rachel had thought more about her relationship with Alex. He was a good man, no question, but his view of life was diametrically opposite to Rachel's. He was an optimist, seemingly able to see the positive side of pretty much everything. The state of the world had deteriorated even further since her departure from Syracuse. Reagan had declared that Iran, Libya, North Korea and Cuba were a 'confederacy of terrorist states'. That had done wonders for international relations. AIDS was on the rise; the war between the Contras and the Sandinistas in Nicaragua had seen the US involved in yet another foreign conflict; James Huberty – after telling his wife he was going 'hunting for humans' – had killed twenty and wounded sixteen in a mass shooting in California. There were forty dead as a result of the suicide bombing in Beirut's US Embassy. Over four hundred American soldiers were taken hostage in Iran. There were assassination attempts on both Reagan and Pope Paul II, Sadat was assassinated in Egypt, and then – back in December of 1980 – a lunatic called Mark David Chapman decided that the world would be a better place without John Lennon.

When Rachel talked about these things, Alex was seemingly unmoved. He saw no reason to concern himself with things about which he could do nothing. Rachel, on the other hand, thought that the prevalent human attitude of *It has nothing to do with me* was the root cause of most of society's ills.

'So you're telling me I'm irresponsible,' Alex had said.

'I'm not saying that you're irresponsible about the things that matter to you, no,' Rachel had replied. 'But when it comes to things outside your apparent zone of influence, then yes, you are.'

'My *apparent* zone of influence? So you're taking charge of everything and I'm living in a delusional world of fantasy and make-believe—'

'Don't do that, Alex.'

'Do what?'

'You know what you're doing.'

'I don't know that I do, Rachel. Why don't you enlighten me?'

'I don't have time for this.'

As was always the case, they would later apologize to one another. Then they would fuck and fall asleep, and in the morning it would be as if nothing had happened. Theirs was not a toxic relationship, but rather a relationship of convenience. Each was aware of an absence of human connection, and for the hours they were together the intensity of that absence was diminished.

One night, perhaps six months earlier, Alex had asked about Carl.

'You've mentioned him a few times,' he said. 'He was important, right?'

'He was, yes,' Rachel replied.

'Am I anything like him?'

'No, not at all.'

'So I'm not a substitute?'

'Hell, no one could be a substitute for Carl.'

'What does that mean?'

'It doesn't mean anything, Alex. We had a relationship. It was ... I don't know, kind of intense. We broke up, we went our separate ways, and as far as I know he's still in New York. He's a father, probably a husband by now.'

'Did you ever consider marrying him?'

'Why are we talking about this?'

'Because I'm interested in what I have to do to get some kind of feedback on where we're going.'

'Why do we have to be going somewhere?'

'Because I think a relationship is either something we're building together for the future, or it's not.'

'And what if we want different futures?' Rachel asked.

Alex paused, just looking at her, and then said, 'You know what? I'm going to go.'

'I thought we were having a conversation.'

'But it's not really a conversation is it, Rachel? It's your viewpoint versus my viewpoint. We go round in circles with no result, and then we sleep together and forget about it until it rears its ugly head once again.'

'Do you want to break up?'

'I'm just going to go,' he said. 'I've got an early start.'

They hadn't spoken for a week. It had happened before – an unspoken challenge to see who would fold first. That time it had been Rachel. She called him late one evening and asked him to come over.

'Are we just going to fuck?'

'We can drink first if you like. Or we can drink afterwards.'

Alex said nothing.

'So are you coming over or what?'

'Yeah, I'm coming over.'

'Get some tortilla chips and a bottle of vodka,' she said. 'And don't buy that cheap shit you usually buy, okay?'

Alex had hit a nerve when he'd asked about Carl.

Rachel could not avoid the feeling that he'd been part of her life for too short a time. She couldn't afford the luxury of fantasizing about what might have happened had they stayed together. What she'd said to Alex was true – as far as she was aware, Carl was still in New York. During that brief coffee shop meeting back in early 1980 he'd told her about the ICU nurse, then a couple of months pregnant. The child would now be almost five years old. Perhaps he'd gotten married; perhaps he'd had another child. She didn't know. A couple of years earlier – a little frayed at the edges, a little worse for wear – she'd made a half-hearted attempt to track him down. Why, she didn't know. To find out if he'd really settled into a regular life? She'd concluded that making contact would do nothing but cause trouble. What if he'd clung to some faint hope about their being together again? What if her intrusion into his life after five years of silence would bring to the fore fissures in his present relationship?

Rachel was thirty-two years old. She'd been a federal agent for four years. She was dedicated, hard-working, motivated, and yet here she was – mooning like some love-stricken teenager about a guy that she hadn't spoken to in half a decade. She gave up trying to find him. He had his life, and it was no business of hers.

That evening of Wednesday 21st, she was grateful to be alone. Much of the time, she was comfortable with her own company. Her work was her life, and she believed that she was on the right road. She wanted to be in Virginia. She wanted Behavioral Science. She wanted to know what she could've done to have prevented the deaths of so many innocent people, first and foremost among them Michael Ridgway. She still thought of him. Not so often these days, but he was there, haunting the back of her mind, if only to remind her of the unpredictability and fragility of life. Michael's death had not been inevitable. That much she knew. Perhaps the most important lesson from her years in law enforcement was how much she didn't under-stand about the true nature of evil – sometimes a scream of human madness that engulfed thousands, even millions, other times quiet and subtle, inveigling its way into individual lives, wreaking havoc, obliterating futures that could have been so bright and bold.

Michael Ridgway had been seven years her senior. She was now older than he'd been when he died. Thirty years was nothing – a blink, a heartbeat – and his life had been snatched away. She'd tried so hard not to imagine what must've happened in those final moments. Did he know he was going to die, or was he so drugged that he was unaware of his life coming to an end? Did he fight, or did he just fade away into nothing, utterly incapable of resisting what was being done to him?

Rachel remembered every name, every face, every crime scene, every detail, and there were so many things that made no sense. The victims of both Marshall and Wagner were now nothing more than yellowing pages and fading photographs in files that would perhaps never again be opened. That feeling – that the investigations had been too neat, too clean – would not leave her thoughts. That each killer had taken their own lives before she'd had a chance to interrogate and understand motive and rationale was an unfinished chapter. Perhaps, if she was completely honest with herself, her departure from the PD had been prompted as much by a need to escape her own responsibility for what had happened.

People so very easily accused others of things of which they themselves were guilty. The lines she used on Alex – *You don't seem to be able to think beyond yourself; you seem to be utterly incapable of taking into consideration that my needs are as important as yours* – were an admission of her own faults. They'd been driven together by the need to punctuate the silence of their lives, to interrupt the constant internal monologue that detailed their own failings. If the strength of a human being was in their ability to deal with everything alone, then perhaps she was not as strong as she believed herself to be. But, then again, perhaps there was a seed of greater truth in the fact that people weren't meant to be alone. Maybe she would go back and see Dr. Burroughs. Maybe she would open up her life to another and see what revelations or changes in perspective could be identified and encouraged.

But not now. Not today. Not tomorrow. Her career had to take priority, and if that meant letting go of Alex, then so be it.

Rachel had once heard that there was a small death in every goodbye. She'd seen enough death in her life not to be overly troubled by one more.

47

News of the death of her father reached Rachel Hoffman on Monday, September 16th.

That it had taken two days for her mother, Muriel, to reach her, and then to discover that they had still been living in Philadelphia just two and a half hours from where she'd been stationed for the previous four years, highlighted how utterly disconnected Rachel had become from her parents.

Edward Hoffman, just sixty-five years old, had suffered a massive coronary in the late afternoon of Saturday the 14th. From what Rachel could understand from the phone call – her mother slurring her words, breaking down, sobbing, then trying to gather herself – it was not the first heart attack he'd suffered. His health had been in decline for some time, and he'd not wanted Rachel to know.

'He cared for you more than you'll ever know,' Muriel said. 'And ... and you just vanished from his life, Rachel. You just vanished and ... and I don't know how to feel about that. I can't help but think that he'd still be alive if you'd been there for him.'

The words washed over Rachel. She refused to give them any credence.

'When is the funeral?'

'Are you going to come?' Muriel asked.

'Are you seriously asking me that?'

'Well, considering how little importance—'

'When and where is the funeral, Mother?'

'I don't know, Rachel. I am barely holding myself together right now, let alone dealing with everything that needs attention. Perhaps you could find the time to come and help me.'

'Of course I'll come. Give me your address.'

Muriel did so.

'I'll try and get there tomorrow,' Rachel said. 'If not, it'll be Wednesday.'

'Oh, don't put yourself to any trouble, Rachel—'

'I'm hanging up now, Mother. I'm sure you could do with another drink.'

Rachel sat back in her chair. She looked at the work on her desk, then up at the ceiling, and then out through the window.

Her father was dead. Left to her own devices, her mother would no doubt drink herself into oblivion in no time at all. Rachel gave her a year, perhaps less. And that would be the end of it – her past, her roots, the history behind her quietly fading into obscurity. She didn't know what to feel. She should have felt grief, loss, sadness, something, surely? All she was aware of was a faint sense of remorse that she hadn't made any effort to reconnect with him. He was crazy, sure, but was he really any crazier than anyone else? He believed in things, despite all evidence that they were unworthy of belief. In his eagerness to seize as much life as possible, he'd seen it slip through his hands and come to nothing. Ultimately, what had been the worth of his existence? An alcoholic wife, an estranged daughter, insurmountable debts, a catalog of failed ventures and projects behind him. That was the thing that warranted sadness – that sixty-five years would be forgotten in a week, and that there really was nothing to show for his endeavors.

Rachel met with Joy Willis that same afternoon. She was granted a week's compassionate leave.

'Do you want to talk to anyone?' Willis asked. 'Dr. Burroughs, perhaps?'

'No,' Rachel replied. 'My father and I weren't close. It's an obligation I need to fulfill more than anything. My mother will be a wreck and she needs someone to help her organize everything that needs to be done. I don't think I'll need a week, but I'll keep you posted.'

Back at home, Rachel called Alex. She told him what had happened.

'I'll come with you,' he said.

'No,' Rachel replied.

'You don't want me to come with you?'

'There's no reason for you to come, Alex. It'll be a clusterfuck. My mother's a drunk. She'll be a nightmare. And you never met my father. You aren't any part of this.'

'You should have someone there to support you.'

'I don't need anyone to support me, Alex.'

'The most significant thing that's happened in your life in the entire time we've been together and you don't want me there.'

'No, Alex, I don't.'

'I can't see that as anything but a problem, Rachel.'

'Okay.'

'What does that mean? Okay? You don't care that I want to be there for you?'

'You need to give it a rest,' Rachel said. 'I don't want to talk about it. I'm going, and I'm going alone. Please respect that.'

Rachel hung up the phone.

Less than an hour later Alex was at the door with an overnight bag.

'We're going together,' he said. 'I've taken the time off work.'

Reluctantly, Rachel let him into the apartment.

'I told you that I was going alone,' she said.

'And I'm telling you that I'm coming with you.'

'What is it that you don't seem to understand? Go home

and unpack your fucking bag and give me a fucking break, why don't you?'

'Is this how you deal with grief?' he asked. 'By being just the meanest bitch on the face of the Earth?'

Rachel laughed. Now he was making her angry.

'I want you to leave,' she said. 'I'm asking you politely. I want you to stop twisting everything around so I'm the bad guy here.'

'You *are* the bad guy.'

'Oh fuck off, Alex. You're behaving like a child.'

'You need to make a decision, Rachel. This is fucking horrible. I don't want to be some guy who just comes running when you feel like getting laid. I'm in this for something real and committed and long-term. But you just go on keeping everything and everyone at arm's-length. It's not right, and it's not fair.'

'Life isn't fair, sweetheart. Get over yourself.'

'Okay, so there we have it. Either I come with you and we work this out together, or that's the end of it.'

Rachel looked at Alex. That expression on his face – so familiar, so weak, so self-pitying. She'd never before felt such an urge to slap someone.

'If you want to fuck one last time before you leave, now's your chance,' Rachel said.

Alex looked down. He shook his head. He picked up his overnight bag and walked to the door.

He paused then for just a second, and from his jacket pocket he took the front door key. He held it for a few seconds, looking at it, and then he turned and threw it to her.

Rachel caught it.

'You know, I think you're going to spend the rest of your life alone,' he said.

Rachel didn't reply.

'You know, there's more to life than killers and junkies and fucking mobsters and psychos. That's the only time I ever see a light in your eyes, Rachel. When you've got . . . what do the

Scandinavians say? When you've got blood on your teeth. That's what you're like, you know? Not all of humanity and life is fucking darkness and death and people doing truly evil shit to one another. It's fucking sad, you know? You spend all your time with the dying and the dead and that's all you'll ever know.'

Alex stopped talking. He was waiting for a response.

'Are you done?' Rachel asked.

'Fuck you, Rachel,' Alex said, almost under his breath, and then he slammed the door as hard as he could as he left.

The only thing Rachel could find was half a bottle of cheap vodka. She poured a good three inches and downed it in one.

Then she poured another glass and stood by the window looking into the street.

She wanted to talk to someone, and the only person she could think of was Carl.

Rachel – knowing better but not caring – called the *New York Courier*. It was unlikely he was still there, but it was the only lead she had. Knowing Carl, he was probably running the crime desk at the *Times*.

Rachel told the receptionist that she needed to reach Carl Sheehan in an official capacity. He was now freelance, but he was routinely on the payroll for investigative work and features. Rachel got the number.

Her hands shaking, she hung up before the line was connected. She got up, walked back to the window, steeled herself and dialed again. She wondered what she would do if the ICU nurse answered. Or maybe the kid. A five-year-old kid might answer the phone. What would she say? How she would feel?

The line connected. It rang twice.

'Hello?' Carl said.

'Carl, it's Rachel.'

There was silence at the other end of the line.

'I'm really sorry about your dad,' Carl said.

'What? How do you know about that?'

'Your mother called me yesterday. She was trying to find you. I didn't know where you were, didn't have your number.'

Rachel couldn't speak. She was trying to get her head around the fact that her mother had had to find Carl in order to find her own daughter.

'I'm glad you called,' Carl said. 'I wanted to ask if it was okay with you if I attended his funeral.'

'Er, yes,' Rachel said.

'Did you speak to your mother?'

'I did, yes,' she said.

'Does she have a date for the service?'

Rachel didn't reply. She focused on her breathing. Around her, it felt as if the walls were moving.

'Rachel?'

'No, she doesn't. I'm going there tomorrow to help her sort things out.'

'You want me to come with you?'

'What?'

'To Philly. Do you want me to come and help you sort things out? I know your mom can be a handful.'

'She's not a handful, Carl, she's a drunk.'

Carl didn't respond. He was always the more tolerant and forgiving of the two of them.

'What about your kid?' Rachel asked. 'What about your girl-friend? I don't think she'd be too happy about you taking off to Philadelphia with an ex.'

'We never had a kid, Rachel. We lost the baby. We're no longer together, haven't been for a number of years.'

'Oh my God, Carl, I'm so sorry.'

It was Carl's turn to be silent. She could hear him breathing at the other end of the line.

Finally, he cleared his throat and said, 'So, do you want me to come with you or not?'

'Yes,' Rachel said. She did not hesitate. She did not ask herself about the whys and wherefores of that decision. She just wanted to see him again.

'Okay, then that's what we'll do. You've got my number now. Call me when you're leaving and we'll meet in Philly, okay? I've got the address.'

'Okay. Yes. I'll call you.'

'It's good to hear your voice, Rachel.'

'Good to hear yours too, Carl.'

At the other end, Carl hung up.

Rachel sat there for a good five minutes without moving, the phone in one hand, the glass in the other.

Finally, as if releasing a long pent-up wave of emotion, she started to cry. She couldn't remember the last time she'd cried. It was not something she did. And yet the tears came – not for her father, her mother, not for Alex or Carl, but for herself. Life – real life – had found her, and with that all her insecurities and fears and emptinesses had been exposed for what they were. The walls she'd built were nothing but shadows, and she had locked herself inside in the belief that it somehow proved her strength, her self-reliance, her courage. But she was not strong, nor was she self-reliant or courageous. She had abandoned her family; she had abandoned her life in Syracuse; she had abandoned Carl, then Alex, and all for what? So she could be alone. She had a life, sure, but she was not living. Not in the true sense of the word.

'Enough now,' she finally said to herself.

Leaving her glass on the kitchen counter, she walked through to the bedroom and started to pack.

48

Carl's car was already outside her mother's house.

It was Tuesday the 17th, early evening, and Rachel sat for a good ten minutes as the engine cooled before she got out and walked up to the front door.

She felt like a teenager – anxious, butterflies in her stomach. She wondered if this would be something she'd regret – asking Carl to be here. What if she felt nothing? What if he was little more than a stranger, almost as much a stranger as her own father?

Rachel tried to stop thinking. What was the worst that could happen? A few uncomfortable days around an ex-boyfriend who now meant nothing and a mother who was too drunk to keep her thoughts to herself? She would bury her father, and then she would go back to Pennsylvania and get on with her life. Perhaps seeing Carl would be the best thing for her. She could finally come to terms with the fact that what they'd shared belonged to a now-irretrievable past. After all, he had lost a child and a girlfriend. Had he needed Rachel, had he even wanted to talk to her as a friend, he could so easily have found her. He hadn't tracked her down because he hadn't wanted to, and it was no more complicated than that.

When Carl opened the door, he smiled. He just smiled and held out his arms, and there was such warmth in his expression and his gesture that Rachel dropped her bag and stepped towards him.

He put his arms around her, and she felt that immediate and undeniable connection.

'It's so good to see you,' he whispered.

In those ten seconds, Rachel felt more needed than she had in her entire time with Alex.

Carl let her withdraw, but he held onto her hands. He just looked at her – directly at her – and the same smile was on his face.

'You kept the beard,' Rachel said.

'You said it suited me.'

She laughed. 'It does, but that's not the reason you kept it, surely?'

'Come in, come in,' he said. He reached down and picked up her bag.

Rachel hesitated. 'How drunk is she?'

'Oh, three sheets to the wind and making good headway to the horizon,' Carl said.

'And how's she doing otherwise?'

'For Christ's sake, Rachel, just get inside the damned house, will you?'

Rachel stepped into the hallway. Carl closed the front door behind her.

'Muriel?' Carl called out. 'Rachel's here.'

Muriel was sufficiently coherent to get up from the kitchen table.

She had aged so very much. She looked exhausted and frail.

'Hey, Mom,' Rachel said.

Rachel hugged her mother. It was like hugging a scarecrow. There seemed to be no substance to her at all.

'I'm so sorry, Mom,' Rachel said.

'I know you are, sweetie, I know you are.'

'Let's eat, shall we?' Carl said.

'Carl has made dinner,' Muriel said.

'I brought take-out,' Carl said. 'I didn't make anything.'

'All the same it was very kind of him,' Muriel said. She turned, placed her hand against the wall to steady herself, and sat down once more.

Carl urged Muriel to eat. She did, but very little. She managed to work her way through three glasses of white wine, and it was all too obvious that she needed to be in her bed.

'I am so very tired,' Muriel said.

'You should rest,' Rachel said. 'Let me help you upstairs.'

It took the two of them, both Rachel and Carl, to maneuver Muriel up the stairs and into her room. Muriel kicked off her shoes and started tugging at the sleeves of her cardigan. Rachel sat her on the edge of the bed and helped her. She didn't undress further. She just lay back on the mattress and closed her eyes.

'Roll onto your side, Mom,' Rachel said.

Muriel was already out for the count.

Rachel looked back at Carl.

'Help me get her onto her side, would you? I don't want her to get sick and choke.'

Downstairs, Rachel started cleaning up the take-out cartons and washing the plates and cutlery.

Carl sat at the table and watched her without speaking.

Once done, she sat down. She poured herself some wine.

'So,' Carl said, 'Special Agent Rachel Hoffman, FBI.'

Rachel frowned. 'How do you know—'

'You don't think I kept an eye on you?'

'We haven't spoken for five years.'

'Well, you could've called.'

'As could you.'

'I thought about it,' Carl said. 'In fact, I thought about it a lot.'

'But you never did.'

'No.'

'How come?'

'Insecurity,' he replied. 'A deep-seated and profound sense of self-loathing and worthlessness that told me I could never aspire to maintain a friendship with such a highly-respected and valuable member of the law enforcement community.'

Rachel laughed. 'Asshole.'

'Because ... hell, I don't know, Rachel. Because I didn't want to be a distraction. I didn't want you to think that I was still trying to hold onto something that was gone. I guess I didn't want to find out that you'd made a complete break with everything—'

'A complete break with everything?'

'Pay no attention,' Carl said. 'I'm tired. I'm rambling.'

'Well, ramble some more,' Rachel said. 'I have no idea what you're talking about.'

'This isn't the right time.'

'For what?'

'To talk about us, about what happened between us, about why we split up.'

'What's there to talk about? We split up. That was eight years ago. We went in different directions and got on with our lives. You started another relationship. I mean, you were going to have a baby—'

'Which we never had.'

'I know, and I'm really sorry about that. I can't even begin to imagine how tough that must have been.'

Carl looked away.

'I'm happy to see you,' Rachel said. 'I really am. I didn't hesitate when you asked me if you could come and help but—'

'But now you've seen me, you'd rather I wasn't here.'

'I didn't say that.'

'Then what are you saying?'

'I'm not saying anything, Carl. What do you want me to say? You want me to say that I still love you, that I've missed you, that I regret the fact that we split up with every breath I take?

Is that what you were hoping for here? Is that why you wanted to come?'

'I'm gonna go,' he said.

Rachel's expression was one of utter disbelief. 'You're going to go where?'

'I've booked a room at a motel a few miles away.'

'Right. Well, okay then. I guess I'll see you tomorrow.'

Carl stood up.

'Why the hell do I feel like I've walked into some kind of emotional ambush?' Rachel asked.

Carl gripped the backrest of the chair. He looked at her, his expression calm and resolute.

'I thought you'd have changed,' he said. 'I thought, maybe, that life would have worn off some of those rough edges and sharp corners. But, then again, the fact that you were so pragmatic and self-assured and inarguably right about your own opinions was always something that I admired about you. Maybe I was intimidated by you. I don't know. Maybe I saw you as some kind of anchor in amidst all the shit and turmoil that went on back then. You know, when Michael was killed, and then later in New York. We didn't exactly meet in a bar, did we? We met because people were being brutally murdered—'

'What do you want from me, Carl?'

'What do I want? Right now, I want to go back about fifteen minutes and not have this conversation.'

'Well, taking into consideration the fact that that's not possible, what do you want now?'

'If I've upset you, I want you to forgive me. If you want me to leave, then tell me and I will go. If you have something to say to me, then say it.'

'I want to ask you a question,' Rachel said.

'Then ask.'

'Did you come here to find out if there was a chance we could get back together again?'

'I came here to help your mom.'

'Was that the only reason?'

Carl hesitated.

Rachel nodded. 'Okay,' she said. 'Well, this might make things a little awkward for the next few days, don't you think?'

'Or not,' he replied. 'It doesn't have to be awkward. You can just tell me straight. I am all grown-up now. I can handle it.'

'I had a boyfriend,' Rachel said. 'His name was Alex Harwood. He was a civil engineer. He worked for the city in Allentown. We split up yesterday. Right after he left my apartment, I called you. Why? That's what I've been asking myself ever since. Why were you the first person I thought of talking to after hearing that my father had died and after having finished a relationship? I'll tell you why, Carl. Because you aren't complicated. Because what you see is what you get, or that's the way I remember it. Because you don't look for deeper meanings and hidden messages and ulterior motives. You just are who you are. That's one of the reasons I loved you. And I did love you, Carl. Really, I did. In all honesty, you're probably the only person I've ever really loved. But that was a long time ago, you know? Things have changed. We've changed. You can't just show up here and expect us to pick up where we left off. That's just crazy.'

'You're right,' he said. 'And I don't think that's what I expected.'

'So what did you expect?'

'I think I wanted to feel nothing.'

'You wanted to see me so you could be sure you felt nothing for me?'

'That would have been the best-case scenario, yes.'

'Well, you were the one who just said it didn't have to be awkward.'

'So, let's not make it so. We can just be here to help your mother.'

'Let's do that,' Rachel said. 'Let's deal with that, and then we'll see what happens.'

Carl put on his jacket. He looked down, smiling, his hands in his pockets.

'What?' Rachel asked.

'Your dad was a good guy, you know? He was batshit crazy sometimes, but he was a good guy. He was one of the smartest people I ever met. He was like a firework going off in all directions. If there'd been a way to channel some of that genius in the right way, he could've done some extraordinary things. But there wasn't, so his life was like a forest fire that he kept trying to put out. And, if you didn't know, he was very proud of you.'

'You're just saying that to make me feel better. From what I could tell, he had a major issue with me joining the police.'

'After a while, it didn't matter what you did. It was just that you did so well at it. That's what he was proud of, that you'd made a decision and stuck to it.'

'He said that?'

'Words to that effect, yes. He also said that he hoped you'd forgive him one day.'

Rachel opened her mouth to say something, but the words disappeared.

'I'll see you in the morning, Rachel.'

Carl walked past her, pausing just for a second to place his hand on her shoulder. She reached back, but his hand was gone.

The front door opened and closed. She heard his footsteps on the drive, the sound of his car, and then the fading of the engine as he drove away.

Closing her eyes, she breathed deeply. The turmoil of emotions she was feeling did not diminish.

49

In the early afternoon of Saturday, September 21st, as Rachel Hoffman and Carl Sheehan greeted a handful of mourners in a small chapel for the funeral of Rachel's father, two Bethlehem, Pennsylvania patrol officers – Luke Morrison and Valerie O'Dowd – responded to a call-out. They'd been on-shift since six that morning, and there was no denying the fact that the request to attend a crime scene, the precise details of which were as yet unknown, was met with some frustration. They had little more than an hour to go before each of them was off until Monday. Morrison was meeting friends for beers and football, whereas O'Dowd, recently engaged, was driving to her soon-to-be parents-in-law with her fiancé.

Bethlehem PD reception had received a cryptic phone message. The caller, a male, had simply given an address and said that a unit should attend. When the receptionist inquired as to the nature of the emergency, the caller had simply said, 'They will understand when they get there.'

Reception contacted Dispatch. Dispatch put out a request for the nearest squad car. Morrison and O'Dowd responded.

The address – in what was perhaps the wealthiest suburb of Bethlehem – turned out to be a very sizeable property set in landscaped grounds. O'Dowd had radioed in for an ID on the residents, but had not yet received a response.

Morrison informed Dispatch that they'd arrived at the property, that they were making an initial approach.

The front door was locked. Repeated knocking and ringing

265

the bell prompted no response from within. Backing up and surveying the exterior, there was no sign of anyone in the lower or upper windows.

'It's a false alarm,' Morrison said.

'Check round the back?' O'Dowd suggested.

Morrison looked at her.

'We have to, Luke. We can't just call it in. What if—'

'I'm right behind you,' Morrison said.

The fence that enclosed the garden had only one door. This was also locked. Morrison hoisted himself up so he could see over the top.

'There's a side door open,' he said.

Dispatch came back to O'Dowd – the residence was owned by a Bernard Clarke.

O'Dowd explained that the property was secured but a rear door appeared to be open. There had been no response thus far. Given authorization to access and determine if the call-out was justified, Morrison climbed the fence and then opened the gate from within.

Approaching the open door, Morrison called out.

'Mr. Clarke? Mr. Bernard Clarke? This is the police! If you or anyone else are in the property, please make yourself known!'

Nothing.

Morrison went through the open doorway into a utility room. Ahead of him was a second door that presumably led into the kitchen.

Glancing back at O'Dowd, Morrison said, 'We need to check inside.'

Morrison knocked. No response. He opened the door.

As he'd suspected, it was the kitchen. There was no one there. Morrison and O'Dowd went left and right, all the while keeping their eyes on the open door at the far end.

Breakfast things were still on the table. Cups of coffee, now cold, sat beside the plates. To all appearances, it looked like there had been two people, interrupted mid-meal, and then they'd left without finishing breakfast or cleaning up.

Something didn't feel right. Everything about the place was immaculately clean and tidy. Whatever had caused them to leave their breakfast unfinished had to have been an emergency of some kind.

'Mr. Clarke!' O'Dowd called out.

Again, there was nothing but silence.

Morrison and O'Dowd walked every room on the lower floor – living room, bathroom, study, dining room, even gaining access to the garage where two cars were parked. Upstairs was the same – four bedrooms, a bathroom, a separate shower room and toilet – and no sign of anyone. The master bedroom was the only one that had been used recently. The bed, unmade, had obviously been slept in by a couple, and yet there were no women's clothes, no dressing table, and no sign of any female beauty products. Back in the bathroom, O'Dowd opened the cabinet above the sink. It was the same. There was nothing to indicate a woman lived there.

'Basement?' Morrison said.

'Didn't see one,' O'Dowd replied. 'We checked every door.'

They headed downstairs again.

They found access to the basement via a floor trap in the garage. It was on the other side of the parked cars.

Opening it, Morrison directed his flashlight down. A wooden stair.

'Mr. Clarke?' Morrison called out.

Silence.

'I'm going down,' Morrison said, and put his foot on the uppermost riser.

O'Dowd watched him go, an ever-increasing sense of tension in her gut. There really was something unnerving about the stillness of this place, the unfinished meal, the absence of anything to explain where the resident had gone.

Morrison's flashlight bounced back off the walls below.

'Luke?'

Morrison didn't respond.

'Luke? Is there anything down there?'

O'Dowd started to make her own way down, and then Morrison's face appeared below her. From his expression she knew something was awry.

'What is it?' she asked.

'You'd best come see for yourself.'

50

Aside from herself, her mother and Carl, there were seven attendees at her father's funeral. Rachel knew none of them, though they each in turn came and expressed their condolences, telling her that Edward was a man of great charm and warmth, that he was 'one in a million', that he had always been so very proud of her.

The days prior had been difficult. Her father's body had been released without inquest. He'd already suffered two heart attacks; there were no suspicious circumstances, and thus a certificate had been issued without delay.

Rachel was relieved to discover that the house was owned outright – no mortgage, no liens, no outstanding charges to be addressed. Her father – it seemed – had also left no will. Whatever remained of his estate, whatever money he might have managed to accrue, would be Muriel's. Rachel hoped there would be enough for her to support herself.

Standing in that small chapel as people she'd never seen before shared anecdotes about a man to whom she'd not spoken for years, a man who was as much a stranger as the mourners themselves, Carl took her hand. He did not look at her, and he said nothing. He just took her hand. It was, in a way, nothing more than a supportive gesture, but – in that moment – she acknowledged how much he really meant to her. Of that first night – the words they'd shared – they'd said nothing further. He had just been there for her, helping her organize the funeral director, selecting a burial plot, ordering flowers. Everything had happened so quickly – too quickly perhaps – but she'd wanted it that way. It was not because she was so eager to return to Allentown, but because she wanted to close this chapter of her life once and for all. She did not ask herself whether she would stay in touch with her mother. She did not think about whether she would find the time to visit, to see that she was okay. That was something that could wait until she was back home. She needed distance and perspective.

The burial itself was over in no time at all. Muriel went to the car.

Rachel stayed back with Carl, the pair of them side by side at the edge of the plot. She had ordered a simple granite headstone, but it would not be ready for installation for at least two weeks.

'When are you going to leave?' Carl asked.

'Officially, I'm back at work on Monday, but if I need more time they'll give it to me.'

'Do you need more time?'

'I know what I don't need, and that's to stay here with my mother.'

'You could come stay with me for a couple of days.'

'Why would I do that?'

'Change of scenery?'

'Is that all?'

'I'm not playing games with you, Rachel. Either you want to spend some time with me or you don't.'

'I want to spend time with you, Carl, just not right now. I need a breather. I dumped my boyfriend, I buried my father, and now I have a concern that my mother is going to drink herself to death.'

'Honestly, I think that's inevitable, and there's not a damned thing you or I can do about it.'

'I know. It's just so fucking sad, isn't it? What a waste of a life.'

'You know, whatever you might think, she loved your father. She was utterly devoted to him. She stayed with him for – what?

– forty-something years. She knew what he was like. She never quit, did she? She believed in him when everyone else didn't.'

'And what did she get for her troubles, Carl?'

'Forty years of adventure and possibility. She got hope. She traveled across half the country with him. There were times when they had more money than they knew what to do with, and then other times they had nothing.'

'That's no kind of life, is it?'

'Maybe that's exactly the kind of life she wanted.'

'I'll leave tomorrow,' Rachel said. 'I'm going back to Allentown, back to work, and then we can speak. I'm not promising anything, Carl. Really. I don't want you to get some idea into your head about how we're going to just start all over—'

'I never asked anything of you, Rachel, and I'm not asking anything of you now.'

'You have my phone number.'

'And you have mine.'

'Okay, so let's go eat tuna fish sandwiches and celery sticks with sad people, eh?'

Rachel left her mother's house late on Sunday evening. Carl had already headed back to the motel to get his things together. He said he'd check on Muriel before he left.

Rachel thanked him sincerely. His help had been invaluable.

Throughout the return journey – two and a half hours along near-empty highways to Allentown – Rachel's thoughts and feelings were a mess. She insisted that others spoke the truth, and yet she lied to herself. She had dedicated herself to the understanding of others, and yet she refused to try and understand herself. Her life was well-defined; she colored inside the lines, followed routines and patterns, never once admitting to herself that those same routines and patterns were perhaps the very reason that she would never comprehend the human condition. The Marshalls and Wagners of the world existed in a reality they themselves had manufactured. How was she any different? Sure, she was on the side of the law; she didn't kill people for the sheer pleasure of killing people; she hadn't fabricated some artificial universe where the innocent were guilty, and guilt was something experienced only by those without conviction and self-belief in the rightness of their actions. All that aside, she was still disconnected, concerned more with whatever might be crossing her desk rather than through her life.

It was as she crossed the Allentown city limits that Rachel knew she'd have to go and see Frances Burroughs. Burroughs was a psychologist, and even though she might have no clear answers for what had happened in Rachel's past, she would at least be a safe harbor. Maybe the truth of her parents' relationship was simpler than she thought. Maybe they were both crazy in their own ways, but they had been crazy together. They had one another, and that had been enough. Meaningful relationships were not fated or discovered, they were created. And what was love? She knew she had no idea.

Arriving home, Rachel looked around her apartment. It possessed no more character than a highway motel. It was a stopover for showers, for sleeping, for sex with a man she'd never loved.

The impulse to speak to Carl was strong. Wasn't it better to give it a chance than to run from it and wonder? Just the thought of it unsettled her. Perhaps it was no more complex than the unwillingness to change. Her entire life had been a balance between avoidance and commitment. She ran from her own needs and yet dedicated herself to the needs of others. She believed she was selfless, and yet wasn't that some sort of twisted vanity? The *need* to be needed; the need to be considered important. The need to be in control of everything to the point of losing control. Equilibrium had been lost and she needed to regain it. She needed to do the things she was supposed to do, and – in time – she would perhaps begin to reconcile the personal with the professional.

Rachel showered and dried her hair. She ironed a shirt for the morning. She put the radio on and listened to music. It was close to midnight when she turned in for the night. She deadbolted the front door, turned out the lights, and just as she was closing the bedroom door behind her she heard the phone.

Her mother, perhaps?

Rachel walked back to the living room and picked it up.

'Rachel?'

'Carl?'

'Rachel. Sorry it's so late. I had to call you. I don't know all the details, but a man called Bernard Clarke and a woman were murdered yesterday in Bethlehem.'

'What are you talking about?'

'Bethlehem, Pennsylvania.'

'I know where Bethlehem is, Carl. It's fifteen minutes away. How do you even know about this?'

Carl didn't answer.

'You have PD sources, right?'

Again, there was no response.

'And what does this have to do with me?'

'Something at the crime scene,' Sheehan said. 'There's a rumor that something was left at the crime scene.'

'Something?'

'A message.'

It was Rachel's turn to say nothing.

'More importantly, I knew the victim,' Carl said. 'Well, I didn't know him as such, but I've spoken to him, interviewed him. He did time on Rikers a few years back. He shared a cell with Charles Wagner.'

51

The murders of Bernard Clarke and Samantha Warner were a police matter. There was no reason for the FBI to get involved.

Hogtied in the basement of Clarke's house, each of them had been suffocated – a plastic bag over their heads, duct tape wound tightly around the neck. Clarke had a record. He'd done a little over four years on Rikers for wire fraud, embezzlement and theft. An accountant by profession, he had falsified loan applications, submitted erroneous accounts to the Treasury, evaded tax, failed to repay numerous corporate debts, and lived his life on the basis that if it was there to be taken then it was fair game. He had never been married, had no children, and – at fifty-seven years of age – had spent his last hours alive in the company of a twenty-two-year-old, three-hundred-and-fifty-dollar-an-hour prostitute.

Rachel spoke to Bethlehem PD Detective John Ingram. Ingram, curious as to why the Feds were even getting involved, was assured by Rachel that the Feds were not getting involved.

'The guy was an asshole,' Ingram told her. 'He was just a rip-off artist, no two ways about it. I don't think he ever actually did an honest day's work in his life. I'm sure we're going to have no shortage of probable suspects. He pissed off a lot of people over the years.'

Rachel then called Carl.

'It's a police matter,' she said. 'It's nothing to do with us. Nevertheless, I am interested to know why you interviewed him.'

'Like I told you, he shared a cell with Wagner.'

'I get that, but—'

'I was considering writing a book,' Carl said. 'About what happened in Syracuse, and then what happened in New York. It was a couple of years back.'

'And?'

'And nothing. He didn't tell me anything I didn't already know, and I got involved in other stuff and dropped it.'

'How much work did you do on it?'

'A fair amount. I was trying to find connections between Marshall and the people he killed. Looking for an explanation, I guess. A motive. And then I got all wrapped around a pole trying to see a link between Marshall and Wagner.'

'And did you?'

'No, I didn't. There just seemed to be nothing to connect any of it.'

'I spoke to the detective who's investigating Clarke's murder. From what I understand, the guy had no shortage of people he'd crossed. You know why he was on Rikers, right?'

'Financial stuff.'

'Well, he didn't seem to have learned his lesson.'

'And the girl?'

'A prostitute.'

'So why kill her as well?'

'Christ, I don't know, Carl.'

There was silence at the other end of the line.

'What about this rumored message? Did you get any more information?'

'I didn't, no,' Carl said. 'Not yet, anyway.'

'Well, if there's nothing, then we're done. I'll give you a call, okay?'

'You alright?'

'Yes, Carl, I'm alright. Now I need to go. I have a week of catching up to do.'

Rachel hung up the phone.

Later that afternoon, Joy Willis asked to see Rachel.

'I just wanted to know that you were ready to get back to work,' Willis said.

'I'm good.'

'And how is your mother?'

'She's coping. She'll go on coping until she stops drinking or dies.'

'That's a very matter-of-fact response.'

'We've never been close,' Rachel said. 'I wasn't close to my father, either. I went there, I dealt with it, and now I'm back. There's not a great deal to discuss.'

'As long as you're on top of things, then so be it.'

'I am. It's all good.'

'There's another matter I need to discuss with you,' Willis said. 'It's come to my attention that you are involved with a man called Carl Sheehan.'

'What?'

'Carl Sheehan. He's a reporter.'

'Yes, I know who he is. I've known him for years. We had a relationship.'

'And he was with you at the funeral.'

'He was, yes.'

'Why?'

'Because he's a friend. Because he knew my parents.'

'How so?'

Rachel was ill at ease. 'Can I ask why you're asking me about him?'

'When was this relationship?'

'Back when I was in Syracuse.'

'And for how long did it go on?'

'A couple of years.'

'And when did it end?'

'Middle of '77.'

'Why?'

'I'm sorry,' Rachel said, 'but I really would like to know why you're asking me about him.'

'He's a reporter, Rachel. He has a file.'

'What did he do?'

'On the face of it, nothing. But he makes noise.'

'Isn't that what reporters do?'

'Sure they do, but most of them don't make enough noise for us to hear about it.'

'Can you be more specific?' she asked.

'Are you involved with him currently?'

'If you're asking if we're currently in a relationship, then the answer is no.'

'And if I asked you to keep it that way, would you have a problem with that?'

'Not at all, but I'd like to know why you think he's a problem.'

'All I can say is that it's not in your interest to be personally involved with anyone from the media. Intimate relationships can be a source of difficulty when it comes to investigations. People drop their guard. People say things without thinking. And when it comes to journalists, they are of a mind to elicit information that should not be in the public domain.'

'So, what you're actually saying is that you're concerned about my ability to maintain professional confidentiality?'

'Actually no, I'm not. I have complete trust in you. So much so that I have already put you forward for promotion.'

Rachel could not conceal her surprise.

'You look surprised.'

'I am.'

'You're a very competent and conscientious investigator.'

'Thank you.'

'It's a statement of fact, not a compliment.'

'Nevertheless, I appreciate the fact that my work has been recognized.'

'It has, and promotion to Senior Special Agent is on the table if you continue to apply yourself with the same degree of diligence and commitment.'

'But I need to adhere to conditions, and one of them is no longer having anything to do with Carl Sheehan.'

Willis relaxed just a fraction. 'Let's just say that it would be appreciated if you kept your communication with him to the bare minimum, and that it remained on a wholly professional footing.'

'Can I ask how you knew I'd seen him?'

'Don't be naïve, Rachel. The responsibility of policing others carries with it a willingness to be policed. We're all under the microscope here, and the higher up the ladder you go, the more your activities will be subject to scrutiny. That is one of the trade-offs we have to make when it comes to a life of public service. I know senior agents here and in other offices who have never considered the possibility of raising a family, simply because they never wish to be put in a situation where their children could be at risk from retaliation or potential blackmail.'

'Are you telling me that my career would be better served if I remained single?'

'That's not what I'm saying, no. You have been in a relationship for quite some time now, no?'

'It ended very recently.'

'Well, be that as it may, there was no concern about him, was there? We didn't have this conversation about Mr. Harwood, did we?'

Rachel laughed. It was a nervous response. 'Wow,' she said.

Willis leaned forward. Her expression conveyed empathy and understanding, but her words were characteristically businesslike.

'We're the highest federal investigation and prosecution agency in the country, Rachel. Look at your training, everything from application submission and job offer through four months at Quantico. What did that include? Eligibility and Qualification

Review, interviews, testing, background investigation, security clearance, all of it through a fine-toothed comb. You don't think we knew about your father's debts and outstanding obligations, about your mother's drinking? You don't think we knew exactly who you were sleeping with, what they did, their background? We knew everything before we took you on, and we took you on because you met every requirement. But that has to be maintained. You're no longer a Syracuse detective, Rachel. You're an agent of the Federal Bureau of Investigation. You answer to me, to my seniors, to the Director, to the President, and if you want to continue to do that then we have to require of you exemplary behavior in everything you do, both inside and outside of your professional remit.'

'Nothing happened between myself and Carl,' Rachel said. 'You have my word.'

'Then we're done here.'

Rachel got up and walked to the door.

Glancing back before she left, Willis was already reading a file on her desk.

Whatever decision she might have made about Carl, it had been taken out of her hands. It occasioned both a sense of resentment and relief. She had indeed been naïve. What had she thought? That the FBI would not invade every aspect of her life, that they wouldn't know everything about her? Well, they did, and that was that. She would have to distance herself from him, irrespective of whatever efforts he might make to engage her in his work. If she wanted Senior Special Agent – and she did – then that was the condition.

52

After a month, Carl stopped calling.

Three times he called her at the office; another half a dozen times at home. He left messages on her machine, but Rachel didn't respond. She considered it would be only polite to explain the reason for her silence, but she was intent on doing nothing that would derail the promotion to which Willis had alluded. Of that, Rachel had heard no more. She began to wonder if it had been a means by which compliance could be obtained.

On Wednesday, November 6th, Rachel received a call from Detective Ingram of Bethlehem PD. He asked whether she remembered the Clarke and Warner murders from back in the third week of September.

'I do yes, Detective Ingram.'

'There have been more,' Ingram said. 'Three others, same MO. One here in Bethlehem, another in Reading, the last in Lancaster.'

'And you think I can help you?'

'Christ, I don't know. That behavioral stuff you guys do, maybe. I've got three different PDs all trying to figure out what the hell we're dealing with here, and … and well, I'm sort of calling you as a last resort.'

'I'm not Behavioral Science, Detective. And this is a matter for the police, not the FBI.'

'Yes, I know that, Agent Hoffman, but you can't even begin to imagine the shitstorm that we're dealing with in the press.

They're saying it's a cult thing, some sort of religious maniac. And I've got a reporter from New York who just won't let it go.'

Rachel knew. In her bones, she knew.

'A reporter?'

'Some freelance asshole called Sheehan. He's making some connection to some murders that happened years ago. He even spun me some line about how you were the investigating officer on something similar in Syracuse. Is that true? Were you PD in Syracuse?'

Rachel was lost for words.

'Agent Hoffman? You there?'

'Yes, I'm here. Detective Ingram, you say that Carl Sheehan has been in communication with you about these recent killings?'

'In communication is a fucking understatement. The man's been a thorn in my side.'

'And what's this religious connection?'

'I don't know. I don't understand it.'

'Tell me what you've got.'

'It's this Sheehan guy. He says these people are being... get this, he says they're being killed because of some book.'

'What book?'

'Some old book. I don't know. Some Italian thing.'

Rachel closed her eyes. A wave of agitation invaded her lower gut. She felt cold. The hairs rose to attention on the back of her neck.

'Were there notes left the crime scenes, Detective Ingram?'

'Notes?'

'Messages. Written messages. Like lines of poetry.'

'Not to my knowledge, no. I don't know about the ones down in Reading and Lancaster. I don't have the files here. On mine, the first one, there was something written on the wall.'

'What?'

'It was an Italian word. I don't know how you pronounce it, but it's spelled a-v-a-r-i-t-i-a. It means avarice.'

'And do you know if there were any similar messages at the other crime scenes?'

'Not yet,' Ingram said. 'I'm following up on that now.'

'Let me get back to you on it,' Rachel said. 'I don't know if this is connected to the cases I investigated, but I need to clear it with my supervisor before I can even look at it.'

'Anything you can do to help us would be appreciated.'

'I understand, Detective Ingram, but I can't promise anything.'

Rachel hung up the phone. She walked to the window. She felt a quiet sense of overwhelm. It couldn't be possible. She didn't even want to consider that it was possible.

Avarice. The financial criminal. A cellmate of Charles Wagner. Once was happenstance; twice was coincidence; a third time was conspiracy. And Carl Sheehan was onto it, wouldn't let it go. Maybe that's why he'd been calling her, to tell her that it had started all over again, that Dante had resurfaced in yet another guise with another name.

No, it was lunacy. It was beyond the bounds of belief. There was no way in the world that what was happening here was a re-run of Marshall and Wagner. But then, hadn't she thought the same thing with the killings in New York? Was this like some sort of virus that kept on spreading? And why five years apart? And here, right here in Pennsylvania, almost as if someone or something was following her, haunting her, dragging her back into the madness of unmitigated violence and brutality.

And yet, despite her dismay and disbelief, wasn't there some part of her that wanted to believe it? Rachel dismissed the thought. She was losing her mind. Why would she want it to be connected? Because it might lead to some understanding of what had happened to Michael Ridgway? So she could finally close that chapter of her life, assuage her own guilt, allay her conscience?

No, that was not it. It couldn't be. Marshall and Wagner were sociopaths, nothing more nor less, and their actions would have continued no matter who might have been involved in the investigation.

No matter which way she considered it, Rachel could not escape the sense that this had something to do with her. It was personal – not for her as an individual, but for her as an investigator. She had tracked both men, and she had found them. Of course, she'd been too late to gain any comprehension of why they did what they did, but she had been the driving force behind those investigations. Had she not worked the way she did, there might have been a great many more victims.

She had to look at it, she had no choice, but she couldn't do it without authorization.

Leaving the bullpen, she headed down the corridor to Joy Willis's office. She knocked on the door, waited to be called in, and then she closed the door behind her.

'I need to talk to you about something,' Rachel said.

'Personal or professional?'

'Definitely professional, but there's a personal aspect to this as well. At least, I think there is.'

'How so?'

Rachel gave Joy Willis the history of the Dante cases – all the way from the February '75 discovery of the body of Caroline Lassiter, through Raymond Keene, the Wilsons and Brenda Forsyth. She told her about Robert Leonard Marshall and the murder of Michael Ridgway. She then detailed the Wagner killings – Christopher Wake, Anthony Yates and Margaret Silva; the notes, the references to *The Divine Comedy*; everything that had occurred prior to her departure from Syracuse PD. She explained how she'd met Carl Sheehan, the articles he'd run for them, the fact that Sheehan – as far as she understood – had continued to look into the cases with a view to writing a book after their separation and her embarking on FBI training. And then Rachel told her that Ingram had called from Bethlehem and requested her help.

Willis listened patiently, and when Rachel was done she said, 'So you're making a leap between what happened in Syracuse and New York to these murders in Pennsylvania because of something that was written at a crime scene?'

'Yes.'

'How is that so? I'm not getting the connection here.'

'Greed,' Rachel said. 'It's one of the seven deadly sins. Bernard Clarke was a thief. A pretty high-class one, but a thief all the same.'

'I know what the seven deadly sins are, but—'

'If the killings in Syracuse were representative of death, and those in New York were Hell, then next would come Purgatory. Purgatory, according to the book, is represented by a mountain with seven terraces, and each of them corresponds to the seven roots of sinfulness.'

Willis smiled. 'You have any idea how crazy this sounds?'

'I do, yes, and all I'm asking is for leave to go and take a look at these murders. If there's any probative evidence that there's a connection, then perhaps we can refer it to Behavioral Science and they can assist. If not, then—'

'This is not your job, Rachel,' Willis said. 'This is a matter for the respective Police Departments of Bethlehem, Reading and Lancaster.'

'Unless it's a cross-state investigation.'

'How can it be cross-state? Marshall and Leonard were both New York, and both of them are dead. You're telling me they've come back from the grave and are now hell-bent on dragging you into yet another multiple homicide investigation?'

'I'm telling you that there might be some other factor at play here.'

'Some other factor?'

'Someone else.'

Willis frowned. 'I'm sorry, I don't—'

'It bothered me then, and it still bothers me. Those investigations – Marshall and Wagner – were by the book. They were concluded as a result of diligent police work. But they were incomplete. No one ever figured out why Marshall chose those particular victims. No one ever asked why Wagner was driven to pick up where Marshall had left off five years earlier.'

'Marshall picked them randomly. Wagner was nothing more than a copycat. Perhaps it's no more complicated than that.'

'A week,' Rachel said. 'I want you to give me a week.'

Willis looked at her unerringly. 'Does it matter that much to you?'

'If I can do something that prevents more unnecessary killings, then yes, it matters.'

'And if I say no?'

'Then I'll abide by your wishes and go back to work.'

'And trust the police to deal with it?'

'Yes, of course.'

'But this Detective...?'

'Ingram.'

'He called you, didn't he? And he said they were getting nowhere.'

'He said he was calling us as a last resort.'

Willis was pensive; her expression gave away nothing.

Finally she nodded. 'A week,' she said. 'At the outside. Having said that, if you determine within a day that these incidents are not connected to either Syracuse or New York, then you come right on back. I am low enough on manpower as it is.'

'Completely understood.'

Rachel left the office before Willis had a chance to change her mind.

53

Directed to a small conference room in Bethlehem PD, Rachel was somewhat taken aback by the degree of importance she was granted upon her arrival.

Detective John Ingram was younger than she'd expected – perhaps in his late-thirties – and he welcomed her as if she was the solution to all of his problems.

She'd called ahead before leaving Allentown, asked him if it was possible to gather all the files from each case along with forensics, toxicology, autopsy, crime scene photos, first responder and witness statements and anything else he thought might be relevant. He had done as asked, and ahead of her on the table was a substantial quantity of documentation.

'You asked about other messages,' he said.

'They were present?'

Ingram had already selected single photos from each of the three cases from Bethlehem, Reading and Lancaster.

'This is from the first one, the Clarke and Warner murders,' he added, sliding a picture across towards her. Clearly visible, scratched into the wall, was the word *Avaritia*.

'And the other Bethlehem case?'

Again, as had been the case with Clarke and Warner, the victim – a male – had been trussed from behind by his wrists and ankles. The rope appeared to be of the same color and dimension as the Clarke/Warner scene. Lying on his side, his body pulled back into what must have been a very painful and constricting position, the victim had a heavy-duty clear polythene bag over his head, and around his neck were several windings of silver-gray duct tape. There was a close-up of the word *Ira* on the wall.

'That means "wrath",' Ingram said.

'Name?' Rachel asked.

'Martin Douglas. Age forty-seven. Divorced, three kids, youngest twelve, oldest seventeen. Three call-outs in the past year alone from the ex for threatening behavior. Never arrested or charged, but according to the ex he physically abused her and the children.'

Rachel reached for the autopsy images. Douglas's face, now visible without the plastic bag, seemed to be badly burned around the eyes.

'From what the coroner said, it seems his eyes were burned out. There were deposits of charcoal in the sockets.'

Rachel looked at the crime scene report. It was dated the 30th of September.

'Clarke and Warner were on the 21st,' Ingram said, 'and the next one was Lancaster.'

Rachel opened the file.

Once again the victim – this time a woman – was hogtied in precisely the same way, her head inside a plastic bag. The way the pictures had been taken gave a clear image of her tortured face, her mouth wide, a final dying gasp for air preserved in perpetuity.

'Carole Sitkoff, twenty-eight, single. Not sure how it fits into any of this, but as far as we can work out she had a history of affairs with married men.'

'And she gets *Invidia*,' Rachel said. 'Which means?'

'Envy.'

'Envious of other women, maybe? Envious enough to steal their husbands.'

'And she gets her eyelids sewn shut,' Ingram said. 'And our most recent was in Reading. Same manner of death. Julian McCullan.'

Rachel looked at the photos. McCullan was a big man, two hundred and fifty pounds or more.

'Thirty years old, lived alone, never had a job as far as we know.'

'Gula,' Rachel said. 'He didn't skip his meals, did he? What is that? Gluttony?'

'Exactly,' Ingram replied.

'So how did he support himself financially?'

'He won the lottery. Not a huge amount, maybe a couple of hundred thousand dollars, but he never moved house, didn't own a car, and from the state of the place he never considered the possibility of employing a cleaner.'

Rachel looked at each of the crime scene pictures in turn – slowly, methodically – trying to identify anything else that would indicate methodology or signature.

'What are the marks around the mouth here?' she asked.

'Salt burns,' Ingram said. 'It appears he was forced to eat a considerable quantity of salt.'.

'Jesus,' Rachel said.

'I don't know what it means,' Ingram said. 'Some sort of ritual, something symbolic, maybe. I've gone through the forensics and autopsy reports. No drugs, aside from Clarke and Warner who both had recreational quantities of cocaine in their systems. But there's nothing else. No abrasions, no blunt force trauma, nothing to indicate that any of the victims were incapacitated. The injuries they suffered – rope burns, bruising – are attributable to the way in which they were tied up.'

'He had to get them tied up,' Rachel said. 'How do you do that? How do you get someone to submit to being tied up like this? One of them must've resisted, fought back, surely?'

'Doesn't appear that way. A weapon?'

'Still, even if the perp had a gun or a knife, how did he do it, especially in your first case where's there's two people to contend with, without encountering some degree of opposition? You don't tie someone up like this one-handed.'

'You think there's two of them?'

Rachel didn't reply. That was the hypothesis she was considering.

'You really think there might be two of them?' Ingram asked.

'It wouldn't be a first,' Rachel said.

'What? Two people working together?'

'You ever heard of the Hillside Stranglers?'

'Yeah, right. Weren't they cousins or something?'

'Kenneth Bianchi and Angelo Buono. Posed as police officers in Los Angeles. Bought retired squad cars at auction, used fake badges. They killed ten that we know of. Youngest was twelve. They raped them, then strangled them, gave them lethal injections, electric shocks, suffocated them with carbon monoxide. There's a whole catalog of couples who've killed together. Charles Starkweather and Caril Ann Fugate killed eleven people in two months in Nebraska and Wyoming, back in the 50s. Raymond Fernandez and Martha Beck, the Lonely Hearts Killers. They killed twenty or so in the 1940s. Henry Lee Lucas and Ottis Toole killed separately and together. Between them, it's estimated that they murdered over four hundred and fifty people.'

'Is this your area of expertise?'

'Oh no, not at all. And, based on my experience, it's no one's area of expertise. There's a huge amount of hypothesis and opinion when it comes to sociopathic motivation, and it varies wildly dependent upon who you talk to.'

'But people turn out this way because of childhood trauma and abuse and all that stuff, right?'

'Some do, some don't,' Rachel replied. 'Sure, there are studies on how those who are abused are more likely to become abusers, but it's not even close to definitive. There are millions of people who have truly awful childhood experiences and then spend their entire lives with no more serious a crime than a parking violation.'

'So what drives people to do this kind of thing?'

'That's the question, isn't it? Simple answer, they're solving a problem.'

'Solving a problem?'

'One that exists for them. They're ridding the world of undesirables. They're taking revenge on people who remind them of some terrible thing that happened to them. The permutations are endless. And these people are inveterate liars. Even when they're arrested, tried, convicted, even those on death row, they're going to keep on lying like their continued existence depends on it. And it's always someone else's fault. It's always because other people don't understand. It's ego and narcissism and an entire construct of imagined reality that is unique in every single case.'

'So where do we begin?' Ingram said. 'We've got five dead in the space of five weeks and if what you're saying is true, then we have at least three more to go, right? Lust, sloth and pride.'

'Tell me about the reporter.'

'What about him?' Ingram asked.

'He's been calling you.'

'And my colleagues in Reading and Lancaster.'

'Saying what?'

'Well, like I said when I contacted you, he was the one who mentioned your name. He told me I should get in touch with you, that you would know all about this. Does this have something to do with the case back in Syracuse?'

'There were two cases,' Rachel said. 'One in Syracuse, another in New York. Five years apart. Mr. Sheehan was working for the *Tribune*, and then for the *Courier* after he moved. He ran some articles for us.'

'So he's not involved as a potential suspect?'

Rachel frowned, shook her head. 'No, not at all. Why would you think that?'

'Well, you hear about people helping to look for missing kids, and then it turns out they were the ones who killed them. Murderers showing up at crime scenes, police press events, all that stuff. He just seemed really insistent, like he wanted to be involved. He also said that there was a connection between Bernard Clarke and one of your perps.'

'Apparently so, yes. Seems that Clarke shared a cell with our New York killer, Charles Wagner. But I can assure you that Carl Sheehan is not a suspect in this or any other case. He's a reporter, first and foremost. His primary interest would be headlines and exclusives.'

'And what's the deal with this book he was on about?'

Rachel gave Ingram a very brief history of the two cases.

'Hence the messages in Italian are significant.'

'Sheehan called me,' Rachel said. 'Twenty-four hours after the first murder was discovered. He knew about the message.'

'How the hell would he know about that?'

'Like I said, he's a crime reporter. It's his business. I can imagine he has no end of contacts inside and outside numerous different PDs. I'm sure he has people in coroner's offices, forensics units, crime scene photographers, God knows who. He's been doing this a long time.'

'And you want him to help us?'

'I don't want him anywhere near this, Detective Ingram. Unless, of course, we need to use his paper for an appeal of some sort.'

'And do you think they're connected? This case and the two previous ones?'

'I don't know what to think, Detective Ingram. There was never any probative evidence for Syracuse and New York being connected, aside from the whole Dante thing. On the face of it, it was a copycat of sorts. Hell, I don't even know what you'd call it. The fact that we never had a chance to question either Marshall or Wagner and that they appeared to be completely unknown to one another meant that we were never able to identify a link.'

'One copycat I get,' Ingram said. 'But two?'

'And then there's the fact that I could be biased by an entirely incorrect assumption. In the earlier cases, notes were left. They were quotes from the book. There's no such notes here. I don't want to fall into the trap of assuming that this guy is somehow motivated by either Marshall or Wagner. This could be entirely unrelated.'

'So where do we begin?'

'At the beginning,' Rachel said. 'We go through everything again. We look for anything that might have been missed. We visit the crime scenes. We canvass neighbors, friends, speak to family members. We unearth everything we can about the personal histories of each of the victims. We see if there's some common denominator, something that links them to one another, or something that connects each of them to someone else. You're going to need to speak to your colleagues in Reading and Lancaster, get clearance for everything, prep them in case we need warrants, interview rooms, back-up, the usual.'

'Right,' Ingram said.

'You have a wife, a family, someone who expects you home?'

'No, I don't.'

'Good, 'cause if there was you wouldn't be seeing them for a while.'

54

Within seventy-two hours it became clear to both Rachel Hoffman and John Ingram that they had nothing. The endless hours poring over statements and photographs, driving back and forth between the three Pennsylvanian cities, discussions with first responders and attending officers and all else that they undertook gave them no substantive correlations between the victims. To all appearances, they were randomly selected, and yet the very nature of their deaths, the fact that each had been considered guilty of a punishable crime – if only by the perpetrator – meant that they were not random at all. They had been chosen, and chosen carefully, deliberately, and with malice aforethought.

Once again, Rachel was dragging herself into bed in the early hours of each morning, though at least – this time – she was returning to her own place each night. Her mind was drawn relentlessly back to the events that had unfolded in both Syracuse and New York. She couldn't escape the feeling that she'd been pursued by the same ghosts, the same unresolved questions, for more than a decade.

Rachel had three or four more days, perhaps a week if she stayed on through the following weekend and didn't return to Allentown until the night of Sunday the 17th. She couldn't return empty-handed. That, if nothing else, would discourage Joy Willis from giving her any leeway in the future. Everything was dependent upon whether this was a progression of the Syracuse and New York murders. If it was, then that lent weight to her theory that there was more than one person involved, and that that person had been there right from the beginning. She remembered the letter that Quinn had produced at the 114th. She recalled how the writer had invited her to the case, congratulated her on her promotion, how he hoped she would appreciate his *contrapasso*.

Elegance and wit. That's what it had said. That his killing possessed a certain elegance and wit.

The letter had been written by an educated individual, someone who'd read *The Divine Comedy*, who possessed a desire for theater. Neither Robert Marshall nor Charles Wagner were highly-educated men. They were men of violence, of brute force. They didn't read fourteenth-century narrative poems about divine justice and spiritual redemption. Rachel had read it, sections of it several times over, and it was no walk in the park.

The more she considered it, the more she gravitated towards the disturbing reality that Marshall and Wagner had not acted alone. There was an unknown identity at work here, and whoever that was had managed to successfully evade her in both Syracuse and New York. Only now, ten years on, was she beginning to grasp this as a real possibility. But why her? Why had she – yet again – been drawn into this? Was this personal, or was she nothing more than incidental? And if she was incidental, then why hadn't she been killed instead of Ridgway? And then there was the fact that Marshall and Wagner had both committed suicide. Had it been suicide, or had they also been murdered once their individual tasks were complete? And why five years apart? What had happened in those intervening years?

It was hypothesis. It could be nothing more than a further misconception that would influence her interpretation of the facts. She had to stay with the facts. She had to stay with the evidence. She had to base her conclusions on what she saw, what could be proven, what could be substantiated. To wander off into a dark forest of theories would be utterly futile.

A little after 2.00 on the morning of Monday 11th, a sixteen-hour day behind her, Rachel returned home. She needed to sleep. If she didn't secure at least one good night's rest, then the likelihood of staying focused would be significantly reduced.

Her sleep – what little she managed – was restless and troubled. She may well have managed a couple more hours had she not been woken by an incessant hammering on the door. Bolting upright into wakefulness, it was as if there was gunfire beyond the walls of the room.

Rachel pulled the cover around her and crossed the room.

'Who is it?' she called out, glancing back at the beside clock. It wasn't even six.

'It's Ingram.'

'What the fuck, John?'

'We've got another, Agent Hoffman. And there's a note at the scene.'

'A note?'

'It's a letter,' Ingram said. 'He left a letter, and it's addressed to you.'

55

On the drive from Allentown to Easton, all of thirty minutes on US 22, Ingram said no more than a dozen words.

'It's bad,' he said. 'The worst yet.'

When Rachel asked for more details, he just said, 'I can't even describe it. Let's just get there and you'll see.'

Heading north-east along the route of the Lehigh River, they passed the Easton Heights Cemetery. On the other side, between Bushkill Drive and Lafayette, there was a warehousing complex and a wrecker's yard. Rows of shipping containers filed out in parallel lines. Beyond that was a large brick-built structure, ahead of it a couple of patrol cars, cherry bars flashing.

As they neared, it was evident that the building had fallen into a state of disrepair. Sections of the roof had come in; most of the windows were gone; weeds had edged around the base of the property.

'What was this place?' Rachel asked.

'It was a factory. They used to make prosthetic limbs.'

'And it's been abandoned?'

'That's what they told me. They thought there was no one in there, but... well, you'll find out.'

'How did you hear about it?'

Ingram came to a stop and switched off the engine. 'Because a couple of days ago I called every PD in a dozen or more nearby counties and told them to alert us if there were any homicides that matched our MO.'

Ingram took latex gloves from his jacket pocket and gave them to Rachel.

Rachel got out and followed Ingram to where the patrol cars were parked up, putting on the gloves as she went.

'When did you come out here, John?' Rachel asked.

'Earlier, as soon as I got the call.'

'And you didn't come and get me first?'

Ingram turned back to face her. 'You were barely able to string a sentence together. You needed to sleep. I wanted to make sure it was our guy before I came and got you.'

Entering a side door of the building, Ingram was greeted by a uniformed patrol officer.

'Agent Hoffman, this is Officer Lance Buckley.'

'Agent Hoffman,' Buckley said.

'You were first on scene?' Rachel asked.

'Me and my partner, yes. He's inside. We're waiting for forensics and the Weegee.'

'You're waiting for what?'

'Sorry, the crime scene photographer. We call them Weegees, you know, after—'

'I know who Weegee was,' Rachel said.

'I didn't mean to be flippant.'

'It's quite alright, Officer Buckley. I get the gallows humor. Sometimes it's the only thing that keeps things in perspective.'

'This way,' Ingram said to Rachel, and started down the corridor towards the rear of the building.

The room into which Ingram showed Rachel could only have been described as makeshift film studio.

Buckley's partner, Dennis Redvers, looked pale and sick.

The first question he asked was whether or not he could step out.

'Yes, of course,' Rachel said, and Redvers went at a run.

Rachel heard the sound of his retching as it echoed along the corridor behind them.

Using scaffolding, a four-sided frame had been built in the middle of a hangar-sized room. The frame was no more than eight feet in height, the internal dimensions roughly twenty by twenty. Over the frame had been hung sheets of heavy black fabric. On the floor inside the curtained area was a sizeable mattress, lighting equipment, a half dozen or so boxes that appeared to contain clothing of multiple different styles and colors, and to the right – in a plastic washing bowl – was an assortment of sex toys. Against the furthest curtain, seated in chairs beside one another, were two men and a woman. Each of them was naked, hands bound to the arms of their respective chairs, the same polythene bags as had been at the earlier five killings over their heads. In each case, the feet were very badly burned, the blackened flesh twisted and peeling.

Rachel turned and looked at Ingram. His face was ashen.

'If you need to go out, just go,' Rachel said.

'You gonna be okay?'

'Well, they're not likely to attack me, are they?'

Ingram turned and hurried back towards the front of the building.

Careful to disturb nothing, Rachel approached the bodies. From the state of them, she guessed they'd been there a week, perhaps more.

The letter that Ingram had spoken of was there on the floor beneath the chair of the female victim. In the same font as had been used for the *contrapasso* letter, the envelope read:

```
Special Agent Rachel Hoffman
Federal Bureau of Investigation
```

Rachel had to step back, to resist the urge to tear it open and read it. She needed Crime Scene here; she needed photographs, prints; she had to have every potential fragment of evidence maintained with complete integrity.

She closed her eyes and breathed. Why was this being directed at her? Who was driving this relentless violence and horror, and why did they feel this need – this obsession – to have her be the enemy? For that's what it was now – a conflict, a war, a campaign of brutality, as if each of them were on opposing sides. She'd been pulled into the orbit of some great darkness with such force that she knew she would never escape from it without finding the source.

There were sounds from beyond the corridor, and then there were voices, footsteps. John Ingram led the way as forensics and crime-scene details ferried in their lights, their folding tables, their tapes and markers and evidence analysis equipment.

Rachel moved back to the edge of the enclosure.

'You okay?' Ingram asked.

'I want to know what's in the letter.'

'I'm guessing this is porn,' Ingram said. 'The mattress, the cameras, the sex stuff over there.'

Rachel didn't reply.

'You need to get outside?'

'I want the letter.'

Ingram nodded. He spoke to the forensics unit. They had the photographer take his pictures, and then the letter was carefully removed from beneath the chair. Rachel watched as it was carried to one of the tables that had been erected to the left. The envelope had not been sealed, but the flap had been tucked inside.

Opening it, the page inside was carefully and slowly withdrawn. It was a single sheet. Unfolding it and spreading it out, Rachel saw the same all-too-familiar font. It bore no greeting; it was brief and to the point.

'Copy that out,' Rachel said. 'The Italian passage. Get that translated for me, would you?'

Ingram transcribed the words into his notebook.

Rachel knew it would be some hours before there was any hope of ID on the victims. She also had to give crime scene and forensics the time and space to do what was required. There was nothing else for her to do here.

She knew she'd have to call Joy Willis and give her an update. She wanted assistance from the Bureau. Whether it would be forthcoming or not was a different matter, but the mere fact that a personal message had been left for her at the crime scene might be sufficient to warrant this becoming official. Perhaps there was now a significant enough connection between Syracuse, New York and Pennsylvania to qualify it as cross-state. If so, and if Rachel could plead the case adequately, then it would become a federal investigation. That's what she hoped for, and to accomplish that she needed as much weight of evidence behind her as she could gather.

56

The Vaill brothers – Eric and Gerald – and the female vic, Judith Whyte, had been dead for a week.

Tuesday morning, a little before ten, Rachel stood in the theater of the Lehigh County Coroner's Office and listened as the coroner, Ellen Beaumont, gave a brief rundown of her initial findings.

The three cadavers were on adjacent tables. The smell was invasive and sickening.

'The presence of smoke and particles of burned flesh in the mouth, trachea and lungs tells us that the feet were burned before the victims were suffocated,' Beaumont said. 'Suffocation was the cause of death, but – in the case of Gerald – there's a clear indication that his heart gave out.'

'Any idea what was used to burn them?' Rachel asked.

'Not definitive, but it was something that emitted a very high temperature. In some places, the flesh was burned away right to the bone.'

'Like an oxyacetylene torch, perhaps?'

'Something of that nature, yes.'

'And what else can you tell me?'

'Not a great deal at this stage. Tox reports indicate alcohol, cocaine, barbiturates, but all in relatively small quantities. That's for all three of them. Judith had bruising in the pelvic and vaginal area, the anal passage too.' Beaumont looked up at Rachel. 'Rough sex kind of bruising.'

'From what we know, the place where they were found was used to make porn films,' Rachel said.

'Yes,' Beaumont replied. 'Your detective told me as much. He also said that this was possibly connected to other recent killings.'

'That's the direction we're going in.'

'Ritualistic stuff, right?'

'As good a word as any.'

'I did the autopsies on Bernard Clarke and the Warner girl,' Beaumont said. 'How many more do you have?'

'These three make it eight in the past five or six weeks.'

'That's some spree. And it's a federal case now?'

Rachel smiled wryly. 'By invitation, yes.'

Beaumont raised her eyebrows.

'It's a long story. There were killings back in Syracuse and New York when I was a cop. The hypothesis now is that the perps back then were not working alone. That's substantiated by the fact that it seems very unlikely that these recent victims would have willingly been tied up and tortured.'

'Indeed,' Beaumont said.

'Can you send all your reports over to Bethlehem PD when you're done? Mark them for the attention of me or Detective Ingram.'

'Of course, yes. I'll get it finished today.'

When Rachel got back, Ingram told her that he had a translation for the letter.

'The weapons of divine justice are blunted by the confession and sorrow of the offender.'

'That's going to come directly from the book,' Rachel said. 'I need to go talk to my supervisor. While I'm gone, see if you can track down a guy called Allan – that's A-L-L-A-N – Cambridge. He was up at Syracuse University. My partner consulted him on this back in '75. He might still be there. If not, find out how we can get hold of him.'

'Sure thing,' Ingram said.

'And chase up crime scene photos, full IDs on the vics, everything you can. Beaumont is sending over autopsy reports later today. Keep an eye out for them.'

Before she left Bethlehem, Rachel called the Allentown Bureau office. Willis was unavailable, but Rachel left a message that she was on the way and needed to speak with her.

On the twenty-minute drive, Rachel rehearsed her proposal to Willis. She had to be specific about what she was asking for – permission to take the case as an official assignment, at least one additional agent, if not two or three, and full access to the physical and informational resources of the Bureau. She would need everything related to the Marshall and Wagner cases brought to Allentown from Syracuse and New York, and that would mean approval from an authority above Willis. It would also mean that Ingram would be sidelined along with the other assigned detectives from Reading and Lancaster, none of whom she'd had time to meet. She would need a full review of the autopsies with secondary opinions from the Bureau's own people. It was a lot to request, and it would require a significant allocation from the budget. Willis, though a very competent investigator herself, was a bureaucrat. Her strengths lay in administration and delegation. She was not personally connected to this; she had not lost a partner; she was not the one who was being taunted and challenged by Dante.

The last vestiges of doubt regarding the presence of a second perpetrator in Syracuse and New York were now just mere shadows. Rachel did not believe that Marshall and Wagner had committed suicide. She believed that whoever was behind this had encouraged, manipulated, engineered and orchestrated the actions of both men, and – once they had served their purpose – they had been eliminated from the game. She used the word *game* advisedly, for that's what it seemed to be. A game. A contest. A battle of opposing intentions and rationales. Here was someone who had selected her as his rival in some grand decade-long chess game where each of the victims were pawns, where Marshall and Wagner were rooks or knights, all too easily sacrificed for some other counter-move or veiled maneuver that would highlight the opponent's weakest line of defense and bring about their defeat.

Rachel had been outwitted and outclassed twice before. She had no intention of allowing it to happen again. There was too much at stake – psychologically, emotionally, personally, professionally – and to lose again would undermine the very foundations of everything she'd been striving for in her life. If she lost a third time, perhaps she would lose herself. It would certainly serve to undermine her self-belief, and if that disappeared, then her own identity would disappear with it. Without her career, what did she have? She had nothing – no family, no home, no love in her life, no future. Everything had been sacrificed in the name of her vocation, and that vocation drove her relentlessly to seek the truth.

There was an abyss, and gazing down into it she understood not only its depth, but the impossibility of ever climbing out again.

She could not fall, and thus she could not fail.

57

'This situation presents me with a number of considerable obstacles,' Willis said. 'The primary one being the simple fact that this isn't, as far as I can see, a matter for this office.'

'Except if my hypothesis is correct and all three cases are connected.'

'In which case it would come under the remit of the National Center for the Analysis of Violent Crime, of which you are not an officer. And besides, that Center is a very new addition to the Bureau's portfolio of units, and they are based out of Quantico. That's Virginia, not Pennsylvania.'

'But they serve nationwide,' Rachel said.

Willis took a deep breath and closed her eyes for just a moment.

'My real concern is that this has become a personal issue for you.'

'Not through my own choice,' Rachel said. 'The perp left a letter for me. It was the same back in New York five years ago.'

'I'm not going to get in a verbal battle with you, Rachel.'

'But if I'm right, then between the schoolteacher in Ulysses in February 1975 and the last three here in Bethlehem, I have a killer who is responsible for the deaths of seventeen people. And those are the ones we know about.'

'But the perpetrators of the murders in Syracuse and New York were both identified and they're both dead.'

'Perpetrators who didn't work alone.'

'Possibly.'

'I'd say definitely.'

'Definite requires evidence, proof, facts. You have a theory, and my worry is that you are so emotionally involved that you're trying to crowbar what you're seeing into a preconceived hypothesis.'

'I don't believe I am.'

'I know you don't believe it, Rachel, but what you believe and what actually is might not be the same thing.'

'And the letter?'

'The people who commit crimes are sometimes just as bright, if not brighter, than those who investigate them. There are tens, if not hundreds of thousands of murders and disappearances that go unsolved each year. What does that tell us? It tells us that there is such a thing as the perfect murder. Your earlier cases are in the public domain. Information on who was involved, whether it was police or federal authorities, can be accessed in any newspaper archive in the country. Your assumption that the New York case was a Syracuse copycat might have been correct. This may be yet another in the same vein. You are tying things together that may have no business being tied.'

'So you're declining my request for assistance on this?'

'I've not said that.'

'So what are you—'

'I am thinking about sitting in front of a budget review board and explaining why I approved what you're asking of me.'

'Then at least give me one more person. Let me collate everything from the last ten years. We can request everything on Marshall and Wagner, we can go through all of it again and see what might have been missed. I have distance now. I have a greater degree of objectivity. Let me put what I know to use and see if I can substantiate my theory adequately to get NCAVC on board.'

'And if you did get them on board, would you let them take over?'

'If that's what was asked of me, yes.'

Willis looked at Rachel. She maintained that gaze as if trying to read Rachel's thoughts.

Rachel looked back at her implacably.

'How is Detective Ingram?'

'What do you mean, how is he?'

'Is he competent, able?'

'He certainly seems so, yes.'

'And you've not yet had an opportunity to speak with the assigned detectives from Reading or Lancaster?'

'No, not yet.'

'Get me the names and numbers of the respective Captains of each precinct. Let me make some calls.'

'What are you thinking?'

Willis smiled. 'Just get me the names and numbers, Rachel.'

Rachel did as she was instructed and then she drove back to Bethlehem.

Ingram was in the office.

'I found the Cambridge guy,' he said. 'He's no longer at the university, but I've got his home number.'

It had been ten years since Cambridge had spoken to Michael Ridgway, but he remembered him without prompting.

'I read what happened,' Cambridge said. 'An absolute tragedy. I am so sorry.'

When she asked Cambridge about the Purgatory section of *The Divine Comedy*, he couldn't conceal his surprise.

'This surely can't be the same case,' he said.

'Not the same, but we think it's connected.'

'And did you ever read the book?'

'I did, yes. I have to be honest and say some of it—'

'It's a challenging work,' Cambridge said, 'and open to a great deal of individual interpretation.'

'I wanted to talk to you about Purgatory. As far as I remember,

Dante and Virgil leave Inferno and they arrive at the island. There's the mountain, and then there's an angel that arrives in a boat—'

'Yes, exactly so. The penitent souls are ferried to Mount Purgatory by an angel. These souls will climb Mount Purgatory with Dante. There's the seven stages of the mountain, terraces if you will, and, as I'm sure you remember, they each represent one of the seven roots of sinfulness. To be even more specific, each of these sins is a distortion of love—'

'Of love?' Rachel asked.

'Gluttony, love of food and drink. Avarice, love of wealth or property. Lust, love of the flesh. You get the idea?'

'Right, right.'

'Anyway, on they go. Dante and Virgil. And on each terrace they find penitent souls who are enduring punishment for their sins. The Prideful are forced to carry heavy weights on their backs. They are permanently hunched over, almost as if the burden they're carrying is to prevent them from standing proudly, you know? Dante himself has to remain in this position throughout his passage along the first terrace.'

Rachel started making notes. As Cambridge spoke, more and more of what she remembered came to mind.

'Envy. They have their eyelids sewn shut. Wrath. They are blinded by a thick, black smoke. Those guilty of sloth are forced to run without rest. The avaricious are laid face-down on the ground, their hands and feet bound behind their backs.'

With each punishment that Cambridge detailed, Rachel saw how these symbolic penalties had been exacted on the most recent victims.

'Gluttony is next, and here the penitent endures agonizing thirst and hunger. Lastly, comes lust, and they are forced to walk in flames.'

Rachel saw the burned feet of the three bodies in the old factory.

'And then Dante himself has to walk through a wall of fire as a last act before he can ascend to Heaven.'

'Paradiso.'

'Precisely,' Cambridge said.

'I can't tell you how much I appreciate your time, Professor,' Rachel said. 'You've been an immense help.'

'Oh, think nothing of it, my dear,' Cambridge said. 'Always happy to help. Do let me know if there's anything I can do in the future, okay?'

'Yes, of course, and thank you again.'

It was less than fifteen minutes before a call came through from the desk.

It was Joy Willis.

'We're going to agree on a compromise,' she said. 'I've spoken with the relevant departments. You and Detective Ingram will be joined by the assigned detectives from Reading and Lancaster. I can't send anyone else from here. This will be a Police and Bureau cooperation. You will have to work out of the Bethlehem Department. In theory, you will oversee it, but how that will work out in practice I don't know. You'll have to reconcile any issues you might run into with the individuals in question. You've got a month, Rachel. If you don't have this concluded, then I'm pulling you back. And I need a full report on progress at the end of each week. Not a novel, and certainly no more opinions and hypotheses. Just a clear and succinct outline of the progress – or not – that you're making with this investigation.'

'Thank you,' Rachel said. 'I really appreciate your support on this.'

'Remember that you're no longer a police officer, Agent Hoffman,' Willis added. 'You're a federal officer and a representative of this Bureau. Don't make waves, don't put peoples' noses out of joint, and do not overstep your remit. You're there in an advisory and coordination capacity, and that's how you should manage it. Is that understood?'

'Completely, sir.'

'I expect your first report by lunchtime on Friday, and every Friday thereafter.'

Rachel was about to say something, but Willis hung up.

She looked over at Ingram. 'I need you to call my old precinct in Syracuse and the New York 114th. We need everything they've got on the Marshall and Wagner cases, and we need it couriered here express.'

58

The first meeting of what would later become known as the *Dante Unit* took place in Bethlehem PD's conference room just before noon on Wednesday the 13th.

The detective from Reading, Diane Brookins, was a heavy-set, middle-aged woman who looked more like a school principal than a seasoned veteran. Her appearance belied the fact that she already had more than twenty years of service behind her.

Clifford Buchanan – the detective from Lancaster – was rail-thin, bespectacled and wore his thinning hair in a center parting. He would prove himself to be a fastidious organizer with a remarkable ability to retain information.

The requested files had arrived from Syracuse, but they were still waiting on those from the 114th. Ingram was chasing up everything he could find on Judith Whyte and the Vaill brothers so that family, friends, neighbors and known associates could be canvassed. Brookins and Buchanan had brought with them all documentation relating to their ongoing Carole Sitkoff and Julian McCullan investigations.

After introducing herself, Rachel summarized her analysis of the overall situation. There were questions from Brookins and Buchanan, and Rachel did her very best to answer them as comprehensively as she could.

When she was done, Brookins was the first to respond.

'So what you're saying is that we're looking for two people. That's my understanding. You've got whoever's doing the actual killing, and then you've got a second person who's ... I mean, what would you even call it? The instigator?'

'Instigator is as good a term as any,' Rachel said.

'And the reason that this wasn't pursued in Syracuse or New York was because it's only now become evident that there may be a second person involved.'

'It's only now become something I am personally certain of,' Rachel replied.

'And, to date, there was no substantive link between the first perp ... Marshall, right?'

'Robert Leonard Marshall, yes.'

'There was no link between him and the people he killed, and similarly, there was no personal link between Wagner and his victims.'

'None that were identified at the time.'

Buchanan raised his hand.

Rachel smiled. 'We're not in class, Detective Buchanan. No need to do that.'

'I have a question if that's okay, Agent Hoffman?'

'Yes, of course,' Rachel said. 'And just to make it clear, we're working on this together. This is a collaborative effort. The Bureau doesn't have any kind of jurisdictional authority. We're the ones who are going to bring it to a conclusion, and we'll only do that if we're on exactly the same terms. So, your question, Detective Buchanan?'

'I want to ask why.'

'Why is this person doing this?'

'I get that we don't actually know,' Buchanan said, 'but it'd be worth our while to ask this question. Potential motives, right? We know the method, though they're different in each case, and the opportunities for the perpetrators to do this are something that they themselves create. But we need to be looking at the motivation behind it.'

'Do crazy people need an identifiable motive?' Brookins asked. 'Isn't the fact that they're crazy enough of a reason?'

'Whether it's enough of a reason isn't what I'm asking,' Buchanan said. 'I'm asking because an understanding of why would give us some idea of the kind of person we're dealing with. If we had that, we can at least narrow the field.'

'It's a very good point,' Rachel said, 'However, I don't know that we'll ever really understand what drives a person to do these things until we get it from their own lips.'

'Do you think it's personal, Agent Hoffman?' Buchanan asked. 'Against me?'

'Against you, yes. This is three separate cases. Each time you've been involved. Granted, the first time was indirect. You happened to be in that particular location when the Lassiter girl was found. But there's been an exchange, right? There have been letters. It almost seems as if every effort has been made to ensure you're investigating this. What 'I'd be asking is whether or not it might be someone I know. Or, perhaps, someone who knows me.'

'I can only speculate as to why he seems intent on dragging me into this,' Rachel said. The line of questioning was making her uncomfortable, not only because she was determined to appear as in-control and professional as possible, but because there was a seed of doubt in her own mind. She'd asked herself the same questions before, and there had been no answer.

'There has never been anything to suggest that it's someone that I've been directly associated with,' Rachel said.

'But we can't rule it out, can we?' Buchanan asked.

'I think it's safe to say that we can't rule anything out.'

Buchanan remained silent for a moment. He looked at Ingram, then at Brookins, then back to Rachel.

'I think our efforts should be directed towards the perpetrator, not the instigator,' Buchanan said. 'If – and it's a significant *if* – there is someone manipulating others to do these things, then that person has managed to stay off the radar for ten years. I'm thinking that the only way to get to that person is through the one he's directing. Find the actual killer, get them alive, and we have a hope. It also means that we're not trying to undertake two separate investigations at the same time.'

'So you think we shouldn't even look at the earlier cases from Syracuse and New York?' Brookins asked.

'I think we should look at them from the viewpoint of identifying whether there's any recurring evidence,' Buchanan replied. 'But beyond that, no, I think we need to focus on what's happening right here and now.'

'So where would you start?' Rachel asked.

'We've got five crime scenes, five separate killings. Granted, one of them was two people, another was three, but it's still five incidents. Judith Whyte and the Vaill brothers was the most recent. As we all know, the longer you leave it, the more things people forget. It's already been more than a week since they were murdered, and that's unfortunate, but we can't change that. They knew people, they spoke to people. Maybe they were abducted, but that seems very unlikely. One person perhaps, but not three. That means they were already there. That tells us that whoever carried out those killings knew the location, perhaps had it under surveillance, maybe had already been in there and decided that this was where they were going to kill them. Tying up three people, burning their feet like that. That was something you'd want to do without being disturbed. We work on building up as comprehensive and thorough a picture as we can of everything that happened in and around that warehouse and the prior movements of the victims. I suggest that Detective Brookins and I start doing the legwork on everyone that these people knew. We make as detailed a list as possible of family members, friends, associates, places they frequented, and then we split them up and start asking questions.'

'Detective Brookins?' Rachel asked.

'I don't have a better suggestion. I'm ready to get to work.'

59

Later that afternoon, Buchanan and Brookins out of the office, the final crime scene reports and evidence bags came in from the Vaill–Whyte killings.

As Rachel had anticipated, there were no prints, not even partial, on the polythene bags or the duct tape that had been used to suffocate the victims. The prints on the chairs themselves were those of the Vaill brothers and Judith Whyte. Everything else was clean.

It was while they were looking through the photographs that there was mention of a key. It had been found in the stomach of Gerald Vaill.

In that moment, Rachel experienced that same sense of being manipulated. The Marshall case had surrendered because of a palm print on a phone booth. The Wagner case had resolved after she and Maurice Quinn had identified the ribbon in New York's Garment District. Yes, she had devoted endless hours to each case, but when she read about the key, she considered the very real possibility that the leads in Syracuse and New York had been given to her. It had been intentional. It had been part of the game.

Rachel said as much to Ingram.

Ingram went through the evidence bags and located it. It was small – definitely not for a door or a garage. Perhaps a padlock? That it had spent a week inside someone's gut meant that there was nothing material on it that could assist in identifying who had put it there. There was no make, but there was a number: 187.

'Locker? Security deposit box, maybe?' Ingram suggested.

'We need to find out,' Rachel said. 'Is there a locksmith you guys use here?'

'I'll check,' Ingram said and headed out to the bullpen.

Rachel placed the key on the desk ahead of her. She stared at it. She was transfixed. The past ten years of her life came up to meet her like a tidal wave. Images surfaced that she didn't want to remember. Time and again, she kept coming back to that Sunday in July of 1975 when she'd found Michael Ridgway. The smell. That coppery, earthy smell. All the emotions that accompanied that scene – horror, disbelief, heartbreak, a profound sense of having failed a colleague, a friend – were right there beneath the surface. It was quicksand. The more she thought about it, the more it dragged her in.

'We have someone,' Ingram said.

Rachel looked up suddenly. She hadn't even heard Ingram come back into the room.

'It's just a few blocks over.'

Rachel didn't say anything. She took her jacket from the back of the chair and put it on. She followed Ingram out of the room.

The locksmith – Vernon Logue – was an independent in a small place off Grant Street.

'The number could be a model number, but – as you say – it could be the number of a locker or a small storage container. I doubt very much that it's for a security deposit box. It's far too insubstantial. This is mass-produced, costs nothing, and whatever lock it's for could be picked in seconds.'

'Can you cut a few of them for me?' Rachel asked. 'Say ten?'

'Sure I can,' Logue said. 'You want them now?'

'If that's possible, yes.'

Logue went to work.

'What are you thinking?' Ingram asked.

'Every school, storage facility, health and fitness club. Every bus station, every maildrop. Anywhere that has lockers. We need as many patrol officers as we can muster to get out there and find what this opens.'

'Jesus, that's—'

'That's what we need to do, John. It was in Vaill's stomach. It was there for a reason.'

'You want me to pull Brookins and Buchanan back?'

'No, let them do what they're doing. We need to get the patrols onto this.'

'I'll call the Lieutenant,' Ingram said. He leaned over the counter. 'Mr. Logue? I need to use your phone, okay?'

In Bethlehem alone, Rachel and John Ingram made a list of more than sixty potential locations. If they covered the entire Lehigh Valley region, there would be hundreds. Add into the equation Reading and Lancaster and their respective counties, and it would likely run into thousands. Ingram's lieutenant was more reconciled than enthusiastic. He understood what was needed, but he said he couldn't afford for it to overtake the day-to-day duties and functions of his patrol officers. Rachel accepted what she was given.

She and Ingram divided the list and briefed the officers who'd be doing the legwork. Additionally, they would each work on their own lists. Rachel requisitioned an unmarked car from the PD garage. It was already past 4.00. Places would be closing.

Leaving the underground garage and pulling out into the street, Rachel knew she was heading back into a spider's web. She was right on the outer edges. She was feeling its pull and pulling back from it. Such a response would only serve to snare her more tightly, but it was instinctive. Nevertheless, she could not allow a revenge impulse to cloud her objectivity. Emotion clouded clarity more rapidly and thoroughly than anything else. The only motivation was ending a killing spree that had already taken seventeen lives. Whether the victims had committed fraud or theft, whether they'd inflicted violence upon others, sold drugs to kids or made porn films didn't matter. No single individual could elect themselves judge, jury and executioner. If she had no faith in law enforcement and the judicial system, then everything she'd done since joining the police would be a lie.

Once again, she knew that Carl would understand. He was a bright and able man, and the urge to talk to him was difficult to resist. But she had been given her marching orders, and she had to obey them.

Rachel drove. She cleared her mind. She had a lot of work to get done, the others too, and the work had to take priority over everything else.

60

Lauren was aware of the guy at the end of the bar. He didn't look up, definitely didn't make himself obvious, but she knew he was watching her. She had that sense, that sixth sense. But then, didn't she like to be looked at? Wasn't the feeling of being the center of attention the most addictive drug of all? He was just a guy. Nothing special, nothing out of the ordinary. He had a beer, and when he was done with it he ordered another one. He'd smiled and said 'Thank you' to the barkeep.

It was after her second drink that he came over. Even as he approached her, Lauren knew it would be lame. But then he smiled and sat down. He didn't offer to buy her a drink. He didn't ask her name. He just said, 'Don't you get tired of it?'

Lauren feigned surprise. She knew exactly what he was talking about.

'Tired of what?'

'The bullshit. The corny lines these guys come out with. The way they treat this place like it's some sort of meat market.'

Right beside her then, Lauren saw him clearly. He was maybe in his mid-forties, a strong face, deep-set eyes. He had on jeans and a khaki combat jacket, beneath it a dark shirt. He didn't seem to be trying at all. Maybe he had no intention of trying.

'If I sit here they won't bother you,' he said. 'You can enjoy your drink in peace.'

'Maybe I don't want to enjoy my drink in peace,' Lauren said.

He looked sideways at her without turning his head.

'Is it loneliness?' he asked.

'What?'

'What you're doing here. Coming out to a place like this on your own.'

'Loneliness? I'm not lonely.'

He smiled. It was friendly, sincere. 'I'm sorry,' he said. 'I didn't mean to sound that aggressive. I guess I'm just a little puzzled by your behavior.'

'My behavior?'

'Maybe behavior is the wrong word. Your attitude.'

'And what might my attitude be?' Lauren asked, glancing towards the barkeep, then back to the door where a security guy stood sentinel. If she needed help, she just had to say so.

'It's superficial,' the man said. 'You wear this face for the world, but it's not your face, is it? I mean, what is it that you do?'

'I don't think that's any of your business.'

'Hey, I'm just making small talk. I'll leave soon, don't worry. I'm just interested, that's all.'

'I'm a cosmetician.'

'You do peoples' make-up.'

'Yes, that's right.'

'So you put on your own mask and then you help others put their masks on.'

'Okay,' Lauren said. 'You're just being weird now. I'm really beginning to feel uncomfortable, mister. I'd like you to leave me alone.'

'Because you're shallow and you look down on people, and you somehow have this idea that you have a greater worth than these guys.' The man looked back around the bar. 'And when they come to talk to you, you make it your business to put them in their place, to make them feel insignificant and worthless.'

'You need to fuck off,' she said. 'You need to fuck off right the fuck now.'

'And there she is,' the man said. 'That's a nasty mouth, my

dear. There's cruelty there. I can see it in your eyes. You think you're a good person, a kind person, but you're a bitch, aren't you?'

Lauren leaned forward to get the barkeep's attention.

The man reached out and closed his hand on her forearm.

He looked at her – dead-straight, his eyes focused, intense – and he said, 'I'm leaving.'

He slid off the barstool. He buttoned his jacket. He took his time, all the while maintaining that stare.

'Take care, Lauren,' he said, and then he walked away.

It was only later, as she was leaving, that Lauren realized she'd never told him her name.

She took a cab, tried her best to shake off that sense of having been threatened, somehow violated. He'd touched her once, just once, but she could still feel the presence of his hand on her forearm.

Once home, Lauren took a shower. She was not in the habit of taking a shower before bed, but she felt... she didn't even know how she felt. As if she'd been infected by something.

The entire exchange in the bar had made her feel anxious. He was an asshole, no doubt about it. He'd spoken to her with one intention and one intention alone: to make her feel bad about herself. Well, fuck him. Who the fuck was he? What did he do that was so goddamned important? What kind of person just undermines people like that? If he was so fucking special and superior, what was he doing dressed in cheap, shitty clothes in a bar by himself?

And how the fuck did he know her name? He must have overheard her telling someone. There had been a guy earlier in the evening. They'd made small talk. He'd asked her name and she'd told him. After a while, she realized the guy was a loser. He was an accountant, for Christ's sake. A fucking accountant. And there was an indent on his ring finger. Either he'd taken it off for the hope of a one-night stand, or he was crawling his way through a divorce. Either which way, she had ditched him.

That weirdo must've heard her. That's how he'd known her name.

When Lauren went to check that the front door was locked, he came out of nowhere.

He grabbed her from behind, one hand over her mouth, the other gripping the back of her neck with such strength that she almost blacked out.

She went down to her knees. She hit the ground with enough impact to bring tears to her eyes. She screamed, but the sound was trapped inside her throat.

Her eyes wide, horror escalating to fever-pitch within seconds, she knew who it was before she saw his face. She was terrified, more terrified than she'd ever been in her life.

She couldn't breathe, couldn't think, couldn't speak. He was going to rape her. That's what he was going to do. He was going to rape her right there in the front hallway of her apartment.

He forced her down until the side of her face was on the floor. For a moment he relaxed the hand over her mouth. She screamed. He clamped his hand even tighter, blocking her nose. She couldn't breathe. She wrestled. He put his knee in the small of her back and leaned down until his face was alongside her own.

'No,' he said. 'Not a sound. Another sound and it ends right here.'

He pulled her to her feet and walked her through to the living room. Still behind her, he sat her in a chair.

'Are we going to do as we're told, Lauren?' he asked.

She nodded instinctively.

'Good, good.'

Slowly, he released the hand over her mouth. She gasped for air, coughing, choking, her chest heaving as she tried to get as much oxygen into her lungs as possible.

That's when he said, 'You shouldn't be afraid, Lauren.'

He spoke gently, as if he was soothing a troubled child. He

323

leaned close to her, brushing her hair from over her ear. And then he said it again – a whisper, a breath – 'You shouldn't be afraid.'

And Lauren was trying desperately to cry, to sob, to plead out her heart, to get him to understand that she was sorry, so very, very sorry, for whatever it was she'd done to make him do this to her. But he'd told her not to cry, warned her what would happen if she did, because he couldn't bear it. It hurt his mind, he said. It hurt his mind deep inside, and if she hurt him like that then he would have to hurt her back. Hurt her more. More than she could imagine.

Stepping around from behind her, he stood for a moment. And then he knelt down, took her hands in his, and looked at her for the longest time.

He was smiling, but it wasn't warm or friendly. It was a smile of bemusement, as if there was a question he had that he hadn't yet voiced.

'Pride is a sin,' he said. 'You know what pride is, don't you, Lauren?'

She didn't respond.

'Lauren?'

'Y-yes. Yes, I know what it is.'

'Then tell me.'

'I-It's … it's when you've done something good … when you've done something—'

He shook his head slowly.

'No, my dear, it's not. Not the pride we're talking about. Do you want to try again?'

Her eyes wide, her breath short and rapid, she couldn't think, couldn't put words together. Everything was moving – the walls, the floor, the face in front of her. She felt the seat grow wet beneath her and she knew she'd pissed herself.

'An inordinate opinion of your own importance. A feeling that you're entitled to special treatment. A sense of superiority.

A sense of self-worth that is not justified. That's the pride we're talking about, Lauren.'

'I-I'm s-sorry,' she blurted. 'I-I'm really s-sorry.'

'For what?' he asked.

'For wha-whatever I-I d-did to up-upset you—'

'Oh, I'm not upset, my dear,' he said. His voice was measured and matter-of-fact.

His expression was almost sympathetic. She felt like a child that was being given bad news – the words used in such a way as to soften the blow.

'W-what d-do you w-want?' she asked.

'What do I want? I want you to understand.'

'I-I understand,' she said.

The man frowned. 'You understand? I haven't even told you what I want you to understand.'

'Th-then tell m-me,' Lauren said. Everything was falling apart. Everything was in pieces. She didn't want to look at him, but she couldn't look away.

'I want you to understand why what happens next is necessary.'

'N-necessary?'

He nodded. 'Necessary.'

'Wh-what's go-going to ha-happen?'

He moved fast. His hand around her throat. She was on her feet. He was behind her then, pushing her towards the bedroom. She stumbled, but he held her up. He was going to hurt her – she knew that much – but maybe that's all he would do. Maybe he wouldn't rape her. Maybe he wouldn't kill her. She didn't want to die. She didn't deserve to die.

He pushed her face down on her bed. He was going to tear her clothes now. That's what he was going to do. But he didn't. He removed each item slowly, carefully, even took the time to fold them neatly and place them on a chair. He tied her hands together behind her back. Where did the rope come from? Then he was tying her ankles together. She was face down, struggling to breathe, incapable of making a sound.

She felt a sudden wrenching pain as he looped the rope from ankles to wrists and pulled it taut. Her back arched, every vertebrae in her spine resisting, every muscle in her torso stretched to its limit. She tried to scream, but he pushed her face down into the bedding.

And then there was something on her back. She felt its cold weight. What was he doing? What was happening to her? She heard the sound then – a familiar sound – as the pressure increased. He was using weights. Where had they come from? From her barbells?

She tried to turn sideways, tried to relieve the pressure that was being brought to bear upon her. She opened her eyes.

His face was right there.

Lifting her head a fraction, he tugged a clear plastic bag down over her forehead, her eyes, her nose, her mouth. And then he was tying something around her neck and she gasped and heaved and the condensation of her breath on the inside of the bag began to obscure her view. She could barely see him. He was growing more distant. She couldn't move. The pain in her body was immense. The weight on her back now seemed like the weight of the world.

Every breath was desperate. Her throat and chest were like someone had lit a fire deep inside her. Her eyes were coming out of her face. That's how it felt. And then the pain increased as he pulled the ropes even tighter. Her spine bowed. She felt something shift and crack. He kept on going, inching her wrists and ankles ever closer until she felt her arms would pull free of her shoulders.

Everything grew faint and dark. Soon there was nothing but darkness. She couldn't see. Her ears were filled with the sound of rushing water, like a storm raging through her head. There was no air, none at all, and she felt the plastic pulled tight like a second skin against her face.

He leaned close. She barely sensed him, barely heard him, but the last words he uttered somehow made it through to whatever remained of her consciousness.

'I know you want to repent, Lauren,' he whispered, his voice like a distant echo from some faraway place. 'So repent.'

He stood up, looked down at her, and gave her that same patient smile.

'Adieu, my dear. I commend you into the hands of God.'

61

A little before 3.00, afternoon of Friday, November 15th, Rachel received a message from John Ingram.

'It looks like we might have it,' he said.

She drove back to the office, was there by half past.

Entering the conference room, all three of them – Ingram, Brookins and Buchanan – were present, and there was a fourth, a uniformed patrol officer.

'This is Officer Meyer,' Ingram said. 'He and his partner were checking schools.'

'Yes, yes, okay, but what have you got?' Rachel asked. 'Did you find something?'

'We think so, yes,' Meyer said. 'To be honest, it's been a hell of a thing because, you know, the schools are closed and everything.'

Rachel raised her eyebrows expectantly.

'Yes, sorry,' Meyer said. 'St. Jude Elementary. It's over near the city library. We think the key belongs to a locker there.'

'You think?' Rachel asked. 'Or you know?'

'Well, it opened a locker,' Meyer said. 'Number 187.'

'And who did it belong to?' Rachel asked.

'I don't think who it belongs to is as important as what we found inside.'

Ingram, sensing Rachel's growing frustration, said, 'There was a copy of the book.' Ingram nodded towards the table to the left. There, secure in a polythene evidence bag, was a copy of *The Divine Comedy*.

Rachel's disbelief was written large in her eyes.

'And there was a bookmark,' Ingram added. 'A business card. It was placed right at the end of the Purgatory section.'

Rachel picked up a second evidence bag. A neat, professional card – deep pink lettering on a white background – said *World of Beauty* with an address and a phone number.

'A beauty salon?' Rachel asked.

'Yes,' Ingram said. 'Here in Bethlehem.'

Rachel turned to Meyer. 'You and your partner go back to the school. Do whatever's necessary to get a list of every teacher, even the ones who cover for sickness and vacations. I need information on maintenance staff, janitors, delivery people, materials suppliers, outside electricians, plumbers, anyone that has access to the school or its grounds, okay?'

'Okay,' Meyer replied.

'So go,' she said. 'Now!'

Meyer, flustered, hurried from the room.

'And we're going to this salon,' Rachel said.

There was a moment's hesitation.

'What the fuck, people! What are you waiting for?'

She turned on Ingram.

'You could have given me the address and I could've met you there! Jesus Christ almighty, let's show some fucking initiative here!'

Rachel turned back towards the door. Reaching it, she realized that only Ingram was following her.

'Now, for fuck's sake! Everyone!'

World of Beauty was a small storefront that offered beauty treatments – hair, nails, cosmetic work. It also stocked skincare items and a general assortment of feminine hygiene products.

The owner and manager, Linda DiMaggio, was completely taken aback by the sudden arrival of a federal agent and three PD detectives.

She had only one customer, an elderly woman.

Diane Brookins calmed the customer while Rachel took Linda aside. Uncertain of the relevance of the store in the investigation, all Rachel could think to ask in that moment was whether or not anything out of the ordinary had taken place in the past few days.

'Out of the ordinary, like what?' Linda asked. 'Am I in trouble? Am I gonna get arrested?'

'No, no, not at all,' Rachel said. 'We're conducting an investigation, and we think that the person we're looking for might have had some contact with you, maybe one of your employees, or even been to the premises.'

'I have contact with a lot of people,' Linda said. 'Can't you be more specific?'

'It would be a man,' Rachel said.

'Well, the only men that ever come here are customers' husbands or boyfriends. As for whether or not anyone's spoken to Lauren, you'd have to ask her. However, fucking pain-in-the-ass didn't show up yesterday and she hasn't shown up today. People just don't seem to want to do a good honest day's work these days.'

'Lauren,' Rachel said. 'Lauren what?'

'Trent. Lauren Trent. She's a beautician. Well, when she bothers to show up she's a beautician, anyway.'

'And she's not been in for two days?'

'No. Why? Do you think something's happened to her?'

'We're just asking questions right now, Linda. I need you to give me her address so I can go talk to her, okay?'

'Er, yes. Yes, of course. She doesn't live so far from here. I'll get it for you.'

Linda did as she was asked. Ingram looked at the address.

'I know where that is,' he said. 'It's no more than five or six miles.'

Rachel told Brookins and Buchanan to stay at the store. She

needed a list of every customer in the past month. She also wanted names, addresses and phone numbers for every supplier. She told them to search the back of the building, the alleyway behind, to look for anything out-of-place, anything that might give some indication as to why the business card had been left in a school locker.

Rachel left, Ingram right behind her.

'Lights and siren,' Rachel said as Ingram pulled away from the kerb.

They headed into the late afternoon traffic, Rachel's heart in her mouth. She sensed what they would find, and she knew they were already too late.

62

Saturday morning – the 16th.

Ellen Beaumont stood quietly as Rachel surveyed the body of Lauren Trent.

Rachel's outward appearance gave away little. Her inner world was on fire – a multiple vehicle pile-up of thoughts, emotions, feelings, and in among all of it was a sense of dismay and disbelief, a profound awareness – justified or otherwise – that she had failed this woman. She could have done more, worked harder, demanded more resources, acted faster. But she hadn't, and now this young, pretty twenty-three-year-old was dead. She was reminded so clearly of Caroline Lassiter, and it hurt her to the core.

Buchanan and Brookins were over at the girl's apartment with forensics and crime scene. Buchanan had already called to let her know that the word *Superbia* had been scratched into the wall behind Lauren Trent's headboard. This was their 'pride' killing. Rachel felt sure they'd find nothing else of consequence.

Ingram had started sifting through every name on the list from the school, crosschecking for criminal records, and any direct or indirect connection to Lauren Trent.

Each aspect of this had been orchestrated to draw her in ever more claustrophobically until she felt the very edges of her mind and emotions pulling at the seams. She didn't know how much longer she could keep it together.

'You look exhausted,' Beaumont said.

'I am exhausted.'

'Are you sleeping? At all?'

'Some,' Rachel replied.

'You know, there's a limit to how much—'

'Tell me about her.'

'Lauren Trent. Twenty-three years old. Alcohol, not excessive. No drugs. Looks like she takes care of herself. There was exercise equipment in her apartment. The weights—'

'That were placed on her back. I know, I saw the photos.'

'They were her own. They had some significance, right?'

'The penalty for pride is to carry heavy weights on your back.'

'But she was suffocated like the others,' Beaumont said. 'That was the cause of death. Estimate between Wednesday midnight and three or four on Thursday morning.'

'Did you find anything inside her?'

'Such as?'

'Christ, I don't know,' Rachel said. 'Gerald Vaill had a fucking key in his stomach.'

'No,' Beaumont said. 'There was nothing like that here.'

'So what else can you tell me?'

'There isn't a great deal to tell. Abrasions on the knees, bruising to the back of the neck, nothing to indicate any great degree of physical force was employed. Incidental injuries to being restrained, held down, tied up.'

Rachel wanted to speak to crime scene and forensics. She wanted to know if there was anything about the way Lauren Trent had been murdered that would suggest more than one person was present. That was a question that would not be answered here.

'Aside from that, I don't know there's anything else I can tell you,' Beaumont said.

'Okay.'

'I'm actually concerned about you, Agent Hoffman,' Beaumont said. 'I understand that you're under an enormous amount of pressure, but physical exhaustion can only serve to exaggerate whatever stress you must be experiencing. They don't use sleep deprivation as torture for no reason.'

'We're close,' Rachel said. 'I can feel it. I can't stop now. And while this is going on, I couldn't sleep anyway.'

'Delegate,' Beaumont said. 'Delegate some of this responsibility, why don't you? I mean, the Police Department must have a number of very capable and competent detectives—'

'This is mine,' Rachel said. '*He* is mine. This has been going on for ten years and I'm the one he's after. He's made it personal, you know? He's got right under my fucking skin and wormed his way into the middle of my fucking mind and there's no one else who's going to stop him. He wants me to stop him. He *needs* me to stop him. That's what this is all about. A battle of wills. A challenge—'

'Do you know how this sounds?'

Rachel looked up at Beaumont. 'I sound like a crazy person, right?'

'It sounds like an obsession, Agent Hoffman.'

Rachel closed her eyes and breathed. She wanted to scream until there was nothing left but silence. She wanted to run, just run as fast as she could, to some place where all of this was insignificant and irrelevant and meaningless. She wanted to go back in time to February of 1975 and find some way to not be in that bedroom with Caroline Lassiter.

She knew this was her Purgatory. This was her penance for her failings. The lives lost, the mistakes she'd made, all the things she should have known or predicted or seen coming before it was too late. Those were the weights on her back, and they had names, faces, lives cut short, families destroyed, the ripple effect of consequences repeating over and again for all these years.

'I have to go,' Rachel said. 'Someone has to tell this girl's family that she's dead.'

*

Back at the precinct, Ingram was coming off a phone call.

'I think I've got something,' he said. 'I found where she was on the night of Wednesday. A bar called Hennessy's. The bartender remembers her, said she spoke with a regular of theirs. The bar guy just knows him as Earl, and there's a Gary Earl who does heating and air conditioning at St. Jude Elementary.'

'He's got a record?'

'Yes,' Ingram said, 'and it's impressive. He did five and half years in Attica for possession with intent to supply. Prior to that he had a string of lesser felonies – B&E, assault, also did time in juvie as a teenager.'

'When was he in Attica?' Rachel asked.

Ingram looked at his notes. 'June of '76 to December of '81.'

'Same time as Christopher Wake.'

'Wake was a New York victim, right?'

'Sex offender. Hung upside-down from the ceiling. Fingers gone, eyes gone. That's where we found the *Dear Friends* letter. He was one of the *contrapasso* killings.'

'Brookins and Buchanan came back from the girl's apartment. I've sent them out to track him down. I told them not to approach him. We need to get some surveillance on him, see if he meets anyone, see if he connects with the other guy.'

'You believe there's another guy, don't you?'

Ingram leaned back. He took a deep breath and exhaled slowly.

'I believe in your belief,' he said.

'And what the hell is that supposed to mean?'

Ingram looked at Rachel. He seemed to be considering his words very carefully.

'Just say what's on your mind, John.'

'I have to look at the evidence, Rachel,' he said. It was the first time he'd used her name, as if he was trying to make some personal connection with her. She didn't know why, but it irritated her.

'Our perp was more than likely armed. He held his victims at gunpoint, had one tie the other, then another. There's very few people that refuse to do what they're told when they're faced with a gun. The earlier cases in Syracuse and New York are closed. They're closed definitively. Marshall and Wagner are dead. It just seems—'

Ingram stopped. He shook his head.

'Seems what, John?'

'Well, it just seems too … too …'

'Too incredible to believe that someone would wait five years and then go through a whole series of killings just to showcase their own ingenuity, their own brilliance, right?'

'And this book,' Ingram said. 'I mean, what the hell, Rachel? Hell, Purgatory, the seven sins thing, it's just fucking insane.'

'You're thinking like a cop,' Rachel said. 'You need to think beyond that. You need to consider the possibility that there are people out there who don't just get off on the killing itself. They want more. They need more. It's a game, you see? Like Berkowitz. Like Bundy. I mean, for Christ's sake, Bundy even represented himself in court. He was grandstanding, proving to the world how fucking smart he was. He even earned some respect from the goddamned judge. What did he say? "You'd have made a good lawyer. I would've loved to have you practice in front of me, but you went another way." For Christ's sake, he even called him "partner" and said he felt no animosity towards him. This was a guy who had sex with dead girls, and he went on having sex with them until the extent of decomposition made it impossible. He cut their fucking heads off and kept them as trophies. And yet he was so smart, so charming, that the judge felt no animosity towards him.'

'I know, Rachel, I know, but I don't see what that has to do with—'

'It has everything to do with this case, John. Don't you see? Can't you get your head around what we're dealing with here?

It's the nature of evil. It's at the very heart of what makes this so important, and not only to me.'

'Okay, okay, I get it.'

'I don't think you do.'

'So I don't, but maybe I will. Maybe I'll have a better under-standing of what the fuck this is all about if we get this guy, whether it's this Gary Earl or not… I mean, whoever the fuck it is that's done these things, we need to get them and find out what happened.'

'I don't think we will,' Rachel said.

'What?'

'Get surveillance on him. Get as close to him as we possibly can. The least we can do right now is ensure that he doesn't kill anyone else. But, if this goes the way I think it's going to go, I don't think he'll be telling us anything. I think he's going to die before we get a chance. Just like Marshall, just like Wagner, we're gonna wind up with a dead perp and a closed case and I'm going to be left with the same unanswered questions.'

'Rachel, I think you need some rest—'

Rachel looked at him. Her expression was fierce and deter-mined. 'When I get the truth. Or when I'm dead, John. That's when I'll rest.'

63

The surveillance of Gary Eugene Earl ran alongside an in-depth investigation into his background, family, personal connections, prior acquaintances, and all else that would give Rachel and the Dante Unit a comprehensive picture of the individual they were pursuing. What they needed, more than anything, was enough substantive and circumstantial evidence to secure a warrant for his place of residence.

Earl's home, a run-down double-wide on the outskirts of Bethlehem, was one of numerous statics that had seen better days. The comings and goings of endless vehicles and visitors to the lot made it easier for those on surveillance to go unnoticed. The number of drug deals and conspicuously illegal transactions they witnessed within the first twelve hours would have kept Bethlehem's PD buried in paperwork for a straight month.

Earl spent much of his time in the unit. He went out for groceries and cigarettes, made a single trip around noon on Monday the 18th to a hardware store, where he purchased two cans of aerosol bug spray and a roll of garbage bags. That same evening he went back to Hennessy's. He was there for four hours. He left at closing time, and he went home alone. There was no doubt in Rachel's mind that he could have been pulled over for a DUI, and that would have given them the chance to search his vehicle, but – for her – that was not enough. She wanted access to the double-wide. She wanted physical evidence that would inextricably tie him to any one of the Pennsylvania killings.

By mid-afternoon on Tuesday, even Rachel was feeling the frustration of watching and waiting. Ingram and a patrol officer were over at the lot. Buchanan suggested they send someone in plain clothes to Earl's place.

'Too obvious,' Rachel said. 'He's had no visitors. He doesn't appear to be dealing or anything else. On what pretext would we send someone there? The last thing I want to do is make him suspicious. If he knows we're looking at him, I think there's a very real possibility he'll kill himself.'

No one challenged her. No one wanted to consider that they were looking at entirely the wrong target. And no one asked Rachel why she thought Earl would commit suicide.

'The primary objective is two-fold,' Rachel said. 'First, we need the guy. Second, we need him alive. We need him here or in Allentown, I don't care where, and we need him in an interview room under strict suicide watch. This one doesn't get away. Are we all clear on that?'

'We know, Agent Hoffman,' Buchanan said, 'but I think we need to be proactive. If sending someone there isn't going to work, then we need to bring him out.'

'Okay,' Rachel said. 'Suggestions?'

'Something that takes him to one of the crime scenes,' Brookins said. 'Somehow get the idea into his head that there's evidence he might have left behind. He acts, and acts in such a way that there's no doubt that he knew where to go. That'd be enough to get a warrant, for sure.'

Rachel didn't speak, but she nodded her agreement. Thoughtful, considering all angles, there was silence in the room for a number of minutes.

'We've got Bernard Clarke's house,' Rachel finally said. 'We've got Carole Sitkoff, Martin Douglas, Julian McCullan, Lauren Trent, and lastly, we have the old factory. Those are the crime scenes themselves. It has to be something that takes him to one of those. So, what would bring him out? What would make him sufficiently anxious to feel compelled to go back to one of those locations?'

'There's another factor to take into consideration,' Brookins said. 'None of the killings were opportunistic. They were all planned. He was prepared. He knew what he was doing. Even the last one, the Trent girl. That wasn't a random pick-up at a bar. He was a regular there, and so was she. He'd seen her before, and he'd already made the decision that he was going to kill her.'

'And we have one sin left,' Buchanan said. 'Sloth.'

'I've been looking at something else,' Buchanan said. 'To do with the dates.'

Buchanan got up and walked to the case board at the back of the room.

'I mean, it might be nothing, but...'

'Tell me what you're thinking,' Rachel said.

'Okay, so we had Clarke and Warner on the 21st. Sitkoff nine days later. Douglas is then sixteen days. McCullan thirteen days after that. Vaill-Whyte is only six days. Then there's a nine-day gap before Lauren Trent.'

Buchanan turned and looked at the gathering.

'Put those days in a row and there's a pattern,' he went on. '9-16-13-6-9. The difference between those numbers is seven-three-seven-three. If that's something more than a coincidence, then the next killing would be seven days after Lauren Trent.'

'Which would be tomorrow,' Brookins said.

'I mean, it could be nothing but coincidence,' Buchanan said. 'But I know that astrological signs and numerology and moon phases and all that have played a part in other investigations, right?'

'I want to believe that nothing is a coincidence,' Rachel said. 'I want to believe that every single piece of this has a meaning.'

'So we ramp up surveillance,' Buchanan said. 'If we're not going to risk tipping him off, then we're at a stalemate until he does something. And if the gaps between the dates aren't a coincidence, we'll know soon enough because he'll be out to kill someone tomorrow.'

'Then that's what we do,' Rachel said. 'He leaves that place tomorrow, we're on him like a shadow. And I know I've said this, but I'll say it again. I want him in custody and I want him talking. We have to know if there's a second party involved in this thing. I'm not willing to accept another dead mass murderer and no fucking answers.'

64

At 7.09, the evening of Saturday the 23rd, Gary Earl exited the double-wide and walked back through the lot to his beat-to-shit Chevy Impala. He carried a holdall in one hand, and in the other was what appeared to be a pair of heavy-duty bolt cutters.

The Dante Unit – Rachel and John Ingram in one car, Brookins and Buchanan each in separate unmarked cars with a patrol officer – were stationed at different points, both inside and outside the lot. There were two exit roads – the first heading back into Bethlehem, the second giving access to the highway. From there, Earl could make his way to any number of surrounding towns and cities. There was always the possibility that he would aim for a location like Reading or Lancaster.

Earl headed north-west, crossed the Bethlehem limits and joined 378. He skirted the edges of Allentown, and at first it appeared that he was going to continue north, but then he turned and joined 22.

'What's ahead?' Rachel asked.

'You've got Myerstown, Lebanon, Hershey,' Ingram said. 'On about eighty miles is Harrisburg.'

Using a system of looping ahead, falling behind, and then coming up behind the Impala once again, the three cars maintained their line-of-sight with Earl. That it was dark played to their advantage. All he would see in his rearview were headlights.

Earl drove within the limit. He didn't change lanes. He kept going for a good hour, passing each of the three turn-offs for the towns Ingram had mentioned.

'It's Harrisburg,' Ingram said, 'unless he plans to go further. Then we've got Altoona and Pittsburgh.'

'I think it's Harrisburg,' Rachel said.

Ingram glanced sideways at Rachel. He'd never met anyone so focused, so indefatigable. She was like a machine. He knew nothing of her personal life, save that she didn't appear to have one. Everything about her – her tone of voice, her manner, her body language – was stressed. He understood the importance of what they were doing – there were people's lives on the line – but just being around her stretched his nerves like piano wire. As far as her theory was concerned – that this was all being orchestrated by some criminal mastermind – it seemed like something from a movie. He'd said he believed in her belief. What he really thought was that her imagination – beginning with an initial assumption – had gone into overdrive. There was no room for objectivity. She'd made that fatal flaw of trying to make every discovery and revelation fit a predetermined notion.

Crossing the limits of Harrisburg, Earl made his way into the city. It appeared that he had no intention of joining another highway.

Now out of the evening traffic, their tailing had to be more considered and cautious. In radio contact, Rachel directed the other two vehicles. Buchanan got ahead of Earl, kept him in the rearview until he turned. Then Brookins or Ingram would pick him up, Buchanan keeping abreast of the new direction and cutting back to join them at another junction.

Earl didn't drive much farther. He slowed and took a left. He pulled up against the curb and switched off both the lights and the engine of the Impala.

Ingram and Rachel were a half block over and to the right. Buchanan was a block ahead. Brookins and her patrol officer were out-of-sight on the other side of an adjacent residential street.

'No one moves until he does,' Rachel said over the radio. 'If you're not already wearing a bulletproof jacket then you put one on now. I'm not losing anyone tonight.'

Ingram reached over into the back seat and got their jackets.

'And if any of you are faced with a weapon and you have to fire, then fire low. Take out his legs. No gut shots, no head shots. Can I get everyone's confirmation of what I just said?'

Confirmation came back on the radio from Brookins and Buchanan.

They waited, and they kept on waiting. Rachel didn't speak. Ingram could hear her breathing. She didn't look away from Earl's car, didn't even seem to blink. It was like watching an animal fixed on its prey.

Just before 11.00, there was movement. An interior light went on in the Impala. It gave Rachel a split-second silhouette of the man, and then it went out.

The driver's side door opened a fraction, and it stayed open for a good thirty seconds before Earl pushed it wide and started to get out. He carried the holdall and the boltcutters.

'Subject on the move,' Rachel said over the radio.

Earl ensured that the trunk and doors were locked. He stood motionless on the sidewalk for a good minute, and then he crossed the street and walked down between two houses.

Rachel radioed Brookins. She gave her the location of the property, told her to get around the back of the houses and wait for further instructions. She instructed Buchanan to come from the far side and make his way towards them.

Rachel exited the vehicle, Ingram right behind her. They kept low along the fence that separated the front yards from the sidewalk. Heading slowly down the alleyway, she saw the chain that had secured it was already cut and lying on the ground. Her back against the wall, she looked around the edge of the brickwork. She pulled back immediately. She motioned to Ingram. Earl was right there at the back of the house. He had not yet gained access. She needed him to get inside. Trespassing and damage to personal property was not enough; she had to get breaking and entering at the very least. She wanted as significant a charge as she could get to justify a warrant for his car and the double-wide.

Rachel tried not to breathe. Ingram was near the ground, crouched as low as he could get. He could feel the tension in his knees, his shoulders.

Rachel was aware of movement at the far end of the yard. Brookins and the patrol officer. She hoped to God they didn't make a sound.

Getting as low as she could, Rachel once again edged towards the corner of the brickwork. Even before she caught sight of Earl, she heard the sound of wood splintering. It was surprisingly quiet, the sound of footsteps on fallen twigs, and she waited, her hand out behind her to keep Ingram in check.

Rachel heard the door creak open. She waited, waited, waited. She held out her left hand so Ingram could see, her fingers like a fan. She went on waiting. There had to be no doubt that he was inside the property, making preparations for whatever he'd set his mind to do.

Rachel gave it another thirty seconds. She then gave a count-down of five, lowering each finger in turn, and then she moved.

Ingram was a step behind her, the pair of them rushing through the back door of the property, Ingram's flashlight illuminating the interior of the empty kitchen.

Sounds from another room, something like a struggle, and Rachel was hollering at the top of her voice.

'FBI! FBI! Get down on the ground! Get down on the fuck-ing ground now!'

She went out of the kitchen at a run, gun levelled at head-height, and into the living room.

Earl was upright, standing behind a figure seated in a chair, and even as Ingram's flashlight revealed what was happening in stark clarity, the seated figure was gasping and wrestling against the constraints, a polythene bag over his head, his feet kicking wildly.

Rachel came around the chair and collided broadside with Earl. The speed with which she moved and with her entire weight behind it, Earl was down on the ground.

Ingram tore the bag from the head of the seated figure.

Brookins was behind him then, the patrol officer too, and within seconds Buchanan and the second officer were in the room.

'Call an ambulance,' Ingram said to one of the officers.

Rachel was on her knees. Earl was face-down, his hands already behind his back. Buchanan handcuffed him. Earl did not resist. He did not speak. He just lay right where he'd fallen.

Between Rachel and Buchanan, they hauled him up and sat him against the wall.

Ingram put on the lights.

Brookins and the second officer helped the man in the chair out of the room and into the kitchen. He was sobbing, still breathing heavily, barely able to stay on his feet.

Earl, however, just stared straight ahead. His expression – seemingly one of calm dispassion – didn't change.

Even when Buchanan read him his rights he did not blink or flinch or utter a word.

Once the ambulance had arrived and the resident of the house had been taken away for examination and any needed treatment, Rachel called the Harrisburg PD. She asked them to send a secure vehicle. She did not want to drive Earl back tonight. Harrisburg could hold him until the morning, and then she would make arrangements for transport to Bethlehem. Perhaps Joy Willis would want Earl interrogated under Bureau supervision. These were details. How it played out mattered far less than the fact that she had Earl alive.

While they waited for the Harrisburg vehicle, Rachel, Ingram, Brookins and Buchanan sat in the living room. Earl was still seated against the wall. There was nothing he could do. There was no possible way out.

The atmosphere was strange, almost an anticlimax after more than two weeks of eighteen-hour days, after all the things that they'd seen, after the horrors they had witnessed, but they were here. Everything they'd done had paid off. Earl was in their custody, and – whatever it took – Rachel was going to get some answers.

Finally, leaning forward in her chair and looking right at Earl, she said, 'Who is he, Gary?'

Earl looked up.

'You didn't do this alone, did you?'

Earl didn't respond, not even a flicker of change in his expression.

'You're not bright enough or capable enough to have figured all of this out by yourself, are you?' Rachel asked, hoping perhaps to goad him into speaking.

Again, nothing.

'Tell me, Gary. Tell me where he is.'

Earl slowly closed his eyes, and then he opened them once more. He looked up at the ceiling, and a half-smile crossed his lips. He opened his mouth to speak.

Rachel leaned forward without even being aware that she was doing it. It was conspiratorial, a secret to be shared between just the two of them.

'He's everywhere,' Earl whispered. 'And he's nowhere.'

There was that smile again.

'Just like the Devil.'

65

Had there been any concern in Rachel's mind that there would be insufficient physical evidence to implicate Gary Eugene Earl in the recent spate of killings, those fears were swiftly assuaged when photos and items from Earl's double-wide started to come into the Allentown FBI Office.

Harrisburg PD had been as accommodating as she could have wished – providing secure transportation and additional officers to bring Earl to Bethlehem. By the end of Sunday, with Earl secure in lock-up, the paperwork required to charge him with nine counts of first-degree homicide was almost complete. Earl had spoken once, and that was to decline his right to a public defender.

Joy Willis spoke with Bethlehem's Captain, and they agreed that the interrogation would be conducted in Allentown. The arrest would be credited to the combined investigative work of both the FBI and the Police Department.

On Monday morning, Rachel gave Joy Willis a full debriefing on the case.

The evidence was overwhelming. There were items of clothing, plastic bags of the same type used in each murder, rolls of duct tape, a portable oxyacetylene burner, a map marking the different locations where the killings had taken place, handwritten notes with some of the victims' names, even a copy of *The Divine Comedy* with certain passages from the Purgatory section underlined. As those items were logged into evidence, Rachel couldn't escape the feeling that it was almost too much. It seemed that

Earl had made no effort whatsoever to hide his involvement in the murders. Even Ingram commented that Earl appeared to be a man who wanted to be caught.

Late on Monday, Gary Earl was formally charged. His arraignment was scheduled for Wednesday the 27th. Rachel had attempted to establish a dialogue with Earl on four separate occasions. Each time he'd remained silent. No matter what tack she tried, she couldn't break through the wall of resistance. Even his manner was infuriating – that same half-smile, the way he watched her with bemusement as she grew ever more insistent that he speak. She knew it was futile to get angry, but he angered her. She knew that Earl had the answers to so many of her questions. She was certain – as certain as it was possible to be – that Earl was just another marionette in this decade-long game of cat-and-mouse she'd played with an unidentified second perpetrator.

That theory – once again communicated with all the circumstantial evidence she could muster – had been put forward at the end of her debrief with Willis.

Willis had listened, had even asked some additional questions, but she'd made it clear that Rachel's job was to secure the conviction of Gary Earl. Her remit was to ensure that a sufficiently watertight case was presented to the Assistant Attorney General to ensure a trial, that said evidence would leave no reasonable doubt in the minds of a jury, and that the state would secure a conviction that had no leeway for appeal. When that was behind them, only then would they discuss further avenues of investigation that Rachel might wish to pursue.

The sense of self-congratulation that others seemed to be experiencing – Ingram, Brookins, Buchanan, other agents within the Allentown office – was not something shared by Rachel. The jigsaw had more pieces, but the full picture remained indiscernible.

*

A little after noon on Wednesday the 27th, Earl was transported in a police convoy to Lehigh County Court. Rachel arrived before the hearing and went down to the holding cell.

Earl had still not spoken. The likely outcome of the proceedings would be referral for psychiatric evaluation. Earl would be moved to State Correctional in Marienville and the weeks-long consultations would begin. If Earl continued to remain silent, Rachel had no idea what would happen. Earl, according to reports, was eating and sleeping. He'd spent the vast majority of his time in lock-up standing beneath the narrow window with his eyes closed. Medical examination had determined that he was in reasonable health, and did not suffer any pathological condition.

Why Rachel felt the need to see the man again – knowing he'd be as unresponsive as each earlier occasion – she didn't know. Perhaps it was simply that it might be the last time. Earl would vanish into the system, and every decision of his life from that point forward would be made by someone else.

Showing her ID, Rachel was allowed into the holding unit beneath the court. The cell in which Earl was housed was open to view. Bars ran floor-to-ceiling, and though the corridor was guarded by four court officers, Earl was still shackled and handcuffed.

Rachel pulled up a chair. She placed it close to the bars and sat down.

Earl was seated. Leaning forward, his elbows on his knees, his fingers laced together, he looked directly at the wall ahead of him. He was motionless, a statue, and Rachel couldn't even hear him breathing.

'I think you want me to call you Dante,' she said. 'You're not the first, and maybe you're not going to be the last, but I think that's how you see yourself.'

Earl didn't move, gave no indication that he could even hear her.

'Virgil guides Dante through Hell and Purgatory,' Rachel

said. 'And the next destination is Heaven. Paradiso, right? Is that where you're going, Gary? Are you going to Heaven?'

Nothing.

'Or are those you killed going to Heaven? Is that how this works? You made them repent, you made them suffer the penalty, and now they're free?'

Earl closed his eyes.

It was something – a change, a reaction.

Rachel pulled the chair a little closer to the bars.

'Help me understand, Gary,' she said. 'Enlighten me. I know I don't understand. I want to understand so badly. I see pieces, fragments, shadows. I need to see how they all connect to one another. You can help me, Gary. In fact, I think you're the only person in the world who can help me.'

Earl smiled. He opened his eyes.

'I'm drowning,' Rachel said. 'I'm being swallowed by this thing. The further it goes, the darker it gets, and I want to step out of the darkness. I want to see the light that you've seen. I want to see what's on the other side of this Purgatory.'

Earl turned then. He turned and looked right at her.

Rachel held her breath. It was involuntary.

She could feel her heart beating in her chest, the blood in her veins, the pressure in her temples, the way each and every hair on the back of her neck seemed to rise to attention in slow motion.

'Until you do what I have done,' Earl said, 'you can never hope to understand.'

Turning back to the wall, he closed his eyes once more.

Rachel knew he wouldn't say another word. She sat there and watched him for as long as she could bear, and then she stood up, returned the chair to the wall, and walked back along the corridor.

66

The internal inquiry would continue for weeks.

Questions would be raised regarding security protocol, prisoner management, whether or not the arraignment of such a high-profile defendant should ever have taken place in a county courthouse. On it went, and it didn't seem that it would ever end.

Newspapers ran headlines – supposition, hypothesis, endless assumptions, wild claims that what happened had been allowed to happen because someone didn't want the Earl trial to go ahead – but all of it was meaningless.

There would be no trial, and thus there would be no extensive psychiatric evaluation to determine the competence of the accused to stand. Even the arraignment – Earl presented before Lehigh County Court Judge Herman Lowenthal – didn't reach a conclusion.

Flanked by two court officers, Earl had been led into the courtroom on the third floor of the courthouse. Judge Lowenthal had instructed that the prisoner's shackles and handcuffs be removed.

Lowenthal's comment – that 'the Lehigh County Court doesn't abide by the Napoleonic Code', and that 'the defendant, irrespective of whatever charges may have been brought against him, is innocent until proven guilty' – were quoted and re-quoted in newspapers and TV bulletins time and again. Though he was criticized, Lowenthal was within the bounds of the law. Earl was innocent until proven guilty, and though there was more than adequate evidence to secure a conviction, though there was no doubt in anyone's mind that he was as violent and deranged a killer as had been seen in Pennsylvania's history, courtroom protocol dictated that the handcuffing or restraining of a defendant, even at arraignment, could be interpreted as prejudicial.

It took seconds, but seconds were all that were required.

Throwing his full weight backwards against one of the court officers, and before the second officer had a chance to react, Earl had vaulted the wooden rail around the witness stand and run headlong for the door.

Pandemonium broke out like a wave, but Earl was fast, faster than his size or weight would have indicated, and he came out through the courtroom door and into the third-floor ante-room.

By the time Rachel got to her feet, Earl was already out through a second door and into the hallway beyond.

Rachel, pushed out of the way by the pursuing court officers, reached the hallway in time to see Earl hit the banister. The banister didn't give, but Earl's intention was never to break through it.

He merely stopped, turned, raised his hands over his head, and went over backwards.

Gary Eugene Earl, all six-one and two hundred and eighteen pounds of him, dropped without a sound. He didn't call out, he didn't scream. He just dropped.

The last thing Rachel Hoffman remembered was being pulled away from the body.

She was later told that she was on her knees, gripping Earl's shoulders with all her strength, that she was shaking him as if she expected him to regain consciousness. Her hands were covered with blood and she was sobbing, hysterical, a desperate sound like that of a wounded animal.

And they told her she was screaming the same thing over and over again.

'Tell me his name! Tell me his name! Tell me his fucking name!'

It took three people to drag Rachel away. She fought them violently, her expression one of rage and defeat, and then she blacked out.

IV

1989

Paradiso

67

The last four years collapsed into a moment.

Carl Sheehan sat across from the *New York Times'* crime editor, Joel Erlewine, and stared at the piece of paper in his hand.

'You know this woman?' Erlewine asked.

'I've known her for years,' Sheehan said, handing back the letter. 'We had a relationship a long time ago. I actually haven't seen her for... Christ, it must be four years now.'

'So, is she crazy, or is there something worth looking into here?'

'She was a cop in Syracuse back in the mid '70s,' Sheehan said. 'A good one. I ran a couple of features for her and her boss. She also worked on a case in New York in 1980. What we now call serial killings, but we didn't have that term back then. Then she went to the FBI, was stationed in Pennsylvania. Like I said, last time I saw her was for her father's funeral, back in '85. She was on another case. Then she just dropped off the face of the Earth. I called her a good few times, never called me back. I got the message, you know?'

'Well, that's all very interesting, Carl,' Erlewine said dryly, 'but none of that answers my question.'

'Is she crazy? I don't believe so. Is this something worth looking into? I guess I won't know unless I go look into it.'

'The thing that doesn't seem right to me is the FBI angle,' Erlewine said. 'If she's still active FBI, then what the hell is she doing writing to us?'

'Maybe she's not FBI anymore.'

'And it's cryptic, to say the least. Marshall, Wagner, Earl. These are the cases she worked on?'

'I know about the first two,' Sheehan said. 'That was Syracuse and New York. The last one, I guess, is Pennsylvania, but I didn't pursue that. I had an indirect connection to a murder victim back then. He shared a cell with the New York perp. From what I later found out, there was another series, but I didn't chase it.'

'And she's saying all three are connected. There's all sorts of God-only-knows-what here. Numerology, something about *The Divine Comedy*. You understand this?'

'I have an idea where she's coming from, yes.'

'Well, for better or worse she remembers you, my friend, and if your name wasn't here on the letter then it would've gone in the file with all the other batshit crazy letters we get.'

'I'm busy with other things,' Sheehan said, 'but if you want me to go track her down and find out if there's anything worth chasing, I will do.'

'All we've got is a PO Box number in…' Erlewine peered at the letter. 'Colonial Heights, Virginia. You know where that is?'

'I can find it.'

'I'll cover your flight and your car rental,' Erlewine said, 'but it comes out at the back end if we get a piece.'

'Fifty percent,' Sheehan said.

'Jeez, you are a ball breaker. Okay, fifty percent.'

'You find out she's a lunatic, then bail out. If she's not, keep me posted and we'll discuss expenses.'

'Can you get Deirdre to make me a copy of the letter?'

'Deirdre is my secretary, not yours,' Erlewine replied. 'Make it yourself.'

In the early morning of Saturday, November 18th, Carl Sheehan took a flight out of JFK to Richmond. He had to rent a car and get out to Colonial Heights before noon. Legally, there was no way to track an address back from a PO Box. There were a couple of people he could call, but that would be a last resort. He figured – in as small a place as Colonial Heights – that asking for Rachel by name would be adequate to find her. After all, how many FBI agents could there be in the locale?

During the flight he read Rachel's letter again. To anyone unfamiliar with what had happened back in Syracuse and New York, it would seem rambling and surreal. Rachel had listed the names and dates of each victim in each city, and then had gone on to list a further nine, the first two of which were Bernard Clarke and Samantha Warner. After Rachel had failed to return his calls and messages, he'd dropped it. He'd been settled in New York, had regular work, much of which was not only interesting but demanding of his full time and attention, and he'd really had no wish to step on the toes of the federal government. She'd dropped the connection for a reason, and he knew her well enough to appreciate that she must've had a good reason. She didn't want him in her life, and that was all there was to it.

And then, four years later – right out of the blue – she'd mailed a letter from a PO Box to the *New York Times*. Along with the names and dates of death of eighteen murder victims, there were numbers, a calculation of the days between each killing, a reference to Dante, to Death, Hell, Purgatory, the seven roots of sinfulness, and finally – there at the end – a single line: *Find Carl Sheehan. Tell him it never stopped.*

She'd signed it *Rachel Hoffman*. No title, no rank, no *Special Agent*. Just her name.

If she was no longer FBI, then why? And why had she gone to Virginia? Why not stay in Pennsylvania? Why not move back to Syracuse?

These were questions only Rachel could answer. She was now thirty-seven, her birthday just eleven days before. He remembered her in Syracuse – twenty-two years old, just a firework in a bottle, all geared up to set the world to rights. Ten years on, her father's funeral, and a decade of law enforcement had taken their toll. She was tougher, sure, but it went beyond the physical and mental. Her emotions had been blunted. That was the only way he could describe it. The readiness to smile, the way in which she would effortlessly knock the seriousness out of him with a handful of words – that was gone. They had been together close to two years, and yes, he'd moved on and had a longer relationship with Suzanne, even prepared himself to settle down and raise a family with her, but then she'd lost the child. He could see that such an event might bring people together – each one bound to the other by a shared loss – but in their case it had been the opposite. Only later, in hindsight, did he consider that they each served as a constant reminder of what had happened. She'd been devastated, as had he, but it had, understandably, hit her harder and more profoundly. After they split, Suzanne had gone back to her parents. How long she stayed there, he didn't know. The chapter was closed, and he knew it would serve no purpose to keep re-reading it to discern some other meaning. Subsequently he'd dated, but whatever life–work balance he tried to establish was too unstable and unpredictable. How many times he'd heard *Look, I care for you, Carl, but I just can't go on living like this* he didn't know, but it had been enough. He'd now been single for over a year. He worked hard. He earned his living. He had no wish to go back to a regular newspaper contract. Of course, as a freelancer, it was feast and famine from one year to the next, but he'd done it for long enough to have never gotten into a difficulty he couldn't get out of. He survived. That was the blunt truth of it. And he survived doing something that gave him a reason to get out of bed in the morning.

As the flight came in to land, Sheehan had no notion of what he was getting into. Maybe Rachel had dropped into the abyss of assumption and conjecture, seeing correlations that didn't exist, inventing connections where none existed. It really was as simple as Erlewine had said – was she crazy, or was there something here?

Of course, half – if not more – of the reason he'd so readily agreed to pursue it was because he wanted to see Rachel. He had no compelling urge to get involved in another serial killer investigation. Unless, of course, it was Rachel doing the asking. Of all the women he'd known in his life, Rachel was perhaps the only one he'd truly loved. How and why it had ended no longer seemed to matter. It was more than twelve years behind them, and she'd made it pretty obvious in Pennsylvania that she had no intention of picking up where they'd left off.

Sheehan rented a car and drove out to Colonial Heights. Though a city, it was no bigger than a suburb of New York. Wide streets, single- and two-story buildings, very little to obstruct a view to the horizon. A sign invited visitors to tour Violet Bank, historic headquarters of General Robert E. Lee, and Swift Creek Mill. Almost at once, Sheehan felt out-of-place. There would be no way for him to remain inconspicuous in such a community.

He located the post office an hour before closing time.

With the copy of Rachel's letter in his hand, he went inside and waited for a teller to be available.

Assuming a respectful and courteous manner, he explained that he was in a predicament and needed assistance.

'I received a letter from my cousin,' he said. 'It was mailed from a PO Box address here. To be honest, the family has been very worried about her and this is the first communication we've received for months. I'm wondering if there's any way you can help me.'

The teller – a middle-aged woman with too much make-up and a precariously ornate hairstyle – was shaking her head before Sheehan had even finished talking.

'I'm really sorry, sir, but we can't divulge any information.

That's the law, I'm afraid. That's the whole purpose of using a PO Box, you see?'

'No, of course,' Sheehan said. 'I understand that completely, but this is something of an emergency.'

'Well, if it's an emergency, the only thing I can suggest you do is go speak with Sheriff Williams.'

Sheehan smiled. 'It's not really a police matter,' he said. 'I mean, it's not like she's done anything illegal. We're just so very worried about her and we want to make sure she's okay. I've flown down here from New York—'

'Like I said, sir, I appreciate the circumstances, but if I give you any information about the person who rented that PO Box number then I'm gonna be having a talk with Sheriff Williams that I really don't want to have. I'd love to help you, but it would be a federal offence.'

'No, I understand, and I really wouldn't want you to be getting into any trouble.'

The woman smiled understandingly. 'You go on down here to the next crossing, you take a right and you'll see the Sheriff's Office up there on the left. You can't miss it.'

Sheehan thanked her and left.

Sheriff Lester Williams was a young man – no more than thirty-five or so – and he greeted Sheehan somewhat reservedly.

Sheehan knew there was no way to get what he needed without telling the truth.

'I'm a journalist,' he explained. 'A letter was sent into the *New York Times* by a federal agent by the name of Rachel Hoffman. She's using a PO Box number from here. Agent Hoffman is a long-time friend. We've worked together on cases in the past and I really need to find her.'

'Well, it seems to me, Mr. Sheehan, that if she's using a PO Box then maybe she doesn't want to be found.'

'I think that relates more to the nature of the things she's investigating rather than not wanting to talk to me.'

'She may not be of the same opinion.'

'Well, if you could just get word to her that I'm here—'

Williams smiled ruefully. 'And what makes you think I have the slightest notion of who this woman is, let alone where she might be?'

Sheehan was irritated with himself. He knew he should have come better-prepared. He could have found the address back in New York. He could have called in a favor and saved himself this hassle. Too eager to see Rachel – that's what it was – and now he was paying the price for his impetuousness.

'I'm not assuming anything, Sheriff. I just know this woman and I know she's in trouble, so I'm asking for any help you might be able to give me.'

'Well, if she's in trouble, how do I know you're not the one who's causing it?'

'My name is right there in the letter, Sheriff. And I can assure you—'

'Let me stop you right there, Mr. Sheehan. I appreciate that you've come all the way down here from New York. I appreciate your predicament too, but I think you're misunderstanding what my job is here. This isn't a Lost and Found office for folks who have a mind to keep themselves to themselves. If what you're saying is true and this here lady's a federal agent, then it sure ain't none of my business to go lookin' for her on behalf of a complete stranger.'

Sheehan nodded. 'You're right, absolutely.' He got up, folded the letter, put it back in his pocket. 'I'm sorry to have wasted your time.'

Sheehan walked to the door.

'Only thing I can advise is maybe get yourself a room someplace in town and see if she comes looking for you.'

'She has no idea that I'm here,' Sheehan said.

'Well, if she put your name in that letter and she's smart enough to be a federal agent, then I'm guessin' she might have expected you to show up sooner or later.'

68

The motel was cheap and basic. It would serve the purpose, but it also served to highlight the potential futility of what Sheehan was doing. He could be here for a day, two, three perhaps, and hear nothing. He could wind up going back to New York only to explain to Joel Erlewine that he'd wasted the cost of a flight and had nothing at all to show for it.

He'd spoken to two people, explained his reason for being there. That would have to be enough. If Rachel had really set her mind to keeping everyone at arm's-length, then further efforts to find her would only diminish the possibility that she'd reach out. The more he considered the situation, the more he needed an explanation. It went beyond his personal connection to Rachel and into the realm of why a federal agent would be writing to the *New York Times* crime desk. That alone could get her reprimanded, perhaps even fired. What had happened during these past four years? What had happened back in Allentown? He should have followed up on the murders of Bernard Clarke and Samantha Warner. He could think of so many reasons he'd not done that – time, the need to make an income, the fact that it was Pennsylvania and he had more than enough to deal with in New York, the simple reality that the very nature of once again being consumed by something so violent and abhorrent was anathema to him – but the truth was simpler. Rachel had withdrawn, and his knee-jerk reaction had been to withdraw in response. If she didn't want anything to do with him, then he – in turn – would have nothing to do with her. And yet here he was in Colonial Heights, Virginia. What had it taken? The mere mention of his name in a letter to the newspaper. It hadn't even been addressed to him. It was some sort of impulse, not only to draw him back to her, but to take him into the darkness that had initiated their relationship. Rachel chased the darkness. That was the simple truth. Perhaps she'd now chased it for so long that she was right in the heart of it and could not escape.

Sheehan left the motel at 7.00 and walked into the first restaurant he saw. He ordered a steak, a baked potato, a side salad. By the time the food arrived, he'd already drunk two shots of bourbon and a beer. He tried his best to eat as much as he could. He had little appetite, but knew he wouldn't sleep if he didn't have at least one good meal. He was tired, but it was not physical. The fatigue he experienced was psychological in nature, a sense that his willingness and motivation were being slowly drained away.

He called for the check, and even as he was counting out his money he was aware that someone was watching him from the bar. He paid no mind to it, but as he got up and put on his jacket, the man came down from the bar stool and walked towards him. Without a word, he sat down. Sheehan opened his mouth to speak.

'Take a seat,' the man said.

Sheehan did so.

The man was in his late-fifties perhaps, bearded, his skin rugged and weatherworn, that of someone who spent far more time outside than in. There was a tiredness about him, however. That's the only word that came to mind. It was as if the man was burdened with something unseen.

There was silence between them for a handful of seconds.

'Can I help you?' Sheehan asked.

'I doubt it,' the man said.

'Who are you?'

'That's not important. I want to know who you are.'

'Who I am?'

The man nodded. 'Ain't such a tough question now, is it?'

'Why should I tell you?'

'Mister, you don't have to tell me nothin' you don't want to. Having said that, if you don't want this to be a wasted journey, then I reckon you'd best answer my question.'

'My name?'

'That'd be a good start.'

'Carl Sheehan.'

'And where are you from, Mr. Sheehan?'

'I came in from New York.'

'And why did you come down here from New York?'

'I came to find someone,' Sheehan replied. 'Look, this isn't right. You won't tell me who you are, so I don't see why I should—'

The man got up slowly, his hand on the edge of the table for support. He paused to withdraw a handkerchief from his pocket. His eyes closed, he wiped his mouth, and then he gathered himself together. 'You have a good visit now, Mr. Sheehan.'

'Okay, okay, I'll answer your questions.'

The man hesitated.

'Sit down. Please. I'll tell you what you want.'

The man eased himself down into the seat.

'I came because someone I know sent a letter to a newspaper. She mentioned my name. It's someone I've known for a long time and I'm worried about her.'

'When did you meet this person you're so worried about?'

'Back in the middle of 1975. I met her in Syracuse. She was a police officer.'

'And what were you doing back then, Mr. Sheehan?'

'I was working for a newspaper. *The Syracuse Tribune*.'

'When was the last time you saw this person?'

'I last saw her in September of 1985. It was her father's funeral.

After that, I tried to stay in touch but she never returned my calls.'

'What was her father's name?'

'Edward. His name was Edward.'

'And is her mother still alive?'

'Yes, she is.'

The man kept on looking at Sheehan. He didn't seem to blink. Though his gaze was penetrating and implacable, there was a deep sadness in his eyes.

'Back in New York, there was a police detective she worked with. You remember him?'

Sheehan leaned forward. 'You know where she is, don't you? You know where Rachel is.'

The man's expression didn't change. 'The detective. His name.'

'In New York... it was Quinn. His name was Maurice Quinn.'

'What was the number of his precinct?'

Sheehan laughed reflexively. 'Jesus, I don't know. I don't remember.'

'Try, Mr. Sheehan. Try real hard.'

'It was in the hundreds. The hundred and... and tenth? No, it was the hundred and fourteenth.'

The man sat for just a moment longer, and then he got up. He looked down at the bills on the table.

'How much of a tip you leave?'

'Ten bucks.'

'Good 'nough.'

'So what now?'

'We take a walk.'

Sheehan followed the man out of the restaurant and into the parking lot behind the building.

Opening up the passenger door of a light-colored pickup truck, the man told Sheehan to get in. Sheehan had no idea where they were headed, but he knew who would be at their destination. He felt a mixture of anxiety and anticipation. He was trusting a stranger to take him to Rachel, and the stranger had needed to ensure that Sheehan was exactly who he said he was. Was Rachel in hiding? Had she gone into some kind of federal protection program? Was she so worried for her own safety that she had to have go-betweens?

The man didn't speak. He pulled out of the parking lot and headed west on 460. The course of the Appomattox River was to their north. They kept driving – on past Fort Pickett, past the sign for Blackstone, and when the highway bore south-west ahead of Burkeville, they took a turn-off away from the lights and houses along the road.

Here the terrain was rough and rutted. The headlights picked out a narrow path between tall banks of black oak and Eastern redbud. Jolting with each furrow in the road, the suspension creaked and groaned. Sheehan felt every jar in the base of his spine. Still they kept driving, and it was a good thirty minutes before the lights picked out a clearing up ahead.

Drawing slowly to a halt, the man switched off the engine. He got out of the vehicle and walked around to the passenger side.

Opening the door, he instructed Sheehan to get out.

Sheehan did as he was asked. He had no idea where he was. He could see nothing but the interminable dark, the trees that reached high above him, the narrow window of deep starless sky above.

'Follow me,' the man said. He produced a flashlight and started walking. It was cold, the air clean and biting. There seemed to be nothing up ahead of him save the vague illumination of the flashlight. He followed the man closely, ever aware that there were dips and rises in the earth that would put him on his back if he didn't follow the foot-worn trail exactly.

They walked a half mile, perhaps more. Every once in a while, the man paused as if to catch his breath.

Concerned that something was wrong, Sheehan asked if he was okay.

'Don't you worry about me, Mr. Sheehan,' was the brusque reply.

After a few hundred yards, they turned right into a wider clearing. Up ahead, almost out of nowhere, a structure was visible. As they approached, Sheehan's eyes – now accustomed to the dark – discerned a single-story wooden cabin. It was wide, at least three or four rooms, and the front and sides were enclosed by a veranda.

Ten yards or so from the steps, the man turned. He shone the flashlight directly into Sheehan's face.

'Wait here,' he said.

Sheehan stood and waited as the man walked up the steps and knocked on the cabin door.

69

Had he passed her in the street, Sheehan would not have recognized Rachel Hoffman.

Thin, drawn, pale, her hair unkempt, she looked as if she hadn't slept or eaten properly in a month.

She was aware of his reaction, and she smiled.

'I've had better days, yes,' she said.

'Rachel,' he said.

'Hello, Carl.'

'What the fuck are you doing out here in the middle of nowhere?'

Rachel turned to the man. 'Carl, this is a friend of mine. His name is Frank Collins. This is his place. He's been good enough to let me stay here.'

'But why? Why are you even here at all?'

'Come on in,' Rachel said. 'You look like you're ready to freeze to death.'

Sheehan took a couple of steps, and then hesitated. 'What the hell am I getting into, Rachel?' he asked.

'You're never going to find out if you don't get inside, Carl. I'm not standing here with the fucking door open all night.'

Sheehan went up the steps. He stepped past her, Collins behind him, and then Rachel closed the door.

She put on the light in the entranceway.

'Down there and to the right,' she said.

Sheehan followed her directions, opening a door into a well-lit and warm room. A fire burned in the grate. Out in the hallway,

Rachel and Collins shared some words. Before long, Sheehan once again heard the front door open and close. Collins was leaving him here. Was he supposed to stay, or would Collins return and drive him back to Colonial Heights?

Rachel came into the room.

'Have you eaten?' she asked.

'I have, yes. Have you?'

'I'm fine, Carl.'

'Seriously, Rachel, you don't look so good. What the hell is happening here? Why all the secrecy? And what the fuck was going on with this guy and all the questions?'

Rachel sat down to the right of the fireplace. She indicated that Sheehan should also sit.

'If you were in my position, you would take precautions, Carl,' she said.

'What, you thought someone would come out here pretending to be me?'

'Who knows, eh?'

Sheehan took the letter from his pocket. 'This is why I'm here, Rachel.'

'I know why you're here.'

'Are you still with the Bureau?'

'Officially, yes.'

'Officially?'

'Things have happened, Carl. Many things. Let's just say I'm on leave for personal reasons.'

'What reasons, Rachel? What happened to you?'

Rachel leaned back and closed her eyes for just a moment. Everything about her body language conveyed a profound sense of exhaustion.

Sheehan could not get over her change in appearance. It troubled him greatly that she looked so fragile and insubstantial. The firebrand that he remembered seemed to have vanished altogether.

'Why are you here, Carl?' Rachel asked.

'Because of the letter.'

'The letter was not addressed to you.'

'No, I know, but my name was there. Joel ... Joel Erlewine at the *Times*, he called me and told me about it.'

'I know what I wrote, Carl. You're still not answering my question.'

'Why am I here? Because I care about you. Because the things you wrote troubled me. Because I got the impression that you were still chasing this ... this whatever, you know? This idea that maybe there were things that happened in Syracuse and New York—'

'And Pennsylvania. Things happened there, too.'

'I don't know what happened in Pennsylvania, Rachel.'

'I can tell you, but I still need to know you're here for the right reason.'

'The right reason? Isn't caring about you enough of a reason?'

Rachel sighed and shook her head. She closed her eyes. 'Try again, Carl.'

'What?'

'Why are you here? That's all I want to know.'

'Christ, Rachel, I don't know. To find out what the fuck is going on with you. To find out if there's any actual substance to what you're saying, what you're thinking. To find out the truth.'

Rachel opened her eyes.

Sheehan looked at her. Something had shifted in her expression and demeanor.

'To find out the truth, Rachel. Once and for all.'

'Do you believe that we know the truth?'

'I don't know what I believe,' Sheehan said. 'The killings in Syracuse, in New York, and now you're saying there were other things in Pennsylvania. You're telling me that they were all connected—'

'*Are* connected,' Rachel said matter-of-factly. 'They're all connected, and it all comes back to me.'

Sheehan felt the seams pulling apart. The emotions he felt were awkward, disjointed. What the hell was happening? He was in a cabin in the woods in the depths of Virginia with a woman he hadn't spoken to for four years. And she was on leave from the Bureau for personal reasons? What reasons? Had she lost her mind? Is that why she was no longer an active agent?

'You're wondering if I'm crazy,' Rachel said.

'I'm wondering if *I* am,' Sheehan replied.

'You want to know what happened to me. You want to know if I was suspended from the FBI because I lost my mind.'

'I want to know everything.'

'Is that the truth? Do you really want to know everything?'

'Of course I do. Why the hell wouldn't I?'

'Because of where it might take you,' Rachel said. 'Because of how fucking dark it is, how deep it goes, and who is really behind all the killings. And they go all the way back to the schoolteacher in Ulysses in February of 1975.'

'And you genuinely believe that all of this, everything that's happened, even with the deaths of Robert Marshall and Charles Wagner—'

'And Gary Earl,' Rachel interjected. 'The serial killer from Pennsylvania. Do I believe that there was someone else behind all of it? Yes, I do, Carl. And I don't just believe it. I *know* it.'

'So why aren't you pursuing this along official lines? And why did you stop talking to me after your dad's funeral? I called, I left messages and I never heard a word. I didn't know what the fuck was going on, Rachel. I figured I'd upset you somehow, and I just had to let go.'

'I didn't have a choice,' Rachel said. 'I had to stop talking to you.'

'Why?'

'Because you're a journalist, Carl, and because I was advised not to maintain communication with you. You were *persona non grata* as far as the federal authorities were concerned.'

'And yet here I am.'

'Yes, you are.'

'So what's changed? You're no longer concerned with what they think?'

'Let's just say my need to find the truth outweighs any other consideration I might have about my career.'

'And why aren't you active? What do you mean when you say you're on leave for personal reasons?'

'Things got difficult after Pennsylvania. I got into trouble. I… Christ, I don't even know what you'd call it. I guess I had a kind of breakdown.'

'And they wouldn't help you? Surely they've had to deal with this kind of thing before. They have psychologists, professionals that deal with agents who get burned out or whatever?'

'The very people that failed to give me any understanding of who I was dealing with? Those professionals? If they can't even understand the motivations and rationales of serial killers, how could I possibly trust them to give me the right advice and help?'

'And they've suspended you?'

'I'm on sick leave. That's the official line.'

'Since when?'

'The beginning of '88.'

'Nearly two years?'

'Yes, Carl. Nearly two years.'

'Okay, so if you're on leave—'

Rachel raised her hand. 'Enough questions,' she said. 'I'm tired. I need to sleep. You're welcome to stay here if you want. There's more than one bedroom. However, if you'd prefer to leave, I can call Frank and he'll take you back to town.'

'And if I stay? What then?'

'We can talk some more. You can hear me out. Then you can make a decision.'

'And that decision would be whether I want to what?'

'Find the truth, Carl. It's as simple as that. Find the fucking truth.'

'Okay, so I stay, right? I listen to everything you've got to say. What if I decide I don't want any part of it? What happens then?'

'I guess you get on a plane and go back to New York and carry on with your life as if this never happened.'

'You think I'd be able to do that?'

'Doesn't matter what I think, Carl.'

'I'm staying,' Sheehan said. 'I want to understand. I really do.'

'Good enough,' Rachel said. She got up from the chair. She indicated the hallway. 'Bathroom's first on the left. Your room faces it. There's towels on the bed. I also got you a toothbrush, and there's a wardrobe of clothes in there. They're Frank's, but he won't mind you using them.'

'You knew I'd stay.'

'I wasn't sure, no.'

'And who the hell is Frank anyway? How do you know him?'

'He's retired. Ex-FBI,' Rachel said. 'And pretty much the only person in the world who believes me.'

70

The silence – punctuated solely by the intermittent sounds of animals, the wind through trees, the creak and yaw of the wooden walls around him – served only to exaggerate the sense of isolation that Sheehan felt.

His mind – crowded with thoughts, ideas, assumptions, conjecture, faces from the past – would not surrender to sleep. He wrestled fitfully, agitated and disturbed, desperate to find some anchor to which he could tether his confusion. He questioned whether he really did want to know the truth. It could be only one of two things: Rachel was right, and there was a great deal more to what had happened in Syracuse and New York, or she had succumbed to paranoia and imagination. If, as she'd said, she'd had some sort of breakdown after Pennsylvania, so much so that the FBI felt it necessary to relinquish her of her active status and put her out to pasture, then maybe he would go the same way if he followed her. And what about Frank? Retired, living out here in the middle of nowhere, unable to reconcile himself to anything approaching a regular life, perhaps he'd gotten involved because he had to feel necessary. Sheehan had seen it with ex-military, ex-cops, all those whose lives were tied inextricably into institutional realities and routines. They couldn't let go. They couldn't walk away. Part of them – a greater part – would always be drawn back into the life they'd once lived.

Sheehan did sleep, but for how long he didn't know. When dawn broke – the light and the sounds of the woods finding him in the narrow bed – he woke with a sense of foreboding.

He hadn't dreamed, could not remember dreaming, and yet that sense of his mind having been invaded by something unknown and unwanted was as real as the room around him.

He put on his own clothes. He needed to shower, but the thought of being naked in this strange place unnerved him. He could've taken some of the clothes hanging on a rail near the bed, but the idea of wearing someone else's things also didn't seem right.

Sheehan opened the door of the bedroom. He could hear movement elsewhere in the house. He smelled coffee.

Rachel was in the kitchen. She stood in front of the window over the sink. The view ahead of her was nothing but trees and sky and space. It was as unlike the cramped and claustrophobic intensity of New York as you could get.

Rachel turned. She smiled. 'Coffee?'

'Sure, yes. Thanks.'

She poured a cup and set it on the table. Sheehan sat down.

'I guess you didn't sleep much,' she said.

'No, not really.'

'That's understandable.'

Rachel sat down facing him.

'If you want, you can leave.'

'I don't know what I want,' Sheehan replied.

'We don't change much, do we? Did we ever really know what we wanted?'

'As in life, or us?'

'Both.'

'I guess it would've been good to know why you never called me back. I would've understood, you know.'

'Would you?'

Sheehan shrugged. 'Maybe I'm only thinking that because I've not seen you or heard from you for four years. I guess it's all a little less raw.'

'I wanted to call you,' Rachel said. 'I wanted to explain. I felt that I owed you that much. But, at the same time, I figured it would be best to make a clean break of it.'

'Did you miss me?'

Rachel smiled. 'Looking back, I think what we had was the closest I ever got to normal, whatever the hell that is. That's what I missed more than anything. And no, there was never anyone else who felt like that.'

'Same.'

'But that's not why we're here, Carl.'

'I know.'

'So, I'm gonna ask you again, and you have to make a decision based on that, not on whatever you might feel about me. There's something here. It's real. I believe that it's real. Frank believes it too. There's too many things that don't make sense, too many unanswered questions, and I don't know that I'll ever be able to have any kind of regular existence until I find out the answer.'

'And if you don't?' Sheehan asked.

'Then maybe someone else will take up where we leave off and figure it out.'

'What do you want from me?'

'I want you to look at something. I want you to hear me out. Then I want you to decide if you're going to help us or not.'

'And what would that help entail?'

'That's something that'll only make sense once you see what I want to show you.'

'Okay. So, show me.'

'You want breakfast?'

'I'm not hungry.'

'You should eat something,' Rachel said. 'I'll make some eggs.'

The back room of the cabin was empty but for a desk and two chairs that centered the room. The only wall that wasn't covered with maps, photographs, notes and diagrams was the one with a window that looked out towards the woods behind the building.

Sheehan stood in the doorway and his mind unraveled. He had never seen anything even close to what was before him. Images of crime scenes, dates, places, photographs of Robert Marshall and Charles Wagner, other faces he recognized but could not place. Everything he'd seen all those years before in Syracuse and New York was here. It was as if the last decade and a half of horror and mayhem had been reconstructed in a single space.

'What the fuck?' he heard himself say. He had no idea if he'd voiced it.

'Sit down,' Rachel said.

'What the hell is all this?' Sheehan asked.

'This is what Frank and I have been doing for the past year and a half,' Rachel replied.

Sheehan walked to the wall facing him. To the far left, a collection of small images was affixed to the edge of a map of Syracuse. A thread ran from each one to a specific location. The names were ones he recalled so clearly – Caroline Lassiter, Raymond Keene, the Wilsons, Brenda Forsyth and Michael Ridgway. To the right was New York, and again a line of images with their related locations – Christopher Wake, Anthony Yates and Maggie Silva. And then there was Pennsylvania, and here he recognized the names of Bernard Clarke and Samantha Warner. But there were others, another seven in total, and their names were unknown to him.

'This is what you were doing in Allentown,' Sheehan said.

'Gary Eugene Earl,' Rachel said. 'That was Purgatory.'

Sheehan turned to look at her. Her expression was matter-of-fact, almost without emotion.

'Take a seat, Carl—'

Rachel stopped, turned. The sound of someone opening the front door.

'That'll be Frank,' she said.

Rachel left the room.

Sheehan could hear them talking in the hallway. He could have misinterpreted it, but there was a tone of concern in Rachel's voice.

Sheehan stayed right where he was. He surveyed the endless amount of information around him, noticing then that beside each Pennsylvania photograph was a small label – *Ira, Invidia, Luxuria* and on it went. To the right were lists of numbers, beside them further lists as if someone had tried to identify patterns and recurring sequences. The time and effort that had been invested in collating this was extraordinary. What it suggested – what Rachel was suggesting – was beyond even that. And he was expected to believe this? That someone had engineered all of this, that some unknown identity was ultimately responsible for killings that had taken place over so many years?

Rachel came back into the room. Collins followed her, carrying with him one of the chairs from the kitchen.

'Mr. Sheehan,' Collins said. 'How you doing?'

Sheehan just looked at him, dismay and disbelief evident in his eyes.

Collins smiled knowingly. 'Yes, it'll do that to you,' he said.

'I'm lost,' Sheehan said. 'I mean, I know we've walked around the edges of this thing before, but this . . .' He looked from one wall to the next to the next. 'This is—'

'This is more than a year's worth of work,' Collins said. 'And a hell of a lot of information that shouldn't even be here.'

Collins placed a chair near the table and sat down. Again, Sheehan saw something in his body language. The man was tired, but this wasn't the fatigue of an insomniac.

'I need to be honest with you, Mr. Sheehan,' he said. 'I don't feel right about this, about you coming here and getting involved, but Rachel is convinced that you're a man of your word. You decide you're not going to help us, then you need to forget you ever saw this. You can't speak about it, not to anyone, and you sure as hell can't ever write about it.'

'Who the fuck would believe me even if I did?' Sheehan asked.

'A good point. Nevertheless, you understand what I'm telling you.'

Sheehan turned to the wall. The more he looked, the more he saw details that raised even more questions.

'Sit down for Christ's sake, Carl,' Rachel said. 'Hear us out. What you then decide is up to you.'

'Yes, sure,' Sheehan replied, his tone uncertain, hesitant.

Looking at Collins, he said, 'So tell me how you got into this? You were FBI?'

'I was Behavioral Science,' Collins said. 'That's where I met Rachel.'

'And you were investigating this?'

'Officially, no. It was never on our books. Rachel came to me for help. She told me what she knew. I listened.'

'And then...'

'And then Rachel went on leave and I retired. We stayed in touch. She needed somewhere to stay, so she came here. That was back in the spring of last year. We got to talking about it some more, and then we decided to do something about it.'

'And how did you get all this information?'

'Let's just say that even when your membership expires you never really leave the club.'

'So there's other people that know you've put this all together? People who are still active FBI?'

'Well, I guess if a bunch of people from different offices all happened to be in the same place at the same time and my name came up in conversation, they might put two and two together. Aside from that no, there's no one who knows that all this information wound up here.'

Collins took a handkerchief from his pocket and wiped his mouth.

'You okay?' Rachel asked.

Collins waved her question aside.

'You want something? A glass of water?'

'Don't fuss,' he replied.

With that, Collins got up and headed back to the kitchen. Sheehan heard the sound of running water.

'What's up with him?' Sheehan asked Rachel. 'Is he sick?'

She shook her head. 'Not now,' she said, her voice a whisper.

Once Collins returned, Rachel said, 'We need to start at the beginning. There's a few things you need to understand before we get into Dante again.'

That name – Dante – hit Sheehan like a bullet. Fourteen years had passed since he'd written that first article in the *Syracuse Tribune*.

'So tell me,' Sheehan said. 'Tell me what I need to understand.'

71

'Back then we knew nothing,' Rachel said. 'In 1975, we didn't even have a term for it. Now we call them serial killers, but we were in the dark.'

'For us, it was always Motive, Method, Opportunity,' Collins said. 'People killed people for many different reasons, but they were, I guess, at least understandable. Greed and need, that's what it was. That's how we viewed things, and it's the way we'd looked at it for as long as investigative technique existed.'

'But things changed,' Rachel said. 'The Nightstalker case back in '85. That was California, the LA County Sheriff's Department. There were a couple of detectives on that – Frank Salerno and Gil Carillo – and they had some guy out there murdering people for no identifiable reason at all. On one day alone, March 17th, their perp kills a woman in Rosemead, then another in Monterey Park. He drags a thirty-year-old woman out of her car, right there in the street, and shoots her in cold blood. She wasn't robbed, so it wasn't greed. And where was the need? She was a total stranger. Ten days later, he commits a double murder in Whittier County. The husband is executed, the wife is raped and then he cuts out her eyes. And just like the earlier ones, these people were unknown to him. Carillo was also investigating a seemingly unrelated series of child abductions that were happening simultaneously. Kids just taken off the street, sexually assaulted and then released at a gas station or near a shopping mall.'

'Victims ranged in age from sixteen to eighty-three,' Collins said. 'No substantive physical evidence at any of the crime scenes. Carillo believed that these two entirely different series of crimes were being perpetrated by the same person. But, how could one person brutally rape and murder grown men and women, and then – at the same time – be sexually molesting children? It wasn't possible.'

'But it was possible,' Rachel said, 'and Carillo finally got a crime scene tech to buy into this theory. And then they got a shoeprint, and the shoeprint tied these completely different crime scenes together.'

'Richard Ramirez,' Sheehan said.

'Exactly,' Collins said. 'And they got him because someone went outside the traditional framework of investigatory protocol.'

'It was firmly established that there were only three ways you would ever find a killer,' Rachel said. 'The perp would make a mistake, someone would get a stroke of luck, or someone would somehow get inside the mind of this person and figure out how he was thinking. The first two were completely unreliable and unpredictable, and the third was something that no one even really had a handle on. What drove someone like Richard Ramirez? That's what I wanted to know. That's where the whole concept of Motive, Method and Opportunity started to fall apart. Here we had a motive that was known only to the person who was committing the crimes.'

Rachel leaned forward, her expression intense.

'Ramirez said "I was in alliance with the evil that is inherent in human nature, and that was who I was. Walking death".'

'Berkowitz,' Collins said. 'He killed people because a six-thousand-year-old demon commanded him to through the body of his neighbor's dog. Who was the neighbor? His name was Sam Carr. Carr himself had two sons, and they were involved in some sort of pseudo-religious satanic cult. They had meetings in Untermyer Park. They sacrificed dogs. They drew pentagrams on the walls of buildings in blood. One of them was called

John Wheat Carr. His nickname was "John Wheaties". That was a name that Berkowitz wrote in one of his letters to the press. And now, evidence keeps coming to light that there was no way in the world that Berkowitz could've killed alone. And then both of the Carr brothers are killed in freak circumstances. One gets his head blown off with a shotgun in Minot, North Dakota, supposedly a suicide, and the other drives off the road into a concrete barrier.'

'I'm sorry,' Sheehan said. 'I mean, I've read about some of this stuff, but I don't understand what it has to do with—' He turned and indicated the walls of the room. 'With all of this.'

'Ed Kemper, John Wayne Gacy, Richard Speck, Zodiac, this guy out in Kansas who calls himself BTK, Henry Lee Lucas, even as far back as Ed Gein,' Rachel said. 'People have been investigating these multiple murders – these serial killers – without ever really coming to terms with the fact that they had no idea what they were investigating.'

'Speaking of Henry Lee Lucas,' Collins said. 'He confessed to hundreds of killings. He even confessed to killings that he didn't commit, couldn't possibly have committed. He wanted the attention. The attention was a drug. He led the Texas Rangers up a long and winding path for years. But, you know, even when they thought he was the worst mass murderer that America had ever seen, they had him interviewed by a renowned and respected psychiatrist. This guy said that Lucas had no conscience, no empathy, that he was a sociopathic deviant with a range of sexual disorders that included bestiality and necrophilia, but he was nevertheless in the normal psychiatric range. It was all based on a completely outdated and utterly unworkable construct that had no relevance to the real world.'

'But there were people who were interested, though not necessarily in law enforcement,' Rachel said. 'Two guys, Morneau and Rockwell, published a book about ten years ago called *Sex, Motivation and the Criminal Offender*. They talked about how some homicides were committed because the perpetrator wanted to see fear. It was a way to obtain complete control of another human being. And then there were a couple of journalists, Stephen Michaud and Hugh Aynesworth. They investigated Ted Bundy from every angle. The only way Michaud got Bundy to open up about the killings was to get him to talk about it in the third person. He talked about his early life as well, how he suffered from a debilitating speech impediment, how he was teased and bullied, how he never really fitted in when it came to social situations, how he loved to scare people. He loved to see that flash of fear in people's eyes.'

'I worked in BSU,' Collins said. 'I knew Bill Hagmaier. He interviewed Bundy, too. Bill asked him why it started, why it continued. Bundy said there was a hunger. He said he was left hungry each time, as if there was something deep inside him that he was trying to satiate. Each time he killed someone he imagined that hunger would go away, but it didn't. And so he'd kill again, and then again. He said that he finally realized he would never be fulfilled. But he also said that he was not an animal, that he wasn't crazy, that he didn't have a split personality. In his own estimation he considered himself to be an entirely normal person.'

'And then there's Syracuse,' Rachel said. 'And then New York and Pennsylvania. No one, and I mean no one, has been willing to consider the possibility that a series of murders, each of them five years apart, could have been orchestrated by the same person. They got their killer, or at least they believed they did, and that was it.'

'Is that why you got in trouble in Allentown?' Sheehan said. 'Because you wouldn't let this go?'

'That was one reason, yes. But I was burned out, I guess. Hell, I don't know what happened. Maybe I just looked too long into the abyss.'

'You know, in the last ten years, violent crime has increased

387

over a hundred and thirty percent,' Collins said. 'Rape has increased a similar amount. Murders are up over sixty percent. Crime has changed, and we haven't changed with it. We're still operating under the same principles that applied when we were chasing bank robbers and Mafia hitmen.'

'Okay, okay,' Sheehan said, 'but what I don't get is why you're even here. I mean, isn't there an actual Behavioral Science Unit? It exists now, doesn't it? It has people and funding and—'

'And an unwillingness to even consider the possibility that we're dealing with one case here,' Collins interjected. 'I know psychological profiling techniques. We did extensive tests on a number of occasions. We reviewed previously solved crimes as profilers, but we gave exactly the same information to police officers, clinical psychologists, even a group of chemistry students, for Christ's sake. After the profiles were done, we compared them to the known perpetrator. In no case did the profilers create a more accurate profile than anyone else. In fact, on several occasions the profilers came up with something that was a great deal less accurate than anyone else. Profiling is based on observations, evidence and conclusions drawn from a crime scene. It doesn't allow for intentional efforts to mislead the investigation. It categorizes offenders as "organized" and "disorganized", and not every perpetrator can be neatly fitted into one or other of those classifications. But the basic flaw, the most fundamental flaw of all, is that the vast majority of information they base their techniques on comes from people who were caught. Even the interviews that Ressler and Douglas did, the interviews that served as a basis for the National Center for the Analysis of Violent Crime, covered only thirty-six offenders. And, like I said, they were the ones who'd fucked up and gotten caught. They were on death row. They were serving life with no possibility of parole. They would say anything that prolonged their own lives or enabled them to get additional privileges.'

'And,' Rachel added, 'they were all inveterate and compulsive liars, narcissists and egomaniacs. We can also pretty much guarantee that the vast majority of them were suffering from some kind of undiagnosed or untreated mental disorder.'

'And yet to meet them you would never know,' Collins said. 'Like Bundy said, "People don't realize that murderers don't come out in the dark with long teeth and saliva dripping off their chin".'

Sheehan looked back at Rachel, then at Collins, and then scanned the walls around him.

'You are convinced, both of you, that Syracuse, New York and Pennsylvania are connected?'

'Right,' Rachel said.

'Tell me why.'

'For so many reasons,' Rachel replied. 'And the first one, perhaps the most important one, is that none of the three serial killers have any history that agrees with any pattern or background that could be considered a flag for such behavior.'

'But you just said that the way in which these psychological profiles have been developed was fundamentally flawed.'

'Not all of it,' Collins said. 'There are common denominators. You look at a lot of these guys, and there are similarities. Socially disconnected, inability to relate to females, a history of parental abuse or institutional bullying. They vent. I guess that's how you could term it. They find an outlet for their frustration and rage. It begins with destroying possessions, their own and others'. They gravitate to hurting defenseless animals. Then it's arson in a lot of cases. Empty buildings, usually. Cars, things like that. Then there's instances of violence against people who can't fight back. Then it becomes murder.'

'And even though Charles Wagner did five years on Rikers Island for stabbing someone,' Rachel said, 'it was the only instance of physical violence in his history. Robert Marshall was a sex offender. Again, no violent history. Gary Earl, the Pennsylvania serial killer, was in Attica for drugs. Sure, he had other things, breaking and entering, one assault, but nothing that was a long-standing pattern of conduct.'

'Their histories didn't add up,' Collins said. 'And then there's the obvious connection. *The Divine Comedy.*'

'Which we assumed to be a copycat in New York,' Sheehan said.

'Have you read it?' Collins asked.

'Back in college, yes. Most of it. Then I started it again, but it's heavy-going.'

'And yet you're an educated man, a journalist, a professional writer. None of these guys had half the education that you have. You're telling me that a trio of petty criminals with little more than a twelfth-grade education between them managed to navigate their way through a fourteenth-century religious text of over fourteen thousand lines of poetry and have sufficient an understanding to model their crimes on its structure?'

'So, if the last one was Purgatory, then what about Paradiso?' Sheehan asked. 'You said the first series represented Death, right, and the second was Hell?'

'That's what we're waiting for,' Rachel said.

'What you're waiting for?'

'It will be five years soon,' she said. 'Each sequence has been five years apart.'

'You're saying that there'll be another serial killer on the loose?' Sheehan asked, now incredulous.

'If we're right about the pattern, yes,' Collins said.

'But you have no idea where or exactly when or who will do these things. And even if you're right, what the fuck does killing more people have to do with Paradise?'

'We don't know,' Rachel said. 'We have theories, ideas, but we honestly don't know.'

'Jesus,' Sheehan said. 'This is just too fucking much.'

'In the final part,' Rachel said, 'Dante is guided by Beatrice. She represents divine revelation. Apparently, Beatrice was based on someone that Dante courted when he was a young man. Beatrice guides Dante through the celestial spheres of Heaven. Here Dante finds the cardinal virtues, one of which is Justice. It's in *Paradiso* that all sins are washed clean and where Dante discovers not only the angels, but the essence of God.'

'So, what are you saying? That you're this guy's Beatrice? That he wants you to deliver justice?'

'It's one among a whole bunch of theories,' Collins replied.

'A whole bunch of fucking craziness,' Sheehan said.

'Maybe.'

'Okay, so say if I suspend my disbelief completely, say I buy into this utterly fucking insane idea, then why Rachel? Why the hell would this guy pick Rachel? Is it someone she knows? Is that what's going on here? Is this some kind of personal thing?'

'Because I was there,' Rachel said. 'I was there for the very first one. Caroline Lassiter, back in 1975.'

'But anyone could've been there instead of you,' Sheehan replied. 'The fact that it was you was entirely random, right?'

'Perhaps,' Rachel replied. 'You're trying to rationalize something that defies reason, at least in our way of thinking. But we're not dealing with someone who thinks as we do. We're dealing with someone who has a construct and an explanation that is understood only by himself. And that's why we're not able to explain it.'

'And yet you're assuming that there's something to explain.'

'We're assuming it because we've considered everything else and there is no other explanation,' Collins said.

'So no copycat?'

Rachel shook her head.

'No other identifiable motive for each of these people to have targeted these victims?'

Again, Rachel shook her head.

'Okay, so why five years apart?' Sheehan asked. 'Why not each year? Why not every six fucking months for that matter?'

'In numerology, five represents the need for experiences in order to feel fulfilled. In the Tarot, five is the Hierophant. This is the messenger between human beings and Heaven. There's five points in a pentagram. There were five wounds in the body of Christ. David had five stones with which to defeat Goliath. There are five books in the Torah. There are five human senses. In spirituality, five is the number of regeneration, the inability to accept the possibility of risk and an innate belief in the power of the universe. In Pythagorean culture it's the symbol of life. The Greeks believed that the universe was made up of five elements. There are five pillars of Islam. In the occult, objects arranged in fives are capable of trapping demons—'

'Okay, I get it. It's a significant number.'

'We don't know why,' Collins said. 'That's the simple answer. But we're looking and we're thinking and we're asking ourselves all the questions that no one else seems to want to ask.'

'I need a break,' Sheehan said. 'I need to go have a drink or look at the sky or take a walk in the fucking woods. Maybe all three. This is all a bit too much to digest in one go.'

Neither Rachel nor Collins replied.

Sheehan got up. He walked around the room. He started to notice things that he hadn't seen before. A pentagram. A list of dates broken down and correlated to other dates. A piece of paper that detailed distances between kill-sites, certain numbers underlined, some of them twice. It was like looking inside whatever universe Rachel and Frank had created for themselves, and now he was being invited to join them.

He stood at the window for a good minute. He breathed deeply, tried to focus, and then he turned back to face them.

'All other questions aside, what do you want from me? Why am I here? What do you expect me to do?'

'He knows who you are,' Rachel said. 'He'll have read your articles.'

'Well, that's enormously reassuring. That makes me feel a whole lot better.'

'If he's anything at all, he's a narcissist. He's smarter than all of us. He's outwitted everyone, every step of the way. He's so ahead of us that no one even believes he exists. And so we want to bait him.'

'Bait him?'

'Yes,' Rachel replied. 'And we need you to set the trap.'

72

Rachel lay awake.

The foremost question in her mind was whether or not she should have involved Carl. He was struggling to come to terms with what they'd told him. This she'd expected, but her concerns went beyond that. She was now, directly or indirectly, responsible for his life and well-being.

Had she honestly thought he wouldn't come looking for her? She knew that there would forever be a connection between them. They'd shared too much, and the demise of their relationship had always been a shadow that haunted her conscience. She shouldn't have let him go. She should've fought for it, but then he should've fought with equal vigor and insistence. But they were young, less cynical, each possessing greater faith in their own ability to create a different, better future. But each of them was still alone. And each of them was driven towards something else – something nebulous, something undefined – and that, above all things, was both a blessing and a curse.

This was a life, but it was not a life. It was a prison – mental, emotional, psychological – and, as yet, she had no clue as to the identity of her jailer, nor whether she would ever be released. She was surrounded by ghosts – the dead behind her, perhaps the dead yet to come – and yet the ghost she feared the most was the one she couldn't name.

She could close her eyes and remember the bound and tortured limbs, the dead sockets where once the eyes had been, the stab wounds and bullet holes, the blackened tongue and bloated features of someone hanged. She had not become inured, but she was – at least in part – familiar with things to which no human being should ever become accustomed. Did each death somehow leave a shadow of death behind? Did the victims leave some small fingerprint of their pain on the soul of the witness? And if she faced this, confronted it, and finally discovered the source of all this darkness, would it then be exorcized from her mind, or would she still be burdened with it forever?

Rachel turned at a sound near the door. Reflex and instinct took her hand to the gun beneath her pillow.

She moved sideways, slipping from beneath the covers until she knelt on the floor beside the bed. Crouching low, she waited.

Frank had gone home. Perhaps it was Carl, also unable to sleep, perhaps out in the kitchen getting some water, perhaps using the bathroom.

She'd spent too long, too many years, looking over her shoulder, all the while anticipating the very worst the world could offer. Trust had long since been replaced with an innate need to be suspicious of everyone, to never put herself in a situation where she was at the mercy of something that could have been predicted.

As the door handle turned, every nerve and sinew tensed in her body.

'Carl?' she said.

The door opened. He stood there, nothing more than an outline.

'I'm sorry,' he said, 'but I—'

'Jesus Christ, Carl. Don't do that, okay?'

'I'm sorry, Rachel. I can't sleep. I have so much shit going 'round in my head.'

Rachel slid the gun back under the pillow. Carl didn't need to see that. She tugged her robe from the chair beside the bed and put it on. Reaching over, she flicked on the lamp.

'Did I wake you?' Sheehan asked.

'No, you didn't.'

'Can I come in?'

'I think you're in already, Carl.'

Sheehan closed the door behind him. He was still dressed, everything but his shoes, and he stood for a moment as if he had no idea what he was doing there.

'What's going on?' Rachel asked. 'Apart from the obvious, of course.'

'You think maybe we could go sit in the kitchen or something?' he said. 'I don't know, it doesn't feel right that I'm in your room.'

'Doesn't feel right? Christ, Carl, we lived together. Everything you could see you've seen a thousand times before.'

'Yes, I know, but—'

'Sure,' Rachel said. 'I'll put some clothes on.'

Sheehan hesitated, and then he turned and left without a word.

With nothing but the light from the hallway, they sat across from one another at the kitchen table.

Beyond the window, the darkness was impenetrable.

'Back in New York,' Sheehan said, 'when you and Maurice Quinn told me about what was happening and I published the Red Ribbon article, I was working on something else.'

'What?'

'You remember the Torso Killings in Times Square?'

'I heard about it, sure. I was a little preoccupied at the time.'

'First one was December of '79. Room 417 at the Travel Inn. Someone lit a fire. Firefighters got in there, saw a woman on the bed, and one goes to give her CPR. Then he realizes she's got no head and no hands. Then they find a second body, just the same, on the adjacent bed. They can't ID them. All they've got is their clothes folded neatly in the bathtub. They dress a couple of store mannequins in these clothes and put the pictures out all over the place. Someone comes forward, a roommate of one of the dead girls. The victim's name is Deedeh Goodarzi. She's a hooker, not a street girl, but an escort, you know? A few hundred bucks a time. The other one was never identified, still hasn't been to this day. They just called her Manhattan Jane Doe. There's no blood spatter, no prints at the crime scene, nothing. I knew Jerry McQueen back then. Sergeant from the 10th Precinct Detectives Unit. I also knew another guy called Vernon Geberth from Bronx Homicide. He'd just got back from doing the profiling course at Quantico. They had no idea what they were dealing with. Anyway, these girls were bound face-down, knife wounds all up and down their backs. Jerry told me they'd been tortured for three days.'

Sheehan paused, looked down at his hands. He took a breath.

'They really had nothing. Went 'round in circles and got nowhere. Then in May of '80, they found another one. Again, the perp had lit a fire. This was in the Seville Hotel off Madison and 29th. Fire guys said that it wasn't done to burn evidence, wasn't even done to burn the hotel down, but to attract attention. Whoever did it wanted the body found as soon as possible. Her name was Jean Reyner. Beaten, tortured, raped, strangled. Again, no evidence, very neat. Jerry said it was the cleanest crime scene he'd ever been to.'

Sheehan paused, looked away for a moment, and then back at Rachel.

'Back then, Times Square was … well, it was like half a dozen blocks of Hell had been dropped right into the city. More than a thousand hookers on the street every night. Peep shows, movie houses, live sex in every other building. Plato's Retreat, the Hellfire Club, the Show World Center. It was madness. And New York laid off over five thousand cops. Most of those properties were either owned or run by the Gambinos. Women were found beaten half-to-death or killed several times a week.

It was a fucking theme park for psychos and predators. And you know, the victims they couldn't identify, and there were a lot of them, were listed as NHI. "No Human Involved". These girls weren't even acknowledged as people. For these hotel killings, the cops looked at hundreds of cases of violence against prostitutes. They couldn't find anything that matched the profile. And then, a little while later, over at the Quality Inn in Hasbrouck Heights, New Jersey, a maid is cleaning a room. The vacuum cleaner keeps hitting something under the bed. She gets down, and there she finds a dead, handcuffed nineteen-year-old called Valerie Street. But this is Bergen County, not New York. The jurisdictions don't talk to one another. Then there's another one, same MO, but she's left in the parking lot of the same hotel. This is thirty minutes from Times Square, you know, just across the river. But they don't put two and two together. Later the same month, May 1980, eighteen days after Valerie Street in New Jersey, just a week after Jean Reyner in New York, there's another nineteen-year-old called Leslie O'Dell. She gets picked up in Times Square, goes to a bar with the john, has a few drinks that he's spiked with sedatives. Then he drives her out to a hotel in New Jersey. He tortures her for hours, but she screams so loud that the staff call the cops. That's when they got the guy. Richard Cottingham. Thirty-three years old, computer operator for Blue Cross Blue Shield. Family man. Married, three kids. Lived out in Lodi, New Jersey.'

'I remember that in the papers,' Rachel said.

'Do you know that even now the only way to get a rape conviction in New York, even if the victim identifies the rapist in a fucking police line-up, is if there is a witness to the actual crime who's willing to get on the stand and testify? Can you believe that?'

'I can believe it, yes.'

'I covered all of that stuff. I wrote so much about Cottingham and those girls. I reported on the 1981 trial in New Jersey, the trial in New York a year and a half later. What started to come to light was that there were many more victims, some say as many as a hundred. There's rumors that he started killing teenage girls as far back as the late 60s. In truth, I don't think we'll ever know. Cottingham got two hundred years. He's out there in Trenton State and he still insists he's innocent, that all the evidence was planted by the cops. And now the New York Mayor's Office and whoever else are doing their damnedest to clean up the city. They have the Office of Midtown Enforcement and they're putting all those sex joints out of business. They made some progress, but the thing that finally put an end to it was AIDS.'

Sheehan looked, up, smiled sardonically.

'Back then the NYPD put out a pamphlet. It was called "Welcome to Fear City" and it had a picture of the Grim Reaper on the front. It was a visitor's guide on how not to get robbed, raped or murdered in New York. Anyway, after that, I'd had enough. I had to get out of there. Only after I left did I realize how my whole viewpoint about people had been ... I don't even know what to call it. Infected? Poisoned?'

Sheehan looked up.

'When I found out about Bernard Clarke and realized that he'd done time with Wagner, I wanted to follow it up. I wanted to pursue that and see if there was any connection, but – to be honest – I was burned out. Then, when you didn't call back, I let it go. I'd had enough of the killing and the mayhem and all that shit. The fact that you seemed to just vanish told me that I'd be doing it alone, and I didn't believe I could.'

'So when you asked me to come stay with you for a few days after the funeral, you had already left New York?'

'I was in Raleigh, North Carolina. Stayed there for a year or so and then came back. I rented a place in the Village, been there ever since.'

'Why there? And why didn't you tell me?'

'Didn't matter where. It could have been anywhere just as

long as it wasn't within walking distance of Times Square. And I didn't tell you because what was happening then wasn't about me, it was about you.'

'And now I've dragged you back into the darkness again, right?'

'You didn't drag me, Rachel. And maybe that's where we're most alike. I'm drawn to it. Why, I don't know. It just pulls at me. Like Jerry McQueen once said, needing to know the truth is the most addictive drug of all. And I want to believe what you're telling me because I don't want to believe the other explanation.'

Rachel smiled. 'The one where I've completely lost my fucking mind, right?'

'Right,' Sheehan said. 'So what really happened in Pennsylvania?'

'Nine dead,' she replied. 'It started with Clarke and Warner, and it ended with a twenty-three-year-old called Lauren Trent. Each murder was meant to represent one of the seven roots of sinfulness. Lust, Greed, Envy, Pride. You know the deal. He killed three in one go. Two brothers and a woman called Judith Whyte. They were making porn films in some old factory, and he tied them to chairs and burned their feet with an oxyacetylene torch. It was fucking inhuman. The guy we arrested was called Gary Eugene Earl. He was a forty-one-year-old maintenance worker.'

'What happened to him?'

'He was arraigned at Lehigh County Court. The judge instructed that his handcuffs and shackles be removed. He pushed the court officers out of the way, vaulted the stand, got out into the corridor and then went backwards over the railings. He dropped three floors and landed on his head.'

'Christ almighty...'

'I spoke to him in the holding cell. I asked him to help me understand. He hadn't said a word up to that point.'

'Did he speak to you then?'

'He said, "Until you do what I have done, you can never hope to understand".'

'And that was the last thing he said?'

'It was the *only* thing he said.'

'So, let's go with what you're saying. We're talking about someone who's capable of getting three separate people to commit a series of murders. Not only that, but those people are then willing to kill themselves before anyone has a chance to interrogate them. Who could do that? And, more importantly, why?'

Rachel got up and fetched a glass down from the cupboard. 'You want some milk?'

Sheehan shook his head.

Rachel opened the fridge, filled the glass and took her seat again.

'God,' she said matter-of-factly. 'Or the Devil.'

'What?'

'The entire construct of religion, whether it be good or evil, is based on faith, right? Faith in something. Faith in an identity. Look at the things that have been done in the name of religion. It's probably fair to say that more people have died in the never-ending battle of "My God is better than your God" than any other single motivation in the history of the human race. Even now, right here in twentieth-century America, you've got fundamentalists who believe that God will protect them from snakebites. Some of them die, for fuck's sake, but that doesn't seem to diminish the fervor that the remainder of the congregation maintain. You convince somebody that their immediate life is nothing but a transitional stage, just one small part of a journey to somewhere better, and it seems there's no end of extremes that a person will suffer.'

'You're saying that whoever's doing this is playing God?'

'Or playing the Devil. He's managed to convince these people that what they did served some greater purpose, and they bought

it hook, line and sinker. They were willing to sacrifice themselves for whatever they were promised in return. Everlasting
life. Heaven. Hell, even. You take an impressionable human
being and you convince them that only they can really grasp the
meaning of what they're doing. Only they can truly appreciate
the reward they will get for doing it.'

'Until you do what I have done, you can never hope to
understand.'

'Exactly.'

'Is that what you think happened?'

'It's a theory.'

'And you have other theories?'

'We have had, but they fell apart when we asked enough
questions. This is the only one that bears up under scrutiny.
The motive was irrational, sure, but it explains why they were
willing to do what they did, and how all three sequences could
be connected. There was some greater purpose that became all-
consuming, and it overrode everything else.'

'It's like a social experiment from hell,' Sheehan said. 'And you
really believe that taunting him will get him to show his face?'

'I don't know, Carl. Maybe it ended in 1985 with Gary Earl.
Maybe that was enough. Maybe he's just vanished into the fucking ether never to be heard of again.'

'But you don't believe it.'

'There's another part to the book, isn't there? Paradiso, right?
I also believe that people have a fundamental need to be acknowledged. Everything we do, everything we say, is driven by
the basic need to have our existence affirmed by others. That's
what drives creation, good or bad. It's like cause and effect. You
make something happen, you want others to know that you
were the author.'

'Even criminals?'

'You think people go back to the scene of a crime for no
reason? You know, there's endless cases of people working their

way into actual investigations, offering to help the police to look for people that have gone missing. Parents who killed their own kids going on TV to plead with the killer to give themselves up. And they're sincere, heartfelt, convincing performances. Some of them are fucking Oscar-worthy. And you can say that offence is the best form of defense. But this is like a challenge, a desire to prove that they're smarter than everyone else, that they've committed the perfect murder, that they will never be discovered. And they keep on believing that until they are discovered. And then, like your Cottingham guy, they keep protesting their innocence even when the evidence is incontrovertible.'

'You think people like that actually want to be caught?'

'Maybe there's an element of that, too. But then you have to believe that human beings are basically good. They know they're doing wrong, they can't stop themselves, so they self-generate a scenario so someone else will stop them. But in my experience, the complete lack of remorse and conscience tells me that's not the case. I've seen too much bad shit, Carl. Let's just say my faith in human nature has been tarnished somewhat.'

'So what are you thinking? That we make less of what this guy believes he has achieved and it will piss him off enough to do something?'

'Narcissism. Self-belief. They're as powerful as faith in their own way. That's faith in self. I am God. Look what I've done. Look how I can control people. Not only can I make people kill others, I can make them kill themselves. How long can someone with that much ego stay unacknowledged? You challenge that, and yes, I think it's going to upset them. You've put them on the back foot. You're wresting back some element of control. They're treating people like marionettes, and all of a sudden the marionette isn't doing what they're supposed to. Maybe that's enough to bring the guy out from behind the curtains.'

'Or maybe that's enough for him to kill you.'

'And Frank. And you. And that's why this has to be your

decision, Carl. I can't choose for you. Sure, we need your help, and if you're on board then all well and good, but it has to be a complete commitment, and it has to come from you. It can't be motivated because you care for me, and it certainly can't be conditional.'

'Like a condition where I help you because then you'll owe me? And maybe, if you owe me, then we can get back together?'

'Like I said, Carl, it can't be conditional.'

From beyond the window, the sound of an owl broke the growing sense of tension between them.

Rachel smiled. 'Not exactly New York, is it?'

Carl closed his eyes for a moment. He'd already made his decision. In truth, he'd made it earlier in the day. He'd been convinced by both Rachel and Frank. He'd just needed time to find his own conviction. It did not manifest itself as a certainty that there was some unknown personality who'd manipulated Robert Marshall, Charles Wagner and Gary Earl, but rather that there was an actual explanation for what they had done that was still unknown. Perhaps Rachel was right with her theory, perhaps she wasn't. Still, there had to be an answer to this, and if they found it then perhaps it would dispel a darkness that had bound them together for a decade and a half.

'I'm going to try and sleep,' Carl said. He got up from the chair.

'And tomorrow?' Rachel asked.

'Tomorrow we get to work.'

73

Collins arrived in time for breakfast.

Sheehan helped Rachel make eggs, toast and coffee. After they were done, Collins said he was going out onto the veranda to smoke.

'Frank, seriously,' Rachel said.

'You're not my mother. Just let me be, okay?'

Once he was out of earshot, Sheehan asked Rachel what was going on.

'He's sick,' she said.

'Cancer?'

'Yes. Lungs, that he knows of. Probably more now. Won't do chemo. Won't do anything but pain management. He thinks he's being tough.'

She looked down, closed her eyes for a moment. When she looked up again there was that same sadness Sheehan had seen in Collins's eyes.

'I've done everything I can,' she said. 'Endless days that turn into endless nights. He goes through phases. Right now, he's better than he's been for a while, but it won't last.'

'How long does he have?'

Rachel shrugged. 'A month, six months, a year. Who the hell knows?'

'He doesn't have a wife, a family?' Sheehan asked.

'He was married, now divorced. They never had kids.'

'And he lives nearby?'

'Maybe ten miles or so.'

'He must be a lonely guy.'

'Frank? No, he isn't lonely. Alone, perhaps, but not lonely. And besides, he has me now.'

'What could anyone else need, right?'

'Precisely.'

Rachel looked up and smiled as Collins came back into the room.

'I want to talk about the double and triple murders,' Sheehan said.

'You're wondering how he did it alone?' Collins asked.

'I can understand how the Wilsons might have been intimidated into doing whatever they were told, but not the others. I'm guessing he had a gun. Got one of the vics to tie up another, then another, then tied the last one himself. If it'd been me, I would've had the Warner girl tie up Clarke, and I'd have had Judith Whyte tie up the Vaill brothers.'

'But it would have been a great deal more manageable if two people were present.'

'Sure it would, but that's not what bothers me,' Sheehan said. 'Killing two people is double the risk, killing three is triple. This is someone who's got everything planned down to the last detail, right? It's precise, almost like a military campaign, and yet here he's adding a considerable degree of unpredictability into the equation.'

'You're forgetting that he wants the perp caught,' Rachel said. 'I think the clues we followed in Syracuse, New York, even Pennsylvania were left on purpose. It was something that always bothered me. Sure, we put a lot of hours and a great deal of work into those investigations, but if we accept that he's as bright as we think he is, then I can only come to the conclusion that it was intentional.'

'Because dying was part of the deal for the killers,' Sheehan said.

'And there's a thrill, a sensation that is experienced only when they take someone's life,' Collins said. 'Bundy called it "getting off". Sometimes that thrill is the killing, other times it's rape, other times it's torture. Maybe there's an energy that manifests itself when someone's in mental or physical pain and that's what they feed off. Here, he's not only controlling the killer, but he's dictating the lives of the people who get murdered as well. It's like twice the rush, right?'

'The control element suggests he knows people, right?' Sheehan asked. 'Like the psychology of people.'

'And we've been through every connection Marshall, Wagner and Earl had when it came to psychologists, psychiatrists, social services, doctors, probation officers,' Rachel said. 'There's not one person that we've found that's a common denominator between them, not even between two of them.'

'And what about the numerology stuff?' Sheehan asked.

Collins shook his head and smiled. 'That, my friend, is a rabbit hole. We've looked at the dates themselves, then the number of days between each killing. We've even looked at the differences between those numbers.'

'We looked at phone numbers,' Rachel said. 'We looked at zipcodes, Social Security numbers, dates of birth. We even looked at map coordinates. None of it came to anything.'

'So we have to go back to Marshall, Gregory and Earl,' Sheehan said. 'There has to have be a connection between the three of them. There has to been some way that he found them. And maybe there were others he tried before, but they didn't take. These guys had to be a very particular kind of person, right? They had to be suggestible, easy to influence and direct. Somehow he manages to get them so certain of what they're doing that they're willing to kill for it. There's a reward for what they're doing. Either that, or there's a greater threat that drives them. Like he somehow manages to convince them that the only way they can be free of guilt or eternal damnation or whatever the fuck is to sacrifice other people and then sacrifice themselves.'

'He's starting to get the idea,' Collins said.

'This is like Manson.'

'In a way, yes,' Rachel said. 'Like Manson, he isn't doing the killing himself. He's motivating other people to do it for him.'

'The thing I can't get my head around is how someone could be so evil,' Sheehan said.

'And you won't,' Rachel said. 'Not ever. And the reason you won't is that you're not a sociopath. As far as they're concerned, this is how things should be. No one else can understand their rationale because no one else even begins to approach their level of intellect. Look at Gacy, Bundy, Ramirez, even this guy you reported on for the Times Square killings. This isn't even a question of moral or immoral, honest or dishonest, right or wrong. This is how they think and what they do as a consequence. I mean, talking about one individual being able to influence another, look at Goebbels and Nazi Germany. Essentially, the vast majority of a population was propagandized to the point that they believed that total war was their only hope of salvation. And right along-side that the necessity to commit crimes against humanity and the Holocaust in order to have enough *Lebensraum*.'

'That takes time,' Sheehan said. 'That's not done in a week or a month. So whoever is behind these guys had access to them for long enough to completely up-end everything that they thought, everything they believed.'

'Not necessarily, no,' Collins said. 'Again, you're looking at it as if it was you. These are not highly intelligent, thoroughly rational people. These are not well-read, educated people. These guys were drifters, losers, into drugs and whatever else. They were the best raw material you could get for this kind of game.'

'A game?'

'What else are you gonna call it?' Collins replied. 'It's a game, sure. He's a grandmaster. He's the Olympic gold medallist of fucking psychos.'

'Can we go in the other room?' Sheehan asked.

'Sure we can.'

'I'm making coffee,' Rachel said. 'I'll bring it through.'

Standing in the back room of the cabin with a decade and a half of insanity covering three walls from floor to ceiling, Sheehan started with Syracuse. Collins had files for each murder – copies of crime scene photographs, incident reports, even interview notes.

What Sheehan expected to achieve was also unknown to him, but he was a fresh pair of eyes. It was the first time he'd seen much of this material. His only real experience had been the little he'd been given by Rachel and Max Kolymsky, beyond that what he'd been told when he spoke to Rachel and Maurice Quinn at the 114th in New York. Everything from Pennsylvania – aside from the little he knew of Bernard Clarke – was new to him.

'I need to know how each killer was identified,' Sheehan said. 'How each of these investigations played out.'

'Well, Rachel's gonna do that a great deal better than me,' Collins said.

When Rachel arrived with coffee, Sheehan told her what he wanted. The three of them sat at the table, and Rachel went through it as succinctly as she could – the palm print on the phone booth that led to Marshall, the ribbons that were used to embellish the crime scenes in New York, the hours that she and Maurice Quinn spent trawling through paperwork at the courier company, the abandoned building on Steinway Street, the name *John Fletcher* and the prints they finally found for Charles Wagner. She told him about the Dante Unit in Pennsylvania, of the killings in Lancaster and Reading, the key they found in the stomach of one of the Vaill brothers and how it led them to Gary Earl. Sheehan had questions, and sometimes he asked her to backtrack and clarify a detail, and when she was done he nodded his head slowly as if he had finally grasped something.

'What is it?' Rachel asked.

'It's like you said. Someone so careful sure as hell wouldn't have left a print on a phone booth or a way for you to find where the ribbon came from in New York. I mean, if the only reason he chose you was because you were there for the first one, then how the hell did he know you'd wind up here? You could've just let it go back there in Syracuse after Marshall was found dead. That could've been the end of it.'

'But he wanted me to be part of it, didn't he? He wrote to me. He left me a note at the scene of the Vaill killings. He wants an opponent. He wants to see if someone can catch him.'

'So maybe we have to get less complicated,' Sheehan said. 'I get that you've looked at every investigation, every individual killing, the whole thing with the numbers and Christ only knows what else, but maybe that's where the problem lies. It's the same thing as researching a feature. There's so much information, so many variables, and you just drown. I get to that point, and the only way out is to go right back to the start and find the most basic question you're trying to get an answer to. I think we need to look at how these guys were selected in the first place. That's the only real connection that we know of, right? That's the only thing that puts these three seemingly unrelated people in the same category. It's not their lives, their hometowns, their dates of birth, their prior criminal convictions or anything else like that. Somehow he got to them and had enough time to do what was necessary to turn them into committed multiple murderers.'

'So what do you want?' Rachel asked.

'You said you'd made lists of all the psychiatrists, doctors, POs and everything else.'

'Yes.'

'Then let's see it. That's where I'd like to start.'

74

There were a lot of names, and each list was detailed with times and places and dates.

As Collins had said, there was no apparent connection between Marshall, Wagner and Earl. Not even their prison terms overlapped. Marshall had been in San Quentin between January of 1970 and August of 1972. Between April 1973 and May of 1978, Wagner was on Rikers Island for a stabbing. Earl did five and a half years in Attica for drug offences between June of '76 and December of '81.

The respective arresting officers, public defenders, judges, prison officers, POs and even the staff at various halfway houses didn't coincide at any point. From all appearances, the three men never seemed to have crossed paths while they were under the auspices of the judicial or penitentiary systems.

'Seemed to me that something was off when I found out that Wagner shared a cell with Bernard Clarke, and then you had the overlapping of Wagner and Christopher Wake in Attica,' Sheehan said.

'We did look into that,' Rachel said. 'We couldn't find anything beyond coincidence.'

'There's also the vigilante element,' Sheehan said. 'Wagner and Earl killed criminals, but Marshall didn't. He killed a school-teacher, a couple of retirees and—'

'And my partner,' Rachel said.

'Right. So that doesn't work as a motive.'

'We looked at Marshall in detail,' Collins said. 'There was

no evidence to suggest that he knew any of his victims, but the fact that there's no evidence doesn't mean he didn't. He could've crossed paths with those people in a hundred different ways that we'll never know about.'

'And maybe he didn't kill Michael Ridgway,' Rachel said. 'Maybe our guy killed Michael, and then killed Marshall. Made it look like a suicide.'

'And he could have been there to make sure that Wagner hanged himself,' Collins said. 'Maybe he didn't actually do it, but he needed to make sure it was done.'

'So the only one we're sure was a suicide was Earl,' Sheehan said. He got up and started pacing the room. 'But we're getting off track again. How could they be connected? Three people, three different prisons, three different periods of time. Who's going to have access to these people?'

'We checked out psychiatrists that were posted at the time,' Collins said. 'They're all different people. And, even if they hadn't been, there's no way that they would've had access to these guys for anything more than an hour a month. Like you said, what was accomplished with them would've taken a great deal longer than that.'

'Okay, but who's to say he worked on them while they were in prison? All he'd have to have done was make his selection, right? He'd only have needed enough time to figure out the best subjects. Then, after they're out, that's when the work begins.'

'That makes sense, but they all saw different people,' Rachel said. 'And they were all government employees. None of them transferred from one prison to another. They were a permanent part of the prison staff complement.'

'Except when they weren't there,' Sheehan said. 'Government employees get vacations, right? There has to be cover when they're sick.'

Collins looked at Rachel. 'We didn't go there,' he said.

'So we need to know who would have been assigned at those three prisons during those periods,' Rachel replied.

'Bureau of Prisons,' Sheehan said. 'They're going to have records, surely?'

'I don't doubt it,' Collins said, 'but they'd be confidential.'

'And Rachel is FBI.'

'I can't do that,' she said. 'Going to a government institution in an official capacity is not an option.'

'Because?'

'I'm not on active duty, Carl. This isn't a federal investigation, and using federal authority to access confidential information for your own ends is a felony. I really have no desire to go to prison.'

'So how?' Sheehan asked. 'How do we get those names?'

'We ask the resident psychiatrists,' Rachel said. 'We have their names. It'd be easy enough to get numbers, even addresses.'

'On what basis? What reason can we give for asking?'

'You're as experienced as either one of us at getting people to answer questions, Carl,' Rachel said. 'Use some of your investigative journalist skills.'

'Yeah, I think that's called lying,' Sheehan replied.

Collins wrote down the names of the three residents – Ernest Frankel at San Quentin, Warren Burnett at Rikers and Sidney Lowe at Attica.

'Marshall was in prison nearly twenty years ago, the others fifteen or thereabouts,' Sheehan said. 'I'm guessing that one or more of them is gonna be retired.'

'Only one way to find out,' Rachel said. 'The phone's in the kitchen.'

Sheehan called Information. The fact that they were all doctors gave him an advantage. Two were listed – Lowe in Buffalo, Frankel in the Sacramento suburb of Oak Park.

Sheehan tried Lowe first, but there was no answer. He then called Frankel, was about to hang up, but a woman answered the phone.

'Hello,' Sheehan said. 'I'm wondering if you could help me. I'm trying to locate Dr. Ernest Frankel.'

'Yes, he's here. And who may I say is calling?'

'My name is Carl Sheehan.'

'Can I ask what this is regarding, Mr. Sheehan?'

'Well, I'm really calling for some advice. It's a professional matter. It relates to Dr. Frankel's work at San Quentin.'

'Please wait there. I'll see if he's available.'

Sheehan heard footsteps and then the distant murmur of voices. It seemed an eternity before the receiver was once again picked up at the other end.

The voice was frail and faint.

'This is Frankel.'

'Good morning, Dr. Frankel. My name is Sheehan. I'm engaged in a study of rehabilitation techniques and recidivism rates in the US penitentiary system. I'm based out of New York, but I'm looking at prisons all over the country. I understand that you worked at San Quentin.'

'I did, yes.'

'Can you tell me over what period you were resident there?'

'Oh, I was there for close on twenty years,' Frankel said. 'Started around '65 and then I transferred towards the end of '84. Of course, I'm retired now, but I did a couple of years consulting work after San Quentin.'

'And I'm guessing you must've seen thousands of inmates during your employment there.'

'Thousands, tens of thousands possibly. Like I said, I was there for the best part of twenty years.'

'And can I ask how much time was allocated to each inmate for psychiatric evaluation?'

'That makes it sound like it was some sort of organized affair,' Frankel said. 'Most of the work I did was in groups, you know? A dozen or so men in a circle, all of them explaining how the world owed them a living or that it wasn't their fault that they raped some girl. There were a few exceptions, of course, but – as I'm sure you know – the one common denominator between everyone in jail is their innocence.'

'So you never really go to work with inmates on any kind of intensive one-on-one basis?'

Frankel laughed. 'A resident psychiatrist in a federal institution is nothing more than a box ticker, Mr. Sheehan. Sure, there were occasions when a formal psychiatric evaluation was required for a hearing or somesuch, or the warden might have needed to know if it was safe to put someone back in general population, but if you think it was hours of Freudian analysis on a leather couch then you're very much mistaken.'

'That's really helpful, Dr. Frankel. And can I ask what provisions were made to cover your position when you took vacations?'

'Oh Christ, they'd just wheel in some half-baked locum from the nearest hospital.'

'Was there anyone that covered for you on any kind of regular basis?'

'I have not the faintest clue, Mr. Sheehan. I took my vacations and left them to their own devices. If you needed that kind of information, you'd have to speak to the folks at San Quentin.'

'Yes, of course. But would you happen to know what hospital or facility the locums might have come from?'

'I'm guessing somewhere in the city,' Frankel said. 'Knowing the government, they're going to want to save as much on travel expenses as they can.'

'From San Francisco.'

'Well, if your geography is the same as mine, that would indeed be the city, Mr. Sheehan.'

'And whatever facility they came from, they'd have to be on some sort of approved list, right?'

'I guess so, but it seems to me that some guy who's coming in for a few hours every three or four months wouldn't be someone who'd be a great deal of use to you in your study.'

'I just need to cover all bases, Dr. Frankel.'

'You want my opinion on this subject?'

'Yes, of course, I was getting to that.'

'It's a shambles. It's a broken system. Hell, I don't know that you could even call it a system. It's lip service, that's all it is. Like I said, just a matter of box-ticking. I spent the best part of my career trying to understand and help people that didn't want any help. If there's one thing I can say about criminals, and this goes for the vast majority of them, they don't have any notion that they did wrong. That's the bottom line. And how the hell do you get through to someone like that, Mr. Sheehan? How do you correct the behavior of someone who doesn't think that their behavior is a problem? You go on and write that in your study.'

'I will do, sir,' Sheehan said. 'This has been really helpful. I appreciate your time and your directness.'

Again, Frankel gave a wry laugh. 'Don't waste your time, son. That's my advice. Doesn't matter how many studies or how many reports you write, the federal government is not interested in listening to anyone but themselves, and they all know best. You want my opinion, most of them politician fellers should in jail too.'

Sheehan expressed his gratitude again and hung up the phone.

'So?' Rachel asked.

'Government approved psychiatric hospitals or clinics in California,' Sheehan said. 'Probably San Francisco. That's where the locums would've come from.'

'Which I can probably get,' Collins said, 'but I'm not calling from this phone.'

'And I guess the same goes for Attica and Rikers,' Rachel said.

'This is a lot of work,' Sheehan said. 'We need to be sure this is something worth pursuing.'

'It's as good as any other blind alley we've gone down,' Rachel said. 'And I agree with you that a connection between Marshall, Wagner and Earl, if there is one, is something we have to know.'

'I'll head out,' Collins said. 'I can make a call from a phone in town and see if this information is available.'

Getting up from the chair, he paused, and then sat down again. Closing his eyes, his face twisted in pain, he took a moment to breathe.

Rachel got up. 'You need something, Frank?'

Collins raised his hand.

'Can I help?' Sheehan asked.

'You can keep trying Lowe and see if there's any other way to track down Burnett,' he said. 'Maybe they can give us something more specific.'

'That's not what I meant,' Sheehan replied.

'I know what you meant, and no, there's nothing you can do to help,' Collins said. 'Don't matter how fast I might run, this thing is gonna catch me eventually.'

75

By the time Collins returned, it was after lunch on Tuesday. He looked as if he'd rested somewhat, a little more color in his complexion, but Sheehan knew better than to say anything. He'd known such men before – a firm belief in their own resilience, almost to the point of self-neglect. To ask for help would be a sign of weakness and fallibility.

'How'd you get on?' Collins asked.

'Not so good. Still no answer from Lowe, and we've not been able to find a number for Warren Burnett.'

'There are a very limited number of psychiatric consultants with government clearance,' Collins explained. He showed Rachel and Sheehan his notes.

'Attica and Rikers both fall within the geographical purview of New York State,' he said. 'You've got a dozen names here, all of them registered with the Bureau of Prisons. San Quentin is under San Francisco, and there's only seven people who have authorization to access the facility. However, there's no name that appears on both lists.'

'Different states,' Rachel said. 'Geographically, as far apart as you can get.'

'And though all nineteen consultants work from only five different hospitals or psychiatric clinics,' Collins replied, 'none of them are owned or run by the same companies.'

'So where do we go from here?' Sheehan asked.

'This doesn't feel like Syracuse, New York or Pennsylvania,'

Rachel said. 'As far as I can see, he's not leaving anything for us to find. And we could be going in completely the wrong direction.'

'Sure we could,' Collins replied, 'but until something else—'

'You ever consider there might be two of them?' Sheehan asked. 'I remember the discussion we had about serial killers working together. Buono and Bianchi, Ottis Toole and Henry Lee Lucas, and we've always looked at Marshall, Wagner and now this guy Earl being in some kind of partnership with someone else. What about if the someone else has a partner? One of them in New York, the second in California.'

'Right about now I'm willing to consider anything,' Collins said.

'So we look at all of them,' Rachel said. 'We need to know which ones were covering which prisons at the times these three guys were inside.'

Sheehan looked at Collins. Collins knew what he was asking.

'I got this information from a source I'm not going back to,' Collins said.

'So we call them direct,' Sheehan said. 'We cook up a story, say we're from the Bureau of Prisons. There's questions about billings, overtime, some fuck-up in accounting or whatever. We take one each and we just ask them.'

'Worth trying,' Rachel said.

'But not from here,' Collins said.

Sheehan frowned. 'What? You think your phone is bugged?'

'I was inside the system for a long time, Carl. I got to the point where I trusted the people I was working for about as much as the people we were assigned to investigate. We'll go into town. And we can't use phone booths. No one official calls from a phone booth. I know someone who owns a bar. We'll call from there.'

*

419

The three of them left in Collins's truck and headed into Colonial Heights. They barely spoke en route, each of them lost in the vast ocean of unanswered questions that accompanied what they were doing. Pulling over in a parking lot across the street from a convenience store, Collins led them back the way they'd come for a couple of blocks and then turned left. Down an alleyway behind a row of buildings, they reached a heavy wooden door.

'You take Attica and Rikers, I'll take San Quentin,' Collins said.

He knocked, waited, then knocked again.

From within came the sound of a bolt being drawn. The door opened just a foot or so.

'Marvin, it's Frank.'

The door opened wide and a bear of a man appeared. Maybe six three or four, he had to be all of three-twenty.

'Frank. How ya doin'?'

'Need to use your phone if that's okay, Marvin.'

Marvin looked over Collins's head at Rachel and Sheehan.

'They're good,' Collins said. 'Friends of mine.'

Collins went in first, Rachel and Sheehan following on.

Marvin closed and bolted the door behind them.

Down the corridor, through a rear store area and into the kitchen, not a word from anyone as they went, they passed through swing doors and entered the bar.

'There's a phone over there, and I got another phone in the back office if you need privacy,' Marvin said.

'I'll take this one,' Collins said. 'Can you show these guys the office?'

'This way,' Marvin said.

The office was barely more than a closet. Stacks of paperwork leaned precariously away from the wall. There was a narrow desk and a single chair against the far wall.

Rachel made the first call to Attica. She did as Sheehan had suggested. There was an ongoing government audit, the usual nightmare of bureaucracy, and she needed to know the names of federally-registered psychiatrists who had covered for the residents between June of 1976 and December of 1981. The woman at the other end, though understanding, said that such information would now be archived.

'We keep only five years of finance records onsite,' she explained. 'Records from earlier years are held in storage in the New York Bureau of Prisons Records Department.'

Rachel asked for the number and was given it.

When she reached the Records Department, Rachel explained that she'd been referred to them by Attica. She gave the name and department of the woman with whom she'd spoken. Equally understanding, the administrative assistant – Peter Marlowe – said that locating such information would take a little time.

Rachel mouthed *phone number* to Sheehan and he went to get it.

'The thing is, Peter,' Rachel said, 'I have this nightmare of a situation. I've got federal auditors breathing down my neck, and you have no idea—'

'Oh, believe me,' Marlowe interjected, 'I know exactly what you're talking about.'

'So, if there's any way in the world you could help me out here, you'd be an absolute lifesaver.'

'Can you give me ten minutes or so?' Marlowe asked.

'Absolutely, yes. I'm staying right by this phone.'

Sheehan came back into the office and handed Rachel a piece of paper.

'Let me give you my direct number, Peter,' she said. She read it back to him, thanked him profusely and hung up.

'I was convinced,' Sheehan said.

'Let's just hope he doesn't check the phone number I gave him, eh?'

Marlowe called back after five minutes.

'You're in luck,' he said. 'It's a good deal better organized than

I expected. I've got two doctors here, both of whom worked at Attica on a temporary basis during that time period. Do you have a pen?'

Rachel wrote down the names she was given and their respective hospitals. She told Marlowe that he was a godsend.

Hanging up, Rachel looked at Sheehan. 'You want me to call Rikers?'

'Seein' as now you've got some experience, that might be a good idea. I don't know that my lying skills are as polished as yours.'

Rachel smiled. 'That I don't believe for a second.'

She called Rikers, gave the same story. It was a runaround, but she finally tracked down someone who seemed willing to help. Rachel was told that the likelihood of finding anything that went as far back as the mid-seventies was the proverbial needle in a haystack.

'Is it possible to look, perhaps?' Rachel asked.

The woman at the other end was silent for a moment, and then she said, 'You know, it might be easier if you just called the hospital direct. There's only one place we'd have brought people over from and they may very well still be employed there.'

'Which hospital was it?'

'That'd be St. Savior in Astoria.'

Rachel expressed her thanks and called Information for the number.

Again, there was an issue with how far back the request went. Wagner had been on Rikers between '73 and '78. They were beginning the exhaustive process of computerizing all their records, but they had yet to go back five years.

'If whoever you're looking for was staff at the hospital,' Rachel was told, 'then Personnel would be your best bet. This isn't a psychiatric hospital as such, but we retain them for post-op and trauma counseling. Let me put you through and see if they can help.'

Rachel waited, all the while feeling that ill-at-ease anxiety that came with the knowledge that she was lying her way through this like a professional. If it ever came to light, there would be a significantly greater penalty than suspension. She remembered Joy Willis's lecture on how federal agents had to be beyond reproach.

'Hello, this is Karen in Personnel. Can I help you?'

'Karen, hi. My name's Linda. I've been passed to you by Accounts at Rikers, and I really need your help.'

'Well, let's see if we can't do that, Linda. What do you need?'

The conversation continued for a good twenty minutes. Karen was as cooperative as could have been hoped. Perhaps Rachel's request was a welcome distraction from the mundane routine of her day; perhaps she responded to another bureaucrat duty-bound to complete some mind-numbing task. Whatever the reason, Rachel ended the call with three further names, all of them current or past psychiatrists at St. Savior's, all of them with federal clearance to access Rikers Island.

Collins had obtained two names, again hospital residents who were called upon to cover for whoever was posted at San Quentin.

'Dates are not absolutely certain, but that's the best I could get.'

'Okay, so we're down from nineteen to seven,' Rachel said. 'That's narrowed the field.'

'So now we get as much background on them as we can,' Collins said. 'Social Security numbers, DMV, maybe a directory of psychiatric practitioners, addresses, phone numbers, anything that gives us more background on these people.'

'I can go through the archives at the *Times*,' Sheehan said. 'See if any of them ever featured in a lawsuit, ever gave expert testimony in a trial, all that stuff.'

'Okay,' Rachel said. 'Then tomorrow we're back in New York.

Me and Frank will work on everything else while you're at the paper.'

'Let's go tonight,' Sheehan said. 'I've got enough space for you at my place. Better to get an early start.'

'Makes sense to me,' Collins said. 'As long as I don't have to sleep on the floor.'

'Do you need anything from your place? You got your meds?' Rachel asked Collins.

'Yes, I've got my meds,' Collins replied, his tone of voice making it clear that no further discussion on the matter was needed.

76

'Six days you've been gone, and not a word,' Erlewine said.

Sheehan stood in the doorway of Erlewine's office. He'd been berated before, would no doubt be berated again. He would just let the man say what he needed to say and wind himself down.

'And I seem to distinctly remember asking you to keep me in the loop, or did I just fucking imagine that?'

'No, Joel, you didn't imagine it, and I'm sorry. Things have been a bit intense.'

'Oh, is that so? And pray tell me, if it's not too much trouble, how this intensity you've been enduring is going to give me a feature worth paying you for?'

'You're gonna have to trust me.'

'Really? Is that the best you've got? You know, hot on the heels of "It'll be on your desk in an hour, chief", that's the most tired line of BS in the journalism business.'

Sheehan stepped into the room and sat down.

'There's a case,' Sheehan said. 'Three, in fact. Here, Syracuse and Pennsylvania. It goes back to the mid-seventies. If this goes how I think it's going to go, you're gonna get an exclusive to rival—'

Erlewine raised his hand. 'I am starved, Sheehan. Starved for good material. You know what the headline is today? Twenty-sixth anniversary of Kennedy's assassination. That's where I'm at right now.'

'It could be really something,' Sheehan said, 'but I need to get into Archives.'

'You're not employed here. This isn't the New York Public fucking Library.'

'I need to get into Archives, and I need some help.'

'You want me to come help you?' Erlewine said sarcastically.

'Eighteen murders,' Sheehan said. 'Over fifteen years. Maybe more than twenty if we add in the guys that were supposed to have committed the murders but then killed themselves.'

Erlewine's expression lightened significantly.

'And this is a real thing?' he asked. 'Not just some imaginary fucking conspiracy from the mind of a penniless hack?'

'It's a real thing, Joel. And I'm not working on it alone. I have help from some other people.'

'Journalists?'

'No, not journalists. Ex-federal people.'

'No shit.'

'No shit, Joel.'

'And when might I expect this exclusive headline-worthy feature from you?'

'I need time. A week, maybe two. A month, perhaps. I really don't know how far this goes or how much more legwork is needed.'

'But right now you need Archives.'

'I really do.'

'Okay, I'm gonna trust you. But you fuck me on this, I'm never hiring you again, even if you have concrete evidence that Jackie was behind the JFK assassination and she and Oswald were fateful lovers involved in a Communist-funded plot to overthrow the United States.'

'Agreed.'

Erlewine leaned forward and picked up the phone.

'Deirdre, grab the first intern you see and send them to my office.'

*

The intern, a recent NYU Journalism Grad called Marcia Roth, wasn't thrilled with the prospect of trawling through years of microfiched newspapers. The time period ran from January of 1970 all the way to December of '81, more than four thousand editions, perhaps four and a half with the supplements and special editions.

She and Sheehan sat beside one another, the list of seven names they were trying to locate on the desk between them. They were not unusual – Black, Maynard, Curtis, Woodward, Doyle, Fleming and Southwell. Woodward alone appeared hundreds of times in every article related to Nixon, Watergate and the subsequent prosecution of those implicated in the cover-up. Though they could have narrowed the search by running both first names and family names together, there was always the possibility that they'd miss a reference to one of them if they were mentioned by family name alone.

The task was laborious and frustrating, but Sheehan could think of nothing that might be potentially more successful. More than two hours in and neither one of them had found any reference to any of the individuals in question.

'What's the deal here?' Marcia asked. 'Why are you looking for these guys?'

Sheehan sat back. His eyes hurt, his neck was strained, and somewhere at the back of his head was the promise of a migraine.

'It's a process of elimination,' he said. 'All of these guys were locum psychiatrists at either San Quentin, Rikers or Attica. We're trying to find some connection between them and three inmates that were held there during these periods.'

'Because?'

Sheehan smiled. 'It's a long story, Marcia, and I really don't have the mental capacity to explain the whole thing.'

'So give me the edited version.'

'Okay,' Sheehan said. 'There have been three series-killings.

The first was in Syracuse, the second in New York, the third in Pennsylvania. Each has been roughly five years apart. In each case the person who was supposed to have committed the killings is now dead. Suicides. At least that's how it appeared anyway. There's a good chance someone else was involved, someone instrumental not only in the original murders but also in the deaths of the killers. That someone has to have had access to these men, and the only way we can see that right now is while they were in prison. We're working on the basis that it was a psychiatrist, and for now we've ruled out the possibility that it was the residents because they were permanent staff and didn't transfer from one place to another. That leaves us the locums who came in to cover for them while they took vacations or whatever.'

'What, so you're saying that someone got someone else to kill a bunch of people?'

'Very simply stated, yes.'

Marcia nodded approvingly. 'That would make a good movie. I'd go see that, for sure.'

'Okay, I'll let you know when I start the screenplay. Now, back to work.'

'So good to be using my Journalism degree to its limit,' Marcia said.

'You can forget everything you learned in school,' Sheehan said. 'A couple of years and you'll realize that reporting the news is getting people to answer questions they really don't want to and ample use of word "allegedly".'

It was mid-afternoon when Marcia found a reference to Dr. Nicholas Maynard from March of 1970. It was nothing but a squib, but Maynard was pictured at a Veterans' Administration fundraiser. He'd been a guest speaker, and was quoted as saying, 'We have so much work to do in the field of veteran rehabilitation. It's a burden we all share, and it's our duty to do all we can to support those who sacrificed so much for the well-being and security of our great nation.'

'Print it for me,' Sheehan said, 'and get me as clear an image as you can of his face.'

Sheehan was ready to call it a day when Marcia looked over at him.

'I've got an obit here,' she said.

Sheehan moved his chair to see the article she was looking at.

Dr. Nicholas Maynard (63), respected psychiatrist, co-founder of the mental health charity "Working for Wellness", died November 2nd, 1971.

The piece detailed his many accomplishments and accolades, and that he'd left behind a wife and two sons, both of whom had followed him into the mental healthcare profession.

Sheehan consulted his notes. Maynard was a locum at San Quentin. Robert Marshall had been incarcerated there between January of 1970 and August of 1972. If Maynard was dead in November of '71, then who had replaced him as locum for the latter part of Marshall's sentence? They were missing a name.

'Print that one too,' Sheehan said. 'And—'

'Make the picture as clear as I can,' Marcia replied.

Sheehan smiled. 'You'll get your Pulitzer yet, Ms. Roth.'

An hour later, most of the day staff having already left, Sheehan and Marcia packed up.

'I might be back tomorrow,' Sheehan said. 'If I am, would you help me again?'

'Only if you name me as a research assistant in whatever piece you're writing.'

'You got a deal.'

Sheehan thanked her and headed back up to see Erlewine. He'd gone for the day.

'Tell him I may be back in the morning,' he told Deirdre. 'If not, I'll call as soon as I have something.'

'Call even if you don't,' Deirdre said. 'Otherwise he's gonna ask me to chase you up and I have way more important things to do with my time.'

Collins and Rachel were already back at Sheehan's apartment by the time he arrived. It was close to 7.00 and hunger seemed to be foremost in everyone's mind. Sheehan rarely cooked, and then only for himself. The time and effort required to prepare a meal for three was beyond his willingness, so he ordered Chinese take-out.

'Fine by me,' Collins commented. 'Enough ketchup and I'd eat roadkill right off the tarmac.'

The food arrived and they ate in silence. Evidently none of them had anything of sufficient interest or urgency that it could not wait.

Rachel asked if Sheehan had any wine.

'Only bourbon,' he said. He fetched the bottle and three glasses.

Seated at the kitchen table, Collins told Sheehan that they'd gotten Social Security Numbers, DMV records and a couple of other things, none of it of any great consequence.

'How did you get DMV?' Sheehan asked.

'I used my ID,' Rachel said. 'I know I said I wouldn't, but...' She shrugged. 'You know, I don't think anyone even asked my name.'

'Speaking of names, we're missing one,' Sheehan said. 'Maynard, the locum from San Quentin when Marshall was there, died in November of 1971. Marshall was still inside until August of the following year. Someone must've come in to replace Maynard.'

'So I'll call San Quentin again,' Collins said. 'But that's gonna have to wait until the morning.'

'I still feel like we're missing something,' Rachel said.

'We're missing a lot of things,' Sheehan replied.

'It's the years that elapse between each series. That's the thing I don't understand. Why five years apart? That has to have some relevance, and I honestly don't believe it's got anything to do with fucking moon cycles or horoscopes or the religious significance of the number five.'

'Okay, so there's a reason,' Collins said. 'And until we find out what the reason is, there's no use thinking about it. The only one who knows is the guy himself, and there may be a chance we'll never know.'

Rachel gave a wry smile. 'Truth is addictive, right? Worse than heroin.'

'I'm not going to think about it,' Sheehan said. 'I'm gonna have one more drink and crash.'

'I'll sleep on the couch,' Rachel said. 'I don't want to kick you out of your own room again.'

'Take the bed,' Collins said. 'You need a good night's sleep. You've been running on fumes for days.'

'It's okay, I can—' Rachel started.

'Do what the man says,' Sheehan interjected. 'End of discussion.'

77

By the time Rachel woke, it was past ten.

Frank had been right. Driven by little but caffeine and adrenalin, she'd ignored all the signs of physical and mental exhaustion. She'd fallen back into old patterns and habits, all of them counter-productive. For a while longer she just laid there, the faint light through the curtains, the sounds of the city beyond.

Perhaps the absence of connection with people had served to further contribute to her own internalization and lack of objectivity. She had gone to some psychological island, and there she'd built walls, and within those walls she'd found a darkened room where she could maintain a safe distance from the world. But everything was still there, would always be there, and ignorance and dismissal would never serve to diminish the ability it had to break through every construct she'd created.

Sliding out from beneath the covers, she sat on the edge of the bed. She looked around Carl's room. Here were reminders of the time they had spent together. She'd missed him, though she was too self-obsessed and defensive to admit it. On paper, they weren't a good match, and yet in reality she could think of no one with whom she was simply able to be herself. In so very many ways they were polar opposites. Perhaps that was the key right there. Where she got frustrated and angry, he remained grounded and calm. When he lapsed into periods of self-criticism, she possessed the ability to direct his attention outward, to focus on all that he had achieved, all that he would yet achieve. They had not separated for any other reason than their respective directions in life, and now – older, a little wiser perhaps – those directions had somehow brought them back together again. Why had she wanted him here? It wasn't because he would necessarily be able to use his media contacts. It wasn't because he had access to newspaper archives. She'd wanted him because he'd been here before, had seen her at her best and worst, and thus carried with him a small part of this history that had spanned a decade and a half. To continue without him would be to continue incomplete.

Rachel showered and got dressed. She was hungry; she needed coffee.

Collins was in the kitchen. 'How d'you sleep?' he asked.

'Like a dead thing,' Rachel replied.

She sat down at the table.

Collins poured her a cup of coffee and took the seat facing hers.

'And you? Did you sleep?' she asked.

'As much as I could, yes.'

'I know you're not going to listen to me, but—'

Collins reached out and closed his hand over Rachel's.

'Enough now,' he said. 'We've been through this a thousand times. I may not say it often enough, but I do listen to what you say, and I do understand that you care, okay? I've never been one for expressing my feelings, and I'm not going to start now. It is what it is. Shit happens. At some point in the not-too-distant future, I will die. That's as straight as it gets. We all die. No one is exempt.'

'I understand that, but—'

'But nothing,' Collins interjected. 'I've spent my career being balked and stopped and sidetracked. I have spent thousands of hours on cases, only to have them collapse because of some administrative or political bullshit. I've been transferred, even given mandatory leave. My faith has taken a battering, just like yours, but over a great many more years. If we do this ... *when* we do this, I will at least feel that it was all worth it. If ending this nightmare is my legacy, then I will die with a fucking smile on my face.'

'I don't want to think about you dying,' Rachel said. 'It breaks my heart, Frank. It just breaks my fucking heart.'

'Then don't think about it.'

'I think that's a little easier said than done.'

'Then I'll change the subject,' Collins replied. 'I called San Quentin. The other locum at Attica just covered for Maynard after he died. They didn't bring anyone new in. However, we might have been looking in the wrong direction.'

'Wrong direction, how?'

'We've been focusing on the psychological aspect of this as a motivation, but we forgot about faith.'

'Faith?'

'The religious connotations.'

Rachel frowned. 'Can you try and be a little less cryptic?'

'We've looked at everyone we could think of who worked inside these prisons. We tried to find a common thread and we got nothing. This thing with the locums was a possibility, but we found out something this morning that Carl has gone to investigate. There's other group therapy meetings they organize in penitentiaries and they're run by priests.'

'Sure, we know about the priests. They were all different.'

'Inside the prison, yes they are, but we didn't think about post-release.'

'Explain.'

'I called Gary Earl's PO. I told him I was BSU. I asked him about Earl's parole conditions after he left Attica at the end of '81. Not only did he have to have meetings with his PO, but he had to contribute to a community outreach program that was run by the diocese. When he had his parole hearing he professed to having found God. He'd been attending services in prison.

He'd gotten baptized. He took communion. The whole thing. That was part of the reason his parole was granted.'

'And what about the others? Marshall? Wagner?'

'We don't know.'

'So where has Carl gone?'

'St. Patrick's. It's the second largest diocese in the country.'

'To see who ran the outreach program.'

'Right.'

'Didn't his PO know?'

Collins shook his head. 'Entirely separate thing. He didn't have a clue.'

'What makes you think someone at the Diocese will tell Carl?'

Collins smiled. 'Well, we'll see how good he is at getting people to answer questions they don't want to answer, won't we?'

'We really are clutching at fucking straws here, aren't we?'

'Doesn't mean we don't pursue other lines, Rachel.'

'And what might those other lines be, Frank?'

'It's an elimination process, and you know it. You did this in Syracuse, New York, Pennsylvania. There's no substitute for what we're doing. We keep looking and asking questions, and—'

'I know, I know. I just wonder how much longer we can do this before—'

'Before what? We give up? Go crazy? Find out we were wrong all the way and that they weren't connected at all? You can't think like that.' Collins leaned forward. 'I'm not telling you anything you don't already know. I don't need to say any of this, and you don't need to hear it. If there's anyone in the world who doesn't need motivating, it's you.'

Rachel didn't respond.

'So, changing the subject, what's the deal with Carl?'

'There is no deal with Carl.'

'Bullshit. You're different when he's around and you know it.'

'I'm not fucking different, Frank.'

'Okay, you're not fucking different. Forget I mentioned it.'

Rachel laughed. 'Okay, so how am I different?'

'You tell me.'

'No, Frank, I want to hear it from you. You're such a master at reading people, you tell me how I'm different.'

'You pair are like pieces from different jigsaw puzzles. The picture doesn't make sense, but you still somehow fit together.'

'So what are you saying? That when this thing is over, *if* it's ever over, we should stroll off into the sunset together?'

'This will end one way or the other, Rachel. It has to. And if you don't have this to live for, then you've got to find something to replace it. My recommendation would be that you replace it with a life.'

'What, a life like yours? No wife, no kids, no grandkids. Living alone in the fucking woods in Virginia like some kind of weird hermit? And now you're all set to die on me and you won't do anything about it? That kind of life?'

'But I never wanted those things,' Collins said.

'And you think I do?'

'I think you've forgotten what it's like to be a regular human being.'

'I don't think I ever was a regular human being.'

'So maybe it's time to find out whether—'

Collins was cut short by the sound of the telephone.

Rachel got up and took the receiver from the wall cradle.

'Hey,' she said. She glanced at Collins and nodded. It was Sheehan.

She listened for a few seconds. A frown crossed her brow.

'But you still don't know if—' She stopped, listened again.

'Okay, right. Sure.'

Rachel hung up the phone.

'Did he get something?' Collins asked.

'He didn't get us a name,' Rachel said, 'but he did find out that this outreach program is nationwide. It's run by the relevant diocese and always from the same church in each area. The priest oversees it, but they don't have anything to do with inmates until after they're released.'

'Okay, so how does this help us?'

'They move them every four years, Frank. If a priest has previ-ous experience in dealing with released convicts, then they take over the program at whichever church they move to. And they're all required to have some sort of basic training in psychology and criminal rehabilitation.'

'So where's Carl now? What's he doing?'

'He's heading back. We need to find out which church Earl went to after he was released and who the priest was at the time.'

'Well, whoever it was will be somewhere else now. Earl came out in '81. They could be anywhere in the country. And you really think this could be a priest?' Collins dismissed the question even as he uttered it. 'Who better than a priest would have familiarity with *The Divine Comedy* and the *Hortus deliciarum* thing?'

'Maybe it's like you said. It's not about psychology, but about faith. There's few things that can inspire people to do things as much as faith. The Crusades, the Inquisition, the Salem Witch Trials. I mean, the entirety of human history is one religious war after another. I had this exact conversation with Carl.'

'And faith is one of the celestial spheres,' Collins said. 'Faith, justice, a final glimpse of the true essence of God.'

'So that's what he's doing. Playing God.'

'I don't know what the fuck he's doing, Rachel, but if history has taught us anything, the people who play God usually wind up becoming the Devil.'

Sheehan was back within the hour.

'They're nervous,' he said. 'I spoke to three different people, and they're some of the most guarded I've ever dealt with, and that's saying something.'

'Well, justified or not, the Catholic Church has had to deal with its fair share of controversy,' Collins said.

437

'Okay, so Earl's PO doesn't know which church and the diocese won't tell us,' Rachel said, 'so we have to look elsewhere for it.'

'The Parole Commission?' Sheehan suggested. 'Bureau of Prisons? Who else holds release records?'

'I don't think it's a case of who holds them, but who can get access to them,' Collins said. 'I'm retired, Rachel's on leave and can't act in any kind of official capacity. We really took a risk with the DMV and I don't think it'd be smart to do that again.'

'We need someone to call the Commission,' Rachel said. 'Not only does it need to be someone official, but it has to be someone who'd have a valid reason to inquire about the parole conditions of a dead perp.'

'Who says it has to be Gary Earl?' Sheehan asked. 'We're trying to find out if the same priest ran the outreach program in three different places, right?'

'Right.'

'So what about Wagner?'

Rachel understood what Sheehan was asking.

'What am I missing?' Collins asked.

'Maurice Quinn,' Rachel replied. 'From the 114th. Officially, Wagner was his case. I was just on loan.'

'When was the last time you spoke to him?' Sheehan asked.

'Not since the case was closed. April of 1980.'

'Well, let's call the 114th and see if he's still there,' Collins said.

'Carl, you call. If he is, I'm just gonna go there. I'm not talking to him about this over the phone.'

78

'I don't want any comments about how much I've aged,' Quinn said.

He sat down in the coffee shop booth across from Rachel.

'Nine years,' he said. 'Nine fucking years. Jesus Christ, I did not expect to hear from you.'

'You look good, Maurice. How've you been?'

'The nightmare continues, but so do I.' He smiled. 'I'll be retired in three years. What I'll do with myself, I have no idea. I don't fish, I don't want a boat, and I sure as hell don't want to live in fucking Florida.'

'But you're okay, right?'

'Sure, Rachel, I'm okay. And you? I heard you defected to the Feds.'

'I did, yes. Still there. I'm on leave at the moment.'

'What, like a vacation?'

'No, Maurice, not a vacation. I have some things to deal with before I go back. That's *if* I go back.'

'It's not working out?'

'It's complicated,' she replied. 'However, even though I'm not here in an official capacity, I'm still looking into something.'

'Okay.'

'And I need your help.'

Quinn leaned back. 'Okay.'

'It's about Wagner.'

'Wagner? That's distant fucking history, Rachel.'

'For you, yes. Not for me.'

'How so?'

'That's also pretty complicated.'

'And I'm too dumb to understand? If you need my help, presumably unofficially, then you're gonna need to give me something.'

'If I'm right, then I'll tell you everything. In fact, if I'm right, you'll probably read all about it in one of Carl Sheehan's articles.'

'Okay, that's another blast from the past. You're still in touch with him?'

'I am, yes. And he's helping me.'

'At least tell me why you're still interested in Wagner, for Christ's sake. Give me that much at least, will you?'

'There was a third series,' Rachel said. 'Pennsylvania. Same kind of shit. Same religious stuff. I investigated that one as well. It was grim. Nine dead. And just like we figured here, I think there was someone else involved.'

'So, you're telling me that you've been investigating the same case for – what? – fifteen years?'

'Pretty much, yes.'

'You do appreciate how—'

'I know exactly how it sounds. And that will give you some kind of an understanding of why I am currently on leave from the Bureau.'

'So what do you need? What do you think I can do?'

'I need you to call the Parole Commission,' Rachel said. 'If needed, get in touch with the Parole Board at Rikers Island. There'll have been terms and conditions for Wagner's release back in '78. I need to know if part of it was to attend some kind of church outreach program. If so, I need to know which church he was supposed to attend.'

'Are you gonna tell me why, or is this one of those "Just trust me on this" things?'

'I just need to know, Maurice.'

'Okay, so are we gonna have a cup of coffee and make small talk or do you want me to go and do this now?'

Rachel smiled. She slid a piece of paper across the table.

Quinn glanced at it. 'That's a New York number. You're here in town?'

'I'm at Carl Sheehan's place.'

'Well, I'll see what I can find out. And give him my best, eh? Considering he was a journalist, he wasn't a bad guy.'

'I'm sure he'd say the same thing about you being a cop.'

Watching Quinn leave reminded Rachel so very clearly of all that had happened here. She remembered the feeling she'd had at the time – that she'd never see him again. And then there was the fear that had preceded it – that she might lose another partner. Thankfully that hadn't happened, and here he was, three years from retirement, going out on a limb for her with no real answer to his questions.

There were good people in the world. Perhaps not so many, but Quinn was definitely one of them.

Back at Sheehan's apartment there was a tangible sense of anticipation. Whether Quinn would come back to Rachel today, whether he would be able to find out anything at all, was unknown. After so many years of questions, uncertainties, those times of genuine doubt regarding the veracity of her belief, the notion that she was now a step closer to the truth seemed somehow the most unrealistic possibility of all. In some way, Rachel expected disappointment, another dead-end, another frustrating reminder that her efforts had come to nothing. But alongside that, perhaps just as strong, was her own faith. There would be an end to this, and if this endeavor didn't open the door, then another one would. And then what? Frank had been right, of course. Once this was over, she would have to find some other *raison d'être*. Whether she would resign from the

FBI, perhaps return to the police, perhaps leave law enforcement altogether, she didn't know. It wasn't the right time to ask such a question, and though it was there at the forefront of her mind, she had to ignore it. As of this moment, the only thing that mattered in the world was a telephone call from Maurice Quinn.

Standing at the window looking out over the city as dusk fell, as the lights of homes and stores and skyscrapers became a universe of earth-bound stars, Rachel closed her eyes and breathed deeply. She cast her mind back to that day in Ulysses, the body of Caroline Lassiter on the bed, that small slip of paper upon which they'd found the first message: *Abandon hope, all ye who enter here.* She could remember all of them by heart, even much of the letter back in New York when she'd first met Quinn.

So, here we are again. It has been a while, hasn't it?

And then the last but one line: *I sincerely hope that one day we will have an opportunity to speak in person.*

Was that day coming? Was that what she had wished for all these years?

Was Dante a priest, a man with access to released convicts, a man who'd manipulated and influenced and coerced people into doing the most terrible things?

And what was his *raison d'être*? To show that it could be done, to play some game of minds and hearts, to be a God in his own right? Or was he driven by some deep-seated and unconscionable obsession to hurt and destroy?

'Rachel?'

She turned at the sound of Carl's voice.

'You okay?'

'Sure, sure.'

'What are you thinking?'

'I was thinking about the first series,' she said. 'I remember speaking to a psychologist called Conrad at St. Francis University Hospital. I took the Dante letter and asked for his opinion.

I remember he commented on the use of the word "Adieu". He said it either meant a kind of "farewell", like the guy knew we'd be meeting again, or perhaps it was the religious meaning. *Ad Deum*. "I commend you to God". And then there was a guy called Boyer at the Institute of Fine Arts. He was the one who told us about the *Hortus deliciarum* book, those images of Hell that were replicated in the killings of Wake and the others. He said that it'd be known to someone who was interested in religious texts, illuminated manuscripts, that kind of thing. The more I think about it, the more it makes sense that this has all been driven by some kind of religious... I mean, what would you call it? He referred to it as a journey. He even said in the letter that he was extending an invitation to accompany him on a journey, that there was a destination, that we wouldn't know what it was until we arrived.' Rachel shook her head resignedly. 'I guess I'm also frustrated with myself that I didn't look into this with more thoroughness—'

'More thoroughness? Jesus, you couldn't have been more thorough. And we don't know it's a priest,' Sheehan said. 'Don't try to crowbar everything into an assumption, Rachel.'

'I know, and I'm not thinking about it that way. I'm just seeing things from a different perspective. I mean, haven't we looked at this from the viewpoint of someone kind of brainwashing people? That's how we saw it. But I think it's just as valid to consider that they were promised something. Maybe that's the *Paradiso* part of it. They weren't manipulated to kill for the sake of killing. They were manipulated to believe that by killing they would somehow attain forgiveness, redemption, salvation.'

'I get that, sure,' Sheehan said, 'and maybe that makes sense when you think about the killings in New York and Pennsylvania, but what about Syracuse? A schoolteacher, a retired couple, some guy who worked at Home Depot? I mean, what the hell did they ever do—'

'What did they do that we knew about,' Rachel interjected.

'Once Marshall was dead we all stopped looking for connections. We didn't need to know the motive, did we? The perp was dead, the killings had stopped, and that was the end of it. And besides, we lost a good detective. One of our own was murdered. That's what everyone was thinking about, Carl. They weren't thinking about why Robert Marshall killed a seemingly random bunch of people.'

'What are you saying?' Sheehan asked. 'You want us to go back fourteen years and look into those murders again? Do we need to know why? If what you're saying is true and Marshall was directed to kill those people—'

Sheehan was interrupted by the sound of the phone.

Collins was on his feet and out into the kitchen before it rang a second time.

Rachel followed him. Even as Collins lifted the receiver, Rachel snatched it from his hand.

'Maurice?'

'I found something,' Quinn said. 'What you were asking about the church thing. It was a condition of Wagner's parole. He had to attend St. Barnabas for some kind of community program. You know, helping out, looking after old folks' yards and whatever.'

'Did you get a name?'

'No name, but I guess if you went there they would have their own records, right?'

'Where's the church?'

'Jackson Heights,' Quinn said.

'I owe you, Maurice.'

'You don't owe me nothin', Rachel,' Quinn replied. ''Cept maybe a beer if you're in the city and you've got nothing else to do.'

Rachel thanked him and hung up.

'Where are we going?' Collins asked.

'St. Barnabas Church in Queens,' Rachel said. She looked at

444

Sheehan. 'You ask the questions. You're doing a piece on offender rehabilitation or whatever. We just need to know who the priest was when Wagner got out of Rikers in 1978.'

The drive up into Queens from the Village took them the better part of an hour. Had they set out later they'd have missed much of the early evening traffic, but countering that was the possible closure of the church and a wasted journey.

En route, no one spoke. There was nothing to discuss.

St. Barnabas Church was off 81st near the Queens Public Library. Lights burned inside.

Collins pulled over on the opposite side of the street and let Sheehan out. Down the block they'd passed a bar called The Kingston. Collins would find somewhere to park up and he and Rachel would meet Sheehan there once he was done.

Rachel watched him cross the street and head up the steps.

Collins pulled away and headed up to the next junction. He turned and went back the way they'd come. It was a good fifteen minutes before they'd found a place to leave the car and made it back to 81st.

The Kingston was a small old-school place. Leather banquettes, a long mahogany bar, a handful of people on stools nursing end-of-the-workday drinks. Collins indicated a booth towards the back and Rachel took a seat. He joined her a few minutes later with a couple of shots of rye.

Raising his glass, he said, 'To the end of this fucking nightmare.'

'You're tempting fate,' Rachel said. 'I'm not drinking to that.'

'Maybe you want to drink to it going on forever, then.'

'Maybe I don't want to drink to anything.'

'You know, I'd like to have known you before you went crazy. I think you'd have been good company.'

'Fuck you, Frank.'

'And fuck you too, Agent Hoffman.'

Raising the glass to her lips, she stopped as Sheehan came in through the door. He paused, surveyed the bar, and then made his way over. His body language said everything that needed to be said. Before he even reached the booth he was trying to catch his breath.

'Ju-July '74 to June of '78—'

'Sit down, for Christ's sake,' Collins said.

Sheehan sat. He took a moment to gather himself together. Rachel passed him the shotglass and he downed it.

'July of '74 to June of '78,' he repeated. 'Four years at St. Barnabas. The guy I spoke to, some kind of curator, church maintenance or something. He remembers him.'

'A name, Carl,' Rachel said. 'Did he give you a name?'

'Eden. Father Virgil Eden.'

'You are fucking joking,' Rachel said. 'Virgil Eden?'

'And did he say which church he moved to?' Collins asked.

'He didn't know, but he told me that before Eden came to New York he was somewhere out in California.'

'San Quentin. It has to be,' Collins said. 'And as for his name, what did we expect? He's not gonna use his real name, is he?'

Rachel sat back. She looked at Sheehan, then at Collins, and then at Sheehan once more.

'Is this our guy?' she asked. 'Can this really be our guy? A Catholic fucking priest who calls himself Virgil Eden? Virgil was the guide, right? He was the one who guided Dante.'

'Who the hell knows, Rachel?' Collins said, 'but he was here at the same time as Wagner, and before that he was on the West Coast. If they move every four years then that's gonna be around the time that Marshall was in San Quentin. Maybe it's a coincidence, but if it is then it's one fuck of a coincidence.'

'So now we have to find where he went after St. Barnabas, and where he went after that,' Sheehan said. 'We need diocese records. There's no way 'round it.'

'That's for tomorrow,' Collins said. 'We're not gonna find

anyone tonight. And we need a strategy. Last thing we want is for him to know that we're looking for him.'

'Oh, I think he knows we're looking for him,' Rachel said. 'In fact, I think he's been waiting for this as long as I have.'

79

Waking from some fractured, savage dream in the early hours of Friday morning, Rachel lay motionless and tried to will her heart to rest. She breathed deeply, slowly, focusing her attention on a single point on the ceiling.

There was blood and fire, fleeting images of burned limbs, the swollen eyes and tongues of those who'd suffocated. She saw the distorted face of her father, pain and terror in his eyes, his mouth open in a silent scream. From deep in her subconscious came twisted thoughts, memories merging one into another. Carl Sheehan lying dead beside Robert Marshall, a wide arc of blood and matter across the wall behind him. Maurice Quinn falling backwards over the railing in the Lehigh County Courthouse. She watched as his body spiraled in slow motion towards the floor below, and all the while he was laughing and repeating her name over and over again: *Rachel, Rachel, Rachel.*

Her body was varnished in a thin film of sweat that cooled and dried as she walked to the kitchen. Rachel took a glass from beside the sink and filled it with water. She stood looking out through the window towards the city. The moon was obscured by clouds, but a thin ghost of light silhouetted the buildings against the sky.

Virgil – Dante's representation of wisdom and reason; the power of intellect left to its own devices without God, without the redemption offered by Christ, and without the influence of the Holy Spirit.

Religion, faith, belief – such things had never played any part in Rachel's life. She had forever discounted them as needful only by those who lacked faith in themselves. And now here she was, challenged and taunted by the faith of another, and that faith – if it could even be considered as such – had been demonstrated in acts that were inhuman, barbaric, founded in such brutality that they defied the imagination.

Father Virgil Eden. A priest playing God. The power of life and death.

Rachel turned at the sound of a door opening in the hallway behind her.

'I heard you get up,' Sheehan said as he entered the kitchen. 'You okay?'

'Bad dreams,' Rachel replied.

Sheehan sat down at the table. Rachel stayed where she was, her glass of water untouched, her attention still directed out towards the darkness. It would soon be dawn, and with it would begin a new day, the fragile hope that there would be another answer, another fragment of the truth, another step towards the end of this thing.

'I'm not sure I'll be able to go back,' Rachel said.

'Go back?'

'To the Bureau. To more of this.'

'There are other departments, other areas you could work in—'

'If I leave, then I leave all of it, Carl.'

'You don't have to make that decision now.'

'I know, but it's there. The doubt is there. I've never felt it like this before. That tells me something, and maybe I should listen to it.'

'Have you spoken to Frank about it?' Sheehan asked.

'He told me that I'd need something else to replace it.'

'What would you do?'

'I have no idea. This has always been what I wanted and what I've done. It makes me wonder if I even understand myself.'

'I don't think anyone ever truly understands themselves,'

Sheehan said, 'and we're changing all the time. From one year to the next, one experience to the next, we're constantly becoming a different version of ourselves. That's life, right? That's human nature.'

'Human nature suggests something natural. The things I live with aren't natural. They aren't even human.'

'You should try to get another couple of hours' sleep.'

'I'm not going to sleep anymore, Carl.'

'Then I'll make coffee. We'll have some breakfast. And then we get to work.'

Rachel set down the glass of water. She turned and started towards the kitchen door. Sheehan rose from the chair as she passed. Rachel stopped for a moment. Her head down, her eyes closed, she was motionless for just a second, and then she put her arms around Sheehan and pulled him close.

They stayed like that – wordless – for a good ten seconds, and then Rachel let him go.

'I'll get dressed,' she said, and then she left the kitchen and walked back to her room.

Collins was up when Rachel returned. It wasn't yet 7.00. Sheehan had made coffee and eggs. They ate their breakfast in silence.

'We have to have a good reason to go back to St. Patrick's,' Collins said. 'Like you said, Carl, for whatever reason they're guarded about giving out specific information regarding postings and assignments.'

'Maybe we're being too defensive,' Rachel said. 'Maybe we go on the offensive for a change.'

'Official?' Sheehan asked. 'Like a Bureau thing?'

'I have my ID,' Rachel said. 'It worked at the DMV. People believe what they see.'

'But on what pretext?'

'Hell, I don't know. We figure something out.'

'And if you're challenged?' Collins asked.

'Then I get kicked out of the Bureau for good and I don't have to make a decision whether to leave or not.'

'There has to be a simpler way,' Sheehan said. 'We have a name, we have a posting here in New York from around the mid- to late-70s. As far as we know, he was out on the West Coast before that. We are assuming that he used the same name, though that's uncertain. If he's a genuine priest, irrespective of his extra-curricular activities, then he'll have been assigned through official channels. That means that a change of name is very unlikely. Sure, we can check with DMV, even look him up in the phone book, but that doesn't give us a history—'

'DMV will have a current address,' Collins said. 'That's if he drives, of course. And how many Virgil Edens are there going to be in the country? It's an unusual name.'

'You remember who you spoke to at DMV?' Sheehan asked.

'I wrote it down somewhere,' Rachel said. She left the room and headed into the back. She was gone no more than two or three minutes.

'Allison Caldwell,' she said. 'I'll call as soon as they're open.'

'She'll remember you,' Sheehan said. 'I'm sure it's pretty rare to get a visit from the Feds.'

'And they'll have his address history on record,' Collins said. 'They'll be able to tell us where he lived right back to when he first got a license.'

Rachel glanced at her watch. 'They're open in forty minutes,' she said.

'So, if that goes nowhere?' Collins asked.

'Back to Archives, maybe?' Sheehan suggested. 'He ran outreach programs for ex-cons. Perhaps he was interviewed for some human-interest feature.'

'Okay, what else?'

'Social Security, traffic violations, credit cards, bank accounts, passport, membership of other organizations, anything that holds your ID,' Rachel replied.

'Maybe he's got a record,' Sheehan said. 'I mean, aside from a traffic violation. We could call Quinn and see if he can find something.'

'He already went out on a limb for us,' Rachel said. 'The guy's three years from retirement. I couldn't live with myself if he got busted for giving out confidential information.'

'You can ask, right? He can always say no.'

Rachel shook her head. 'Maurice is not the kind of guy who'd say no.'

'Okay, so DMV first,' Collins said. 'If that doesn't fly, we find some other way that doesn't sabotage someone's pension.'

'I've gotta say, this sure isn't how it seems from the cop shows,' Sheehan said. 'I thought it all got figured out in forty-five minutes. Where's the flash of genius? Where's the implausible coincidence that cracks everything wide open?'

Collins smiled. 'Oh sure, most of them are like that. And the bad guy realizes he's been busted and he gives himself up without a fight. Except if there's a car chase, of course, and then there's an awful lot of damage to piles of empty cardboard boxes and hot dog stands.'

Rachel got up. She hesitated for a moment, and then she went out through the door and down the hallway.

Carl got up.

'Leave her be,' Collins said.

'I was just going to—'

'Trust me on this, Carl. She's every kind of stressed you can imagine. She's not sleeping or eating enough. She's got a trigger like a two-dollar pistol.'

Carl sat down again.

'The road to Hell is paved with good intentions, right?'

'I know, I know,' Carl replied. 'But she's tough. She's gonna be okay.'

'Sure she will, but it'll take time. This thing is an obsession, and it's driven her for as long as I've known her. When this ends, and it will end, she's either gonna be dead or completely adrift.'

'Dead?'

'It's a very real possibility. I know I'm gonna die so it doesn't matter a fuck to me, but you've got to take that on board as well. This guy is a fucking maniac. Directly or indirectly he's got eighteen murders under his belt. Add another two if Marshall and Wagner didn't commit suicide. And then there's Gary Earl. Sure, he threw himself over a banister in a courthouse, but because that's what he believed he had to do. And this is the guy that got him to believe it. You imagine someone like that would think twice about killing Rachel? Killing you, me? We're the only three people in the whole fucking world who even believe he exists. He's a ghost. We vanish, he burns this place to the ground, what's left to say that he was even here? You gotta understand, Rachel was put on indefinite leave because she wouldn't drop it. No one wanted to know. They thought she'd cracked. They told her she needed psychiatric help. They made it a condition of her return to active service. She told them to go fuck themselves. They didn't have grounds to fire her, but I guarantee they looked, and real fucking hard. You're dealing with someone whose certainty has been challenged for years. She's in no-man's land, out there in the fucking darkness with nothing but dead people for company.'

'She has us,' Sheehan said.

'Me? Not for so long, but she has you, yes. But this is her thing. It's never been anything but her thing. If you and I walked out of here today she'd keep on going by herself. Could you say the same for yourself?'

Sheehan shook his head. 'No,' he replied. 'I'd leave it right where it is.'

'I've known a lot of people in my life,' Collins said. 'Most of them law enforcement of one sort or another. Hard people. Bitter. Frustrated. Kicked in the teeth by the legal system, the judicial system, by DAs and prosecutors and plea bargains and crooked fucking cops who were paid to lose evidence. I knew one guy, a Fed, who worked on a case for three years. He had a witness, a real solid witness, and he was all set to bring down a major crime outfit. This witness had a coronary less than a week before trial. Dead before he hit the ground. Without him, there was no case. End of story. The guys my buddy was after? Well, they felt this wasn't good enough. They killed his wife. Left her body in a dumpster outside his house. Two weeks later he shot himself in the head. And he was a twenty-year veteran of the Bureau.'

'Fuck.'

'People don't choose this life, Carl. They get chosen. There's something in them that just won't let go. The crap she's had to deal with, it amazes me she's still standing. She makes it through this, not only is she gonna have to deal with the consequences of running an unofficial and unauthorized investigation, of using her Bureau authority to influence people, of all the other shit she's done that she's not supposed to have done, but there's gonna be a hole in her life like the fucking Grand Canyon. She's gonna be empty, hollowed out, and that's when she's gonna need all the time and all the support she can get. Until then, we work. That's all we do. No sympathy, no anxiety for her mental state, nothing. We just keep on going until we're done.'

'And you?' Sheehan asked.

'What about me?'

'You aren't gonna do anything about getting well?'

Collins shook his head. 'I'm too far gone, my friend. This is it for me now. This is what I'm doing, and that's all there is to it.'

Allison Caldwell remembered Agent Rachel Hoffman of the FBI. The challenge she faced, however, was the fact that there were over three hundred Virgil Edens on the DMV system.

Rachel had neither a date of birth, nor did she have any information as to locale.

'What about occupation?' Rachel asked. 'I know it's not specified on a driver's license, but do you have it on file?'

'That's not something we record, Agent Hoffman. People change jobs all the time. There'd be no way to keep track of it.'

Considering the fact that the first series of murders had taken place in 1975, Rachel estimated that Eden had to be no younger than twenty-five or thirty at the time. If so, he would now be in his early to mid-forties.

'Can you narrow it down to people born before 1950?' Rachel asked.

'Sure I can. Let me check.'

Rachel waited, tension twisting in the base of her gut.

'That still gives me over two hundred names.'

'For fuck's sake,' Rachel said, and then caught herself. 'I'm sorry, Allison.'

'Oh, it's quite alright, Agent Hoffman. I can only imagine how frustrating this must be for you.'

'Okay, how about previous addresses? I know that the person I'm looking for was based in New York somewhere around the mid-seventies. I doubt he'll be in New York currently, but can you check that?'

'Unfortunately not, no. I don't have that level of access. To be honest, I really shouldn't be doing this without some sort of official authorization, but considering that you came here with your partner and we spoke in person ... well, I'm just trying to be as helpful as I can.'

'I know, Allison, and I really appreciate it.'

'Well, is there anything else at all that you know about this person?'

'In truth, I know very little. He's a priest—'

'A priest? Like an ordained minister?'

'Yes, he's a Catholic priest.'

'They have special dispensation,' Allison said. 'Like a doctor, right? They can park in a no parking zone if they're dealing with an emergency situation. You know, how a priest is sometimes called on to give the last rites or whatever? The police can check the license plate through us and it'll come up. Let me run that and see what we get.'

Rachel closed her eyes. Her knuckles whitened as she gripped the receiver.

'I've got a Father Virgil Eden here,' Allison said. 'Date of birth is June 15, 1935.'

'There's only one?' Rachel asked, wanting to believe with everything she possessed that they'd found the man they were looking for.

'That's what it says.'

'And you have an address?'

'I do, yes. It's 1312 Garland, Asheville, North Carolina.'

Rachel wrote it down, her hand shaking. She told Allison how grateful she was for her help. Allison barely had time to tell Rachel that she was welcome before Rachel hung up the phone.

'We got it?' Sheehan asked.

Rachel held out the slip of paper. 'Asheville, North Carolina,' she said.

'I'll check flight times out to Raleigh,' Collins said.

'Wait up,' Sheehan said. 'We still don't know for sure that this is our guy. We haven't verified that he was actually in California—'

'This is him,' Rachel said. 'I believe it. I fucking know it.'

'Just pack your bag, Carl,' Collins said. 'Whether you like it or not, we're going.'

80

The flight out of JFK to Raleigh was just after 10.00 and would land before noon. They could then take another flight to Asheville Regional, but the first available wasn't until 5.00 and they wouldn't arrive until 8.00. If they drove, they'd be in Asheville around 4.00.

'We'll rent a car,' Collins said. 'That'll give us time to check the address, see if he's there. If not, we'll need to find the church he's working out of.'

They made the flight with minutes to spare. Just out of self-preservation, Rachel knew it would've been wise to take a gun, but that would have required Bureau ID and signed documentation. She had no wish to leave a paper trail behind her.

Sheehan rented the car in his name. Rachel sat up front, Collins in the back. Traffic was light and they made good time. Reaching Winston-Salem by 2.00, Sheehan suggested they stop and get something to eat.

'I'm not hungry,' Rachel said. 'I want to keep going.'

'We need to stop,' Collins said, 'and we all need to eat.'

'But—'

'Rachel, just do as you're fucking told for once, will you?'

Rachel glanced back at Collins. 'Yes, sir.'

'We can do without you passing out from malnutrition,' Collins said. 'And we can do without the sarcasm, too.'

Considering her professed lack of appetite, Rachel ate more than both men combined. The meal was done in little more than three-quarters of an hour.

It was as they were leaving that Collins lost his footing in the doorway. Clutching his hand to his chest, he slipped sideways and went down to the ground.

Rachel and Sheehan were there to help him up. He started to cough then, and the sound that wracked through his chest and throat was fierce.

A waitress came out of the diner, asked if everything was okay, if she should call an ambulance.

'I'm okay,' Collins gasped. 'No ambulance.'

'Frank, you need—'

'I need to stand up,' Collins said. 'And get me a glass of water.'

The waitress headed back inside, returned moments later with the water.

From his coat pocket, Collins took a bottle of pills. He struggled to open it. Sheehan took it from him.

'How many?'

'Two,' Frank said. 'No, give me three.'

Sheehan did as he was asked.

Collins leaned against the railing. He took the pills, took a drink of water, then another.

'You gonna be okay, mister?' the waitress asked. 'You sure you don't want me to call someone?'

'It's okay,' Rachel said. 'Thank you for your help.'

Rachel and Sheehan helped Collins down to the car. He got in back, Rachel beside him.

Sheehan, up ahead in the driver's seat, looked at Collins in the rearview.

Collins sat with his head back, his eyes closed. His breathing was shallow and rapid.

'I really think we should get to a hospital,' Sheehan said.

'No,' Collins said. 'Just drive for Christ's sake.'

Sheehan turned and looked at Rachel.

Rachel nodded. 'Go,' she said.

Within minutes, Collins's breathing slowed down and he was asleep. Rachel didn't move or speak. She just held onto his hand.

In the mirror, Sheehan could see her looking sideways out of the window, almost as if she didn't want to know what was happening beside her. Her friend was suffering, and there was nothing she could do to stop it.

Collins didn't stir until the car finally came to a stop near the address they'd been given by Allison Caldwell. It was a little after 5.00.

'We're here?' Collins asked.

'Yes,' Rachel replied. 'How are you doing?'

Collins sat up. He took a moment to focus. 'I'm okay.'

'You sure?'

Collins nodded. 'I'm sure.'

Garland Street was in a middle-income suburb of Asheville – well-maintained yards, modest houses, nothing to differentiate it from a million other small city residential areas. The streetlights were on, as were lights in many of the homes.

Looking from the rear window, Rachel could see a house number. She counted the adjacent properties one after the other until she identified 1312. The place was in darkness.

'I don't know what I expected,' she said. 'Something less... less innocuous.'

'What did you hope for?' Collins replied. 'A lawn sign?'

'So, what now?' Sheehan asked. 'I guess we're not gonna just walk up there and knock on the door, right?'

'That's exactly what I'm going to do,' Collins said. 'I doubt very much he knows who I am.'

'And if he answers the door?'

'Then I'll make up some bullshit. Tell him I'm a gardener or something looking for work.'

'I don't think he's there,' Rachel said.

'Only one way to find out,' Collins replied. He was out of the car and crossing the street before the others had a chance to respond.

Sheehan and Rachel watched and waited. Collins was at 1312 for a good three or four minutes. He knocked twice, waited, even pressed his ear to the door. There was nothing.

Collins approached the house to the right of the property. Lights were on out front and upstairs.

Within a handful of seconds, the door was answered. An elderly woman exchanged a few words with Collins. Collins was smiling, grateful, and then he returned to the car.

'St. John the Evangelist,' Collins said. 'According to his neighbor, he should be there now. He takes confessions Monday, Wednesday and Friday evenings until 8.00. It's about six blocks up here and then to the right.'

Collins started the car.

'You have a game plan?' Sheehan asked.

'I'm gonna go confess,' Rachel said. 'First time for everything, right?'

The last time Rachel had been inside a church was for her father's funeral. She was anxious, aware of how vulnerable she was without a sidearm. Sheehan and Collins came with her, but stayed back near the door. The place was empty but for a couple of people in pews to the left.

The sound of her footsteps on the stone tiles of the aisle reverberated up into the vaulted ceiling. She could not describe how she felt – a confusion of hope, fear, anger, anticipation, a profound sense of emotional disturbance and inner turmoil. With each step she took she believed that she was nearing a conclusion of fifteen years of her life, but – at the same time – she couldn't help but believe that she'd got it all wrong. She would find some mild-mannered priest, a man who knew nothing, a man who had no inkling of why she was there, and she would leave no closer to an understanding of all that had happened to bring her to this place.

By the time she reached the last row of pews she was ready to turn back. She wanted to know, but she didn't want to be wrong. More than anything she needed the truth, but was acutely aware that the truth could be something so very different from what she'd imagined.

There was silence but for the hammering of her heart in her chest, her temples, and the sound of her rapid, shallow breathing.

She reached the confessional. Her hand against the wooden paneling of the door, she stopped.

There was a small, unlit bulb above her head. She could only assume that once someone was inside the bulb would be illuminated to signify that a confession was in progress.

The wrought iron handle was cool against her fingers. She turned it slowly, stepping back then to open the door. She understood that once she was inside, there was no going back.

Within, the light was subdued. The wooden latticework to her left gave no clear indication of who was on the other side, but there was someone there. Of this she had no doubt. She could hear breathing, a faint sound of movement. She closed her eyes, and her entire body was filled with a sense of dread and misgiving.

'Welcome.' The voice was calm, measured, even gentle.

Rachel didn't speak.

'Are you ready to make your confession?'

Rachel swallowed. Her hands were shaking.

'Is … is this Father Eden?'

'Yes, my child. Are you here to make your confession?'

Again, Rachel didn't respond.

'The penitent is to begin,' Eden said. 'Bless me, father, for I have sinned …'

'I have never made a confession before.'

'You are not a Catholic?'

'I think you know who I am, Father Eden.'

There was movement on the other side once more. Rachel instinctively reached for the door handle. The movement stopped.

'And why would you think that?'

'Because I know who you are.'

'I am Father Eden. I am the priest here at St. John's.' There was a smile in Eden's tone as he responded.

'I want to know why,' Rachel said. 'Why did you choose me?'

'Choose you for what, my child?'

'For your journey. For Hell, for Purgatory, for all of this. All this death and pain and horror.'

'Are these the things you have suffered by the hand of another, or have you brought these upon yourself?'

'You brought them. These are the things you have caused.'

'You are mistaken, my child. I have caused no harm. Whatever you believe has happened has been the will of God. Everything that happens is the will of God.'

'You haven't asked my name,' Rachel said. 'You know who I am, don't you? And you know why I'm here.'

'Perhaps you are here to find the truth. Perhaps you're here to find salvation.'

'I'm here because of Robert Marshall and Charles Wagner. I'm here because of Gary Earl. I'm here for all the people they killed.'

'A man alone is responsible for his actions, good or bad.'

'You're not asking who these people are. You know these names, don't you?'

Eden didn't respond.

'You are responsible for what they did. They did these things because you told them to. You made them what they became.'

'God created Man in his own image, my dear. It is only through God that human reason and purpose is created. Does a man twist the heart and soul into some other shape or form, or is a man merely capable of guiding what is already there?' Eden paused. His voice then grew louder as if he'd leaned towards the partition between them. 'Are you here for them or are you here for yourself? Or perhaps you are here to find the essence of God.'

'I am here for you,' Rachel said. 'I'm here to find out what you have to say. I want to hear the truth from your own lips.'

'There's no such thing as the truth. At least in no one's mind but their own. You can say whatever you wish, you can accuse me of whatever flights of fancy your imagination has conjured up, but I am just a priest. I am nothing more nor less than a servant of God.'

Rachel moved quickly. She wrenched open the door. Reaching for the handle on the facing door, she then had to step back suddenly as the door opened from within.

Eden emerged slowly, his eyes never leaving hers, a faint smile on his lips. Whoever Rachel had imagined him to be, he contradicted all her expectations. Little more than five seven or eight, an aquiline face, his hair thinning, his eyes deep-set, in any other situation he would have been immediately innocuous and forgettable. And yet there was something – a dark intensity in his expression, a presence that somehow made her want to look away. And yet she could not. There was something in his eyes that transfixed her. Eden faced her, seemingly untroubled, even bemused by the nature of this confrontation.

In the field of vision to her right, Rachel was aware of Collins and Carl Sheehan. Frank was heading up the aisle, Sheehan on the far side of the church.

'They can stay where they are,' Eden said. 'This is a moment for you and me alone.'

Rachel raised her hand. Both men stopped walking.

'You know who I am, don't you?' Rachel said.

'I know who you think you are,' Eden replied. 'That you're the sword of justice, here to set the world to rights. And yet you're nothing but a frightened little girl.'

'I'm not frightened of you—'

'And so you shouldn't be. You should be grateful for what I've done. You're here, aren't you? This is your destination. This is everything that you've wanted for as many years as you can remember. I led you a merry dance. I even showed you the way when you were lost. I made you who you are, my child. Perhaps that's something you will only come to understand in time.'

'I'm here to arrest you—'

Eden laughed. 'Arrest me? For what? For something you've imagined? For some wild conspiracy you've concocted? I'm not the one who's on leave because I suffered a nervous breakdown.'

Rachel couldn't conceal her reaction.

Eden leaned forward. 'I know everything about you,' he whispered. 'Without me, you would be nothing.'

Rage fueled Rachel's reaction. She raised her hand, her fist clenched, unsure even in that moment what she intended to do. Whatever it was, Eden reached out and grabbed her wrist. His grip was vice-like. He pushed back suddenly, violently, and she went to her knees.

Collins was running then. Sheehan called out to the parishioners at the back of the church.

'Get out! Get out of here now!'

Alarmed, confused, they did as they were told. There was the sound of running feet, and then the church door slammed shut behind them.

Collins hit Eden with the full weight of his body. Eden went down, Rachel with him. The pain through her wrist was excruciating, but Collins managed to wrench Eden's grip away. Down on his side then, Eden did not resist. He even stretched out his arms in submission.

Collins took the car keys from his pocket and tossed them to Sheehan.

'Glove compartment,' he said. 'Handcuffs.'

Sheehan ran back down the church and out through the door.

Collins hauled Eden up into a sitting position, his arms locked firmly behind his back.

Rachel was on her knees. Looking at Eden, their eyes level, she said, 'Say my name, Virgil. Say my fucking name.'

Eden smiled. 'To me, my child, you will never be anyone but Beatrice.'

81

Free of his outer vestments, beneath which was a plain black cassock, Eden sat handcuffed to a chair in his own kitchen.

He'd offered no resistance as he'd been led out of the church and down to the car. During the short journey to his home, he'd not spoken. Seated between the two men in the back, Rachel driving, Eden had looked at nothing but the rearview mirror. Every time she'd glanced at it, there he was – that same intense expression, that same unspoken humor in his eyes.

Not wishing to leave the car outside Eden's house, Rachel had pulled up to the curb before the last turning.

Collins had got out first. Sheehan had stayed right behind Eden until he was out of the car, and then the pair of them had walked Eden down the street.

The keys were in the pocket of Eden's robe. Collins opened the door, and they hurried inside. Before closing and locking the door behind them, Collins glanced back and forth down the street.

Sheehan and Collins led the priest down to the kitchen, told him to remove his cassock, had him sit on a chair before handcuffing his left hand to the crossbar beneath the seat. Eden offered no word or action to resist or challenge them. His seeming willingness to cooperate was unsettling. It was as if he had been expecting such an outcome, perhaps had planned for it with as much care and attention as everything that had culminated in this moment.

Once everyone was seated, Eden looked at Rachel, then at Sheehan, and then turned to Collins.

'You are unknown to me,' Eden said.

'You don't need to know who I am,' Collins replied.

'As you wish.'

Eden turned back to Rachel. He smiled. 'Time and travail have aged you, my child,' he said. 'You have carried the weight of the world on your shoulders, no?'

Rachel closed her eyes for a moment. She breathed deeply. She opened her eyes again.

Eden was smiling. It was an expression of such patience and sympathy.

'You want all of this to end, don't you?'

'I want you in prison,' Rachel replied. 'Actually, I want you in Hell.'

'As Milton said, "The mind is its own place, and in itself can make a Heaven of Hell, a Hell of Heaven". Perhaps the worst Hell of all is to be ignored, ridiculed, abandoned by those who professed to trust you. And yet here you are, in the presence of truth, the very foundation of Paradise, and all that you've imagined has been shown to be exactly what you believed.'

'Enough,' Collins said. 'Enough of this bullshit. You have the murders of innocent people to answer for—'

'No one is innocent, friend,' Eden said. 'Not a single man, woman or child across the length and breadth of God's Kingdom is truly innocent. Not until they have accepted Christ as their Savior, not until they have repented, atoned, been washed clean of their sins. Only then can they enter the gates of Heaven and find eternal peace.'

Sheehan got up and walked to the doorway. 'I can't listen to this insane crap,' he said. 'We need to get this guy into custody. He needs to be interrogated by the authorities. Rachel, you need to call someone, and you need to call them now.'

'And tell them what, Mr. Sheehan?' Eden asked. 'That you have kidnapped a priest? That you believe he's responsible for a whole host of murders that go back a decade and a half, but no, you have no evidence, and no, there's nothing to corroborate this wild and fantastic theory? I can tell you anything I wish, but you have no authority here. You haven't read me my rights. You haven't arrested me. You have no means of recording what I am telling you. I am whatever you believe me to be, but you are the only people in the world who would consider this anything but madness.'

'So what do you expect to have happen here?' Sheehan asked. 'You think we're just going to let you go?'

Eden looked back at Rachel. 'Do I deserve to die for what I have done, Agent Hoffman?'

'Deserve to die? You deserve to die a thousand times over.'

'Then that is the decision you have to make, my child. You believe you're the sword of justice. So wield the sword. Set us both free. Here. Now. Release us both from the agony and the horror of everything we have suffered together.'

'Together? What the fuck do you mean, together? We're not in this together, you sick fuck.'

Eden looked at Collins. 'There,' he said, 'in the drawer beside the sink.'

Collins opened the drawer. He paused for a moment, and then reached in and took out a .38 revolver.

'A moment,' Eden said. 'Just a second, a heartbeat, and it's over. You want it to be over, don't you, Rachel?'

'Is that what you think is going to happen here?' she said. 'You think I'm going to kill you?'

'But what else can you do?' Eden asked. 'You aren't here, are you? I don't exist. I am ghost, a phantom. And I can't kill myself, can I?'

'And what about Marshall? What about Wagner? They killed

themselves, didn't they? Where is the paradise that you promised them?'

Eden just looked back at Rachel. He didn't say a word, but it was there in his eyes. Marshall and Wagner hadn't killed themselves. Eden had been there. He had killed them, too. And Earl? He had convinced him that there was no other way out, that his own salvation depended upon never revealing the truth of what had happened.

'The world needs to know who you are,' Rachel said. 'The world needs to know what you've done.'

'And, then again, it could be so much simpler. Wracked by guilt for crimes unknown, perhaps a loss of faith, a lonely priest, burdened by shame and despair, takes his own life. It wouldn't be the first time and it won't be the last. But you cannot ask that of me, Rachel. Suicide is a mortal sin. You want me to deny myself the eternal salvation that I deserve? But you could do it, couldn't you? I could die right here and you could drive away, go back to New York, to Syracuse, wherever you wish, and no one would be any the wiser.'

'I'm not gonna fucking kill you,' Rachel said.

'Then what do you want with me?'

'I want you to answer my questions. I want to know the truth. I want to understand why you did what you did.'

'Some of us are born to carry the light, my child. Some of us are in the service of God for no other reason than to illuminate the sins of Man. Some of us are Wrath, some are Vengeance, some are here to show the way to salvation. You question the nature of Man. You ask yourselves how people can be cruel or wicked, how they can take another's life. We each have our calling, and we fulfil our duty—'

'Enough,' Rachel said. 'People have died. So many people have died. You coerced and manipulated those who trusted you, those who believed you were a good man, and you made them

469

do terrible things. People were killed for no other reason than to satisfy some sick, demented obsession—'

'Wicked people. People who had no right to walk on God's green Earth—'

'Innocent fucking people, you crazy, crazy fuck! What possible reason could you have had for killing a fucking schoolteacher?'

'I killed no one.'

'Yes, you fucking did! You killed them. You were just as responsible as Marshall for that woman's death. More responsible, in fact. Without whatever brainwashing bullshit you fed him, he never would have done what he did.'

'I am disappointed,' Eden said. 'I believed you would understand by now, but I see that you—'

'Understand? Understand what, for fuck's sake! Tell me why. Why did Marshall and Wagner and Earl have to kill people? And why did they have to die?'

'To understand the power of life and death, my child. To be free of the constraints of the physical, the corporeal. The Lord giveth, and the Lord taketh away. And why would you grieve? If they were truly innocent, then they have all passed over into the Kingdom of God.'

Rachel got up. She stepped away, looked down at Eden, and then at Collins.

'What the fuck do we do with this crazy, crazy motherfucker?' she asked. 'This is no different from Berkowitz hearing the voice of a demon through his neighbor's fucking dog. All this misery and fucking horror, and here we are, in the kitchen of some fucking house in Asheville with a lunatic handcuffed to a fucking chair.'

'When I die, everything will become clear, my child,' Eden said. 'But I have to die by your own hand, you see?'

Rachel lunged for him, her hand around his throat. Her face inches from Eden's, she said, 'I am not your fucking child, you insane fucking asshole, and I am not going to fucking kill you, you understand?'

Collins stepped forward. He put his hand around Rachel's wrist.

'Stop,' he said. 'Don't let him do this to you.'

Rachel gripped even harder for just a second, and the she let go.

Eden looked at her, and then he gave that same unsettling smile.

'You are nothing,' Rachel said. 'You are nothing to me. You are an evil piece of shit with some fucked-up God complex. You are a worthless excuse for a human being. You're no better than Bundy or Gacy or any of the other narcissistic sociopaths who get some kind of sick thrill out of hurting and killing people. I don't believe in your God. I don't believe in any fucking God. This is one time I wish I did because I know you'd burn in fucking Hell for eternity.'

'Rachel, enough,' Sheehan said. 'Let's get out of here for a minute, okay?' He looked at Collins.

'Go,' Collins said. 'Just go into another room.'

Sheehan took Rachel out of the kitchen and down towards the front door.

She didn't speak. She leaned with her back against the wall, and then she slid down until she was on her haunches. She wrapped her arms around her knees and lowered her head.

Sheehan sat on the lowest riser of the stairs.

A minute passed, perhaps two, and then Rachel looked up.

'So what the fuck do we do now?' she asked. It was a rhetorical question. Sheehan didn't venture an answer.

'We can't arrest him. We can't take him into a fucking police precinct. I can't call my boss and say, "Hey, you never guess what? All that shit I told you is true and we have the guy". They didn't believe me then, and they won't believe me now. He's right. We have nothing.'

'He's made no denial,' Sheehan said. 'Not a single thing. Everything you believed he did, well he did it. How he fucking did it, I have no idea.'

'You heard him, Carl. I can see how some weak-minded, impressionable, half-crazy fuck might buy into all that God and Heaven-and-Hell shit. He selected them. He manipulated them. He told them that redemption and salvation were right on the other side of it. And I think he was with them, you know? When they did those killings? He probably absolved them before they killed themselves, and they committed suicide believing that—'

'Rachel,' Sheehan said.

She stopped, looked at him.

'We need to make a decision. That's the only thing we have to do right now. We can't just leave him handcuffed to a chair, can we?'

'I know, Carl, I know.' She shook her head. 'And I don't know what to do. All these years, everything that's happened, I've been heading towards this moment, and now I'm here and...'

Sheehan reached out and placed his hand on her shoulder. 'We have to take him in,' he said. 'What other choice do we have? We're not his judge, and we're certainly not his executioner. We kill him, no matter the justification, and are we any better than him? If you don't have faith in the law—'

Rachel looked up. There was bitterness in her eyes. 'Faith? How can you expect me to have faith in anything? All of this has happened because of faith, for fuck's sake.'

'This isn't just his life we're talking about,' Sheehan said. 'This is your life, your whole future. You kill him, and everything you've worked for, everything you've accomplished will be meaningless.'

'And what about the lives he's taken? Don't they mean something? Are they meaningless, too?'

'No, they're not, but what you're considering now is driven by anger, by hatred. This is nothing but revenge, Rachel. It's the old saying, isn't it? If you seek revenge, you should dig two graves.'

Rachel got to her feet. They stood there in the hallway of Eden's house. The tension and the silence were oppressive.

'It's not revenge,' Rachel said. 'It's justice.'

'Sure, but it's not the fucking Wild West, Rachel. You can't just hang the guy or shoot him in the fucking head, can you?'

'Then what would you have me do?' she asked. 'I have nothing. Fifteen years of murders and I have nothing.'

'Then we make something. We do whatever it takes to get enough circumstantial evidence together—'

'And meanwhile? We just let him go? Who's to say he won't go out in a blaze of fucking glory and kill as many people as he can?'

'I don't know the answer, Rachel. There's other people, other agencies we can approach. We can keep him under surveillance—'

'How? How are we going to do that, Carl? Are you going to do that?'

'Listen to me for a moment—'

Pushing past Sheehan, Rachel walked back to the kitchen.

Eden turned as she came through the doorway. Collins stood against the sink, the gun in his hand.

Without a word, Rachel took the gun from Collins. He didn't try to stop her.

For a moment, she just looked at the weapon, and then looked at Eden.

Sheehan came through the doorway.

'Rachel, no—'

'Leave her be, Carl,' Collins said.

'But this isn't the way. You just can't do this, Rachel.'

'Carl!' Collins said emphatically. 'Enough!'

Rachel glanced back at Collins, and then looked at Sheehan for just a moment. She took a step closer to Eden. Raising her hand, she pressed the muzzle of the gun against his forehead.

Eden smiled. 'And there she is,' he whispered. 'My Beatrice, my light of truth, my savior.'

'You killed my friend,' Rachel said. 'You were there, weren't you? You killed Michael. Tell me you killed Michael.'

Eden closed his eyes.

'Say it, you sick fuck! Just fucking say it!'

Eden breathed deeply.

Rachel's left hand around his throat, the gun in her right, now pressed hard against his brow.

'Look at me,' Rachel said, her voice hard and sharp. 'Look at me and tell me you killed Michael.'

Sheehan took a step forward. The color had drained from his face. His eyes were wide with fear.

Sheehan looked at Collins. Collins shook his head.

Eden opened his eyes.

'The old order has passed away,' he said, his voice a whisper. 'Welcome me into Paradise, where there will be no sorrow, no weeping or pain, but fullness of peace and joy with your Son and the Holy Spirit forever and ever.'

Rachel stopped breathing. Her hand was shaking, her finger tightening gradually on the trigger.

She closed her eyes.

Eden smiled. 'Father, into your hands I commend my spirit.'

Steeping back suddenly, Rachel lowered the gun.

Sheehan exhaled audibly.

Collins reached out and put his hand on Rachel's shoulder. Turning towards him, she let him take the gun from her.

Eden looked up at Rachel. In that moment, all she saw was a profound and desperate sadness in his eyes.

'I am not you,' she said. 'I am nothing like you.'

'We are all, each and every one of us, created in God's image, my child.'

'You can keep your God,' Rachel replied.

'Take the gun,' Eden said. 'If you don't give me peace, you will never find peace yourself.'

'This is the end. I intended to find you, and I found you. If you think that I'm going to free you from this, then you are so very wrong. You can go on suffering in the Hell you've created for yourself.'

'Beatrice,' Eden said. 'My Beatrice...'

Rachel did not respond. She turned to Collins.

'Let's go,' she said. 'Before I change my mind and put this animal out of its fucking misery.'

'You should go,' Collins said. 'Both of you.'

Rachel frowned.

'Do as I say, Rachel. Go. Do it for me. Just leave the house, get in the car and drive away.'

'What are you going to do, Frank?'

Collins closed his eyes and lowered his head. He stayed like that for just a few seconds, and then he looked up at her again. The resolve and determination in his expression told her everything she needed to hear.

'Frank... no...'

'Carl, take her out of here,' Collins said.

Sheehan didn't move.

'I need you to do what I'm asking of you,' Collins went on. 'I need you to do this for her, you understand? This isn't about you or me. This isn't about what you think is right or wrong. This is just the way it has to be.'

Rachel took a step forward. There were tears in her eyes, and when she spoke her voice cracked with emotion.

'You don't need to do this, Frank.'

'Oh, sweetheart, this is just exactly what I need to do.'

Collins held out his arms. Rachel walked forward and he hugged her. He held her for a small eternity, and then he released her.

Collins raised his hand and held it against her cheek.

'After all the noise has died down, you come visit, okay?'

'Okay,' she said, and then she started crying, her breath hitching in her chest, her hands shaking.

Sheehan walked forward. He puts his arm around her shoulders and walked her to the door.

In that final moment, he glanced back at Collins.

'Take care of her,' Collins said. 'Give me your word.'

'I give you my word,' Sheehan replied.

Collins waited until he heard the sound of the front door closing, and then he looked at Eden.

'You're not the only one who knows your Catechism,' he said. 'It is God who remains the sovereign master of life. We are stewards, not owners, of the life God has entrusted to us. It is not ours to dispose of.'

'You think I'm going to take my own life? Is that what you think?' Eden laughed coarsely.

'Oh, it doesn't matter what I think, does it? It's how it will be seen. As loss of faith in divine forgiveness. The fallen priest. The murder of self is a violation of the sixth commandment. No last rites. No consecrated burial for you. God will not call you home.'

'You can't—'

'Can't what?'

Collins stepped forward. He unlocked the handcuffs, and before Eden had a moment to resist, the gun was in his hand, the barrel beneath his own chin. The force with which he was held kept him rooted to the chair, unable to move.

'Think of Michael Ridgway,' Collins said. 'Think of all of them. Think of every face, every name, every single life you destroyed.'

Eden looked up, his eyes cruel, his expression one of arrogance and hatred.

'I am a man of God,' he said. 'And you are nothing. Kill me, and you will burn forever in Hell.'

'Is that so? Well, I'll see you when I get there, you worthless piece of shit.'

V

1994

Epilogo

82

Frank Collins succumbed in the early hours of Friday, January 19th, 1990.

Rachel was with him to the last faltering breath.

After he'd gone, she sat alone with him for a long time. Her tears were spent. Her heart would now have to heal. That would take time, but she had time. It was perhaps the most valuable thing she possessed.

She did not wish for things to be different. She knew it would serve no purpose. She did not imagine how the present might have been had she made other decisions or taken other actions. Such an activity was futile.

All she had was the future, and she had long since determined that the future would be very different from the past.

How that future would be could wait for another time, another moment. This time was for Frank. For a man who had released all of them from a decade and a half of nightmares and despair.

Frank had turned himself in. He'd called the police and waited right there in Eden's house until they arrived. He didn't try to convince anyone that the man's death was justified or in self-defense. He simply stated that he had killed Eden. He gave no reason, no motive, no explanation.

After arraignment, he was held in the state pen. His condition worsened rapidly, and he was transferred to a hospice. The DA knew that Frank wouldn't make it to trial. The FBI wanted to do whatever was necessary to avoid a public scandal. There wouldn't be any public statements or newspaper reports. They were going to let him die quietly.

During those final weeks, Rachel visited ever more frequently. Often, Frank was so subdued by painkillers that there was no conversation at all. She would just sit and hold his hand, talk to him even when there was no sign that he could hear her. She believed he could hear her, and that was enough.

Four days before he died, Frank spoke for the first time in a week.

Much of what he said made no sense as he drifted in and out of the haze of sedatives and painkillers, but at one point he seemed to focus on her very clearly. He just looked right at her and said, 'You know, I always wanted a daughter. And if that had happened, I'd have wanted her to be just like you.'

'Like me?' she'd replied through the tears. 'I don't believe anyone would want a daughter like me.'

Frank had smiled. He'd squeezed her hand as he closed his eyes.

It was the last time they spoke.

83

Rachel stands at the window overlooking the yard.

Beyond the far treeline flows the Satilla River. On, past Woodbine, the river meets St. Andrew Sound and joins the Atlantic. All up and down the Georgia coast, as far west as Kings Bay, as far north as Savannah, out across the Sea Islands and Blake Plateau, there is nothing but light and space and distance. Heading west for four and a half thousand miles, she would finally reach Morocco and the coast of Africa. For some reason she cannot explain, the feeling of separation comforts her.

Closing her eyes, she breathes slowly, deeply, willing her heart to be nothing but a murmur in her chest.

The images she's worked so hard to dispel from her memory return every once in a while. Sometimes awake, sometimes in her dreams. They appear in slow motion. They are faint and fragile, but still they hold sufficient substance to evoke emotions she'd hoped never to feel again. But they are there – like ghosts, their shapes and colors faded like photographs left to bleach in the sun. She knows that they'll forever possess the power to haunt her.

It is four years since Asheville, four years since she resigned from the Bureau. It's more than three since she moved to Georgia and started a new life, a different life, a life so far-removed from everything that she left behind. But she didn't truly leave it – not all of it – and the ease with which a single moment can bring it all back sometimes scares her.

She has new friends. She meets them every once in a while – a cup of coffee in town, a dinner party, a birthday celebration. They know who she was before she came here. They are fascinated. They ask questions. They all want a glimpse into the abyss. She has accommodated them a handful of times, little more than a few anecdotes, and perhaps for no other reason than the belief it would somehow exorcize some of her own shadows. It had not. Regardless, the people she now knows remain unaware of the depth of darkness that separates their world from the one to which she once belonged. It's something she hopes that none of them will ever come to understand.

After Frank's death, she was lost for a long time.

'You must kill only what you can eat,' Frank had once told her.

She'd understood what he'd meant. The burden of guilt she'd have carried if she'd ended Eden's life in that kitchen would have finished her. There was no way she could have survived. None of them could have survived. No, it was not right. It was not just. It was not fair. But the world was never fair, never equitable, never just. People died who did not deserve to die, just as people lived who had no right to live.

And so Frank shouldered that burden for her, and for this she owed him everything.

Rachel looks up at the sound of the car pulling into the driveway.

The key in the front door, the murmur of voices. She walks out to the hallway as Emily comes through ahead of Carl.

'Mommy!' Emily shouts. Rachel stoops down, her arms wide, and lifts her daughter.

'Hey, sweetie,' she says.

Rachel looks at Carl. He smiles, steps forward and kisses her.

'How was it?' Rachel asks.

'Oh, we had fun,' Carl says. He reaches out and ruffles Emily's hair. 'We had fun, didn't we?'

'We had ice cream!' Emily proclaims.

'Did you now?'

Rachel looks at Carl disapprovingly.

'It was small, okay? A really, really small ice cream, and we shared it.'

'Such a bad liar,' Rachel says. 'Is that all she had for lunch?'

'I'm taking the Fifth. Any more questions and I want a lawyer present.'

'Life without parole for you,' Rachel says. 'And probably too far away for us to visit.'

'Well, I'm glad we got that resolved. And now I need to get to work.'

Carl pauses for a moment. 'You okay?'

'Sure. All good. Off you go, Mr. Ice Cream Man. Me and this little monster are going to make a terrible dinner together.'

Rachel pulls Emily close. She feels her warmth, that sense of pure and unconditional love, and she prays – for her daughter, at least – that life will never be consumed or corrupted by pain. She knows that it's a vain and impossible wish, but she wishes it all the same.

Some lives were blessed, of course, but those never reached by the darkness of the world were rare indeed.

Some lives were swallowed into the abyss, never to be seen again. Some clawed their way back out and brought the darkness with them.

And then there were those who teetered on the edge – drawn and transfixed – and yet never lost their balance.

Through death, through hell and purgatory, Rachel had found her paradise.

It was here.

It was now.

And she was never going to leave.

Acknowledgements

With so many books behind me and so many acknowledgements to those who have given their support over the years, this book is dedicated simply to my readers. My appreciation for your kindness, your loyalty, and your endless encouragement knows no limit. Without you, I would not be able to spend my life doing something I love, and for this I am – and always will be – eternally grateful.

Credits

R.J. Ellory and Orion Fiction would like to thank everyone at Orion who worked on the publication of *A Darker Side of Paradise* in the UK.

Editorial
Emad Akhtar
Sarah O'Hara
Millie Prestidge

Copyeditor
Patrick McConnell

Proofreader
Jane Donovan

Audio
Paul Stark
Jake Alderson

Design
Tomás Almeida
Joanna Ridley

Publicity
Leanne Oliver
Jenna Petts

Contracts
Dan Herron
Ellie Bowker
Alyx Hurst

Editorial Management
Charlie Panayiotou
Jane Hughes
Bartley Shaw

Finance
Jasdip Nandra
Nick Gibson
Sue Baker

Marketing
Tom Noble
Javerya Iqbal
Hennah Sandhu

Production
Ruth Sharvell

Operations
Jo Jacobs
Dan Stevens

Sales
Jen Wilson
Esther Waters
Victoria Laws

Toluwalope Ayo-Ajala
Karin Burnik
Frances Doyle
Rachael Hum
Ellie Kyrke-Smith
Sinead White
Georgina Cutler